WHERE SHE LIES

Also by Caro Ramsay

DCI Christine Caplan Thrillers

THE DEVIL STONE *
IN HER BLOOD *
OUT OF THE DARK *

The Anderson and Costello Series

ABSOLUTION
SINGING TO THE DEAD
DARK WATER
THE BLOOD OF CROWS
THE NIGHT HUNTER *
THE TEARS OF ANGELS *
RAT RUN *
STANDING STILL *
THE SUFFERING OF STRANGERS *
THE SIDEMAN *
THE RED, RED SNOW *
ON AN OUTGOING TIDE *
THE SILENT CONVERSATION *

Novels

MOSAIC *
THE CURSED GIRLS

* *available from Severn House*

WHERE SHE LIES

Caro Ramsay

SEVERN
HOUSE

First world edition published in Great Britain and the USA in 2025
by Severn House, an imprint of Canongate Books Ltd,
14 High Street, Edinburgh EH1 1TE.

severnhouse.com

Copyright © Caro Ramsay, 2025

Cover and jacket design by Nick May at bluegecko22.com

All rights reserved including the right of reproduction in whole or in part in any form. The right of Caro Ramsay to be identified as the author of this work has been asserted in accordance with the Copyright, Designs & Patents Act 1988.

British Library Cataloguing-in-Publication Data
A CIP catalogue record for this title is available from the British Library.

ISBN-13: 978-1-4483-1409-6 (cased)
ISBN-13: 978-1-4483-1410-2 (e-book)

This is a work of fiction. Names, characters, places and incidents are either the product of the author's imagination or are used fictitiously. Except where actual historical events and characters are being described for the storyline of this novel, all situations in this publication are fictitious and any resemblance to actual persons, living or dead, business establishments, events or locales is purely coincidental.

No part of this book may be used or reproduced in any manner for the purpose of training artificial intelligence technologies or systems. This work is reserved from text and data mining (Article 4(3) Directive (EU) 2019/790).

All Severn House titles are printed on acid-free paper.

Typeset by Palimpsest Book Production Ltd., Falkirk,
Stirlingshire, Scotland.
Printed and bound in Great Britain by TJ Books,
Padstow, Cornwall.

The manufacturer's authorised representative in the EU for product safety is Authorised Rep Compliance Ltd, 71 Lower Baggot Street, Dublin D02 P593 Ireland (arccompliance.com)

Praise for the DCI Christine Caplan Thrillers

"Dark, unsettling . . . A fine choice for fans of Ian Rankin and Val McDermid"
Booklist on *Out of the Dark*

"Unnerving"
Kirkus Reviews on *Out of the Dark*

"A taut, suspenseful police procedural with plenty of dark twists to keep fans riveted"
Booklist on *In Her Blood*

"Gripping . . . Ramsay has created a fascinating character in Caplan"
Publishers Weekly on *In Her Blood*

"Breathtaking"
Kirkus Reviews on *In Her Blood*

"Caro Ramsay fully deserves a place in the upper echelons of Scottish crime writing . . . top-notch"
Financial Times on *The Devil Stone*

About the author

Caro Ramsay was born and brought up in Glasgow, and now lives in a village on the west coast of Scotland. She is an osteopath, acupuncturist and former marathon runner who devotes much of her time to the complementary treatment of injured wildlife at a local rescue centre. She is the author of thirteen Anderson & Costello thrillers, one standalone novel of psychological suspense and the DCI Christine Caplan thriller series.

www.caroramsay.com

PROLOGUE

22 December 2001

There is before.

There is after.

There is in between. Here lies a pause, a stillness where a breath is held as life teeters in the balance. The pendulum can swing this way or that. The wheel stops then turns again, and there's another breath to take.

And then the platitudes come.

I have some bad news for you.

Please have a seat.

The doctor will be with you soon.

The pendulum swings again.

The wheel takes one more turn.

Will he turn left, or right? Will she live or die?

Daisy Evans is exhausted and bruised from the 'before'. She is excited by the 'now'. But the 'after' remains undecided by the gods.

It doesn't depend on the moon coming out from behind the clouds. It won't be determined by the subtle interplay between lunar phases and the oceans, the ancient pull and push of gravity.

Maybe it was the light of the full moon that had alerted her as she approached the caravan. That prescient sense of danger, a prickle on the back of her neck, maybe the scent of his cigarette in the still, dark air. Or had she heard a noise where there should have been silence? Whatever, whyever, Daisy pulled back into the shadows as soon as she had stepped off the path.

'Daisy? Is that you?' His voice was quiet, gentle even, in the tranquillity of the night. How had he got in? She'd only nipped out to get her dry clothes from the laundry, ready to pack before her lift came. Tomorrow would be a new day, another turn of the earth, another turn of the wheel.

'Daisy?' Louder this time, getting angry.

He wasn't supposed to be back until lunchtime and by then she had hoped to be lost in Liverpool. Her new suitcase was ready. Ironically, it was one he'd bought her for a holiday in Tenerife, a holiday that she'd spent in hospital after another fall down the stairs. Now the case was lying open on the table, her handbag was sitting beside her rucksack, in plain sight.

Errors of speed over caution.

Daisy inched her way round the side of the caravan until she could see in the rear window. Leaning forward, she peeked into the room that had been her safe haven for months.

He was there, leaning back on the sink, arms folded, waiting. As she watched, he turned his head slightly, as if he'd heard something.

Heart thumping, she pulled back. She knew.

He knew.

That old moon playing tricks again. This time the trick was on her.

Then she'd heard footsteps within, a movement of the shadows.

And that was the 'before'.

Now she was on the beach with nowhere to hide and he was somewhere, watching and waiting.

'Daisy?'

He's shouting, words escaping on the breeze. She can pretend she never heard.

Before she'd had a chance of getting away but now, after the baby, he'd become so much worse. It didn't matter where she went, he would always find her. She'd spend a lifetime looking over her shoulder; she didn't want to walk into any more doors or trip over any more rugs. No more nights in casualty, no more stitches, no more blood, no more holidays in a foreign hospital.

She looked at the waves, at the silver shimmer of the moon on the glistening sapphirine sea.

Daisy thought how beautiful the moon was tonight, bright but treacherous. She tucked herself behind the largest rock she could reach. The waves raced in behind her, erasing her footsteps in the sand, keeping her secret.

She looked up the beach, along the top of the distant cliff, the ruin of Mary's Tower rising like a finger pointing to the sky, telling her to wait.

So she waited.

When he was gone, she started the walk, the first steps to a new freedom.

Then his words roll over the noise of the deceitful waves and the whispering breeze funnelling between the rocks.

'Hello, Daisy.'

ONE

Christine Caplan was ignoring her family and the remains of the Eton mess on the table. Sitting as she was, with her back to the Ben, she had the best view, looking out to sea watching the dying light of the longest day settle over Kerrera and Mull. The iridescent display of blue around the witching hour was surviving another Highland sunset. She was making the most of a rare still point in her life. Time sitting outside in the garden with her family, time to savour.

The twenty-second day of June had been long and unbearably hot. Caplan was relieved the heat had worn off; she might get some sleep tonight instead of tossing and turning, before going out to stand on the balcony to cool down. The ever-present cooling breeze that blew in from the Sound had deserted them. Scotland had turned into a furnace.

She was enjoying the changing colours on the horizon when she realised that Mags, her daughter's boyfriend, was tapping a glass of water with the tip of his spoon. As he got to his feet, Caplan realised, with a chill of horror, what was coming and quickly rearranged her features into some semblance of neutrality.

Christopher 'Mags' Allanach had the kind of private school education that made him accomplished at public speaking, so he appeared to be at ease while he waited for silence. Even Caplan's son Kenny, who hadn't been quiet since the moment he was born, realised that he was supposed to be now.

Caplan looked round the table. She and Mags were the only two totally sober. She was on call. He didn't drink. She caught the eye of her daughter, Emma, who beamed back at her with pride and with something sheepish, a little guiltily even. Emma tucked her brown hair behind her ear, her tell since she was a wee girl. But at the moment, Emma was so pleased with herself that she could hardly contain it.

Caplan looked back out to sea but the waves, darker against the rainbow of colours above, remained distant and calm.

Mags cleared his throat. 'Earlier this month I asked Aklen for the honour of Emma's hand in marriage and I'm delighted to say that he agreed. And so did she.'

Kenny broke out into whooping and screeching, then dancing

and singing 'My Brother-in-Law is a millionaire, I'm skint and he doesn't care,' to a tune that Caplan almost recognised. Aklen and Mags shook hands, firmly and genuinely. The handshake developed into a hug. Kenny immediately asked for a loan of ten grand 'as we are family now'. Jade, Kenny's girlfriend, was clapping her hands together like a demented seal. Caplan hoped this celebration wouldn't give Jade any ideas. She got up, gave her daughter a hug and her new son-in-law-to-be a kiss on the cheek and then, out of nowhere, Aklen produced a bottle of champagne.

Caplan's phone went. Instinctively, she lifted it to reply. Emma glared at her. She put the phone back down.

Jade went over to Emma and asked, 'Oh my God, what about the dress? And where's it going to be? I mean, like when? Oh, my goodness, you could get married up at Torsvaig? Imagine that? A fairy-tale wedding in a castle! My mum said they had guests arriving by helicopter last month. Imagine how cool that would be.'

Caplan saw Mags, an eco-warrior, wince.

Emma said, 'I think we'll be getting married on the island – quiet wedding, just family.'

Caplan's phone went again.

A few minutes wouldn't make any difference. She'd get back to them in a quiet moment. DS Craigo could hold the fort.

Mobile in hand, Caplan settled back round the table with the rest of her family. Enthusiastic conversation bounced between weddings, venues, dresses, then houses and future plans. Then how awesome the refurb of Challie Cottage was, then to Aklen's fledgling business, Toaty Houses, then back to weddings. The increasing intensity of the glow from the citronella candles, hanging on tall iron spikes placed round the table to ward off midges, emphasised the lateness of the hour.

Jade and Mags sat back and listened to Emma and Kenny, alcohol fuelling the sibling banter that had been the mainstay of their relationship, before Aklen was forced to end the bickering by asking if anybody wanted tea or coffee. He rubbed his hands together eagerly as he offered but didn't stand up. Caplan resigned herself to her role of waitress while Jade looked on, considering and absorbing everything she was hearing. Kenny leaned in, telling her another anecdote about his sister without stopping to draw breath. When he nipped off to the toilet, Jade helped herself to the white wine from the chiller and topped up her glass, then settled back in her seat, now watching Caplan but not offering to help.

As she was going up her new stairs for the ninth time that day,

Caplan made a mental note not to invite any more guests until the balcony was finished and any alfresco dining could take place out there. But then, she hadn't exactly invited any of these guests to party in the garden at the side of the house – that had been her husband's doing. Still, she thought how lucky she was to be surrounded by her family. Now the kids were young adults, she and Aklen were seeing less of them. When they did meet up, they had been living their own lives and had their own stories to tell.

Toni Mackie, her constable, had buried her mother that afternoon in the bright sunshine of a summer day. Today had been another scorcher and if the weather had had any respect at all, a lonely cloud should have passed over, dulling the day for the interment, a sign that nothing was wonderful forever. She put on the kettle and checked her phone: two missed calls from control and a text from Mackie thanking her for the flowers. Then a second text a couple of minutes later that read: **I'm going off my head. Mum's pals won't leave. They keep asking what I'm doing with her pearls and who's getting the tea cosy.** That was followed by a screaming face emoji.

Caplan was placing cups, milk and the cafetière on a tray, thinking that Mackie was probably doing exactly the same thing, albeit in different circumstances. Still considering the circle of life that was weddings and funerals, she descended the stairs and walked into the warm evening air to rejoin her guests.

She sensed a change in the happy mood of the party.

Kenny was trying to persuade Mags that he needed a professional taster for the gin they were producing on the island, but the conversation was slightly forced. Caplan took her time placing the cups on the table, trying to sense the source of the disquiet, when she heard Emma ask Jade, 'What do you do for a living?' Jade replied, as she always did, that she worked in the media.

'Yes, but doing exactly what?' asked Emma, her persistence rather surprising her mother. 'Are you a nepo baby?'

'No, she's a Scorpio,' quipped Kenny.

Nobody laughed.

'After uni, I did a few things, but if you mean am I following Mum into journalism, then yes, I am. I've got a column in an online magazine, nothing big as yet. I got that through my TikTok content, not because of Mum. But I've started on my first novel.'

'So has Kenny, but he's reading one rather than writing one,' said Emma, flicking a small piece of meringue at her brother.

'Sorry,' asked Caplan, 'Who's your mum?'

'Carrie Cowie-Browne, the journalist.'

Emma's eyes met her mother's, sharing the tiniest of eyerolls.

'We do discuss social affairs, gender politics. Mum prides herself, you know, on the zeitgeist. She's always where it's relevant.' Jade narrowed her eyes a little, looking at Emma over the top of her glass. Then, like a thunderstorm, what had been a polite chat gave way to vitriol. 'There's so much that women have to put up with these days, and it's expected of us to accept the role of victim as our lot, and to keep quiet.'

Kenny pulled himself deep into his chair, and as he raised a glass to the others, he pulled up a cushion to hide his face. He had witnessed this before. 'Here she goes.'

Jade's taloned fingernail was pointing at Caplan. 'Let's consider some of the recent police screw-ups?'

'Is this you keeping quiet about it?' asked Kenny, with an air of innocence.

'What about that man who lay dead for months in his bed? The police had visited his flat three times, got no response at all but they still reported that all was well. A sixteen-year-old is photographed by her father to produce soft pornographic images, and the police do nothing. And that's just off the top of my head. I mean Police Scotland? They're getting such a bad rep at the moment.'

'When do they ever get a good one?' muttered Aklen.

Jade wasn't finished. 'I mean, Peter Maxwell. Kills his mum, serves nine years then gets out, kills his dad. Or like, Angus McLeerie, kills two women, maybe three? Gets tried for one. David Goss, rapist and police officer. He raped three women, women who he knew would be alone because he was a constable on their beat, I mean, like . . .' Jade gave a long and deliberate blink, her eyelashes dancing, '. . . how can that even happen?'

Caplan tried to appear unperturbed. 'Maxwell was a mental health issue, McLeerie was a decision by the Fiscal, and Goss? Well, he applied to the service with the specific agenda of having access to vulnerable people. He's clever, he had his forensic awareness long before he became a cop.'

'And was selected for promotion, I believe.' The taloned fingers spread out like knives, and Jade's eyelashes opened like flowers, revealing the darkness of her pupils.

And the colour of her soul, Caplan thought unkindly. 'He wasn't selected for promotion, he applied for it, and he was proving that he could do the job. Or so everyone thought. Like I said, he was bright.'

'Cleverer than the average cop, but that's a low bar!' Kenny said, laughing, giving Jade a gentle bump in the ribs with the cushion to ease the mood. 'But my mum's not average,' he said.

'No, she's not. Your mum has an incredibly high clear-up rate,' said Aklen, supporting his wife.

'I've always worked with good people,' said Caplan.

'Certainly lucky that you didn't face a disciplinary in the Brindley case.' Jade took a deep breath to let that sink in, ignoring the ice-cold atmosphere descending on the table. 'Was that how you ended up here, in the back end of nowhere? And there was that other cop who was having sex with the victim of the domestic violence he was supposed to be investigating. Isn't that against the law? I mean, the poor guy was traumatised. Being battered almost unconscious by your partner? Not exactly a speeding ticket, was it?'

Caplan regarded the remains of the dessert on the table, slightly confused at the turn the conversation had taken and thinking how Jade would look wearing the cafetière.

Jade, however, took the slight pause as an admission of guilt. The taloned nails tippy-tapped on the tabletop, emphasising her point. 'Just to be clear, the constable had gay sex with the householder who had been abused and violated, thus taking advantage of a vulnerable victim when he was supposed to be taking a statement.'

'Anything you say will be taken down and used in evidence. Pants!' Kenny tittered like an end-of-the-pier comedian.

'Serving officers can't comment on ongoing cases,' said Caplan.

'Can't? Or won't?' snapped Jade.

Emma looked at the darkening sky. 'So, Jade, what is your basic complaint about? The fact that he was having sex on duty, the fact he was gay, or his abuse of a position of trust?'

'I thought it was compulsory in the force these days, being gay.' Kenny rolled his eyes.

'Each to their own,' said Aklen, taking a very long sip of champagne.

'And unfortunately police officers are people, like everybody else. Some do their jobs well; some leave a lot to be desired. I know. I have to work with them.' Caplan stacked the two plates nearest to her and made to stand up.

'But they're not, are they? That's my point,' said Jade.

Caplan settled back in her seat.

'They're not *people like everybody else*. They should be held to a higher standard.'

Drunkenly Kenny raised his hand. 'I can confirm that my mother is "a people". She peopled us very well when we were wee. Homework had to be in on time, we could never stay out beyond curfew, and we had to sing. A lot. And wear curtains.'

'What?' asked Emma.

Kenny burped. 'Sorry, that was *The Sound of Music*. But it was a very similar regime.'

'You talk so much shite,' muttered Emma to her brother.

Caplan watched Jade picking at bits of meringue with those bloody fingernails. Aklen too was studying Jade, no doubt trying to work out which one was real: the friendly guest excited about the wedding, or this entitled, argumentative squirt. Out of the corner of her eye, Caplan saw Emma shrug her shoulders at her dad.

Deciding that removing herself might be the best way to create a more comfortable atmosphere for the coffee and chocolate mints, Caplan stacked the rest of the plates and got up, saying that she'd put the dishwasher on. Mags gathered the empty glasses and followed her.

'The young people of today, eh? I don't think I've ever been that confident in my entire life,' said Mags.

'Who does she think she is?' Caplan spat, ramming plates into the dishwasher rack, glad to have some moral support even if it was from the sandal-wearing vegan who was her prospective son-in-law.

'One to be watched, I fear. Her mother has been known to castrate sheep with a glance.'

Caplan smiled, then saw the glasses in his hand. 'Can you put them in the sink for now?'

'Are you okay?'

'Yes, I'm fine,' she nodded. 'Thank you.'

'Did Kenny not tell you that Jade was Carrie Cowie-Browne's daughter?'

'No, he forgot to mention that. Still, it can't be easy being the daughter of a powerhouse feminist who writes for a tabloid. I presume mother and daughter are both very clever, but Jade can't be all that bright if she's putting up with Kenny.'

That got a rare smile out of Mags. 'Your son has his own charm.'
'I think he reinforces Jade's superiority complex.'
'Emma's furious that Jade has ruined the party and upset you.'
'I'm not upset.'
'Well, I think Emma's tempted to punch your other guest. She was so looking forward to telling you our news, she wanted you to be thrilled.'
'Have I let her down by not being? She knows I don't like surprises.' And now, in her new kitchen, the sink full of glasses, she analysed why she was so hurt by the engagement, given that this man clearly loved her daughter. Was it because Aklen had known and had not said a word? Neither had Emma. Neither had Mags. Or was it the fact that Mags had asked Aklen for their daughter's hand in marriage, as if Emma was a second-hand Volvo with a low mileage and Aklen was glad to see it going to a good home?

They stood in the kitchen, the doors on the balcony open, as the conversation of the guests below, working their way through the champers, floated up. Kenny's stories getting ruder, Emma and Aklen laughing loudly; the family closing ranks so that Jade couldn't get a word in edgeways.

But something was off.

Mags followed Caplan onto the balcony. 'So Aklen didn't tell you about the engagement?'

'No, he didn't. He must be old fashioned that way and I've never noticed.'

'I do love your daughter very much.'

'Yes, I think you do.' Caplan followed him, watching the handsome face of her future son-in-law soften as he looked down to see Emma, and the beam of happiness on Emma's as she looked up.

Caplan spoke without looking at him. 'If you hurt her, in any way, you'll see a side of me that you won't like.'

There was a spike of hilarity as Kenny finished telling a filthy joke about a nun and a blind man.

Caplan felt her phone buzz.

Mags smiled. 'You forget, DCI Caplan, that was the side of you I saw first. I'm not likely to forget it. If that was your phone and you need to go, we won't be offended. You might be required to enforce the fascist police state against the will of the populace.'

'Again?' she muttered and opened her phone.

TWO

When Caplan walked down the stairs of Challie Cottage to say goodbye to the guests, her face must have betrayed her reaction to the news from Control. They sat in silence; she simply said she had to go. Aklen gave her a hug, and as she got in the car, she heard Mags saying, 'I guess duty calls.'

Then Aklen's weary response: 'It always does.'

Caplan was relieved. The satnav said the drive would take her nearly an hour and, at that moment, she felt the greater the distance between her and the lovely Jade, the better. She'd thought the new navy-blue linen trousers and white blouse, confidently bought now there was an area of the house free of plaster dust, was a bit formal for the dinner, but it meant she didn't need to change. She was also suitably dressed if the hot weather continued, and her presence at the scene rolled into the next day. All she had had to do was tidy her hair into its low chignon, grab her rucksack, and she was ready.

The coast road going north was single track with boulders on either side to stop tired drivers ending up in a field with angry sheep or in the freezing water. The first twenty miles had been flat, but it was now undulating, an indicator of the Munros to come. Control had reported that there had been a potentially fatal incident, on the cliff at Torsvaig Castle. The location pricked a memory in Caplan, something that Jade had mentioned, an advert for something? Certainly not a memory of serious criminality. The more immediate problem was that her satnav couldn't find the location and the station had not responded to her request for a more precise address. She had simply been told to head for the village of Limpetlaw, and that was what she was doing, hoping that she was driving in vaguely the right direction.

Control had mentioned that air-sea rescue had been alerted but both the lifeboat and the helicopter were already deployed, one to an incident on the Sound, the other to a climbing casualty in the Glen; such were the challenges of a scorching summer in a tourist destination with mountains that demanded respect and lochs that remained bitter cold, no matter the weather. The last update from the Torsvaig incident was that a drone was now sweeping the bay. Caplan checked the clock in the car; it was 01.07, and a search had already been initiated. The chain of investigation was underway, although basic details, like exactly who was involved and what had happened, were suspiciously absent. Generally, that meant confusion at the scene, many witnesses, maybe intoxicated, everybody with a different story. This wasn't like Glasgow where any situation could be processed by the uniformed branch who could then gather information from multiple sources to reach a definitive narrative.

The female voice on the satnav had been sulking for a while now. Twelve miles along this road, the graphic showed, then turn inland to skirt the landward side of the rise that she could see vaguely in the distance. It was too far for her to see any evidence of a castle but that's what she had been told to look for, on the basis that *you can't miss it*.

The drive itself was not unpleasant. It was a clear night with a full moon, and this far north, it wouldn't get completely dark. There was always a taste of daylight on the horizon, a warm orange glow to the union of sea and sky.

Caplan sighed a slow breath out, letting go of the pressure of the meal, the engagement, Jade, and Mags being so bloody understanding about it all. And why had he asked Aklen for his permission to propose to Emma? Why had he not asked them both? What did they expect her to do? Refuse?

More worryingly, Jade made Kenny very happy, happier than Caplan had ever seen her son. He had grown, matured, but was still a dreamer. He was happy in his flatshare in Glasgow, living with two male friends, but career-wise he still had a few decisions to make. Caplan had waited until injury terminated her dancing career before she went to university; only then had she joined the police. Aklen had always been involved in studying, teaching or practising architecture and design before he had burned out. Kenny was very happy working in a city-centre bar where his easy charm came to the fore.

But Jade? Caplan couldn't quite work her out. She was both mature and juvenile, often simultaneously.

The road swung inland, keeping to flatter terrain as the land hugging the coast began to rise. There was still a long way to go. Caplan looked around for signs of life but could see no lights, no houses, no other traffic around. As if proving a point, a cloud appeared from nowhere and crossed over the moon, dulling her view. The road rolled on, twisting and turning. She glanced at the satnav. Her route was taking her through no man's land. It appeared she was on a journey to the end of the world.

Torsvaig? The satnav blinked in ignorance. She called back to the station, asking if they had an update. They hadn't.

She pulled into a lay-by when her mobile rang. She tapped her screen hoping to be told *all is well, you are not needed.*

It was Adam Spencer, her new Detective Superintendent. 'Sorry to get you out on a Saturday night.'

'Sunday morning,' she corrected him, 'and believe me, this, whatever it is, is preferable to being at home.'

'Is Aklen okay?'

While being slightly perturbed that her new boss had done his homework, she was impressed by the directness of the question. He had a reputation for being a boss who ran a tight ship. 'Oh yes sir, nothing like that.'

'I hear he's designing small houses now.'

'He certainly is. So, what's happening? No matter what, it's got to be better than children in their early twenties flicking Eton mess at each other.'

There was a snort of agreement. 'Wait until the grandchildren appear.' The voice over the speaker changed timbre. 'Do you know Koi McQuarrie?'

'The supermodel? Not personally, I tend not to move in those circles.'

'Your call out was due to an unsubstantiated report that she's lying at the bottom of the cliff at Torsvaig Castle, dead.'

Caplan was confused. 'Was she staying there?'

'No, she owns it.'

'My satnav can't find it. Is it a house somewhere round here?'

'It's Limpetlaw Castle, renamed, befitting its status as a celebrity wedding venue. Limpetlaw wasn't seductive enough for the McQuarries.'

'What are we thinking? Substance abuse? Partying too hard?' Caplan's mind worked through the options.

'Information is limited but it's the old fall, jumped or pushed scenario.'

'But definitely dead?'

'There might have been some hope if she'd landed on sand, but the beach is in a cove formed by the Five Sisters, very nasty rocks. She landed on those. Information coming through is sketchy. There's a presumption that she did not survive but no confirmation.

'Get there and do everything, I mean everything. Take nothing for granted. This case will go viral no matter what has happened, given who she is, or was, and who she's married to. And who the kids are.' He sighed. 'My daughter follows one of them on the socials, thinks the sun shines out his backside.'

Caplan knew that Koi McQuarrie had been married to a celebrity photographer whose name eluded her for the moment. She glanced out the window where some sheep were staring at the car indignantly. 'I didn't know the world did supermodels any more. What does she do now?'

'Nothing, she's just Koi McQuarrie. Her son is a personality.'

'So's mine,' muttered Caplan.

'And her daughter, or stepdaughter, is EB, the influencer. Considering the media frenzy you'll have from the get-go, you can use Pilcottie. The station's small enough to be under the radar. We'll send the media flak to Oban.'

'Okay.'

'We want you front facing and professional. You'll get dragged into the mudslinging, being a cop makes you an easy target. But we want, we need, everything explored. Everything. Nothing left open that can come back to bite us on the bum at a later date, at the inquest.'

'Inquest? Are you thinking suicide? Unlawful death?'

'We don't know anything yet. But if she's at the bottom of a cliff, then I really hope it was an innocent fall.' She heard him sigh. 'Actually, I hope it's all a mistake and she's fine. I've always liked her; she was my favourite of the Sunflower Girls.'

'Yes, sure, the tall blonde with a famous bottom. Was it her personality that attracted you and every other man on the face of the planet?'

'Hey, they were the kids who never tried to be cool.' He became serious. 'Be wary though, nothing'll be as it seems up there. These people lead a different life from us, so tread with caution.'

'The Sunflower Girls? Have the other two already passed away? I have a vague memory?'

'Indeed they have, DCI Caplan. Keep that fact to the front of your mind when you're working the case. Social media will think that one's an accident, two a coincidence, but all three? The conspiracy theorists will be all over this.'

She thanked him and put Limpetlaw Castle into the satnav. It responded with an unnamed road on the right. Pulling out, she drove very slowly, looking for a gap in the drystane wall, any sign that there was a junction ahead. Ten minutes later, she was still driving, still looking, thinking that she had missed the turn-off but not understanding how that could be.

Then she saw it. The moon slid out from behind the lone cloud letting the castle reveal itself, sitting proudly on the headland with a tall tower pointing to the sky. Slowing to walking pace, she spotted the turn in the road and a small black sign that said only guests and authorised visitors were allowed beyond this point.

The road here was bordered by thick hedgerow with individual rocks on the margins of the tarmac; intermittent signs gave the precise distance to the next passing place or lay-by. It felt ordered and cared for.

The road was climbing now as she drove up to an area of flat land, and a sign saying 'Car Park'. Another sign had an 'H' on it and an arrow. She thought about parking, lining the Duster up with the few cars already there. She recognised the red Hilux parked next to a battered brown Jeep. The blue Corsa also looked familiar, but she reasoned there must be other official cars further on; it looked a long walk from here. The hedgerow gave way to trees, saplings at first then into a deeper, older wood. Within a few minutes, the branches of the substantial oaks were meeting overhead, creating a tunnel of green where the darkness was absolute. She got the rather eerie sensation that the woods extended a long way on either side, and if left to Mother Nature, this strip of tarmac would be entirely reabsorbed. The sense of disorientation was unnerving; the castle, the sea, the sky were not visible through the leafy canopy. Caplan shuddered, sensing something was watching from the trees, something hiding deep in the dark. Then the ancient wall gained height: eight feet, ten feet, twelve feet. The Duster was now on a narrow road across an inclined lawn, approaching a set of ornate gates, open enough to allow access for a vehicle. The words 'Failte' was arched over the top of each gate, but Caplan noted the spikes that were functional as well as decorative.

She was still driving at a snail's pace when a ghost, a flash of bone and flesh, darted out in front of her. She stamped on the brake.

No noise, but there must have been an impact. In the ensuing silence, a small skull appeared over the bonnet, spindly twiglet fingers stretching out towards her.

Caplan nearly screamed, clamping her hand over her mouth as she leaned towards the windscreen, peering at the stick-thin arms, the scrawny neck. Hair hung in ringlets around the features of a small wretched face, jet-black eyes, sunken cheeks hollowed to shadows. The girl steadied herself, but not before Caplan saw the tear marks that streaked the skin, the fear and the horror behind the eyes that now opened, like a wraith surrendering to capture.

Caplan fumbled for the door handle now, getting out, not taking her eyes from the girl running down the grass and into the wood under the cover of the trees. She got out, setting off in slow pursuit, tracking the flashes of white linen, an easy target, easy to follow. Somewhere behind her, Caplan heard an engine stop, a door slam, a shout that sounded like 'roe'.

Somebody was looking for this distressed young lady, so close to a location where a life had apparently been lost a matter of hours before. The two had to be connected.

The ghostly figure was now weaving between the trees, too tired to run properly, resting behind each tree trunk, hiding from whatever, whoever was in pursuit. Caplan was determined to get there first and offer protection to this terrified girl.

She found the hunched figure of a young teenager cowering behind a broad tree trunk, her thin arms, barely bone and skin, hugging her knees, head down, a keening noise slipping from her lips.

'Hello,' said Caplan, treading carefully, not getting any closer. This person was seriously ill. That degree of weight loss was neither natural nor healthy. 'Are you okay?'

No response. Into her field of vision appeared a woman, half Caplan's age, jogging through the trees, wearing what looked like a white evening dress, matched with an overlarge blue jumper and untied trainers. She saw Caplan and stopped, then bent over, hands on her knees, sucking in deep breaths of fresh air.

'Is she there?' she asked quietly, the woollen cuff backhanding her tears from red, puffy eyes. Her fingers made a curved gesture, indicating behind the tree before retracting into the sleeve.

'Yes,' said Caplan, stepping forward, placing herself carefully, professional instinct telling her to intervene between a distressed individual and a determined, but equally distressed pursuer.

The woman in the evening dress straightened up, placed her hands on her hips and looked like she was counting to ten, slowly, then wiped the sweat from her forehead with her cuff.

'Morrow?' she called loudly. 'You need to come back; you're not making this easier for anybody.'

'I hate them all,' came the strangled voice from the bottom of the tree.

The woman tucked her tousled hair behind her ears, shoved the sleeves of her jumper up her arms and sighed, 'Yes, well I hate them all too, but it doesn't exactly help the situation does it? I'm heading back now.' She sniffed loudly. 'This lady here'll bring you up. She's the one they're waiting for so don't keep her too long. This is not about you!' She shook her head at Caplan in abject apology before turning and walking back to the road, the white hem of her dress darkening as it dragged through the leaves.

Caplan looked down at the teenager, now uncoiling herself from the bottom of the tree and standing up, her dark eyes showing no surprise at all.

'Are you okay?'

'Fuck,' the girl said, and started walking back the way she had come.

Her name was Morrow. That was all Caplan got out of her during the short drive up to the castle, that and heart-wrenching sobbing, then a stony silence which was more difficult to bear.

She drove slowly up to the impressive wall that curved around the hill, only broken by the wrought iron gate, noticing that two rearing unicorns held up the words 'Failte: The Welcome Gate'. The view through the gate was the long driveway to the castle itself. Outside was a small group of people – not the police, Caplan noted – but more like fans paying their respects, or journalists clutching their recording devices. Caplan looked at the time. It was not yet two a.m. Somebody had made whatever had happened here public very quickly. She now understood why Spencer had been concerned. Caplan saw two security guards; the older was obviously ex-job as he tipped his head in salute as he waved her through the gate, while ushering a small overweight man out. But not before one of the onlookers had snapped them with a phone.

As she stopped at a smaller, second gate, the other security guard opened the passenger door and bent over to nod at Caplan before addressing the teenager now sitting with her arms looped round her knees, scowling. The DCI noted that Perkins, according to the ID round his neck, had wet trousers.

'Morrow? Get inside,' he said sternly, but not without kindness. His attitude suggested he knew her well and that this wasn't an uncommon occurrence. Then she was dismissed with a gesture to go in the direction of the main castle door, and he closed the smaller gate behind them.

'You better go with her, Joe, don't leave her on her own with all this going on,' said the older security guard.

Caplan noted the phrase, *with all this going on*. 'DCI Christine Caplan. I've a team around here somewhere; there's some familiar cars down at the car park.' She shook hands with him, and he introduced himself as Frank Pickering, ex-DC from Oban.

'There's been an incident at the cliff. Koi, Mrs McQuarrie-Samphire? She's . . .' He shrugged. 'Dead at the bottom of the cliff. We don't really know. Scene of Crime are on-site already. Callum's about somewhere.'

'Callum?' asked Caplan.

'DC McPhee. He caught the call, was first on the scene. He'll know what's going on.'

'Good,' said Caplan. Of course, these guys would know her team if they were ex-job; they would have known them for longer than she had. 'How do I get to the cliff?'

Pickering sniffed and thought for a moment. 'Get the layout of the place straight in your head first. Go back down to the outer gate, there's a path there that runs round the outer wall and up to the clifftop. There's a flat headland called the King's Reach.' He waited until she nodded her understanding. 'I'd better stay here; we've just moved the rubberneckers.'

She pointed at the small gathering. 'How is this public so early?'

Pickering shrugged, 'Curse of social media. If the Samphires sneeze, somebody has it on their content.'

'Oh right. Can I get directly to the top of the cliff from here?' Caplan asked.

He shook his head. 'No way. It was built to deter invasion from the sea.' He pointed to the high wall, an impressive structure, fifty feet high at this point. 'This huge wall circles the castle, the bailey – well, the entire courtyard really, including the chapel, the living areas and the wedding venue. If you think it looks high now, it was much higher back in the day. The family are safe inside.'

'Just the family?'

'Yes, no guests, no wedding party, just them. If you want to visit the castle first,' he pointed, 'follow this path, the door is open.'

Caplan began to walk up the gravel drive. The lawns on either side were cut very close, the verdant hue showing they had received the constant attentions of a sprinkler during the heatwave. She wondered who their gardener was, and how often he visited. The old, wide driveway swerved to the right to lead up to the castle, the entrance marked by magnificent oak double doors, heavily patterned with diamond-headed wooden nails, a flaming torch fixed to the wall on either side. At the moment one door was open, the other closed. A familiar figure was tapping one finger on his tablet, his paper notebook between his teeth. He was sweating profusely, getting gently toasted by the heat from torches on either side of the stone portals. As she watched he took a step away from the naked flames before his scalp got roasted.

'Callum?'

He looked at her with an anger that stemmed from frailty. She had seen him bleeding from a stab wound to the chest, ending up on the operating table needing thirty pints of blood transfused; he'd been haemorrhaging as quickly as he was receiving it.

With that one knife wound, the brave but daft DC McPhee was gone, and had been replaced by this stony-faced facsimile.

'I guess you weren't at the party either.' He gestured to their similar attire: dark trousers, flat boots, thin jackets hanging over their shoulders.

She smiled. 'Do you know this place?'

'The locals call it Koi Castle. It was Limpetlaw Castle for a thousand years, then Torsvaig when the Palmer Hotel chain took over.'

'Does Koi own it now?' Up close, even with the rosy glow from the flaming torches, McPhee looked gaunt. He looked as though he'd aged ten years.

He frowned in concentration. 'I don't know for certain, but it'll be a shell company or a sister company to keep the tax bill down. I can only tell you what I've surmised from a quick look online. You've seen their security; they have motion-sensitive lights and cameras there.' McPhee nodded at the gates. 'You'll know all about the family from what you've seen in the media.'

'You know, I've been living in an old caravan with dodgy Wi-Fi for the last couple of years,' Caplan replied. 'I'm in need of an update.'

'It's Koi McQuarrie,' confirmed the young detective in hushed tones that made it hard for Caplan to hear against the gentle rush of the flames.

'Yes?' Caplan stood for a moment, looking up at the closest of the four towers, and the single narrow stack that tapered towards the sky. Over the top of the castellated walls, high above her, was a sky that was still undecided about darkening. Or lightening. Her neck hurt. 'And, what's happened?'

'They had a family gathering in the bailey – eight of them from what I can ascertain. A bit of dancing, some drinks. Koi left on foot, went past Frank and Joe at the Welcome Gate, and then walked up the path to the cliff and went off the top. No witnesses. I was just about to make my way up there.'

'If there were no witnesses, how do we know what happened?'

McPhee looked a little uneasy. 'She left the party, then minutes later her husband followed. They heard a scream as soon as he was out the gate. He had no time to get up the Queen's Rise path, to the clifftop. That was my first thought. He didn't have the time. She was alone up there.'

'Did they tell you that?'

McPhee looked a bit sheepish.

'Why did she go? Alone? In the dark?'

'To jump off the top?' offered McPhee.

'Has anybody said that?'

'My deduction.'

Caplan thought for a moment. 'So, a family party? Drink? Drugs?'

'They're celebrities, so I wouldn't be surprised, but nobody was out-their-face drunk, if that's what you mean.'

'Why did she go? It's a fair walk. Down to the lower gate and back up the other side. Was she meeting somebody?'

'Not established that yet.'

Caplan looked up at the gradient.

'It's a bit of a leg-stretcher,' McPhee said. 'DS Craigo has been trying to gather statements from the family, when he can find people. This place is huge, ma'am. The wedding venue hotel bit is lovely. There's the wing where the family live but some of it is old, stinking, damp and dark, like scary dark.'

She caught a slight smile pass his lips.

'Yes?'

'Made me think of Scooby Doo, that's all. They even have the big dog.'

'Okay, Shaggy.' She nodded. 'Meet you at the top of the cliff once you're finished here?'

He nodded. 'Boss said to get media liaison on it straight away.'

'The fans have wind of it already, so keep an eye on the situation. You're the one with the real authority here, don't forget that.' Caplan gave him a rueful nod of dismissal and walked through a smaller gate down to the Welcome Gate, to start her ascent to the cliff. It was the summer solstice, just after two in the morning, yet it had been so bright when she left the cottage, away from the effects of light pollution, it could have been early dawn already.

She slid out through the Castle Gate, avoiding the attention of the small crowd as Pickering moved them slowly backwards. At the larger Welcome Gate, she walked round the meagre collection of flowers and candles before starting up the path, wide enough for three people, maybe more if they were close together and super slim. The dense shrubs on either side had recently been trimmed back, leaving a slab-stone track that was bordered by grass and low gorse, substantial trees and a wall beyond that. She looked down at how smooth the slabs under her feet were. Well worn with centuries of soldiers tramping up and down them, guarding the castle.

The coast at this point was a cove, a sandy beach to the north, then a sharp rise to a rocky cliff that varied in height up to nine or ten metres. It'd be an easy place to defend. There was something very impressive about the location. To the right, the ancient walls of the castle rose above her to disappear into the subtle darkness, ancient stone upon ancient stone, some minerals glinting in the moonlight. To the left was an ever-increasing drop to the sea.

Then the landscape changed as the path took a turn inland, the noise of the waves below growing immediately louder, the salt scent of the sea stronger. Through the foliage, she could see lights at the edge of the tall cliff. Unsure of her footing, she put on her phone torch and followed the path round the bend of the circular castle tower. The trees thickened, forming a hedge between her and the top of the cliff, but she knew she was close to the edge. Over the rhythmic hush of the cresting waves, she could hear voices carried through the night air.

Was it a crime? That she fell off a cliff? Because it was Koi McQuarrie, this incident would be subject to intense public scrutiny. They needed somebody with some rank to be seen to investigate. Jade was right: the public's faith in the police service was at rock bottom, morale was at an all-time low and once word of 'an incident involving Koi McQuarrie' had worked its way up the chain of command, the case had priority stamped all over it.

Caplan came across a flagstone platform, the Queen's View, which afforded a view across the bay and the treacherous rocks below that encompassed the north and south of the cove. Nobody could survive a fall onto those. Where she stood, the cliff edge was protected by a solid wooden fence with a metal plaque detailing that it was 2,320 miles to the North Pole and 3,170 miles to New York. She tested the fence, making sure it was firm before she leaned on it and looked out, getting as good a view as she could. The uplift of sea spray on the breeze kissed the skin of her cheek.

To her right the cliff dropped in height, the castle being built on the highest promontory – the distance from the top of the castle wall to the bottom of the cliff was an eye-watering drop. It was hard to judge it in such faint light, but Caplan guessed the drop was over ten metres. The Scene of Crime guys were already working on an area of grass, bordered by thick ancient walls to the north and the east; the south side was partly bordered by the castle wall and then the path. To the front of them, heading west, was the sheer drop to the rocks below, now buffered from the waves by a band of wet sand.

Caplan captured the image in her mind as two people stood together on the flat land at the top of the cliff, on the King's Reach, looking out to sea. She realised that it was a version of an image she had seen many times recently: a full-page ad in one of the Sundays, with the two scene techs being replaced by Koi and a man, a male model probably, posing on the clifftop with the sunset behind them. In real life, the composition would have been enhanced, or dominated, by the tall, elegant ruin of the ancient tower, little more than a spindle of rocks that reached to the sky in an ever-tapering turret. She recognised it as the feature she'd seen from the road. That tower had been airbrushed out of the shot, probably because it would have drawn the eye away from the beautiful couple. It had been photographed during a perfect single moment of the setting sun. In that image, the tumbling lace train of the designer wedding dress had been dramatically splayed in front of the bride, some of the lace cascading down the cliff, filigree over rock. The photographer would have been Koi's husband, and he would have been standing where she was now, to take that picture. He had a biblical name like Noah or Jeremiah, and he'd been married to Koi for a long time. It looked like the events of the morning had put an end to that.

The cliff that faced her was fearsome. She could imagine any invading army who had marched up the hill behind her would have little energy left for fighting. Looking down to the rocks, she saw the white of the waves, the patches of sand and seaweed left to dry at the waterline, abandoned by the receding tide.

The drop was sheer, and deadly.

Caplan shivered.

The rolling pattern of the waves was disrupted by a light dancing on the surface. The annoying buzz got slightly louder as a drone came into view, sweeping over the bay. She followed the clifftop path, walking towards the group of crime scene techs working under the strong lights.

Caplan didn't dare to go any closer to the edge. Instead of looking down, she looked out to sea, to the drone now hovering over the narrow beach and the retreating waves. 'DCI Caplan. Can somebody update me?' she asked, addressing the five or six people who were gathered, discussing something around a tall man with a very powerful torch. He promptly got down on his belly on top of a polythene tarpaulin and shone the beam over the edge.

He shouted over his shoulder, his face pale against the night sky. 'She's gone, you know. The body's gone.'

THREE

'Gone?'

'McQuarrie went over the cliff right here, landed on those rocks and we think the tide carried her out.' The technician pointed with his torch, and stood slightly to the side, allowing Caplan to take the few steps to the edge. 'The body was gone before we got here.'

Ignoring the drop-induced nausea, Caplan nodded.

'And if she survived the fall by some miracle, she wouldn't have been able to get to the safety of Limpetlaw beach because of the rock formations. You can walk round them at low tide, but at high tide you'd either be bashed against the rocks or drowned. Fatal either way. We're just combing the bottom of the cliff to make sure she's not managed, somehow, to get herself to a safe spot.'

Out of the corner of her eye she saw McPhee at the top of the path, stopping to catch his breath, so she gladly took a step back. Then another. She'd been too far out on the ledge of crumbling earth for comfort.

'When did you get here?' she asked her constable.

'About twelve forty-five? When I arrived, all they had was a drone. Wattie, the local cop, had already called out rescue response. Mr Pomeroy called him. It wasn't safe for a smaller boat to attempt it due to the rocks.'

'Who's Pomeroy?'

McPhee pulled a face. 'Koi's manager? Seems to be in charge.'

Caplan looked at the time on her phone, almost half-past two, then at the horizon where the faint orange line was increasing in depth and luminosity. She said very quietly, 'And who's that? Sitting with their feet over the edge? Watching?' She nodded her head to the cliff at the north side of the cove. 'Are they safe there?'

'Oh, I did point them out. Triton—'

'Pardon?'

'Tron for short. One of the children – well, teenagers. Pomeroy told us to leave him alone.'

'It's a bit worrying the way he's sitting.' Caplan looked round. 'So, who raised the alarm?'

'Samphire did.'

Caplan nodded in encouragement. 'Koi's husband? First name?'

'Gabriel, Gabriel Samphire.'

Caplan turned and pointed at the top of the path. 'Let me get this straight. McQuarrie had walked away from the party, come up the Queen's Rise. Samphire went after her but had only got as far as the gate when he heard the scream. He could hear her scream from here?'

'Yes, ma'am. The gate is really just over the wall here, but it's a long walk round. When he heard the scream, he came running up and found her dead on the rocks at the bottom of the cliff.'

'He saw the body?'

'Yes.'

'Have you?'

'No.'

Caplan shook her head and said quietly. 'So, we are looking for a body that nobody has actually seen apart from the husband?'

'Oh. Shit.'

'Have the crime scene guys found any sign of a struggle? Blood? Hair? Drag marks?' She tapped her heel on the dry earth. 'There'll be no footprints with the ground this hard.'

'They've had good light, good visibility and they've found nothing ma'am, so I doubt there was anything to see.' McPhee was almost apologetic.

'Well, a lack of evidence is sometimes evidence in itself.' Caplan started to walk towards the tower of the castle, getting McPhee to fall into step with her, moving further away from the techs on the cliff.

'Ma'am, Samphire got up here – he wasn't really making much sense to be honest – then went back down and raised the alarm. Pomeroy called it into Wattie at Pilcottie station. I got here early, within an hour, but I didn't come up here. Samphire said the waves were already moving her when he saw her, he said it looked like she was waving goodbye. So, I presume the water floated her from the rocks.' He stopped, taking a deep breath, then gathered himself. 'Oh, and when I spoke to Pomeroy, he said . . . I think it was him . . . that Samphire and somebody else, I can't recall who, had attempted to get access via the beach but the tide was too high. So, if they were trying to access her, she must have been there,' he added lamely.

'That's the path on the outside of the gate?'

McPhee shook his head. 'No. You can only get on the beach via the woods down closer to the car park. The beach is public – that sign about only guests and authorised visitors beyond this point is a bit cheeky – but the Welcome Gate is kept closed. It might be possible to get round the rocks on the beach now – the tide turned two hours ago.' He put his hands to his face, breathing in hard. 'I'm sorry, so sorry. They were all talking, and I couldn't get a straight answer. I felt out of my depth.' He winced slightly at his phrasing, his eyes drifting out to the waves and the Tinker Bell light from the drone that danced on the surface.

'Callum, you were dealing with people who spend their lives spinning a story. Don't worry, we'll find out what happened. We've no body, no trace of a body and no witnesses to what actually happened.' Caplan placed a comforting arm on his shoulder as they walked downhill.

'CSI want me,' he said, looking at his phone screen in response to the silent notification.

'Let's hope they've found something of interest, eh?' said Caplan, and McPhee was off, taking the steps two at a time, with the vigour of youth, leaving her with the sinking feeling that everything was too little, far too late.

She looked up at the sky, at the castle defences. Three cordons of solid ancient stone kept this place safe, and the drop in the land was steep. This climb, following the jog through the wood after the skinny girl, had been more than enough for her after a hard day preparing for the dinner party. She'd talk to Samphire and this guy Pomeroy, find out what actually happened.

As the path led her into the dark shadow of the castle wall, she heard an alert on her phone. Opening up the screen, she saw an image of a woman lying on rocks, surrounded by waves, her long white dress a wavering halo. Her blond hair swirled like the snakes of Medusa in the ocean; blood poured from wounds on her face; her eyes were open and staring at the sky. With her arms outspread, she was fair Ophelia in her watery bed, about to be swallowed by an approaching wave.

Caplan recognised that face immediately.

It was Koi McQuarrie.

* * *

Caplan blew out a long, slow breath, and leaned against the rough stone of the castle wall. Had these people posted a picture of the dead body of their wife, their mother, on social media within minutes of calling the police? Heartless bastards? Or getting their story out to the public first?

There followed a text message from Spencer to say that this photograph was now viral on social media. As if she needed to be told.

Celebrities didn't think like normal people. These days every life event was recorded. Had Samphire documented Koi's death as he had everything about her life? A fit young man running might take half an hour to get up and down the Queen's Rise. It had taken her twenty minutes to get up; she didn't think Samphire would be much faster. Why stop and take a photograph before getting help? Because he was a photographer? Or? She couldn't figure out an 'or'.

She jumped as McPhee came round the corner.

'God, Callum!'

'Have you seen the picture ma'am? We've all got it.'

'Yes.'

'Well, you need to come and see this. We don't need to go all the way back up.'

She followed him up onto the platform that looked over to the King's Reach to where two of the crime scene guys were lying on their stomachs, watching the light on the drone as it swept back and forth over the rock face with a slow metronomic rhythm.

'What is that over there?' Caplan lifted her phone from her pocket and took a picture of the cliff. 'It looks like a bit of material.' She opened the image on her mobile and zoomed in.

McPhee looked at her phone screen. 'The description of her clothes was a long white dress and a lemon scarf, like a pashmina.'

No matter how far they leaned out, those on the King's Reach couldn't see it from their viewpoint. The material had been snagged on a sharp point of rock directly below them. Had that happened as Koi fell past?

Caplan looked back up just as the bright beam of a torch focused on the rock face, picking up the lonely figure of the Samphire child on the King's Reach. At least somebody was checking that he was still there.

Caplan swore as she saw a crime scene tech shuffle forward on his stomach to dangle the top half of his body, trying to see the scarf waving on the cliff face below him, far beyond his reach.

'Get over there quickly and tell them we'll retrieve it when we have qualified help. I don't want anybody else going off that cliff.' She watched her DC walk away, her eyes drawn to the lone figure of Tron at the far side, hunched over, not engaging with any of it.

'Dear God,' muttered Caplan, throwing a last look at the brightening horizon and the billowing material snagged on the rock. It waved like a flag of honour. Or a flare of distress.

Koi McQuarrie: a Cinderella story, plucked from obscurity at Stansted Airport to worldwide fame. A beautiful face and sparkling blue eyes, a good and decent woman according to her public image. Caplan looked up at the dark walls of the castle, forbidding and foreboding. Keeping the public out.

Or keeping the family in?

This was a terrible thing. This would punctuate people's lives. People would always remember where they were when the last of the Sunflower Girls died.

Originally, there had been three Sunflower Girls. Two had passed away and, if Caplan's memory served her correctly, their children had been brought up by Koi and her husband, Gabriel Samphire. Rosie was the eldest child, the woman who had followed Morrow into the woods. Caplan wanted to talk to her to make sure that Morrow was okay and find out what she could about Tron, the boy sitting on the cliff. That accounted for three of Koi's children. Given the age of Rosie, some of those children would be, should be, independent adults by now. Given the state of Morrow and Tron, they were not without their challenges.

Caplan went back down the path, noticing the lights on the rope posts at the side, there for aesthetic reasons rather than with any thought to safety, as the slab stones under foot were so smooth and shiny that they'd be treacherously slippy on a wet, winter day, in a strong wind, after a few glasses of wine or while wearing a long dress.

These thoughts made her doubt the viability of the castle as a profitable wedding venue; then she remembered that photograph of the bride and groom on the clifftop. That had seared its way into her psyche, yet she had no memory of ever paying it any particular attention. Maybe that was the effect of Samphire's photography, drawing the viewer to beautiful things: the light catching the white lace against the ebony rock, and the composition of the image, with the loving couple looking so small and insignificant against the majesty of the castle and the cliff. If the image was created to sell a wedding dress, then it failed, as the dress itself was lost in the beauty of the landscape.

She made her way down the Queen's Rise, taking four or five strides for each step, thinking how huge weddings were now, costing a fortune. Hen parties were not a night at the bingo but a long weekend in Marbella. Stag nights were a bier fest in Berlin. Weddings needed chocolate fountains, pipers, street-food vendors. A dog chaperone was needed to look after the family pet for the day, bringing Rover along for inclusion in the photographs. Thank God Emma was sensible, and of course Mags was a 'careful' millionaire. Their wedding would be a quiet affair, Caplan was sure of that. Then she wondered if the lovely Jade would still be on the scene by then, and guiltily found herself hoping not.

At the bottom of the path, she slinked along the outside of the wall, moving quickly but keeping to the darker shadows. She saw Pickering addressing the ever growing gathering of journalists and fans, taking a bunch of flowers and placing them against the wall, joining others that were already there.

He opened the Welcome Gate when he saw her coming.

'Has your colleague come back?'

'Not yet. He'll be settling Morrow with Rosie, she's the only one staying sane at the moment. Wee Morrow's nice, calls us Pinky and Perky. Hard to think that she's what? Seventeen? Eighteen?' He dropped his voice. 'I've seen the picture.'

'Who do you think put that picture out in the world?'

'Any of them would have done it. It's the way they are.' Pickering shook his head in disapproval, the wrinkles in his face creasing to show every one of his sixty years. 'She landed right on the rocks. Brutal.' He shook his head.

Caplan cast a glance around her. 'What did you actually witness?'

Pickering pursed his lips. 'Nothing really, we were hanging around in the driveway between the two gates, there's a nice bench there, it gives us a good view. We have a wee hut here and we turn the camera monitor round, so we can see everything. They need that level of security. Anyway, we were listening to the music coming from the party. It was a nice night, warm, barely dark, so our vision was good.' Pickering glanced around, as if looking for his colleague. 'Koi came out the bailey, came through the gate, she was her normal cheery self. She came through here, and walked up the Queen's Rise, where you've just been. About ten minutes later, Gabe came out and asked us where she'd gone. We heard the scream before he was out of our sight, so he was nowhere near her when it happened. There's a camera on the gate as well so it'll be recorded. It's motion sensitive and catches everything.'

Caplan nodded, knowing that she could put this together later.

'So, you were here, and Koi came out? She definitely seemed normal?'

'Yip, she'd popped out earlier to give us some beer, alcohol free before you ask, and a tray with pizza, olives, garlic bread and a burger. We were sitting on the bench at the hut, enjoying the food when Koi came through the Castle Gate, like I said.'

Caplan turned to look, judging the distance, thinking about the light, what they could actually see. 'You saw her come out the door?'

'That door makes a huge squeak and bangs when opened or closed. She was wearing a white dress, easy to see, a floaty long thing. And a big scarf wrapped round her, her hair was pulled up on top of her head and kind of falling down. She looked like the ghost of Lady Mary – she's a portent of doom that hangs around here.'

He seemed serious so Caplan said, 'Time?'

'Like I said to Callum, just before the fireworks. Midnight? Gabe went after her, he wasn't in a hurry or anything, he said he wanted to know where she was.'

'To backtrack for a moment, a woman on her own went up a path to the clifftop at midnight? Did you not think to stop her?'

'We're security, not their guardians.' Pickering put both hands up. 'There was no suggestion of anything odd, like I said, she was her normal self. They have their eccentricities as all rich and beautiful people do. I presumed she was going to look at the sky at the solstice. If you ask me, she fell. She wasn't the type to take her own life. She didn't drink, didn't do any drugs, said she'd lost too many good friends that way.'

'She didn't seem upset or annoyed?'

'No. More like she was going to get some sea air, or to look at the sky, look at the moon and all that. She waved at us before she went round the corner. She was in a good mood.'

'And sober, you think?'

'Yes. Some of them though . . .' said Pickering, giving her a wee nod, '. . . take a few things recreationally.'

'Who?'

'EB. Mostly.'

'I didn't get that from you,' Caplan smiled. 'No suggestion that Koi was meeting somebody else?'

'Nobody else walked past us.'

'You're sure of that?'

'I am. The place was built to give those on the Welcome Gate a good line of sight. It's slanted, facing the sea. Nobody can get past.'

'Okay, so Gabriel, Mr Samphire, came out maybe ten minutes later. Asked where she went then he followed her. There was a scream and . . . Did you go up after him?'

'No, we waited here. We thought he had bumped into her on her way down and given her a fright. It was a light scream, if you know what I mean, not a blood-curdling screech. It seemed ages before he came running up to the gate, shouting something like, "She's fallen." He was running, you know, upset, and then he set off towards the beach.'

'She's fallen? He said that?'

'I think so. We didn't ask, we just assumed from his actions that she was in the water, so we ran after him. He got through the wood and into the water before Joe dragged him out and slapped some sense into him. It was bloody stupid. The current is lethal at high tide, those rocks are deadly. Before I followed him into the wood, I raised the alarm with Pomeroy, he called Pilcottie. Wattie called out the emergency services, but we haven't seen or heard a helicopter. He sent Callum round, and then the CSI appeared, then Finan Craigo, then you.'

'There's an incident up the Glen, another out at sea,' Caplan informed him. 'They'll attend as soon as they can. The information here was of a reported fatality, they'd prioritise elsewhere.'

'Aye. We heard, a yacht sinking out in the Sound, and a kiddie taken a tumble in Glen Coe, head injury. I mean taking young kids on a hill walk? They don't realise the dangers,' said Pickering, rubbing at the bridge of his nose. 'I was in mountain rescue for years, that's where I met Joe. But Koi gone? That's hard to take. She was so full of life.' He shook his head. 'Still, you'd better hope that the fall did kill her. If not and the delay did, then you have the shitshow from hell on your shoulders.'

'Who saw the body?'

'Well, Gabe did. Did any of the crime scene guys?'

'No,' said Caplan. 'If you know these waters, where is she likely to wash up?'

He thought for a moment. Caplan was going to repeat the question, thinking that he had not heard. 'One body I know went in on Limpetlaw beach and was washed back up a few days later. Two from a fishing boat out on the Sound washed up there too. Better asking the Coastguard. But there's one thing – we were told, asked, to do a walk round the perimeter of the property, the woods, the cliff, including the Woodwall that runs from the castle to the clifftop. We did a walk round before the party tonight.'

'Was that unusual?'

'It was when there was only family here. But yes, I'd say there was a wee ramp-up of security.'

'Any reason?'

'Pomeroy said it was due to the Unterweger wedding last month. That put Torsvaig on the map as a venue.'

'The Unterweger wedding?' asked Caplan, exaggerating her ignorance.

'The star of the film *The Skin Game* married the director here. It was very successful, our eighth wedding, hence the celebration tonight. It was a private affair due to issues with their ex-spouses, their age difference and the paparazzi. If Torsvaig can keep a celebrity wedding like that quiet, this business will be made for life,' Pickering said, shrugging. 'Then there's Koi's stalker. You should have that on record. Calls himself the Fisherman.'

Caplan made a mental note. 'But to clarify, there's no way in or out except past you or off the cliff. Nobody could sneak past you or down to the beach, over the wall? While you were enjoying the beer and the burgers? No way the stalker could have got to her?'

'No.' He pointed, 'The security cameras are at the front of the castle, in the wood and on the drive up to the big gates.'

'But none overlooking the King's Reach?'

'No, none.'

Caplan gave a small nod, muttering, 'Handy.'

Pickering's radio crackled, a quick message that Caplan couldn't make out. Then he turned to her. 'Is Callum still up on the clifftop?'

'Yes.'

'Aye. He's up there,' he said into the radio, and then stopped the call. 'Rosie's asking for Callum.'

'I'll send word up,' said Caplan, not wanting her train of thought interrupted. 'And Tron?'

'What about him?'

'Well, he's up on the King's Reach so he must have got past you?'

The first look of doubt flickered over Pickering's face. 'Well, I guess he must have slipped out in all the panic of Samphire running for the beach. We'd left Pomeroy covering the gate.' He shrugged. 'It'll be on the footage. I'll make sure you get it.'

'Thank you. And Rosie?'

'Came out in the car to get Morrow.' Pickering leaned forward to speak quietly out of the corner of his mouth. 'She's not exactly normal, and to say the rest of them are a tad eccentric would be putting it mildly.'

Caplan looked around her and said quietly, 'I'm looking at all this security. Tell me about the stalker, cop to cop?'

'We are non-disclosured up to our eyeballs, DCI Caplan. But Koi McQuarrie was a beautiful woman and this world's full of weirdos. There's been unwelcome attention in the past. Pomeroy jokes that Gabe keeps a dick-pic diary for the photos they get from nutters. But the Fisherman? You didn't hear this from me, but I think there's been death threats, rape threats. That's the reason they moved here, to the middle of nowhere, from London.'

'To hide behind these walls?'

Pickering gave her a brief nod; this was as far as he was prepared to go.

Caplan looked around, a little awed by the castle. 'What would normally happen, security-wise?'

'We shut the two gates, this big Welcome Gate and the smaller Castle Gate. Nobody can get through those, and nobody's getting over that wall, are they?'

Caplan was about to point out that might not be true when a small round man waddled his way up the path from the direction of the car park.

'Oh, here we go,' sighed Pickering.

'Hello, son. Thank fuck yer here.' The man's light-grey jacket hung over a well-developed beer belly and his flat cap was frilled with wiry grey hair. He looked as if he had spent the day walking the hills searching for a stray lamb for his dinner. 'Right, whit's happening?' he said, hands on hips, 'did that daft bint take a heider aff the top? Pished, wis she?'

Caplan flashed her warrant card in front of the newcomer. 'And you are?'

He ignored the card, 'Aye, it's okay, hen, Ah know who Ah am. Wattie from Pilcottie station. Well, Ah've a sofa and a phone. It's a one-man band and that's me, so whit's up that warrants a DCI? The missus fell aff the cliff? Drunk? That's what Ah wis telt. She okay?'

'Nope,' said Pickering.

'Did you bring anybody else with you?' asked Caplan.

'Nope, it's just me. Ah wis told folk would be here.'

'Okay . . . Wattie, can you help get statements from those present, please? We need to make a timeline of tonight's events.'

Wattie snorted. 'You've got two hopes of that, hen. Bob Hope and no hope.'

Pickering translated, 'He means they are too eccentric to get much sense out of.'

'That's one fucking word for it,' said Wattie, circling his forefinger on his temple. 'Bloody film a shit while it's in the pan. Putting her body out there on the phone – their missus? Their ma? Where's yer common decency, eh?' He snorted. 'Right, hen. If yer heading up tae the castle, ask them tae put the kettle on. Wee Cosy Rosie'll see you right. Easiest way in there, go through the back gate tae the bailey, roon the hedge and through the paytio doors.' He turned round, 'Right Pinky, you can tell me whit we have here, once Ah've shifted the motor.'

Caplan turned and walked away, sighing deeply. It was easy to imagine the mechanics of it now she was seeing it in person, the scale of the cliff and the castle, the difficult access, how long it would take anybody to get to the site of the incident, and during that time the body had been carried out to sea. Who would you alert in the event of an incident like that? The body had not been accessible from the cliff, and climbing down would need an expert with equipment. So, they had called the emergency services, mountain rescue plus the Coastguard. Pickering seemed sensible and observant. He had been chosen well for the job, which made Caplan wonder about the level of threat that required such a skill set. Security, at its basic level, could be done by anybody who could walk and hold a torch, but these two might be a cut above that. Pickering had years of experience in law enforcement, while Joe Perkins, well, he looked as if he had seen action.

Was this the state of celebrity nowadays?

The answer to that was obviously yes.

FOUR

The giant wooden doors of the castle were both slightly open, the flames still burning on either side throwing orange shadows onto the cobbles of the drive. The whole scene was eerily quiet. She knew there were many people about, but from where she stood, she could neither see nor hear them. If she closed her eyes and listened hard, she thought she could hear the swish and rush of the waves. Behind the castle wall, probably less than forty feet from where she was standing now, were those who had attended the party. The family had been celebrating the success of the business – dancing, drinking. From here she couldn't hear a sob, a wail, a scream, not even a fan arguing with Pickering on the gate.

Was there something that might drive Koi McQuarrie to take her own life? Was there somebody out there with intent to harm her, as Pickering thought? Morrow, the silent skeleton Caplan had brought back from the woods, looked as though she'd been living with her demons for a while. Tron, the figure on the edge of the clifftop, dicing with death, and the staff's casual acceptance of that behaviour suggested it might be habitual. What was going on with Koi herself? DC Mackie would know all about the family; this celebrity stuff was right up her street.

The other two Sunflower Girls, back in the day, had certainly been troubled. The memory that had been scratching at the back of Caplan's head flexed its limbs and came to life. The Sunflower Girls: three teenagers who had made one famous advert, and the advert had made them famous in return. Caplan thought back to the beach that bordered the woods; the advert had been filmed in a place exactly like this. The three of them, Koi, Ecco and . . . she had to search her memory – Ray? Rhea? – and a big carthorse, had splashed their way through the surf, soundtracked by a George Michael song. She couldn't recall what the advert had been for.

The carefree, laughing teenagers in that advert. All dead now.

It could be interesting to find out who inherited what. As Spencer had hinted, one Sunflower Girl dead was a tragedy, two was a coincidence but three sounded like a plan.

Caplan had pulled her phone from her pocket and was looking down, scrolling for the most recent call when she saw a pair of hand-made shoes neatly sidestep to avoid colliding with her at the doorway.

Caplan apologised immediately. The older man's harassed demeanour and his reddened eyes evidenced some distress at McQuarrie's demise, while the expensive blazer, the white chinos belted under an overhanging belly denoted that this was a man who lived the good life. The collar-length white hair was swept back off his handsome suntanned face. He looked sixty at least. Too old to be Gabriel Samphire.

'Police?' he asked, in between gasps. He was breathless, maybe even older than he had first appeared and not in good shape.

'Yes – DCI Caplan, and you are?'

He shook her hand, a warm firm handshake that jangled his gold identity bracelet. Rose gold, Caplan noted, with a designer tag with medical alert information. 'Philip Pomeroy – Pip, the manager. The young chap said you'd arrived.' He snuffled, guiding her back out of the arched doorway. 'Gabriel's very upset, as you can imagine. He saw her lying . . . down . . . there . . . And Morrow's in a terrible state. I'd like to get our doctor in, Dr Rowe. I say "like", I mean "demand".'

'Morrow's the girl who ran into the woods?'

'Yes,' he sighed. 'If you have met her then you'll understand why we are concerned. We need management of her situation here; the girls were everything to Koi.'

'How old is Morrow? She looks about twelve but somebody else said she was seventeen?'

'Yes, something like that. They grow up so quickly. Gabe's in pieces. So, yes, I think the doctor's the right thing to do. I just want to find him – Gabe, I mean. Have you seen him?'

Caplan shook her head, the heat from the torch warming her face before Pomeroy walked on, leaving the flames to lick the air.

'It's not our intention to cause any further stress. I presume Morrow and Rosie are Koi's children?'

'Pearl Lilac Rose is her full title.' Pomeroy turned to look her straight in the eye, then gave her a very charming smile that creased the tan lines round his brilliant blue eyes. He blinked, looked up to the sky, sighed and relaxed his shoulders, a slight smirk playing round his lips. 'They're so incredibly famous, and we get the one copper who knows nothing about them?' He looked comically offended.

'I've no preconceived ideas. I don't listen to gossip; I'm not impressed by celebrity. We all die with our final breath, princes and paupers both, Mr Pomeroy.'

'Pip, please,' he corrected, walking again but now at funereal pace. The faintest suggestions of shadows on the landward side of the castle were showing how much unnatural light there was around on the shortest night of the year. 'If you ever leave the force, you should join me in PR with a turn of phrase like that. I left Gabriel round here.' He gestured and called the other man's name softly. 'It's the one place that's very quiet.'

At the carved stone alcove on the side of the inner castle wall, the bench was empty. A faint damp mark showed that somebody had sat there in wet clothes very recently.

Pomeroy stood and looked round, twirling a three-sixty, nimble for an overweight man. 'Where's he gone?' He took a few quick strides, before guiding her back to the castle doors. As they stepped on a flagstone floor with thick red carpet, Pomeroy walked quickly on, leaving Caplan to survey the magnificence that was the Great Hall of Torsvaig Castle.

Along the walls of the entry hall the naked flames of three torches burned on each side. Glancing up she saw the yellow and gold pennants and pennons hanging from the arched ceiling and wondered what kind of health and safety certificate this place had.

The only sound was some gentle jazz that seeped creepily from somewhere, and then echoed elsewhere.

Caplan sensed Pomeroy was doing his job. Being a PR manager, he wanted to be present when she talked to Samphire, and Caplan was content to play along, at first.

Pomeroy was on his mobile, paying her no attention. She drifted across the hall, exploring, feeling the castle's homely warmth. The air was scented with peat, amid the aromas of garlic and pesto. She passed a closed door with a brass plate saying 'The Stewart Room' and then looked into the next room. There was a huge unlit fireplace full of logs; a large oblong table that could sit twenty was decorated with intertwined variegated ivy and white oriental lilies down the centre. Long red curtains, tied back in swathes, hung from bars above the windows framing ancient glass and wrought iron squares.

She looked up, taking in the torches, the armour, the muskets, the wooden musicians' gallery, the struts and crossbeams. The vaulted ceiling was three or four floors high, neck-achingly so.

At the bottom of the red carpeted stairway, sitting in the shadows, was a young man, his white linen shirt almost open to his navel, his bare feet matching his bare chest. Dark hair, tinted to auburn by the sun or by some designer hairstylist, was fashionably messy. He was breathtakingly beautiful. And very drunk. A bottle of Chivas Regal nestled against his leg.

Cosmo Samphire.

She recognised him from the front of *GQ* and a TV advert for an aftershave where he stood, dressed much as he was dressed now, balanced on an ice floe. He had the best genes of his mother and his father. The swaying of the heraldic pennants in the draught had hypnotised him. Then, spell broken, he lowered his head, dropping his face between his knees and clamping his hands round the back of his neck. He was an actor but this act of grief was not entirely convincing. This was more akin to relief. Relieved about what, she wondered.

Caplan looked up at the portraits of the clan MacDougall hanging on the lower part of the high-beamed ceiling. Then she saw movement, heard the quiet tempo of light footsteps moving quickly. A hand moved swiftly on the handrail above then a lithe figure appeared at the turning at the top of the stairs, stunning in a white dress, short at the front, ankle length at the back. A mandarin collar curved high round her neck and the sleeves were cut up to the shoulders. On anybody else it would have looked ridiculous, but on her, it was the armour of Boudicca. And she had the longest legs Caplan had ever seen. Her skin the colour of latte, she had the sides of her skull shaved, and the middle section had her lush black hair pulled into a ponytail that fell beyond her waist – too long to be real, surely. This beautiful creature had paused at the top of the stairs by habit, as if this was what she did, and she did it even if there was nobody there to admire her. Then she started making her way down, step by step, with the hip-swaying, head-high, face-forward walk that catwalk models had down to a fine art. Once next to Cosmo, she folded herself into him, her arm round his neck, dipping her head next to his, murmuring something in his ear. Then she gave him a kiss on the head and dropped her chin onto his shoulder. For a moment they looked like two children lost in the wood, hiding from the big bad wolf and unable to find their way home. Would this be

EB, the influencer? Another of Samphire's children, or was that a rumour?

Turning at a bad stage cough, Caplan saw DS Craigo standing in his crumpled beige jerkin, his fair hair stuck up like he'd had a close encounter with the resident ghost. He had emerged from behind a pillar. He waved his clipboard and nodded slightly.

'Update?' Caplan asked.

'On what?' he asked.

'The situation.'

'The situation remains unclear, ma'am, and I've been spending my time . . .' he dropped his voice even lower, '. . . researching this family. That's Pomeroy on one of his many phones, ma'am. The manager and director of the Sunflower Linen Company. They all work for him in some way, as yet . . .' his beady eyes darted up and around the vaulted ceiling . . . 'unclear.'

'And those two?'

'Best to go in order, ma'am. We have Rosie, the daughter of Mrs McQuarrie and Mr Samphire. That's their son, Cosmo, who does, um, dancing? And that lady is the daughter, she's . . .' he looked at his notes, 'Eee Bee, the daughter of Ecco, the other Sunflower Girl. She's lived with the Samphires for twenty years or so.' He leaned forward. Caplan bowed so he could reach her ear. 'It's very peculiar.' He nodded with the judgement of a village gossip.

'Yes.'

'Morrow, the very slim young lady. I think you met her. She belongs to Mr Samphire and Mrs McQuarrie. Then Tron, actually named Triton after the Greek god.'

'Parents?'

'Poseidon and Amphitrite. He ruled the deep sea, half human, half fish.'

Caplan held Craigo's gaze.

'Oh yes, he's the son of Rhea Doonican, the redheaded one of the Sunflower Girls, if you remember them, ma'am.'

'I do remember them. Is there any chance you could get the family together in this room?'

'No, ma'am.'

Caplan smiled. 'That was an order.'

Craigo blinked. 'That was an honest answer. I tried. It doesn't work. I have three very good collies on the farm and even they couldn't. Slippery fish, ma'am. Herding cats.'

'Okay, okay.' Caplan's eyes were on Pomeroy, now scowling at his phone. He said something to Cosmo, who didn't answer, but there was a message in the returning look. *Not now?* Pomeroy went back to dialling. 'Samphire?' asked Caplan.

'Very handsome chap, I think, long black hair. Now, see the ropes on the brass stanchions.' He indicated one at the top of the stairs, pulled to the side. 'Red is for the wedding venue. The blue is the house. And I'm not sure about the black one, that's the older parts, maybe being kept for historical—'

'Get on with it, Craigo.'

'Mr Samphire slid down there.' He nodded to a small passageway that Caplan hadn't even noticed, little more than a gap in the wall. 'Mr Pomeroy went off in the opposite direction to find him.'

'Slid?'

'Covertly, ma'am.'

'Did he now?' Caplan walked across the red rug, passing the bar area along the panelled wall, checking that Pomeroy was still on the phone, muttering to himself. She lifted the thick braided cord from the brass hook then heard the tap tap of footsteps coming down from overhead. A man stumbled from the gap in the wall.

Samphire's long glossy black hair hung down, covering his face. His white linen shirt was crumpled, his trousers wet and dirty up to the waist.

He was weeping. Deep, emotional, heartfelt weeping.

And he was out of breath.

'Gabe? Gabe? Come on, now.' Pomeroy strode over, placing an arm round Samphire's shoulder. 'Come on. The police are here, this is the detective in charge, she wants to talk to us. I've explained about Morrow. I've called Dr Rowe. Everything else can wait, eh?'

Samphire looked up, and Caplan recognised him immediately. The intense brown eyes that had featured on a Tuesday night TV series about photography – Aklen had watched every episode. Now those eyes were tear filled and unfocused. He addressed his manager. 'Where is she?'

'They're still looking with the drone. It's scanning the lower parts of the cliff. She might have managed to get some protection from the waves. They're sure she's not swimming out in the bay. There's still hope, so let's be positive, eh?'

Samphire collapsed into a heaving mass of sobs.

'Mr Samphire? DCI Christine Caplan, I'm sorry to disturb you in such tragic circumstances but I do need to speak to you. Maybe we could sit through here?'

Craigo stood back, opening the door to the Stewart Room.

Samphire was cold. As Caplan shook him by the hand, she registered the skin of a dead man. He looked up at her, flicking his long black hair over his shoulder. They were the same height, both of them taller than Pomeroy. 'Sorry? What did you say your name was?'

There was an intensity behind his question that set off alarm bells.

'DCI Caplan – Christine. Please, have a seat,' she said, longing for a seat herself. She ushered Samphire through the door, keeping behind him so she could indicate to Craigo that she wanted him note-taking. As she turned, looking out to the hall she caught a slow-motion tableau of Rosie appearing, her hands out to Pomeroy, pleading, her face red and puffy with tears. Then the palms of her hands were on Pomeroy's chest, but he took her by the wrists and pointed back the way she came, telling her to get back to the kitchen. Then Pomeroy turned back to Cosmo and EB. The young man looked ready to get to his feet, ready to comfort or defend his older sister, but some gesture or a word from Pomeroy had him back on the stairs. As Pomeroy followed Caplan to the door, both EB and Cosmo were looking daggers at him.

If looks could kill.

Craigo raised an eyebrow in surprise.

Samphire had sat down on the far side of the huge table. 'Gabriel Samphire,' he said, his eyes running over Caplan's face. 'Most people call me Gabe.'

Caplan gave him a tight smile, knowing that she would never call him anything but Mr Samphire. She sat at the angle of the long oak table, judging that sitting across from him and Pomeroy on such a wide table might look too confrontational and would necessitate speaking loudly.

Samphire looked up at her. 'Has anybody seen Tron?'

Pomeroy sighed. 'Rosie said he was sitting on the cliff edge, refusing to come down.'

'He knows, then?'

'Yes, Gabe, he knows. And Dr Rowe is on the next flight. Harley Street,' explained Pomeroy, leaning forward, blocking the sightline between Samphire and Caplan.

Caplan shuffled her chair round a little. 'Can you talk me through what happened, Mr Samphire?'

Samphire tilted his head, appearing to scan her face, as if he wanted to never forget her features. 'There was a scream. No. Well, yes, there was, but I'd already gone to find her as she was about to miss the fireworks, and she was the one who had wanted the things in the first place. Silent ones, you know. Because of the dogs.'

'Where were you exactly when you heard the scream?' asked Caplan gently.

'He's been over this many times. He was at the gate, weren't you Gabe?' prompted Pomeroy.

'Actually, out of the gate by then. Just starting up the path. I didn't know if it was Koi or not – sound carries at night, don't you think? I wasn't sure but I did . . . panic a little, so I ran up the path, and then . . . I mean that's not the first thing you think, is it?' He shook his head, as if trying to get rid of the painful images that danced behind his eyelids, trying to unsee them. 'She wasn't there. She wasn't there . . . There's nowhere to go, just the wall. I put my phone torch on.'

'So, you looked over the edge, Gabe? You took a photograph,' Pomeroy reminded him.

'Oh yes, I'm sorry,' he handed his mobile to Pomeroy. The manager's podgy fingers dabbed over the keys, not needing to ask for the password. Caplan now knew how close these two men were.

'Did you see her fall, hear her fall?'

'Gabe went up to the clifftop and looked down. This is what he saw,' he said as he handed the phone over.

Samphire folded into himself with pain.

Although she'd already seen the picture, Caplan took the proffered phone. It was a top of the range iPhone. Samphire had snapped this image during the stress and the shock of seeing his dead wife lying on the rocks.

Pomeroy read her mind. 'It's an instinct,' he said, catching the look on her face. 'He was a war photographer in his younger days, before he moved on to more artistic work. He learned to take his chance, might never get a second one.' He shrugged in apology.

'I thought it might help – it shows where she was, her exact position. Do you think she could've survived?' Samphire jabbed his finger at the screen. 'We showed it to the men at the top of the cliff.'

'Mr Samphire, we're still investigating. The drone's up; air-sea rescue have been contacted.' She neglected to say that they were busy elsewhere. 'Was your wife able to swim?'

Both men nodded, a hope they could hold on to. 'Koi was a very good swimmer. She swims in the cove there, sometimes when there's nobody else about.'

'Is that not dangerous?' Caplan looked confused.

'Only dangerous at high tide. There was—' began Pomeroy.

Samphire interrupted him. 'She's not been swimming recently, she'd injured her knee.'

Pomeroy turned to Samphire. 'Yes, she injured her knee recently doing pole work in the gym, but before that she was swimming almost every day.'

It was, Caplan was sure, a very rare rebuke.

Gabriel Samphire looked at her, and for the first time she saw his face in full, with his expression of grief and concern, and something close to confusion.

FIVE

An old-fashioned mower had left perfect stripes on the lawn, their precision emphasised by the glow thrown from the Victorian street lamps. A filthy police Land Rover was abandoned, half on the gravel and half on the lawn, leaving four deep gouges of tyre track on the manicured grass. Caplan presumed this was the vehicle of Wattie – whatever his second name was – the local cop. He was well known, there was an easy familiarity, a respectful familiarity in the way Pickering talked about him. If Wattie was hopeless, then Caplan would have picked up the vibe.

Craigo followed her out. 'That was weird.'

'It was. I'm going into the kitchen to speak to Rosie, but I might try and have a word with EB or Cosmo on the way past. What does Pomeroy actually do for them all?'

'Dealing with the press, protecting the family. They're very close, ma'am, like father and son, Pomeroy and Samphire,' he said, and walked back into the Great Hall, folding his notebook and slipping it into his jacket pocket.

Caplan took a moment, distilling the internal rivalries and alliances she'd just witnessed. And she'd been aware of Samphire watching her; studying her, looking at her cheekbones. Once a photographer, always a photographer. She'd been under that cold scrutiny before when she'd done some modelling work related to her ballet. She could remember the pain of holding a glow stick while moving through different ballet positions, always on point, always holding the glow stick in her outstretched hand. The studio was low lit, she was wearing a black tutu, her dark hair tight in a low chignon. In the finished pictures, the lights were bright comets streaming around her, she was caught in a spiral cage of gold filaments. Her toes were bleeding by the time they had finished. Her calf muscles took a week to recover. Her lasting memory was of the photographer telling her to do it again and again and again, as her mother glared at her to do as they wanted and not to complain; there were plenty of other girls at the ballet class who would grab this opportunity. Caplan knew she'd felt her skin blistering and the dampness of blood oozing from her toes. But they still wouldn't stop.

Maybe to be a good photographer, you had to be a hard-hearted bastard, but that explanation of why Samphire had photographed his wife at the bottom of the cliff had felt a little prepared.

On the pretence of being on the phone, she looked back into the hall. The stairway was empty. Quickly she googled 'Ecco Sunflower Girl' confirming that she had died in a fall from a height during a rooftop party. That's what had been niggling at her: a fall. Wikipedia confirmed the date of death as the eighteenth of December 2004. She'd died after a very long and public battle with heroin, leaving her baby daughter Ebony Blanc to be brought up by Koi and Gabriel.

Back in the Great Hall, Caplan slowly followed the scent of cigarette smoke that hung in the still air, up the three long, shallow steps, wide enough to photograph an entire wedding party. Cosmo was nowhere to be seen but EB was leaning against the wall, rather than standing at the bar, blowing cigarette smoke out the open window above her head, the smoke curling into the freedom of the night.

Close up, Caplan could appreciate the true beauty of EB. She had tiger eyes, golden flecked with brown, and as she stared into the middle distance, oblivious to Caplan, the detective noticed that her pupils were pin pricks despite the dull light. Caplan resisted getting her notebook out, or her recorder, and asking politely what she remembered of Saturday night. It was obvious that EB was under the influence of something.

Instead she asked, 'Are you okay?'

The response was slow, as if EB was thinking about it. Her accent, when she spoke, was broad south London, not what Caplan was expecting at all.

'Yeah, fine.' The model bit her lip and sighed, whether through weariness or boredom was unclear. 'A bit of a shock.' The words were quite clear, spoken as if there had indeed been some thought behind them. She arched her back against the wall a little, putting her hand to her forehead.

'Do you know what happened? Earlier?'

EB shook her head, her eyes now studying the flagstone floor. 'Koi said something odd to me. She said . . .' there was a pause while she steadied her nerves, 'She said that she was so, so sorry for my mother's death . . .' The eyes, their flecks of amber burning, flicked up to look at Caplan, then narrowed. 'What did she mean by that? Did she have something to do with it?'

Caplan let her rucksack fall from her shoulder and pulled out one of the bar stools, perching on it, 'Do you think she did?'

EB snorted. 'I was less than a year old. I've heard many theories. Even more rumours. I've heard my mum was wild, a party girl who got out her skull constantly. That she was so loaded with coke her heart arrested.' She took another draw on her cigarette, another slow breath out the window. 'And for a long time, I believed that.'

'And now?'

Another slow, thoughtful draw. 'I wonder. Koi's dead.' EB smiled like she was seeing Caplan for the first time. 'The answer to your question is no. I was dancing in the bailey. I might have been laughing. I don't do that often. Nobody does round here. Then all hell broke loose. I don't know who said Koi was dead. I think Pinky took over. They were sober. I wasn't. I'm not. I don't know what happened.'

'How long have you lived here?'

'Two years, a bit more. I travel a lot. There was a three-line whip to be here this weekend.'

'Has that happened before?'

She shook her head, the ripple of hair flowed like a bore wave. 'Not since we left London. Pip wanted the photograph. Us all in the photograph. Like a happy family. Which we are not.' The feline eyes struggled to focus.

'Here's my card. Put it somewhere safe. Call me any time and I mean any time,' said Caplan.

EB took it in her beautifully manicured hands with a languid, graceful motion. Then, looking round, she tucked it into her shoe with extreme haste.

'There was nothing weird. Except Koi said that. Said she was sorry about Mum.' Her lips pursed, she took yet another long drag on the cigarette, a true addict. 'There was the scream, from the distance, you know. I heard it. We all heard it. We kept dancing. Can you believe that?' The amber eyes closed slowly, then opened up again with a degree of effort. 'We just kept dancing.'

'Maybe you should go to bed and get some sleep. Tomorrow will be a long and difficult day.'

A sly smile, maybe a sad smile. 'Yeah. I've pills to go to sleep. I've pills for long and difficult days. You look tired too.'

'Part of the job. Do you know where Rosie is?'

'Cosy Rosie the Wonky Donkey? She'll be in the kitchen. She's always in the fucking kitchen.' She leaned forward to reach the window better.

Caplan thought that EB was going to fall but like many drunks, she had a very acute self-righting mechanism, so Caplan said goodbye, thinking about the use of the word donkey.

She tried to recreate Pomeroy's path, past the bar, turning up a narrow corridor in the faraway corner, looking for the kitchen. It'd be good to chat with a sober person, to get an overview of the situation as it had unfolded. Experience of many years told her that there was usually one witness who designated themselves the sensible one. They opened the door, recalled people's names, got the facts mostly correct. Rosie might be able to shine some light on the private life of Koi McQuarrie, the ex-model who had ridden high on the rough tides of popularity and celebrity for the last twenty years. With Ecco Middlemass and Rhea Doonican, Koi had been launched onto the nation's TV screens on the back of that big horse. It came to her now, what the advert had been for: the Little White Dress from the Sunflower Linen Company.

She turned left into a short, wooden-panelled, carpeted corridor, usually protected by the blue cord that was now hanging from its brass hook. This was the source of the smell of coffee, garlic, basil pesto. It was a sharp contrast to the cold passageway that Samphire had emerged from. Caplan yawned. It was getting on for three o'clock. She really needed a cup of something hot and refreshing.

The lower ceiling here signalled the modern part of the castle. After another sharp turn she went down some stairs.

Suddenly, she was in a large modern kitchen, a huge oak table to her right, an eight-burner range cooker to her left. Beyond that, standing at a marble worktop was the woman she'd met in the woods.

'Hello,' Rosie said, still in her white floaty dress. Slipper boots had replaced the trainers, but the overlarge jumper was in place. 'Sorry for leaving you with Mo but she responds better to strangers. If I'd tried to get her in my car, I'd still be having a screaming match with her. I gave up with Tron. We all give up on Tron eventually.' Her hand rested on the kettle as it rumbled to the boil. 'Do you want a cuppa? I'm on my fourth. I keep putting them down and they go cold. Do you want anything to eat? We're not allowed usually but with the party there's some nice stuff upstairs and we could eat tonight – well, within reason,' she said, half to herself.

'I'll be fine with the tea,' Caplan assured her, thinking over the woman's use of the word *allowed*.

'I've been up and down the stairs so many times. I put Morrow to bed and Tron wanders off to sit at the top of a cliff. As soon as I find him, Morrow's out of bed and has disappeared into a dark corner, literally and figuratively. Are you happy with English Breakfast? Green? Earl Grey?' She sniffed loudly, steadying herself to ask a question. 'What's going on out there?'

Caplan sat at the table. 'Green, please. Then you should sit down. The search is ongoing, we're doing our routine. Who was where et cetera, you know?'

Rosie nodded, walking back to the huge stove, her arms folded so tightly she was hugging herself. In front of Caplan was a biro and a spiral-bound notepad; Rosie had been making a list of some sort. Just lost her mother and she was making a list.

Caplan watched her. Their shared silence was soundtracked by the noises outside, the odd shout or a door closing. Every so often the young woman would look up at a voice, but she didn't move. The only time she unfolded her arms was to scratch at her scalp, clawing at the hairpins that were irritating her. Her face, her neck in particular, showed signs of excess skin which made Caplan question if she was older than she had first appeared, if she had undergone some kind of surgery or if she had lost a lot of weight recently, either by illness or by design.

Caplan smiled at her, placed her own notebook on the table beside a plate of plain rice cakes, pouring herself a cup of steaming tea.

'The guy outside, can't remember his name, asked me to make a list of everybody who was here for the party.' Rosie sat down opposite the detective, then tore the page out. 'It's not much, just the family, and that includes Pip. Have they found Mum yet?'

'No.'

'Do you think they will?'

'I've no idea, to be honest,' said Caplan. 'Those who know about tides think that they will, but it depends on many things. We'll keep looking.'

'Could she have survived the fall? Could she swim from there?'

'The drone can't see anything. She was wearing white, I believe?'

Rosie looked down at her dress. 'We all were.'

'And you know the cliffs – are there any small caves, recesses, ledges that she might have managed to get onto?'

'Not here, no. I saw that photograph.'

Caplan searched her face for a sign of revulsion, but all she saw was puzzlement. She took a sip of tea, considering the question, wondering at the disconnect. 'Mr Samphire said he was keen to mark the place, with the tide turning. But as to surviving the fall? Again, I don't know.'

'She did fall, didn't she? Or did she jump?'

Did she have a reason to? Caplan shrugged, looking at the bit of paper. 'I can't answer that.' She raised her head, regarding the young woman across the table who seemed as bright and as practical as Emma.

The woman got up, slowly took the two steps across the red tiled floor towards the kettle, then returned and sat down at the table. The biggest dog that Caplan had ever seen came meandering around the corner, nose in the air, following the scent of something appetising. It sauntered up to them and sat, leaning against the legs of the young woman, dusting the white linen in either sand or mud. She didn't seem to mind.

Caplan looked around, at the framed photographs and the posters hanging on the red walls. 'Who are these people?'

A faint smile played on Rosie's lips. 'Are you one of the few people on the planet who don't know us?'

'I've been living in a caravan for two years.'

'I envy you.'

'And I'm a bit too old to know about influencers and such.' Caplan smiled. 'The girl in the woods doesn't seem well?'

'That's Morrow, my wee sister. She's the one who does the Calorie Diary podcast, although Pomeroy drafts them, a journalist writes them and the actor Lynda Becaul reads them. Do you know her?'

Caplan shook her head.

'She's very good. Have you heard the new podcast about us? By MisChief666? She really is a bitch.' An uncomfortable look shrouded Rosie's face, her eyes narrowed. She looked spiteful for a moment, then said, 'Oh yeah, nothing that appears to be from us ever is. There's a whole office in London giving us quotes to say or Insta to post, scripts for TikTok. It's all about content. The photo shoot today was about the Little White Dress of 2025. A future retrospective. Does that even make sense? Oh, we're well rehearsed in being spontaneous. But if you're given someone else's words to say for most of your life you forget you've the ability to speak your own.' Rosie ruffled the hair on the dog's head. 'Pip's either raising awareness of anorexia or making money out of my sister's anguish. I'm never sure which.' She took a mouthful of her tea and placed the mug back on the table, very deliberately, but her eyes were on the rice cakes. 'Sometimes I think that's what we do in this family, make money from the misery we cause each other. And that's a never-ending supply. You hear EB spouting all that inspirational stuff, "Beauty begins with the authentic you." What a load of shite. It's all made up by AI somewhere in Ealing. She's hasn't had a genuine thought in her life. Cosmo is more sincere, but even then, everything he says and does is filtered. But you don't want to hear about that.'

Caplan did, but said, 'What about your mum?'

Rosie gave a little laugh. 'She got into trouble once for talking to a local school unscripted. They loved her. She was the real deal.'

Caplan kept her concerned look on her face, hesitating to ask the questions that were rolling in her mind. Pearl Lilac Rose, aged twenty-two, the oldest of the 'Sunflower children'. Rosie was an attractive young lady but nowhere near the supermodel sculpted beauty of her mother, or father for that matter. She looked curvy, pretty, but nothing more. She wore the jumper and the trainers more easily than she wore the single diamonds that hung around her neck and on each ear. The hand stroking the dog's head had rough skin on the fingers, the nails were neat, French manicured. Her other jewellery was a plain silver bracelet and a ring on the middle finger of her left hand.

She saw Caplan looking. 'Mum gave me that bracelet only last week, it was one of her favourites.' Rosie threaded the silver band with the thumb of her opposite hand, then without looking up, she said. 'What'll we do without her?'

'You'll find your way through. It's a terrible thing losing your mother.'

Rosie gave a derisory snort. 'Except she wasn't.' The woman reached into her jumper pocket and pulled out an iPhone.

Caplan cursed herself. 'Sorry, I thought you were the eldest daughter of . . .'

'Oh yes, I'm Rosie, the adopted child of Koi and Gabe. It was a very happy adoption, a good career move for them.'

'Gabriel and Koi were your parents in all but DNA.' Caplan felt this conversation was not going the way she had hoped.

'Not so easy when you're so different. Listen to this.' She tapped the screen on her phone. 'From MisChief666, who has just said that my "mother" was one of the most beautiful women in the world: "*I suspect she sits up on the ramparts of the castle, preferring to listen to the happy chatter drifting up to her from below, because then she can imagine that they are small and fat and ugly like her.*" That's what they think about me.'

'But—'

'And if Koi's really dead, why was Gabe messing about up there?' She shook her head, suddenly overcome with emotion. She swallowed hard, and Caplan resisted the temptation to reach out and hold her hand.

'Messing about where, Rosie?' she asked softly.

'Well, he was up there, took that picture, of Mum. You know?'

Caplan watched her intently, listening to the odd shout from outside. She took the moment to orientate herself. She realised that she was looking at the French windows that led out onto the big patio; she could see a hedge and the garden. The bailey would be beyond that. The ground level at the front had the main entrance to the big hall, the dining room, the event space and the main stairway that led upstairs to the left and the right, to the balconies and floors above.

'Where were you when you heard the scream?'

Rosie pointed through the French windows. 'Out at the firepit. Or I had come in here for something. I don't remember seeing her go.' Rosie looked at her phone, then took a deep breath. 'I think I might have killed her. You see—'

There was a loud knock on the French windows. It was the knock of a police officer. The handle was then rattled up and down. The dog stood up, taking its time to go and investigate.

Caplan watched as Rosie shuffled across the red tiles, unlocking the second panel, the one where the handle had been rattled. She opened the door and put her head out.

Caplan heard a familiar voice ask if she was there.

'Yes, she is,' replied Caplan.

DS Craigo came in, looking not unlike a scarecrow who had come off worst in a fight with a particularly belligerent crow. He scraped his boots on the step before he stood on the tiles. Caplan, not for the first time, wondered how he managed to appear at the wrong moment, in the wrong place so often.

Over the last two years Caplan had tried to get used to Craigo interrupting her at exactly the wrong moment but this time he had excelled himself. Rosie had clammed up, refused to expand on her statement and busied herself boiling the kettle, as Craigo took a seat at the table and started talking to the dog. Then he casually mentioned, in passing, that Pomeroy had declared Cosmo too drunk to be interviewed and had sent the young man to sleep it off.

To this, Rosie had muttered, 'Again?' and Craigo had started wittering about folk dealing with pressure.

Caplan had said goodbye and left. She had learned that witnesses thought Craigo was no threat and tended to talk openly to him. So, she'd leave them to have a wee chat, another cup of tea that Rosie wouldn't finish. Caplan sensed that what Rosie had been going to say about killing her mother was emotional rather than literal; Rosie had shouted at her, or not made her a coffee or not done some mundane everyday task and the guilt had swollen that small, inconsequential action into something that led her mother to take her own life.

To Caplan's mind, Rosie killing her mother was highly unlikely.

She retreated into a quiet corner of the bailey, beyond the patio door and behind the hedge. This area was designed to shield the private quarters of the house from the wedding guests in the bailey. She checked her messages; there was a two-word text from Emma, Jade!? Jesus! with a cross-eyed emoji. Caplan smiled and was about to text back when she saw a message from DC Mackie, announcing that she was down at the car park and had just met McPhee. Where did Caplan want her? Caplan thought that she wanted Mackie at home resting, on compassionate leave.

'What are you doing here, Mackie?' Caplan said as she approached the Duster, her constable now leaning on the bonnet, her face beaming with excitement. 'You buried your mother yesterday, which I'm sure you've not forgotten.'

Mackie smiled at her boss. 'I'm here. I'm ready, so if that's okay with you it's okay with me. I'd like to be back at work as from right now. You're dealing with the celebs that live up at Limpetlaw and that's pure exciting. It's the most exciting thing that has ever happened to me in my whole life.'

'You're on compassionate leave.'

'I'd rather be at work, so I don't need compassionate leave, do I?'

Caplan whispered back. 'The fact you can say it like that means that you're still processing it, so no, you can't come back.'

'I'll tell them that being at work will aid my recovery. I can't eat any more egg sandwiches, ma'am. You need me on this, you need me to give you all the background.'

'I've McPhee for that.'

'Being stabbed hasn't made him more intelligent. . . Okay, so I know that Limpetlaw is the real name of Torsvaig Castle. What else do you know? I mean, do you know about the beach and the woods? The Palmer Group did the refurb from castle to hotel. They wanted the caravan site at Limpetlaw beach closed and they've let the trees grow wild. Public access to the beach is almost impossible now, bunch of bastards. I met Wattie who knows Pickering, and he's talking about Koi's stalker and the death threats? Did you know about that?'

'Fact or gossip?'

'Gossip, ma'am, The stalker called himself the Fisherman. Out to catch Koi. See? Still, enough to make them ramp up security.' Mackie rolled her neck, cracking it.

'That's interesting. I still think you need to go home.'

'I need to be not at home. Too many visitors. I need to be here.'

'You want to be here. That's not the same thing. Why would I let an officer who has just lost her mum return to investigate a case where a family has lost their mum? Especially when that officer was granted compassionate leave. You'll get pulled under, Toni, you'll lose objectivity and make mistakes.'

Mackie smiled like she had checkmate. 'Well, I could bond with the Rosie one, couldn't I? I know what she's going through. She'd open up to me and 'fess up that she'd chucked her mum off the cliff.' Mackie puffed out her fat cheeks. 'That's a tough shift, being the daughter of a model, eh?'

'You're serious, aren't you?'

'Ma'am, I've been a fan of Koi for years. I read the celebrity glossies. I know about *Strictly*, the drugs, the porn pics and AZed. Even if I wasn't operational, I could run the room, ma'am. McPhee's hopeless, you know that.' She nodded up at the castle, pulling a face of total innocence. 'But can I go up just once? I might bump into Cosmo, you know accidentally, like, if I'm there right where he is?'

'He's a very pretty young man,' confirmed Caplan.

Mackie whispered back. 'He's a sexy motherfucker!'

'Mackie!' chastised Caplan.

'Sorry,' she said, not sounding very sorry at all. 'But he is. He's doing *Strictly*, as is his girlie. She's a talentless stick insect.'

'How old is he?'

'Twenty-one, ma'am.'

'And how old are you?'

'Not quite old enough to be his mother, but I really need a break.'

Caplan thought for a moment. Mackie would be a PR disaster if she was out and about, left to her own devices. One conversation with a journalist off duty and that would be it. 'Okay, you can do the board at Pilcottie.'

'I'll get a new box of markers, ma'am; I'll colour-code the board and you'll be impressed.'

'Timing will be important on this case. While we're here, from your own celebrity expertise, is there any reason why Koi McQuarrie would take her own life?'

'Nothing that's obvious, except the stalker. I'll find out what was reported to Police Scotland.'

'Or to the Met, when they were living in London. She might have been running away from something, somebody. Chances are it's social media being toxic.'

'She *is* dead though,' replied Mackie, scrolling through her phone.

'What does Dr Ryce, our friendly pathologist, always say? Death cannot be confirmed until there's a body.' Caplan looked at her watch. 'If you go home now, can we meet at ten a.m. at Pilcottie? Tell McPhee and Craigo. Can you get a presentation prepped by then, background stuff, but I'd guess you're already halfway there?'

Mackie sprang from the side of the car and squealed. 'Ma'am, I could kiss you.'

'Please don't,' said Caplan. 'I'm looking in at Pilcottie on my way home. If I need help, I'll shout.'

'I'll meet you there and see what we'll need. Knowing Wattie, it might need a hazmat suit and antibiotics.'

SIX

Caplan had driven down the hill to the first lay-by she found and pulled in. Alone, with dawn ever creeping over the horizon, she studied the image of Koi on her phone screen. Caplan could recall being in a bar somewhere, she had no memory of where, but the neon lights, the loud music, the purple and glitter walls were very clear. As was the song coming through huge speakers, matching the video on the numerous TV monitors round the bar. On came the charity single 'He's Got the Ohhh' by Three to Please. The popular three-girl band singing very seriously, and then the Sunflower Girls appeared, at first singing the backing vocals, dancing abominably, making a total mockery of the sexily writhing, pouting singers at the front. Rhea, slyly glancing at the other two, pretended to swig from a bottle when nobody was looking. Koi pulling out a mirror, acting bored. Ecco miming deliberately badly and having an argument with somebody off-camera. But the song, the dancing, all came together at the end, and it was, even now, very catchy. It raced to the top of the charts and raised a fortune for Comic Relief. There was something – an energy, a charisma, a sense of engaging with real people – about the Sunflower Girls. And now they were all gone. Koi was gone. Her kids, young adults like Caplan's, were now going to roll along the road of life without her. Rhea and Ecco had left their children in the care of Koi and Gabriel. Surely that showed a degree of trust deeper than being close pals. Caplan was fortunate: she still had her children, she had her friends Liz and Sarah. She rolled her head back onto the headrest and closed her eyes. She could hardly bear to look at the picture of Koi, her white dress soaked, her blood-spattered face, those beautiful eyes just staring at the sky. Even in death, she was quite, quite stunning.

DCI Caplan looked at the small building. It stood on its own patch of weeds, set a little way back from the high street of Pilcottie. The village was too small to have any kind of permanent police presence; the station was there as a conduit between the rural populace and the larger Police Scotland hubs. The small strip of land, the garden of the station, was full of wildflowers – a colourful rainbow of petals bisected by a concrete path that had cracked and buckled over time. It was a single-storey building, painted white sometime in the last twenty years, the dark blue on the door matching the dark blue round the frosted windows, two on either side of the door. In italic blue paint on the white above the door was the date 1923.

The plaque was clearly marked with the Police Scotland logo and the opening hours: ten to four, Mondays to Fridays, and then a mobile number if there was no response or the door was locked, plus a central number if needed. The door was opened with an old-fashioned thumb-press lever on top of the handle. The gap at the bottom must have let fresh air through but that was not enough to dispel the stink of the interior.

A Land Rover rumbled slowly along the narrow road past her, the scent of diesel fighting with the smorgasbord of smells that had already assaulted her nose. The driver waved, recognising her. Two vehicles, a brown jeep and a ubiquitous red hatchback, were caught behind the slow-moving Land Rover, as they would be for the next twenty miles. She watched them go, wondering what they were doing out at this time of the morning.

Caplan opened the door and walked in. She wasn't good with bad smells at the best of times, but this place was rank rotten; damp, with an all-pervasive odour of decay that suggested the building was about to collapse.

She decided to keep the door open, hoping that the early-morning breeze would find its way into the small building and chase the stench out. Hopefully there was another door at the back for a refreshing flow-through.

How could the local guy, Wattie, work in a shithole like this?

The lino on the floor had been black once, and was now scuffed to grey or even white at the counter, though remained polished ebony under the wooden bench at the window. The bench had no doubt been stolen from a church somewhere by some lads on a good night out and, when arrested, they had brought it with them to the police station, and it had never found its way back to where it belonged.

There was a Formica counter, burned with cigarette ends and stained with so many coffee mugs, it looked like somebody had had a go at redesigning the Olympic rings. On top of the reception desk was a blank pad of yellow paper. The chain for a pen hung loose and spun on the fresh draught floating in from the open door. A plastic shutter was pulled down to cut off the rear part of the building; on it, a small handwritten sign said that Wattie would be back soon. The door at the far end looked new, made from thin plywood that had not been painted yet, with a single hasp padlock looped round a steel ring. Caplan reckoned that she could force it open by leaning on it, or maybe a gentle gust of wind could do the job for her. There was no reason for it to be there, as all anybody wanting to gain access to the office at the rear of the station needed to do was pull up the flimsy shutter and climb over the counter.

How careless was Wattie?

But Pilcottie was a small place; everybody really did know everybody, and no doubt there were doors around here which were never locked. The best thing about Pilcottie was its location in the middle of nowhere – difficult to get to while being equidistant from the places of importance.

Wattie would have good local knowledge, but those who lived up at the castle weren't local. She was sure that only their inner circle knew the truth about anything they did or said. Everything was for effect. The image of the close-knit family unit was a little at odds with what Caplan had seen with her own eyes – and that acquaintance had been merely a matter of hours.

She turned her attention back to the station, where everything seemed dark and depressing. Deciding that the smell had dispersed enough for her to safely go in further, Caplan walked up to the counter, slipping her hand across the top until her fingers found the edge. Then she felt around until she found a series of metal hooks, the final one holding a fob with three keys. She unlocked the padlock easily, the key selection made easier by the plastic tags that said outer door, front door and back door. A hook on the wall showed how the door stayed open, and a flat hatch lifted to gain access to the area behind the reception desk, presumably the office where Wattie worked. She noted the lack of Perspex guard behind the shutter, with nothing to protect the officer standing at the desk. Whoever stood there on duty was fairly confident that they would not encounter violence.

Behind the reception counter was a free-standing desk with two piles of paper on top, and a couple of battered bookcases. The swivel chair sweated foam, and the rug under the wheels was worn through to the floorboards. A narrow cupboard, maybe a key cupboard, was on one wall. There was a desk phone next to a dust-covered printer. The wall above the two bookcases was covered by a huge map of the area, adorned with Post-it notes and arrows. There was a calendar, still open at May, with a picture of an Aberdeen Angus bull looking very pleased with himself. Down the side was a marker hanging by a string.

Caplan walked round the desk and through the door at the far wall, to the other half of the building. The short narrow hall ran to a toilet at the far end, a source of one of the smells. At the back was a staff kitchen, the worktops covered with the detritus of takeaways and empty cans. The rings of scum layering the edges of the cluttered sink echoed those of Saturn. Caplan turned towards the front, through another open door to a room with an old, dented kettle, sachets of milk and coffee, small sticks of sugar, and English breakfast teabags held together with a small elastic band. There was an old black plastic sofa against one wall, a small dining table for two people, and a couple of chairs tucked in under it. Another door towards the front of the building led her back through to the reception desk. She wondered what this room was for. Relatives waiting for mountain rescue? Holidaymakers whose hired car had broken down? Or locals coming in for a chat or complaining about lost sheep? Caplan had been up here for nearly three years now and still had a lot to learn about the demands of policing a community like this. Theft from whisky-carrying lorries and theft of heavy farm machinery were big problems.

The glamour of the McQuarrie-Samphire life was a million miles away from this squalor, yet Koi's death, if she was dead, had brought her here to a dirty toilet and scuffed lino.

'Jesus Christ!' Caplan jumped as Mackie burst through the front door.

'Sorry, did I give you a fright?' Mackie sniffed. 'Oh, holy Mary, just look at the state of this place. I started off my career in a shithole like this – it was the longest six months of my life.' She looked around quite happily. 'Easy to go crazy in these wee stations, and Wattie was halfway there anyway.'

'Do you know Wattie, then? Was he normal before they sent him here?'

'Nope, always been Wattie Weirdy, WFP as I know him. Craigo knows him better. They both have sheep.'

Caplan didn't ask. 'Detective Superintendent Spencer wanted a place away from the media, but I doubt very much that anybody can work in this tip. Can you dig around and see if you can find any cleaning materials? There must be some bleach somewhere.'

'He's certainly not used any.'

'Can we steal a whiteboard from Oban or Cronchie?'

'Or use paper like we did in the old days. I'll set up an incident room in reception and get the landline checked. I'm presuming Wattie has a laptop that he carries about with him for security. We could put McPhee in charge of tech, give him something useful to do,' said Mackie without a trace of irony.

Caplan went outside and phoned Spencer, leaving a message that she wouldn't let her team work in there, as it was a health hazard. If he was intent on using it as an incident room, then they needed time to put the building right. Then she thought that her statement might get Wattie into trouble when she could do with him being onside. 'I think it has maybe been used for retrieval of lost livestock – it smells like a vet's waiting room.'

Caplan drove back home, making much better progress than she had on the way out. She was coming to the conclusion that any investigation of the incident at the castle was simply a salve to the media; it was to keep the Jades of this world quiet. Koi had apparently been on the cliff alone and the investigation team would test that theory vigorously. If found to be true, she had either fallen or had jumped. That was a decision for the Fatal Incident Inquiry. Not her.

She drove carefully, aware of traffic on the narrow road even at this hour of the morning. She wasn't sure if she was looking forward to going home, not knowing who was there, what kind of atmosphere she was walking into. She was too tired to care. It was her house, and if she couldn't get any peace at home, then what was the point? And, deep inside, she was concerned about what the stress of this was doing to Aklen. It had been Emma's night, and it had been hijacked by Jade and her nonsense.

Maybe Jade was just a young woman, brought up in a #MeToo environment, sensing misogyny everywhere, especially in the police. She would have grown up thinking that toxic masculinity rides roughshod over any sense of feminism or gender equality. Caplan had seen her fair share of women betrayed, beaten, battered and killed by their male partner and it had been down to her to nail the perpetrator. And while she had seen many women killed by men, she'd seen many men taking their lives over a woman, especially young men, especially when there were kids, and a separation involved . . . And now the police were dealing with increasing numbers of teenage suicides caused by social media getting hold of a malicious rumour and not letting go.

Jade could have asked her, as a DCI in the police, a female police officer in a Major Investigation Team, what did she think? Were things changing? If not, what could be done? But Jade had not asked that. She had gone into attack mode straight away and that was worrying. It gave her concern for Kenny and their future together. Somebody had once described Kenny as a black Labrador kind of person: good natured, a bottomless pit of a stomach, a bit daft but give him something to do and he'd do it. He just had to be prodded.

Jade had changed personality over the course of the meal. Would the real Jade please stand up?

And that took her thoughts full circle back to Koi.

And what deception and duplicity had been happening up at Torsvaig? Even the name – Limpetlaw for hundreds of years – was now reinvented.

Who was the real Koi McQuarrie anyway, where did that persona come from? One thing that Caplan was sure of was that she had not been born Koi McQuarrie.

She knew nothing of Koi's history save that the seventeen-year-old was spotted by the thirty-year-old Samphire. The minute he saw her, he'd found his muse, or his meal ticket. That was part of her legend: being plucked from obscurity.

Samphire was already a famous photographer, with an eye for both the absurd and the beautiful. Pomeroy was already his manager. They had always sidestepped any questions about where, and who, Koi had been before that. It added to her mystique. Caplan reckoned that would be the question when they got back to the castle: who was Koi? Until they knew who she was, who she had been, what hope did they have of finding out what had happened to her? If Samphire thought that he had created her, maybe he thought he could erase her just as easily. Did he have the kind of ego that could make her feel that she was yesterday's news, overtaken by those who used to depend on her? The focus was now on the next generation. Caplan needed to find out how influencers make their money.

Samphire was distraught when they had spoken. She was wary of Pomeroy, the puppet master. If he had something to do with the invention of Koi McQuarrie, then he'd no doubt put every legal block he could on normalising the goddess he'd created; all important documentation would be tied up in legalese. She suspected that he'd hold on to the drama and suspense of the current situation for as long as he could; it would be good for business. The only thing that would earn more money than Koi alive was Koi dead.

Why, in thirty years, had nobody popped up, hand out for a tabloid payment to say '*Ahh, you see, I knew her before she was famous.*'

Maybe they would now.

At this rate, Caplan would be home by six a.m., catch a little sleep, get a hot shower and then head back. Time was passing; maybe Craigo had been able to speak to Morrow and Tron. Hopefully they'd be able to interview Cosmo this morning. She needed a firm timeline on who had been where.

Her mobile rang. She answered it on the hands-free. It was Spencer again; he sounded a little apologetic while asking her for an update. It had been only three hours since they had spoken.

'I'm going home to change clothes,' she said slowly. 'Are you sure this is the best use of resources? I've been there since two this morning. It seems tragic but nothing criminal.'

There was a short pause. 'I owe your team an apology.'

Caplan took a guess. 'Somebody very tired on night shift was told to send the team at Limpetlaw a picture of Koi? And they sent out the one of her body that CSI had just sent in.'

'Near enough. A civilian, second week on the job, processing evidence.'

'I thought that, when Mackie didn't get one. She wasn't on the contacts for this incident.'

'However, we've been alerted to other versions of it appearing over the socials. I'll get somebody on to it. Meanwhile we have ACC Sarah Linden taking the heat at the press conference, they'll be like vultures over this. The Sunflower business empire has its own security, its own media people, we don't want it controlling this investigation.'

'The investigation into what? That's my point.'

'Into whatever happened. What was involved? Drugs? Drink?

Was there turmoil within the family? We'll be scrutinised over this to the nth degree. Put on your best public face, dress well. Although Sarah Linden is heading up the PR machine, you'll get papped at some point. Our PR has to be better than theirs. A beautiful blonde at the bottom of a cliff totally outplays our police service harbouring a rapist among our number or not doing our job properly. We need to claim back some of the moral high ground here.'

'Well, you know what they say about the moral high ground? It's rough but the view is good. Let media liaison deal with it. Is that not their job?'

'We need more than that, we need the confidence of the family, and this family are experts at manipulating the media, never forget that.'

'It seems they are manipulating Police Scotland already,' Caplan said drily. 'I need to concentrate on the events here to ensure there's no criminal case. There are mental health issues that should be treated with respect. There'll be a full inquiry by the Fiscal. We need to know what really happened, not what they want us to believe. The odds are that she fell, or she jumped. Either way, unfortunate but not criminal.'

'Any evidence to the contrary?'

'Nothing yet. We'll be reviewing the footage from the security system later today but it seems nobody else went up there with her.'

'What's your instinct?'

'Too early to say. So far, I've walked along a hilltop path and looked down at a small beach with some very big, nasty rocks. The more detailed interviewing starts later today when the family are sober or feeling better.'

'I'll call you later today for an update. Keep ACC Sarah Linden informed of everything she's not to say at the press conference.'

'Will do.' She ended the call and looked at the open road ahead, doing some mental rescheduling about when she had to be where, and how many plates she was trying to spin without dropping any.

SEVEN

It was ten past six on Sunday morning by the time she pulled the Duster up the rough track that the Caplans called their driveway. The sun was casting light around, making the world a brighter place. The cottage, however, looked like the *Mary Celeste* – as if the family had got up from the table the previous night, or earlier that morning, and vanished from the face of the earth. Dirty cutlery had been gathered, but not taken upstairs. Half-empty glasses were being investigated by busy insects looking for a sugar rush. The chairs were pushed back, one had fallen over. Caplan righted it as she approached the house, her mind, just for a moment, playing with the idea that something awful had happened here and there would be a terrible scene inside, a bloodbath on her new oak flooring. Then the cats, Pas De Chat and Pavlova, trotted out to greet her in the hope of an early breakfast. Pas was so domesticated he almost insisted on a napkin when eating. He was winding his way round her legs, tripping her up. Pavlova, the feral female, kept her distance, yowling enough to waken the dead, but probably not enough to waken Kenny after what he'd had to drink last night.

Before she went near the cottage, Caplan followed the narrow verge of grass to the caravan and listened, hearing the vague noises of life inside. Mags's green van was still parked beside Aklen's; Mags and Emma had decided to stay the night in the caravan. She hoped they hadn't sat round the table until the small hours, waiting for her to return.

Caplan retreated and went up to her new front door, stepping over the sacks of plaster in the hallway. Again, she heard subtle sounds of life. The lower ground floor was still very much a building site, everybody would be upstairs. The door to the dining room, a bedroom at the moment, had a large glass panel and through that she could see her son and his girlfriend lying in the double bed, dead to the world, enjoying the deep sleep of the innocent.

Or the very drunk.

Caplan smiled to herself and walked into her kitchen where she and Mags had been hours ago, before Jade had made her speech, before she got the call, before Koi had died. Or went missing.

She looked through the glass panel on the living room door. Aklen was asleep on the sofa with one of the kittens, who was not supposed to be in the house at all. She retreated to the worktop and slipped the kettle on. There was a change of clothes in her car, so she didn't need to go into the 'bedroom' to get underwear from the suitcase, or a fresh blouse from the clothes rail they used as a wardrobe. She was determined not to disturb Jade, or Kenny.

Filling the cat bowls with Felix and fresh water, she went downstairs and watched the cats eat their breakfast before getting her bag out of the boot of the car and heading back to the house for a shower.

Afterwards, she made herself some toast and a cup of tea, taking it outside with her laptop to sit on the balcony and admire the view, watching the morning sun highlighting the bright water, the mountains and the sky beyond. It was a view she'd never tire of.

She opened her laptop intending to google 'Torsvaig Castle wedding venue' but soon found herself reading about the tragic deaths of Ecco and Rhea. The fact that Ecco had fallen from the roof of a three-storey building, during a party in St John's Wood, didn't make her feel any easier about the case. The inquest into Rhea's death had ruled it a suicide after drinking red wine laced with a toxin, unspecified. She had been having a meal with Gabriel Samphire, he'd been called away, and she'd died, 'apparently' by her own hand. At the inquest, Samphire had said she was depressed and desperate. Her medical history had backed up his testimony. Then she looked up EB's YouTube channel. EB was promoting a dress she was wearing from the Sunflower Linen Company, saying something about the colour of it, white but not white. Then the door of the room in the video opened. EB looked over to her right, smiled, then looked back at the camera and said that the company also did a colour that enhanced white skin; brilliant white on pale white skin was not flattering. She held up a finger and leaned forward to press play. The song 'Addicted to Love' blasted out and Koi appeared, posing at the back of the set. EB struck a pose at the front and off they went. EB posing and pouting, being very serious. Koi was acting her age, dancing very badly, pointing her fingers and smiling. Caplan found it funny, she'd engaged in similar daftness with Emma but . . . But . . . was Koi publicly making a mockery of her cool stepdaughter? EB was – Caplan couldn't put her finger on it – false, definitely, but fragile at the same time, scared that reality might come along and bite her. She typed MisChief666 into her phone and the link to the *Living Their Life* podcast popped up. She pressed play, surprised at the soft, plummy English voice and more surprised at the content.

Today on the Living Their Life *podcast we are continuing to look at the famous, or should that be infamous, family who now reside at Torsvaig Castle.*

Oh, to be born into the McQuarrie-Samphire empire. Oh, the stresses of that family, being so beautiful, so slim, so lovely. Too perfect. That's the first generation. The second generation tend to suffer. I'm sure that you, like me, and every other person on the face of the planet, was shocked at the appearance of Morrow on Instagram recently. She's what, nineteen? Twenty? She looks twelve.

Youngest daughter Morrow spends her time kneeling on the bathroom floor somewhere high up in the ancient castle; because her mother is too busy being everything but a mother, Morrow will be cradling the toilet bowl.

It's reputed that she throws up more than she eats. Is that how her mother stays so slim? There have been specialists and Harley Street doctors.

We've all known people who suffer from eating disorders. We've all heard the stomach growling, the retching, the coughing.

It's been over two years since they moved up to Scotland for the good of the children. Was it for the good of Morrow, having a wedding venue full of celebration food, celebration drink and beautiful slim brides?

Maybe that was the best choice. But just not the best choice for Morrow.

It's heartening to know that through all this trauma, she churns out an episode of the Calorie Diary *every week. Except she doesn't. Most days, she doesn't have the strength to get out of bed.*

From MisChief666 causing Mischief 24/7.

Laters

Caplan turned it off. That was nasty. How would she feel if somebody had written that about Emma? She made a mental note to get Mackie on to it; she appeared to have the stomach for social media bile.

* * *

The difference in Pilcottie police station was amazing, Mackie had done a marvellous job, putting her restless emotional energy to good use. Two horizontal strips of lining paper were pinned to the wall in the reception room with the name 'Operation Sunflower' along the top in Mackie's handwriting. There were pictures, printed off the internet, of all the major players; the beautiful EB was mostly covered by five pictures of Cosmo. Above 'Operation Sunflower' was the picture of Koi on the rocks, just to focus their minds.

Caplan looked at the highly stylised black and white photograph of the family that had been taken hours before Koi died. If she didn't know better, she'd think it was four adults and a child, but the extremely slender figure on the left of the picture was Morrow. Caplan took a long time to look at that face, the huge eyes full of ... fear? She looked so fragile she could break with a slight breeze.

The photographs had been taken on the King's Reach. The family were dressed in the trademark white linen of the Sunflower Linen Company. At the front was Koi, lying on her right side with her face turned to the left so she was caught in profile. Cosmo stood at the back with his dark hair straight, hands on hips, straight legged, tall and fine limbed, his shirt unbuttoned, showing a smooth bare chest. It might have been the same clothes he'd been wearing when Caplan had seen him on the stairs. Beside him stood EB mimicking Cosmo's posture, one arm straight out to lean her hand on his shoulder, echoing the way Koi's legs framed the bottom of the picture. Caplan could see Samphire's talent in posing them this way, drawing the eye to the three of them. Morrow was crouched low on the left. Towards the middle, wearing a white fedora, was, she presumed, Tron in front of Cosmo's feet. She could see the evidence of inherited genes, beautiful ones in this case. Then she realised that Rosie wasn't there.

Both sofa and printer bore the legend: 'I'm broken'. The laptop had not been located. They were rather short on tech. McPhee had gone home to his parents and would return with goods borrowed from the incident room at Cronchie; his list went onto a second page of A4 and was headed by a working lock for the door.

The office looked old, well used. The desk was free of crumbs but still stained with rings from a hundred coffee cups. The toilet was now usable without an oxygen mask and while the kitchen stank of bleach, it was safe enough to boil the kettle. McPhee had mugs on his list too. The reception room was now the incident room; two tables and some chairs had appeared. The windows had been cleaned; the curtains were open.

On the top of the 'board' was an aerial photograph of the castle, which fixed the geography of it in Caplan's mind. The grounds of Limpetlaw were protected by two walls; the castle itself was nestled in the northwest corner. The grass between the walls would have been used to bring the animals in overnight, back in the days when the castle would have been a small village. The fiefdom of the MacDougalls. Its position relative to the clifftop explained how the scream was heard by everybody. It was close as the crow flies but a long way round.

The place was a fortress.

The door clonked ominously on its hinges heralding McPhee looking tired but happier than Caplan had seen him in a while, carrying a monitor screen and a laptop. He heeled the door open for Craigo who was carrying a parcel in his arms as if it was a sickly baby.

With an instinct for the essentials of a good investigation team, McPhee announced that he'd brought the office coffee machine from Cronchie.

After thirty minutes of plugging in laptops and printers, the four of them perched or sat or leaned as Caplan took up position at the front of the new incident room, whatever that incident turned out to be.

'I see we have the major players up on the wall. It's good to focus on Koi McQuarrie.' She tapped on the picture of the body on the rocks. 'We need to keep in the front of our minds that she's missing.'

'She's dead, ma'am, look at the picture,' McPhee said, pointing.

'Everybody keeps assuming that but, for the record, she's a missing person until a body washes up. I'm sure it will, but for completeness, let's consider alternatives. We're looking at the movements of those who were present. We also need her mobile phone. What was her state of mind? Who was in her life? If life in that castle was driving her mad, or if she was scared, who did she share that with?' Caplan tapped the desktop. 'Any ideas?'

'Well Rosie has a healthy disconnect from the celebrity aspect of it all. And she's old enough to be a friend as well as a daughter,' said McPhee. 'I saw her early that morning, she was genuinely in shock.'

'Rosie's adopted and harbours some anger towards Koi. Too conflicted to be the friend,' pointed out Caplan.

'I doubt it would be any of the others. They'd have sold it to the papers by now. It's Pomeroy they turn to, not their mum. They're like stage children. What about Cosmo?' asked Mackie.

'There's something off between him and Pomeroy for sure. And Cosmo was devastated by his mum's death.'

'Robyn?'

'Who?' asked Caplan.

'She looks after the horses, she came up from London with them.'

'Okay, can you expand the list to who comes and goes at Torsvaig? We're looking for any of Koi's acquaintances. And get Pickering and Perkins on the list, for completeness.'

'I'm on it,' said Craigo, retreating to his laptop. 'And the security footage is through.'

'Okay, let's get that set up before we go any further.'

Caplan nipped into the small kitchen to ensure the water in the kettle was fresh, Mackie following close behind.

'I confess I'm a bit confused by this, ma'am.' The rising heat in the small room was making the sweat pour down Mackie's face. She dabbed at her chin, pulled her fingers through her unruly damp hair. 'If there's a woman, you know like her, like Koi or whoever she really was, and she gets paid, let's say a million dollars to get her photo taken walking up and down wearing stupid clothes just because she's a skinny bitch who has never enjoyed a fish supper—'

'A million pounds?' asked Caplan. 'Really?'

'Not all at one time, but Limpetlaw Castle wasn't free in a lucky dip, was it? You've seen the size of it. When you look at the clothes, the kids, the song, the castle . . . Koi was the name that was pulling that kind of money in. She had a hand in designing the clothes, choosing the fabric and all that stuff. Well, it's believed that she did.'

'And your point is?' Caplan switched on the kettle.

'Well, who's exploiting who? I mean men are as thick as shit when it comes to a pretty face – not something I've ever suffered from,' said Mackie, hoping for a contradiction from Caplan.

Caplan was about to say something about force of personality but didn't.

'Craigo says that it's more a calmness he looks for.' Mackie folded her arms and stared into the middle distance.

'Toni, he wants a woman who doesn't talk back.'

'His mother was a nightmare. But being calm is good for the cows. You can't have hysterics about eyeliner when there's milking to be done. He's not taken in by looks.'

'I'm glad to hear it, Mackie.'

'Does that make him a feminist?' asked her constable.

'I think that makes him a farmer.' Caplan smiled at her, thinking about setting up a dinner party with Craigo, McPhee and Mackie on one side of the table and Jade on the other. The poor lassie wouldn't stand a chance.

'Right, did you manage to speak to Tron?' Caplan asked Craigo, once they were all settled with a refreshing cup of something, except McPhee who was downloading a program to view the footage.

'I found the young gentleman eventually, but I had to have a good look round first,' Craigo said innocently. 'While trying to locate him, obviously.'

'Obviously,' repeated Caplan with a touch of sarcasm.

'The wedding venue is over at the North Tower. It's very lovely, ma'am, soft towels and very thick carpets. I think they get in a company for cleaning, laundry and . . .' he pursed his lips, '. . . wedding plans and management. Then I went over to the family quarters. Rosie's bedroom has an awful lot of stuffed toys, so many I didn't think it was that of an adult. EB's looks like an explosion in a clothes shop, suitcases lying around half opened. Tron and Morrow's rooms are nowhere near anybody else's. Cosmo's is military clean and tidy, Koi's is all natural wood and cream rugs, a lot of fluffy pillows on the bed, books and a big dog basket – well, two big dog baskets. I didn't see her phone.'

'Did you touch anything?'

'Oh no, ma'am.'

'And then you came across Tron?'

'I did, yes. I tripped over him. He was on the stairs, very drunk. Not in a fit state for interview. He kept repeating that Pomeroy was a . . .' He blinked as he got his recollection straight, '. . . a bastarding bastard. He talked in the same vein for some time. I thought it best to leave it at that. And I told Rosie where he was in case she wanted to intervene, but she didn't seem to bother.'

'He was Rhea Doonican's boy. It's known that he's had either mental health issues or a drink problem since he was thirteen.

Nobody knows who his dad is. Well, his mum did obviously but she's not around to ask. He's a very troubled young man,' said Mackie, 'but "pushing his mother off a cliff" type of troubled?' She shrugged.

'Of them all so far, most likely. He was on the clifftop,' said McPhee.

'But the commotion that allowed him to get there was after she had fallen, remember. If he sneaked through the gate beforehand, by some means, then he'll be caught on the party phone footage or the security footage.'

McPhee said, 'Just to clarify the Tron issue, this security footage is from Pickering. Pomeroy doesn't know we have it. Pickering said to ask EB or Cosmo for their phone footage as they film everything. He suggested, again, that it'd be better if Pomeroy didn't know.'

'Let's have a look.'

Five minutes later they were watching the night-tinted images. The huge gates were slightly apart. The time in the upper right corner read 23.31, and they could see Perkins and Pickering, the former being the taller, broader of the two. He stood, Caplan thought, like a soldier. They were talking, both drinking from cans – the low-alcohol beer Koi had given them.

They walked off the visual field of the camera, and the time stamp stopped then jumped forward to 23.34 when Koi came past, like an angel slipping through the gates of hell. She turned to wave at them.

'I wonder if their conversation was just out of shot,' said Caplan.

Neither of the security guys followed her. They walked around. They took a drink. The clock ticked on. At 23.45, they were both in view, leaning on the gate, chatting, when Samphire appeared on the right of the screen, moving slightly quicker than Koi had. Was there an agitation, an air of irritation about the way he moved?

'He's asking where Koi is,' said Caplan.

The answer was an arm pointing up towards Mary's Tower and the King's Reach beyond. Samphire followed Koi's route out of the gates.

Then the two men reacted to some noise from the seaward side of the gate, both of them turning their heads. Another question asked. Perkins went out of the gate. Pickering stayed there, on guard, waiting.

Then Perkins reappeared, a shrug and a shake of the head indicating that nothing was out of order. Again, they strolled out of view. The clock stopped. Then restarted.

'There's nothing there,' said Caplan.

'Oh, it's a wee fox, he's lovely,' said Mackie.

'That shows how high tech the motion-sensitive sensors are. Oh, oh. What's that now?'

Samphire appeared through the gates like a wild man; Perkins stopped him in his tracks, holding him.

'What's he doing?'

'Listening to him, I think. Where's Pickering?'

It looked like Samphire and Perkins were hugging each other, then Samphire dropped out of Perkins's grasp and was away down the lawn. Perkins ran after him, shouting something over his shoulder. Then a few moments later Pickering ran across the screen, with Pomeroy, his phone to his ear, plodding after him. The manager staggered to a halt and bent over, hands on his knees. Gasping for breath, he leaned against the open gate, keeping the camera sensors active.

'Samphire's running to get to the beach and the boys are stopping him.'

'If that's the time, then that's Pomeroy calling it in.'

'That gate was never left unattended. Not once. McPhee, watch the whole thing again. Watch it right up to us, me arriving. If Tron got out there, it wasn't by the gate.

EIGHT

Caplan wished she had an office of her own. This was the still point in an investigation where she wanted to sit in the quiet, away from the rest, look at the ceiling and think. At the moment McPhee and Craigo were arguing about the internet connection for some more footage that had arrived, and Mackie was slurping at her tea while tapping on her tablet.

'Mackie? What did the locals think of the set-up? Were the McQuarrie-Samphires liked? Resented?'

'Well, I know they employed local people. So they were preferred over the multinational chain who owned it before. They'd basically closed the caravan park and the beach and that made them very unpopular. Torsvaig does small weddings. But yeah, they scored a lot of brownie points by engaging Louise Kendall as their wedding planner and coordinator.'

'Because?' asked Caplan.

'Because old Billy Kendall was ill, he had carers in four times a day. He'd been the minister for many years, and there was Louise in Edinburgh, doing well at her career. She contacted the Sunflower Company when she heard the place was going to be a wedding venue and they gave her the contract.'

'We get Louise up on the list as well.'

'And Robyn, the girl who looks after the horses,' said Craigo.

'What are we thinking about reactions to the incident? I think Samphire was upset in a way that Pomeroy wasn't.'

'I got that vibe too,' said McPhee.

'EB was struggling. She's the young star, eclipsing the old star, Cosmo seems very close to EB, and he was genuinely distraught.'

'I saw him in that police drama, he's not that good an actor to fake it convincingly,' said McPhee.

'I can interview him once he's sober, ma'am,' said Mackie. Caplan ignored her.

'Who is EB?' asked Craigo, 'In the family?' He pointed at the picture almost covered by Cosmo's face.

Mackie jumped in, 'She's Ecco Middlemass's daughter, Ebony

Blanc, known as EB, as it's such a stupid name. Her father was unknown but now the world knows she's Gabriel's daughter.' Mackie pulled a sarcastic smile, 'That's a wee bit handy! She's a model and an influencer and does all kind of shit for TikTok, or Instagram or something. She's famous for a revenge sex tape, not nice, but she's coming out of it strongly. Her new boyfriend is called AZed and he's a poet.'

'Who was on the revenge tape with her?' said McPhee.

'Some other arsehole boyfriend.' Mackie shrugged dismissively. 'One of her scandals, but she was only furious because she looked three pounds overweight in it. Then there was that photo with her bare bottom, known as the butt cheek pic. Taken by her dad. She was sixteen and four days old. Make of that what you will.'

'So, the rising star maybe not keeping in with the wholesome brand,' said McPhee, his eyes fixed on the bare rear of EB in the photograph.

'Wholesome! She'd flash her tits to anybody who asked,' scorned Mackie, getting a stern look of disapproval from Caplan. 'I mean that's a very famous picture of her. We all knew her age.' Mackie pointed at the picture stuck on the board, mostly covered by pictures of Cosmo. It was shot in sepia, the tones emphasising the colour of her skin. The portrait was from the back, upper body, her head half turned so her profile was visible. The long, glossy ponytail dropped down her spine like a waterfall. Her hair over the left ear was shorn, her shoulder and shoulder blade were covered by white tattooed flowers, each leaf and petal highlighted by a crystal resembling a rain drop. Just visible in the picture was a pair of small sunflowers rising up from her left buttock.

Caplan looked closely, 'Two sunflowers for the two that have died?'

'She must have been psychic because she's left room for the third one,' said McPhee, peering at EB's buttock, earning another glare from Mackie.

'Recap, please.'

Mackie pointed at the photographs on the wall. 'Flame-haired Rhea Doonican was a Belfast girl. Ecco Middlemass was a mixed-race Londoner from Peckham. Middlemass died on Christmas Eve in 2004. Rhea Doonican died in 2008. Middlemass fell from the roof terrace of her flat in London during a party, which might be of significance, though she had a history of substance abuse. Rhea

Doonican passed away from an apparent accidental overdose of prescription medication.' Then Mackie looked at her notes. 'But there had been deliberate contamination of the wine she was drinking, by the prescribed medication, probably by her own hand. It was something she did.'

'Was Samphire present at both events?' asked Caplan.

'No idea. Why?'

'Just interested. It's fine. Adam Spencer said that he'd send over the details from the Met. He called the Sunflower Girls the cool kids, "the kids who never tried to be cool". Am I right in thinking that each time, after the death of the mother, Koi and Gabriel take on the child?'

'Oh aye,' confirmed Mackie. 'And this is where it gets a bit lovely, or a bit bloody weird depending on your point of view. Ecco Middlemass and Rhea Doonican have no family to speak of – they have the same lack of backstory as Koi. In fact, I was talking to one of the journalists outside the castle this morning.'

'Mackie,' warned Caplan.

'He said that Police Scotland doesn't have the money to break through the legal red tape to find out who Koi is. Or was. Pomeroy has it sealed like a duck's arse. It's worse than looking for somebody in witness protection. He was being helpful.'

'Nice of him. Is that the same for all the Sunflower Girls?' asked Caplan.

'Exactly the same.'

'So, to confirm, they have no past. Any of them?' asked McPhee. 'It's like they were born when they met Samphire.'

'Aye, he photographs women in the scud and calls it art. Then he spots Koi and "discovers" her, like she's an island. Or a disease. Or a wee beastie.' Mackie was not impressed.

Caplan ignored her. 'Confirmed, DC McPhee. A new identity, for whatever reason, costs money. And necessitates knowing people with that nefarious skill set.' She scanned the board. 'Rosie? She interests me. She said something about how she'd killed her mother, but she was talking figuratively. Who wants to interview her again?'

'I can do it,' offered McPhee. 'There's something going on. She's twenty-two, the oldest child, and while she's on the payroll of the brand and plays a huge role in the parenting of her siblings, she seems to be the family dogsbody.'

'Rosie did comment that the family commercialises their tragedies. She talks as if the family is a commercial enterprise. That must be hard to live with. Rosie was adopted by Koi and Gabriel?' asked Caplan.

'That's not common knowledge, ma'am,' said Mackie. 'No podcasts or documentaries about that.'

'Could somebody look into that? It might be useful to dip into a podcast from MisChief666. I quote, "The Samphires are all tall, elegant and beautiful. Where did Rosie come from? The answer is that Samphire is not her dad." Unquote. That's insulting, and a breach of privacy if the adoption isn't in the public domain. Mackie, can you sniff around that podcast, it sounds . . . well it sounds as if it's by somebody on the inside who's not happy. It's bitching rather than content.'

Mackie was very enthusiastic. 'I'll do that. And there's Cosmo! The totally hunky and delicious male model, the eldest son of Koi and Gabriel. He's just gorge, has a huge future in front of him.'

'From what I saw, he was the one who seemed genuinely upset this morning. EB was comforting him. They looked close.'

'Weird, or brother-and-sister close?' asked McPhee.

'Brother and sister, I'd say.' Caplan thought about it. 'Maybe bordering on weird, but if they live, work and have been educated together, their navigation of emotional relationships with the outside world might not be the best.'

'Okay, so today we explore the family relationships, we track Koi's phone, we look at Rosie's adoption. And we talk to Cosmo and Tron. Today we go down that narrow passageway and find where Samphire was. With everything that was going on, he was in there pronto. Let's find out what he was doing?'

'Do we trust Pickering and Perkins?'

Caplan smiled. 'Maybe cognitive bias, but I do trust Pickering.'

'And his story gels with Perkins's version.' McPhee nodded.

'How did the tech boys get on?'

McPhee scrolled through his tablet. 'Nothing on the interim reports, still no blood at the scene, no signs of a struggle. They tore the scarf getting it up, but it's been confirmed as Koi's.'

They all looked at the board.

'And the rumour is she's Scottish. Could she have been coming home?' asked Caplan.

'What kind of Scottish though? Posh Edinburgh or cheery islander?' asked McPhee.

'Let's ask Pickering and Perkins, as locals they'd notice. Call them now, Callum, and don't let them confer.'

'That gives me an idea,' said McPhee. He turned his back to the rest of the room, and got on his mobile.

Caplan sighed. 'I always saw Koi as the strong one of the Sunflower Girls but as you say, we don't know. The image of Ecco was as the wild party girl; Rhea was emotional and sensitive, Koi was the earth mother. But who knows the truth?'

'We don't know anything apart from what they tell us. Pomeroy controls the information, he controls everything,' said Craigo.

'It's well known that she and Samphire marry, split up and get married again. During the split, he fathers EB with Ecco Middlemass.' Caplan waved her pen in the air.

'I've found a boyfriend of Ecco Middlemass, DeVries. There's an interview where he says he wanted Ecco to leave the Sunflowers, but Samphire got Ecco pregnant. DeVries walked and she remained with the band, then she died a year later. Samphire goes back to Koi,' said Mackie in the hushed, rushed tones of the village gossip.

'How did Samphire and Pomeroy meet?'

'In rehab. It started as an agent/photographer relationship as Samphire wasn't going back to his dangerous work. If he'd witnessed all kinds of shit shows around the world, suffered with his mental health as a result, that could explain Pomeroy's protective role. Craigo thought there was a father/son thing,' said Caplan. Her sergeant nodded in agreement.

'Now Pomeroy looks after the entire Sunflower business empire. Including Torsvaig,' said Mackie. 'It all started with that advert.'

'And that was filmed right here,' said Craigo.

'What?' asked Caplan.

'Well, on the beach at Limpetlaw, not here in the station.'

'That's weird.' Caplan nodded her head slowly. 'Are you sure?'

'Maybe they saw the castle when they filmed the advert, and when it came up for sale, they bought it. No mystery,' said McPhee, ending a call.

'Can I see the advert, ma'am? It seems so popular, but I don't watch TV,' said Craigo.

'It's on YouTube,' said McPhee, taking the laptop.

'Mackie, try and speak to the boyfriend, DeVries, he'll have an outsider's view. But for now, we need to confirm the ways of getting in and out the castle. If we find a big drain or a dungeon with a broken grate, then we need to re-examine everything. We really do need to chat to Tron.'

Caplan decided to let them get on with it and intended studying the timeline but as soon as the music sounded out of the laptop speaker, she too turned to watch.

Melancholy fell over the small room as they knew that, in that short film clip, only the horse had died in old age. The three women, still teenagers. The giant horse plodding along the beach, waves splashing at his huge, feathered hooves, the sun shimmering on his deep-brown coat. The long black mane and tail flowing in the wind were matched by the long hair of his three human companions, mere stick insects next to him. Koi's blond locks blew in the breeze, Ecco Middlemass's black hair was loosely piled on top of her head and Rhea Doonican's messy Titian pleat dangled over her shoulder. They were splashing through the surf, two walking, one on the horse, dressed in the white linen of the Sunflower Linen Company. Ecco was deeper into the waves, Rhea holding on to the luxuriant mane. The horse had no saddle, no bridle. Koi was perched high on his broad back like a doll. Then one rogue wave hit a little harder. The horse, feeling the slap of cold water on his belly, sidestepped a little, which in a Clydesdale was a long way and caught Koi unawares. She slowly began to slip off, her body weight pulling her round the horse, her laughter infectious in the air, even on the small screen and twenty plus years later. Rhea was the next to go down, her hand up to her face, succumbing to the next big wave. Then Ecco belly-flopped into the water for the sheer hell of it. There were six long shapely legs in the air, faces resurfacing in hysterical laughter. They held each other as they lost their balance again, staggering. Ecco had her hand out in an attempt to protect them from the tide like Canute trying to hold back the waves.

'They are all dressed in white. They were dressed in white at the time Koi died,' said Craigo.

'There was a photo shoot earlier,' said McPhee. 'Rosie said they had to get dressed up.'

'The Sunflower brand is the home of the Little White Dress,' explained Caplan.

'And Charlie Campbell,' said Craigo, nodding at the paused video.

'Who?'

'He died last year, he was thirty. Marvellous age, ma'am, just marvellous.'

'Who are you wittering on about?'

'The horse. The horse was called Charlie Campbell.'

'Why?' asked Caplan.

'Because that was his name,' answered Craigo.

Caplan realised that she had asked the wrong question. 'How do you know that?'

'He was famous. With a heart shape on his shoulder. He was one of the Kinglass Clydesdales, a good bloodline. They, the Samphires, bought him after the advert and took him to London. When they bought the castle, he was stabled along the road here.' The other three looked at their sergeant. 'As I said, only put to sleep last year. And there's also Kinglass Aberdeen Angus, fabulous bloodline there. I know about them too.'

Caplan was still looking at him when Mackie started speaking. 'The advert was famous because this was 1995 and the pouting, sour-faced supermodels were still around. Along come the three of them, fresh faced, hair all over the place, not perfect in any way but very beautiful . . . and all five feet nine plus and weighing about three stone. The Sunflower Linen Company decided that the clip where Koi falls off the horse and goes head first in the water was the one to head the campaign. And all to the sexy sax solo of 'Careless Whisper'. As a serious advert, it would have been average, but as a funny advert, it was hysterical. And made them very famous.'

'Aye, the bit where they all climb out the water soaking wet, with very little clothing on underneath the transparent white frocks, is one of the most paused videos of all time,' said McPhee. He became aware of the other three looking at him and added, 'So I believe.'

'Pervert,' muttered Mackie, closing the laptop on the caption Sunflower Linen, Perfect for Any Occasion.

'Hey, they made a poster of it, it was a very famous thing. Like the tennis lassie scratching her arse or *Pulp Fiction*.'

'Can I just say something about the money?' said McPhee. 'This is second-hand info, but it seems to have all stayed within the company. The endorsements, advertising, the clothing range, perfume, all that kind of shit remains with Pomeroy and Samphire. The kids stay with them. The kids have been home-schooled. They are now famous or infamous in their own right. But the money they earn goes into the company.'

'That's . . . interesting,' said Caplan. 'And the kids are young adults, they'll want the freedom to spend their own money.' She pointed at the smiling picture of Koi. 'Was Koi a depressive? Any history? Is there a reason for her taking her own life?'

'I've sent out a couple of emails re the stalker. The two reports I can track are a threat of rape and a threat of death. Not considered anything more than average celebrity nutter stuff, but the timing is interesting. They're mostly from before Covid lockdown, then they started up again once the family moved here. Do you want me to track down the originals?'

Caplan nodded. 'Get the IT boys on it if needed. Pomeroy might have them all behind a wall for a reason, if they moved here to get away from it all. Then Koi goes for a walk in the dark and is found dead.'

'Not found. Not dead,' said Craigo.

'Maybe a castle felt secure,' said Mackie.

'Then why open up as a wedding venue?' asked McPhee.

'Mrs Samphire buys a castle to protect herself and the children, then Mr Pomeroy develops it as there's money to be made.'

Caplan nodded her head. 'You read people very well, DS Craigo. Look into the financials a little more. How many weddings would be needed per annum to keep that financially viable?'

McPhee added, 'You know, I think of Koi as a woman who did the right thing. She wasn't born into any of this. Maybe there's a reason for the secrets about her past – she was seventeen, maybe getting away from a troubled background. Did you say that the other two were on their own in the world? Maybe there's something there. The Sunflower Linen Company made her famous. Years later, when it got into financial trouble she bought the company, reinstated the workforce. Which brought about increased profile, and the clothes started to sell again. Koi McQuarrie re-invented the iconic Little White Dress, it became an instant classic. She saved those people's jobs.' He waved a pencil in the air. 'Is the brand the family. Or is the family the brand?'

'She was the face of the brand, and, you know, the heart of the brand. Remember she had to snog Jeremy Clarkson for Cash for Kids,' said Mackie. 'She was happy to make fun of herself. Ecco and Rhea rarely did anything like that.' She shrugged. 'Maybe they didn't live long enough.'

'And now she's dead on the rocks. Why?'

'Not dead. No body found,' said Craigo.

'I think she was brought up in care. Samphire comes along.

Money. Success. Now she's had enough. Tells the rest of them to look after themselves. They now have their own income stream – as a family, I mean. The castle will make them money. She jumped,' said McPhee.

'It's worth a thought but I doubt she'd leave Morrow in the state she's in.' Caplan shook her head. 'Unless she saw herself as part of Morrow's problem. I like that idea that her own upbringing was troubled. Hence it being hidden behind a legal wall. If she had been born near here and all was lovely, Pomeroy would have opened a coffee shop and put up a wee blue plaque. You'd be able to buy Koi mugs and posters of . . . Charlie Campbell.'

'Cosmo's awake, he's just sent in his phone footage,' said McPhee, tapping at the screen on his mobile.

Koi was dancing on the wooden dance floor near the firepit. Tina Charles's 'I Love to Love' came through the speaker of the laptop. Somebody shouted 'Mum'. Pomeroy, Morrow, EB and Rosie waved their hands in the air, singing along. They sounded happy.

Then she walked out of shot to the right. The next time she appeared she was looking up, gesturing to somebody. She had her arms out as if to catch somebody falling. The screen was filled with Pomeroy dancing badly. It looked like Pomeroy said something to the off-screen Koi. When the camera panned back, Koi was holding Tron in a long, deep cuddle.

'He's holding on to her for dear life. That's so sad.' Mackie put her hand over her mouth, tears ready to fall.

'It shows that he's there when Koi's there.' Caplan sat back.

'And he looks sober to me, he's not under the influence of anything, judging by the way he's moving,' said Mackie.

The music moved on to 'Sweet Caroline' and the focus of the video moved, Koi now only visible in the outer part of the screen, then disappearing before dancing back in. Samphire appeared, dressed in white. The team leaned forward. Husband and wife danced together, laughing.

Then something changed; Caplan watched carefully, her eyes narrowing.

Koi danced away and placed something on the table.

'That's her phone, ma'am,' said Craigo. 'At least we know it's not at the bottom of the cliff.'

'But watch,' said Caplan.

There was an almost imperceptible change in the movements on the screen. A wrong word said? A step on a toe? The focus moved away but not before Samphire grabbed Koi's upper arm. He stepped in, said something in her ear, then she moved away, the entire length of her arm running through his closed fingers. They paused when their fingertips were about to separate. Then she was gone from view.

Mackie paused the film. Samphire was turning away; Pomeroy was mid-step in front of the firepit. 'That was the last time Koi was seen, apart from by Pickering and Perkins of course.'

'Go back. That was a long, weird kind of handshake with Gabriel. She walks away while he's still holding on to her hand. Does Koi say something before she leaves?'

'Is she saying goodbye?'

NINE

The Welcome Gate was now festooned with flowers. A small crowd of people stood quietly, some holding candles, some holding pictures. Lying against the drystane dyke was a framed picture of Koi, the focus for the offerings. The car park was busy, the air heavy with genuine grief and sorrow, people taking their turn and their time to place their gift and then retreat back to the crowd to continue contemplation of a woman they had never met.

The sense of loss was palpable. Caplan walked a few feet in front of Mackie who was already struggling on the incline. Craigo was up ahead, his short legs striding out as if he had a purpose that the other two had no knowledge of.

She turned round and waited, concerned about how this outpouring of grief would be affecting her colleague so soon after losing her mother. 'You okay?'

'Fine, ma'am.'

She didn't look fine at all. Caplan flicked her eyes over to the celebrity mourners.

'I can cope with everything this morning. I'm at my work,' said Mackie. Her eyes were not visible behind the sunglasses, but her mouth betrayed a little unwelcome emotion.

'But you don't need to—'

'Hey, youse two!' A voice shouted to them.

'Oh Christ, it's Wattie. I might bugger off now, if that's okay,' muttered Mackie.

He came striding over, looking hot and sweaty in his black T-shirt, his belly hanging over his utility belt.

'Good morning, ma'am.' He sounded just on the right side of insolent. 'Good morning, ya wee nugget, what the hell are you doing back at yer work? Have you not just planted yer maw? These folk are all gaping at mair death, need their heids looked at.' He took a breath. 'And who's been cleaning ma office?'

'We have, you dirty wee sod.'

'I'll leave you to explain, DC Mackie. Craigo and I are going to chat to Mr Pomeroy, eventually.' Caplan turned and continued up the hill with renewed vigour.

They walked up to the castle, where the main door was lying open. The big dog was resting across the steps, facing the sky, his eyes closed, enjoying the sun. To Caplan it didn't look like the same dog that she'd met the day before. This one had a darker coat, it was larger, and the pink tongue lolling out the side of its mouth just emphasised the size of the teeth. She wondered how many of them the family had, and if they were all friendly.

The Great Hall was deserted; she had that feeling again that they were on their own. No noise from anywhere, no sign of life apart from the sleeping dog ineffectually guarding the door.

'What do you want to do, ma'am?' asked Craigo, standing so close behind her he gave her a fright.

'I suppose we should phone somebody and tell them we're here.' She pulled her mobile from her pocket slowly, looking around her, once again taking in the details of the armour, the muskets and the pennants. Paintings of the MacDougalls still looked down from the walls. She wondered what they thought of the current residents with their Wi-Fi and vegan burgers. A trophy head of a sixteen-point stag regarded her with watchful glass eyes.

Craigo whispered to her, 'I think we're being watched.'

'I was just thinking that too,' she said, tilting her head at the magnificent antlers.

'No, I mean we're being watched. From the narrow corridor, far side of the bar.'

Caplan took her time looking over the ceiling then dropping her gaze across the gap in the stone wall. At first, she saw nothing, then in the blackness of the shadow was a movement. There and gone.

Caplan kept moving, kept looking, until she was facing Craigo, saying quietly. 'Who was that?'

A whispered answer. 'Tron, I think.'

'Well.' Caplan put on a defeated expression. 'Well, we agreed that he had mental health issues and that we needed to interview him.'

Craigo nodded. 'Sober, anyway.'

'So would you agree that we'd be better following him, make sure he's okay?'

'We could just phone somebody, ma'am . . .'

'Or we could follow him.'

A slow smile spread on Craigo's face. 'Oh, I see what you mean, ma'am, yes, oh yes.'

She took one final look around, up the balcony, to the musicians' gallery, to the stairways above. Nobody to be seen. Then she walked across the red carpet, onto the flagstone floor and into the narrow gap that was delineated by the black cord hanging between the two brass stanchions. Quickly unclipping it, she stepped into the darkness. Craigo followed.

The temperature immediately seemed to drop by twenty degrees. An effect of the lack of light, the closeness of the walls, the lack of fresh air. The total, enveloping darkness. Caplan felt something soft touch her arm and jumped.

There was a thick velvet curtain, gathered up in the corner. She had not seen it before. Then she heard Craigo say 'Hello,' feeling his warm breath on her cheek.

'We tried to have a chat yesterday.'

No response. But in the darkness, something moved, sliding away, along the short corridor, footsteps barely audible on the flagstones.

Craigo already had his torch on, pointing at the ground, the beam of light showing wear from the many feet that had passed this way over the last, how long, eight hundred years? Caplan pressed herself into the wall, letting Craigo get ahead of her. McPhee hadn't been wrong when he thought it was all a bit Scooby Doo.

She followed Craigo, who was following the lithe figure who paused at each corner to let them see where he had gone, then was away again. They'd turned left, gone along a passage, then turned right to go up some spiral steps.

Caplan reluctantly went up them behind Craigo, suppressing her phobia of spiral staircases.

Craigo moved the torch beam up and to the side, highlighting the twisted old rope that hung between the old iron hooks in the wall. Even before she touched it, it was moving slightly. Tron was holding on to it as he made his way up the steps, to wherever he was going.

'Tron?' she called, her voice wavering a little. As they climbed, visions of a deep hole where they would both plummet down to the dungeon crossed her mind. They would fall to their deaths and be eaten by rats. Then they were back on the flat again, and then Craigo was heading up another set of treacherous, crumbling steps.

'Craigo, no!' whispered Caplan as her colleague and his torch rounded the curve, plunging her into darkness.

'It's easy, ma'am.'

Steeling herself, she followed him up. It was getting colder, and the lack of light was now absolute. Caplan, unable to cope with the narrowing steps, stopped. 'I'm not going any further.'

'Come on.'

'No.'

'I'll go up, you stay here.' She heard Craigo's light footfall going up, over her head, the sound echoing down the centre of the stairway as it receded somewhere up in the darkness. She knew if she placed her foot close to the central column, she'd fall all the way down, and she had no way of knowing how far 'all the way down' was. Certainly, the ground floor, the Great Hall, was not the bottom of this staircase. So, she stayed still, holding on to the rope, her back to the curved wall, both feet on the widest part of the step. And waited. Then she attempted to find the step beneath her by stretching her foot down, pointing with her toe, but it only reached into the abyss, so she retracted it. And waited.

And waited. She was sure she could hear rats, mice, God knows what. She thought she could hear the breathing of a huge animal, a rasping breath in and out. Then she realised it was the sea. She turned her head, listening to the noises coming from above. She could make out the call of seabirds. Slowly she slipped her rucksack from her shoulder, something she'd done a hundred times before, but this time it seemed in danger of unbalancing her. Scrabbling around, she got out her mobile and turned on the torch.

And let out a yelp when the first thing she saw was Craigo's shoes on the steps above her.

'I think you need to come up here.'

Caplan didn't speak. She was already terrified at the thought of coming down, but she forced herself to move, both hands on the rope, playing step up, catch up with her feet.

It seemed to go on forever. But it was only two, maybe three complete spirals later when Craigo turned off to go through a passage. There was a roof fall at the entrance, rubble on the floor, but the smell here was better – fresh air. And heat.

'It's just this bit, ma'am. Scramble over it.'

She sat down on the largest of the stones and swung her legs over.

Each step they took brought them into warmer, fresher air.

'Where are we?'

'We're about to find out.'

He walked along into the light, more confidently than she would have.

And then there was the natural light of a window opening, a hole in the wall, high up in a tower. She walked towards it and looked out to see the lower parts of the castle below, the grass, the wall and the sky. Not the best of outlooks in a castle surrounded by beautiful views.

'Through here.'

She followed him into a small circular room with four windows. The glass was old, green-flecked with leaded surrounds. In the room was a deck chair, a corkboard. On an old easel was a tin box of ink and pen nibs. It was labelled, 'Love, Koi'. The wonderful quality of the daylight picked up drawings and more drawings, papers and pencils and charcoal. Behind the archway of a door was a pile of vodka bottles and beer cans, all empty.

'Bloody hell,' said Caplan. 'Look at that.' It was a fine drawing of Koi, curled in a chair, a book in her hands, a dog at her feet. 'That's lovely, that's how I imagine her to be.'

'He's caught the real person there.' Craigo pointed at the drawings on the other side. 'Here, he's mapping the castle, ma'am: every single one of these is a drawing of a passage or a room, the Great Hall, the dungeons. Look at the detail. These are more than maps, these are works of art.'

The drawings reminded her of Aklen's detailed sketches of the tiny houses, before any measurement or calculations were done. Craigo picked up an open sketchbook and started flicking through them. Caplan walked to a window and looked out. Almost a full one-hundred-and-eighty-degree view. They were high up, looking along the ramparts. Ahead and to the right was the sea and a little bit of the Woodwall with the dense forest behind. To the left she could make out the trees, the sea beyond. She heard Craigo taking photographs on his phone as she leaned as far forward as she could, seeing the path down from the King's Reach and a narrow strip of the grassy Reach itself. She'd need to be out on the ramparts themselves to see more. She guessed this was some kind of lookout.

'Did you draw all these yourself?' Craigo's voice was soft. 'It's okay, you haven't done anything wrong. I was just admiring this.

It's the end of the Woodwall, isn't it? With the large coils of wire. Stops anybody getting round the seaward end of the wall. Do you see that, ma'am?'

Caplan came over to look.

'Oh, that's very good. You have a real talent for this,' she said to the teenager standing just outside the door. He looked very different to his photograph; this face was acne scarred, he had the pasty skin of a teen who spent his life in darkness. At least his altered image had made the final cut, unlike Rosie. 'Does it take you a long time to do each one?'

He eyed her, not with suspicion or fear but something else. Hope?

'Depends,' he said quietly. Like EB, he had a strong London accent.

'Can we have a word, Tron, just between the three of us?' asked Craigo.

'Depends.'

'This picture. That's from the top of the cliff, isn't it?'

He nodded.

'Those are the crime scene technicians in their suits?'

Another nod.

Caplan could hardly keep quiet, but Craigo was very good at this introvert talk.

'So, I was over here,' Craigo tapped the picture. 'You must have been—'

There was a noise, like a muffled bang, as if a door had closed deep below them.

And Tron was gone. He didn't even make a sound.

'This way, ma'am.'

'This is the only way down?'

'Yes. Of course.'

Craigo had taken a few more photographs and then they left, going back down the way they came. Into the cold, then back into warmth as they descended. Caplan took each step very gingerly, ignoring the feeling of dizziness as the curved wall in front of her seemed never ending.

Then Craigo stopped on the second landing, his finger to his lips. He pointed along a passageway to the left and to the collapsed walls with rocks sticking out like teeth. Then to the right, to a narrow bar of light on the floor. Craigo lifted the torch to show a wooden door, relatively new compared to the staircase they had just navigated.

The handle was tantalisingly shiny in the harsh beam.

'Should I?'

'If we get caught we'll say we were looking for the way out.'

Craigo placed his hand gently on the brass handle and Caplan thought that this was the point when she would be grabbed from behind, thrown into a dark dungeon and never seen again.

The door was locked.

Craigo shrugged, tried again with the same result, then shone his torch around, seeing the drape of a red curtain. He made his way forward, unclipping the black cord that hung between two brass stanchions before he pulled back the folds of velvet.

They were on the musicians' gallery. Looking down they could see the red carpet of the Great Hall. In front of them the big door was still open. The dog was now indoors, lying in the shade. The pennants were much closer now, so close Caplan thought she could touch them if she just leaned over the handrail a little.

'Where did Tron go?' she whispered.

'Shall we go back and find out?'

'I'd rather be where I can see my hand in front of my face.'

'Hey,' shouted a voice from far below. It was Rosie in the middle of the hall. 'How did you get up there?' She sounded almost amused.

'Tron,' said Caplan vaguely.

'That explains it. Sorry I missed you. You need to go straight on and come back the way you went up.'

Caplan thanked her. Rosie had presumed that they had come up the main stairway.

They walked onwards, to another door, with a blue-corded rope this time, and then onto the main staircase, over twelve feet wide, with a pristine central runner of deep red and gold borders, and down they went, side by side. Caplan was getting a glimmer of what it would be like to be married in a place like this, walking down these stairs in a wedding dress, arm in arm with your new husband. Friends and family gathered below. How wonderful it would be in the winter – dark, candlelit, tartan and the torches burning over the door. And even some snow . . .

'What the hell do you think you're doing here?' Pomeroy's voice boomed at them; he was just this side of furious.

'Investigating the disappearance of Koi McQuarrie, as I think you well know, Mr Pomeroy.'

He took a breath. 'I mean, what the hell are you doing here on the landing?'

'Investigating the disappearance of Koi McQuarrie, Mr Pomeroy. Where we are does not change what we are here for, does it?'

They were now on the first floor at the junction of the stairs and the east and west wings of the castle. He had no idea where they had been, but he was more suspicious than Rosie, which was interesting.

'We were looking for Tron actually. We saw him come this way. Any ideas? We don't have a formal statement from him,' said Caplan, fighting authority with authority.

'No idea where he goes. Why are you here?'

Caplan put her hands out as if to say, *What, again?*

'Better question. Why does he have his torch on?'

'Xestobium rufovillsum,' said Craigo, without missing a beat.

'Pardon me?'

'Death watch beetle. Do you have problems in the oak timbers?' He shone his torch down. 'There.'

Pomeroy looked from Craigo in his beige jerkin and cream chinos, his hair sprouting over his bald patch. Caplan then felt his eyes on her, taking in the good suit and smart boots. She felt dirty and covered in dust, but Pomeroy didn't seem to notice. He dropped his eyes to look at the skirting board.

'You should pay attention to him; his farmhouse is as old as this. You should get somebody out,' Caplan advised. 'But it's fortunate we bumped into each other. We haven't got a statement from you yet either.'

'This way,' said Pomeroy, sighing and heading into the public part of the castle, muttering something under his breath.

TEN

'DCI Caplan, please do take a seat. Sorry about that. Not the first time I've caught wedding guests wandering around, trying to catch a glimpse of Cosmo. It's always Cosmo.' Pomeroy's mobile phone rang. He glanced at it, rejected the call and slipped it back into his pocket. 'I'm afraid I didn't catch your name yesterday?' He held a hand out to DS Craigo, giving him a warm and firm handshake as Craigo introduced himself. Pomeroy indicated the three deep-red Chesterfield sofas placed round a low oak table at the far side of the room. One was covered by a thick tartan rug that was strewn with dog hair. The room was dominated by three canvases on the olive-green walls, each one six feet tall and three feet wide, bearing photographs of the Sunflower Girls dressed in their white linen, posing in a luscious meadow somewhere.

Pomeroy pulled another ringing mobile from another pocket. 'Excuse me, avoid that sofa. It belongs to the dogs; you probably met them downstairs.'

They turned as the door opened again and a big black nose pushed in. The large dog entered, his wiry coat the warm colour of bracken in autumn. He regarded them both with an air of mild interest, took a sniff then climbed slowly onto the rug on the spare settee, circled round twice then flopped down, laying his huge head on his front paws, and gave Craigo a doleful stare, which prompted a look of apology from the detective sergeant.

'Is that a wolfhound?' asked Caplan.

'Scottish deerhound,' corrected Craigo, 'bred for hunting deer since the 1500s.'

'Bloody dog, sneaks in here the minute my back's turned. It knows I don't like it.' Pomeroy sat down opposite them. 'I was very drunk yesterday – this morning – and at my age I don't sober up quickly, not the way I used to. I hope everybody was cooperative.'

Caplan recalled the nifty sidestep when they had almost collided with each other at the castle doorway. Not that drunk, she thought, just a useful excuse for any odd behaviour. 'They were.'

One of his mobiles rang again. 'Sorry, you know what it's like.'

He glanced at the number, swore quietly and swiped it back off again. 'Have you found her?'

'Not yet,' Caplan looked round the room. 'It's a lovely set-up here. How's business?' She was thinking that if a big hotel chain could not keep this place running at a profit, then what hope did an ex-model with no experience of the wedding trade or hospitality have.

'We were in the right place at the right time.' He leaned back, ready to pontificate. 'Koi and Gabe wanted out of London. I wanted a place with thick walls for my wine cellar. My own collection is in a secret passage behind that.' He nodded at the large image of Koi. 'Very Sherlock Holmes! Anyway, the house in Chiswick was worth a fortune. There's a waning fashion for huge weddings. There was one in London with nine hundred guests last year. Imagine that.'

Craigo pulled a face, clearly wondering how anybody could know that many people.

'How do you get out of that? If you're a parent in a society that expects the nine-hundred-seater wedding. Or maybe it's a second wedding where the couple want a few quiet days with their friends. We offer bijou weddings, intimate, and of course, we offer that landscape.' He nodded out the window. 'If you think that family is important, then get married at Torsvaig. We like to think that we have brought the wedding back to bride and groom.'

'How often do you make that speech?' asked Caplan.

Pomeroy laughed; it was a heartfelt laugh. 'Not as often as I thought I'd have to. The place actually sells itself. The press were invited for a photo shoot, we got a fabulous write-up in three of the dailies. Hutton, Cowie-Browne and Marshall, three lifestyle journos we like to keep sweet, and Andrew Knox for the great unwashed – same text but rewritten for the different demographic.' He gestured with his hand. 'We've only twelve bedrooms, that's enough for most families. The Stewart Room is a lovely space, the interior design was all Koi's influence. It's a room that makes memories. The Great Hall, the stairway. Who doesn't want their wedding pictures taken by Gabriel Samphire? That's the big draw.'

He fell quiet. 'Any further forward to finding out . . .' he struggled a little for the right words, 'what happened to Koi?'

Caplan assured him they were still investigating. 'What exactly was your relationship with her?' Her eyes drifted across to the wall over the desk, to the photograph of a bride standing on the stairs they had just come down. She was looking out of the window, her back to the room, the train of the dress falling as a bejewelled white teardrop over the stairs. Caplan could recognise the Samphire touch – simple yet beautiful.

Pomeroy stared at the floor, a long white lock of hair flopping free from his fringe. 'We've a commercial relationship. I'm the manager of the entities that are Koi McQuarrie, the Sunflower Linen Company, plus the cosmetics and skincare ranges that are coming through. EB's launching a haircare range for ladies and gents of mixed ethnicity. Cosmo's skincare and fragrance will be in the top five for their demographic next Christmas. We've another product in development for the very young, a more fun-filled approach. Morrow will front that.'

'I've met Morrow. I would hardly describe her as fun filled. Has she seen the doctor yet?'

'Yes, thank God. Good job, as Gabe has a crippling migraine with the stress. He's had an injection. He'll want to talk to you once he can be upright without being sick.' Pomeroy smiled at Caplan, dropping his voice like an avuncular family friend. 'His grief response. But you asked about Koi. I think of her as a daughter-in-law. I view them as my family, with everything, the good and the bad, and the tragedy that comes with that.' He looked up at the print opposite his desk, the image that he looked at every day, not quite the image that the Sunflower Girls were famous for, but one that must have been taken earlier on the same shoot as the advert in a nearby field. Ecco had her mouth wide open in genuine surprise. Rhea Doonican was holding on to Charlie Campbell. And Koi, with a huge smile, held her hand up to her lips as if she had just uttered something she should not have. They were holding wildflowers, the three of them were seductive and sexy, each in a different way, because they weren't trying to be. They just were. 'They view me as the boring old fart who makes them behave.'

'Who controls the money?' she asked.

He smiled, showing his perfect veneers. 'I do. I also have all their passports, including Koi's. Believe me, I need to. I also oversee all the social media. They don't do anything unless it's authorised by me or the PR team. Gabe's an artistic genius, hopeless with money. Koi's not interested. She prefers to be reading with a mug of tea rather than partying with a glass of Veuve Clicquot. Cosmo and EB know that they're the face of a whole generation. They've no expertise in contracts, due diligence, travel plans and logistics, VAT, tax. That's all down to me. I work very hard, plus the staff at the Sunflower Linen Company's London office of course. The family get well paid by the business.' He looked round the room. 'What do young people today aspire to? A holiday in the Maldives? An Aston Martin? A wardrobe of designer gear? Cosmo and EB have all that by being who they are.'

'Really?' asked Craigo, genuinely intrigued.

'Oh, a holiday company will give EB a week in the Maldives if she takes a few selfies in swimwear, or a range she's promoting. She has over five million followers on TikTok. They can't buy that kind of publicity. Well, they can,' he laughed, 'but you get my drift. Kids of her age see her as a role model. She's mixed race, attractive, intelligent. She's one of them. People know where she came from and what happened to her mum. It's all part of the brand.'

'And the revenge tape?'

'She's a young woman. It's an issue that faces young women today. We'll do what she wants us to do and I'll back her decisions 101 per cent. Remember, I've known her since before she was born.' His eyes met Caplan's. He looked away first.

'So does the young gentleman get an Aston Martin for doing nothing?'

'Well . . . we had the Aston for a week.' Pomeroy picked up a sheaf of papers and started flicking through them. 'There, look at that. There's Cosmo looking like a god, using the Aston as a sun lounger. His shirt's open, he's barefoot, he's reading a book. The advert is for the trousers. It's the lifestyle that they're selling. That picture was taken out in the bailey.' He tapped on the image. 'That face will not last, his modelling has a shelf life. He's moving into acting. Morrow, Rosie and Tron will need to be cared for until their earning potential can reach that of their more marketable siblings. They'll all benefit. Even Rosie, and Rosie does not have the appeal that the others have.'

'Not as immediately attractive, you mean?' asked Caplan.

'God, fat and ugly would be some of the nicer things said about her. She's already had a few attacks from the nastier voices on social media.'

'She is neither fat nor ugly,' said Caplan coldly.

'Oh, I know that.' He pointed up at the pictures, 'but she's not that either, is she? She doesn't have what those three have. But I've plans for her.'

'They would seem to have it all, these youngsters.' Craigo looked around the room.

'They have peace and quiet and—'

'There're rumours of a stalker? As yet we can't find any original reports to the police about that.'

'The Fisherman.' Pomeroy blew out his cheeks. 'No, we decided to keep that within these walls. Initially I thought it was Koi's imagination, but the death threats seemed very real. Real in the sense that they existed, not real in the sense that they meant any physical harm.'

'Can I see them?'

'I destroyed them but have the pictures on my phone. They arrived in the mail, would you believe? How quaint, none of this cyberstalking for him. Or her. They had stopped for a few years then restarted when we moved up here. I'll get them forwarded to you.' He looked at his array of phones before deciding which one to pick up, then started pressing buttons. 'We made sure that Koi never went anywhere on her own. She declined any event that involved the public.' He scrolled until he found one particular image then read, '"*Your friends didn't live to an old age, neither will you.*" It's all rather tame.' He sighed. 'It had no bearing on what happened to her.'

'You seem very sure of that.'

'I am. She was not depressed, not anxious. She didn't end her life. She fell.'

'Morrow and Tron are ill; she didn't live a stress-free life.'

'We have a different view. We think they can help others who are suffering, as they are.'

'You're commercialising their mental health issues?'

'You can put it like that. They've agreed to it, of course. But maybe a few kids out there who aren't eating, who are having real doubts about their self-worth and their self-belief will think *if Morrow McQuarrie-Samphire can feel like that and recover, then so can I.*'

Caplan frowned.

'I don't make the rules. Ask the Beckhams or the Kardashians or the producers of the programme about that farm. Our lives are so boring nowadays we like watching other people live a non-boring one. We'll take advice on it all of course, but that's what I see coming along the line. Anyway,' he let out a long sigh. 'I know you're talking around the subject, but I can put my hand on the Bible and state that I've no idea what happened to Koi, and I truly wish I did.'

'Who's MisChief666?'

His answer was instant. 'Some bitch who really is making money out of our misery. There's one about Koi's death just come out. Vultures, DCI Caplan, evil parasites.'

Caplan nodded. 'Where exactly were you last night?'

'Drunk as a skunk in the bailey. There'll be film of my dad dancing.' He blinked, pausing. They gave him a minute or two to collect himself. 'It was a great party. Our eighth wedding had gone really well. Phil Brightman married Donna Unterweger here. Have you seen her film, *The Skin Game*?'

'No.'

'Our first helicopter wedding. There was no press. That means that all the photos can be sold as exclusives.'

Caplan had memorised a name. 'And Betty Wilson's?'

'Yes. That was a nice family party, older. We proved we could do both, so we threw a wee party to celebrate with all the family together. Koi was enjoying herself; she must have slipped. But I don't know why on earth she went up there in the first place.'

'Mr Pomeroy, is there any possibility that Koi took her own life?'

And there it was, that tiny flicker of something. Grief? 'I'm sure it's a possibility but there was no reason for it. I'm sure she fell.'

'What about Rosie's adoption?'

'Why's that relevant? It was a private adoption, nobody's business but ours.'

'Rosie thinks she might have upset Koi when she asked about it.'

'Why would she kill herself over that?' asked Pomeroy, in what seemed genuine confusion. 'Koi always knew Rosie was adopted – she adopted her! Rosie can . . . exaggerate things. She feels she needs to keep up.'

'Can you tell us what happened with Ecco Middlemass and Rhea Doonican? Their deaths, I mean.'

'Both fully investigated at the time.' Pomeroy held his hands out in defence. His gold bracelet jangled.

'Three women, all connected, die premature deaths? We police tend to look into that kind of thing.'

He looked confused for a moment, then looked rather hurt. 'Yes, of course. You're asking me to revisit the darkest times in my life. They were like daughters to me.'

'I realise it's difficult for you.'

'I don't see it at all. Koi loved the children. Rhea and Ecco were very different personalities.'

'And Koi adopted their children?'

'Ask EB and Tron. They'll tell you how Koi has looked after them. Don't take my word for it. Both those kids have had a much more stable life with us than they ever had with their respective mothers. They were dumped with Gabe and Koi more often than not anyway.' He sniffed. 'But Ecco? Christmas party 2004, watching fireworks on the roof of her flat in St John's Wood, heart issue caused by her addiction. She fell from the roof, was dead before she hit the ground. It'll be on your system. Ecco was stormy, crazy, loveable, bloody annoying, entertaining and passionate. Not the personality to live to an old age. It wouldn't have sat right with her world philosophy. Die young, stay pretty.'

'And Rhea Doonican?'

'Yes, Rhea.' He looked thoughtful.

'That wasn't so straightforward, sir, was it, the way she passed away?' asked Craigo, leaning forward, his notebook out.

Pomeroy glanced at Caplan to see if she was going to object.

'Can you answer the question, just for background?' she smiled sweetly.

'Yes,' said Craigo. 'Much more interesting that one, wasn't it? I mean, if you yourself hadn't phoned when you did, if Mr Samphire had not left the company of Miss Doonican, they might both be deceased.'

Caplan managed to keep her eyes on Pomeroy, despite a huge temptation to glare at Craigo. Pomeroy had not anticipated that question. 'Gabe, well, you will find out all this anyway, had affairs with both Ecco and Rhea—'

'At the same time?' asked Craigo.

'No. It was nothing really. I had to work very hard to keep the thing from blowing up the image, upsetting the fans. The kids have always known that he's their father. Koi has always known. There's never been an issue. One of the reasons why I'm keen to keep everything on an even keel. EB's parenthood is common knowledge but Tron's is not. Please only share that with those who really need to know.'

'Why?'

'Timing. With EB, Gabe was not married. Gabe and Koi split up for a while. With Rhea, he was with Koi. It puts a different slant on things. You have children, DCI Caplan? Two, isn't it?'

She detected the implied menace in that statement. 'How do you know that?'

'I have a fully staffed PR office. DCI Christine Caplan née Murray, Conservatoire Ballet, Tulliallan Police College, husband Aklen. Quite the highflyer with your MIT, then came the case against Grace Brindley and it all fell apart. And you landed here, just a few miles away as the crow flies.'

Craigo, totally missing the change in the atmosphere, asked cheerily, 'So, Mr Pomeroy, is it all like those American programmes where there's one man and different wives and everybody gets on?'

'I suppose so,' said Pomeroy, giving Craigo the side-eye as if he was the village idiot. 'Gabe's a very handsome man who spends his post-conflict career photographing very beautiful women, but it's always been Koi and Gabe. When Rhea had Tron, she was never the same, she suffered from terrible depression. She did hate Gabe for a while. She had two or three relationships after that, leaving Tron with us while she was away living with another man. Then, that night, she invited Gabe over to have something to eat.' He breathed out, 'Thank God. We had negotiated a deal for Rhea, she was celebrating. She bought me a bottle of Penfolds Grange 1999. And this needs to be kept away from the ears of Tron, please.'

'Of course.'

'Gabe went round to have dinner with her. I was working through a contract, there was a time-critical signature needed, time differences and all that. Gabe had only taken a few sips of wine when I called him to get himself back to the office. I was still on the phone to him when he got in the taxi. Then he got severe stomach pain and collapsed so the taxi took him to hospital.

'Later the drink, well, the bottle of wine was tested. It had been laced with tri-glucosomething or other. Rhea had drunk most of it, was dead by the time the police got there.'

'Mr Samphire's prints were on the bottle,' Craigo explained to Caplan. 'If Mr Pomeroy had not called Mr Samphire when he did, there would have been two bodies, looking like a murder suicide.'

Pomeroy looked at Craigo for a long moment while the dog yawned noisily then chewed at the fresh air.

'It was all very tragic, DS Craigo.'

'Why?' asked Caplan, 'Why would she do that?'

'She was getting too old to model, thought it was all over, she was depressed. She knew that Tron preferred Koi. Even as a baby, he preferred Koi.' He shook his head again, then turned to look out the window, hearing a regular 'whop' sound from somewhere outside. 'Rhea had been in therapy for a long time and decided to stop. It all came out at the inquest. We let it be known publicly that she took an accidental overdose. It's kinder to Tron. But all the reports are there for you to read. I can even tell you the name of the investigating officer – Barraclough.'

'Barrington,' corrected Craigo, without missing a beat, nodding and smiling, pleased with himself.

'He was very thorough, as are you, DS Craigo. He's probably risen high in the ranks, if the police force is any kind of meritocracy.' Pomeroy leaned back in his settee, turning to look at the three pictures. 'Beautiful, young, talented. Being born that lucky, something was bound to go wrong. Can we leave it there?'

He looked out the window again as the whop-whop became more pronounced. 'That's the helicopter.' Pomeroy snatched at his phones. 'She's early. Always far too early or far too late.'

'Who?' asked Caplan.

'Shazamtina Orlean, Cosmo's girlfriend. Flown in from Paris, via London and Glasgow. I need to make sure that the photographers get good pictures of the tearful reunion, even if we have to drag Cosmo out his bed. In fact, it'll be better if he looks terrible. Was there a crowd at the gate when you came in?'

'Yes.'

'Good.' He got up. 'If you'll excuse me.'

'One more thing,' Caplan said. 'Tron gets out of the castle without going through the gate. How?'

'He doesn't.'

'He does.'

'I sign the insurance that this place is safe for those who live here. He doesn't, for God's sake, he sneaks past Pickering and Perkins when they aren't looking. He can climb the gate. He's a sneaky wee monkey. I need to go.' He was off.

'Oh, cheerio, then,' said Caplan to the rapidly closing door.

The dog sighed and went back to sleep as if he had seen it all before and was bored.

Caplan and Craigo looked at each other. 'Craigo, you go for a look around, walk the ramparts and see for yourself if there's any way down. Nobody'll see you if they are at the landing pad. I'm going to find Rosie or Robyn if she's here. See what they say while Pomeroy's busy with Cosmo's girlfriend.'

'Shazamtina's Cosmo's media girlfriend,' Craigo corrected.

'Pardon?'

'Media girlfriend. There's no romantic relationship. Rosie was telling me.'

'Oh, right.' Caplan got up; the leather of the settee was making her back damp with sweat and she wanted to get to the cooler parts of the castle.

'How do you think the others feel about that?'

'The family? Well, they think it's great because it brings in money and gives them airtime, column inches and all that.'

'It keeps them relevant. But there's Cosmo's real girlfriend and there's Shazamtina. There's the other lady's real boyfriend. That could cause ill will.'

'Who is Cosmo's real girlfriend, then?'

'Robyn at the stables. He was why she moved up here.'

'Really?' Caplan adjusted her opinion of Cosmo. 'Is it a game they all play and nobody gets jealous?'

'Then there's Cosmo and EB.'

Caplan turned round. Her sergeant was looking at her like the smart kid who had arrived in the headmaster's office for being too smart. 'Cosmo and EB? You know they're related?'

'Yes. They are still very . . .' his weaselly little eyes flicked to the window. 'Affectionate?'

'How affectionate?'

'Very.' He pursed his lips, a sly little tell when he knew something his boss didn't. 'Is that worth throwing somebody off a cliff for? Somebody who might take the moral high ground on an incestuous situation rather than ignore it just because it's good for business.'

'Koi might have been really upset by it. Your son and the daughter of your husband . . . you know what I mean. Never mind the PR fallout if it became public.'

'Either way, ma'am, it could have been the end of her,' said Craigo almost tenderly.

Caplan nodded, recalibrating her initial interpretation of the hug that EB had given Cosmo on the stairs. 'What were the names of those tame journalists again?'

ELEVEN

Caplan walked out the door into the cool of the dark hall and made her way back to the stairs, through the archway and across the flagstones, relishing the dim light and the chill in the air, thinking how lonely this place would be to live in permanently. The nearest village had an unmanned police station and a population of two hundred. There had been an article in *The Times* explaining that the population had temporarily doubled with the death of Koi, mostly via the one hotel and a few B & Bs. Walking across the wooden floor to the passageway that led to the kitchen, Caplan ignored the glassy-eyed stare of the sixteen-point stag that still regarded her from the ceiling beam. Her phone pinged: a message from Sarah Linden with an attachment. She opened it, and her own face, grim through the window of her car, looked back at her. The first line of the text below said something about her being moved sideways rather than promoted, and now leading the investigation into the death of Koi McQuarrie under the supervision of Detective Superintendent Adam Spencer. She growled as she deleted it, cross about the 'death' and the 'supervision', both inaccurate.

She guessed correctly that Rosie would be in the family kitchen with the old dog, avoiding all the fuss outside. In fact, Rosie was sitting at the table, holding a mug of tea in both hands. There was no evidence of any activity, but a growing pile of dishes and plates showed somebody had been eating. 'Hi Rosie.'

'Oh, hello. Has Pomeroy finished with you, then?'

'The attraction of the helicopter proved too much.'

'Do you want a bite of lunch? I have some cucumber, I can do a sandwich. But if you hang around out there, you'll be given a glass of champagne and a salmon blini.' She pulled a wry face. 'Mum's dead and they invite the photographers in.'

'Your mum was very popular. People, the general public out there, seem to be concerned about you.'

Rosie gave her a twisted smile. 'Not about me, it's Cosmo and the *Strictly* girl they are concerned about. Don't know how to pronounce her name. Morrow pronounces it B. I. T. C. H. I'm quite worried about her – about Morrow, not Shazamabitchface. That cow can look after herself. Have you seen Tron?'

'I was about to ask you that.'

'I've no idea where he is. He's wandered around this castle since the day we got here. I'm sure he's mapping every passage and dead end – he's eighteen and has bugger all else to do. He'll be staying away from Shazamabitchface. She hates him. He hates her. Tron likes Robyn, Cosmo's real girlfriend who works at the stables in the village. Shazamabitchface is an actor, singer, dancer, model and a complete cow.' She looked at Caplan expecting some recognition. 'She's doing *Strictly*. For fuck's sake.'

Caplan smiled. 'With Cosmo?'

Rosie leaned forward, as if about to say something in confidence. The lines on her young face were deep. For all the riches and the castle, the fame and the fortune, Pearl Lilac Rose Samphire McQuarrie had not led an easy life. 'Sometimes I'm not sure where this family ends and the cast of a mockumentary starts. It's getting cold in here, I'll open these doors to let some heat in.' She stood at the double patio doors, gripping the handle. 'Have you found her body yet?'

'No.'

'What happens if you don't?'

'What do you mean?'

Rosie shrugged. 'Pip was saying yesterday that it can get very difficult if we don't have a body.'

'What can?'

'Wills, insurance, stuff.'

Caplan noted the comment but refrained from saying what she was thinking, so settled for, 'Well the Coastguard know about tides and currents. Don't let it worry you.'

'Can we have a funeral without a body?'

'I wouldn't worry about that either at the moment.' She waited until Rosie had opened the doors to the patio; it felt like she'd opened the door to a furnace. 'We were interrupted yesterday. You said something like you'd killed your mother. I'm presuming that you meant that metaphorically rather than literally.'

Rosie sat down at the table and looked up at her. 'How can you be sure?' she smiled.

'We can't be 100 per cent sure about anything. Were you down here when you heard the scream?'

'I could have been anywhere in the castle.'

'True, but there are timelines and locations that we're double-checking. Your family photograph themselves constantly. That's a bonus to us. Somebody's piecing together the bits of film from various phones and from the security cameras and the family pictures from your dad's camera. You were very busy. Dealing with food, pouring the drinks, you were dancing with your mum. I don't think you had time to leave the bailey, go out the main doors, through the Castle Gate, sneak past Pickering and Perkins at the Welcome Gate. Those two are certain they would have seen anybody leaving the property to go up the cliff path. They were hanging around, eating. The gates were open – anybody leaving the front doors of the castle is easily visible as they cross the drive and the lawn to get to the bottom of the Queen's Rise. That's the only way up to the clifftop.' Caplan waited for Rosie to respond then added, 'Unless you know different?'

'I don't. If there was a short cut, I'd use it with the dog. Did Pip tell you that Lady Mary's been wandering around?'

'Lady Mary?'

'The ghost. She walks when there's a death. We should've known something was going to happen. Pip could get *Ancient and Haunted* to come up and film us for TV.' Then Rosie shook her head, 'Pip keeps talking about trying to get access to the clifftop from inside the castle, so brides don't need to go the long way round for the big photograph, but it's a bloody castle, for God's sake. It was built to stop people getting in if they invaded from the sea.' She sighed, closed her eyes, succumbing to tiredness. 'And there's that old Scottish custom of running up the path in bare feet. It makes sense to leave it as it is. And the servers follow them up with champagne. It's no hardship.'

Caplan smiled. 'I think somebody would have seen you, or somebody would have missed you, so let's just take it as read that you did not physically push your mother off the cliff.'

Rosie shook her head. 'I didn't do that. None of us could. We were all down here, all the time.' She turned her head slightly, looking very earnest. 'Do you think Mum might have seen the ghost? She fell backwards, didn't she? She was backing away from something. Or someone? She fell ten metres. Internet says it's too low for a body to turn.'

'I think she fell.'

Rosie bit her lip and held back tears; her fingers began to gather and separate the red cloth on the table, working faster as she became more tense as she thought about her mother's final moments.

'I presume there was something said between you, and you think that that comment made her jump. Or was it something that somebody else had said?'

The tears began to flow. 'Koi's been my mother for as long as I can remember. I was adopted way, way back, before the real celebrity stuff. I mean Koi and Gabe were well known but not in the way they are now. Koi decided to adopt me, of all people. She has given me a great life. I've travelled the world. I've been blessed, but something makes me want to find my natural parents. I need to know where I come from. Is that wrong?'

'All perfectly natural. Did you and your mum discuss it?'

'That's what I thought. I thought she would be okay about it. But she went absolutely mad. Said something weird like she would sort it out. I really can't remember. She just didn't react the way I thought she would. But she was calm the day before the party, right back to her normal self. She didn't even mention it. I thought she had thought it through. Now I think I said something that pushed her over the edge. Now she's dead. Did she think I was rejecting her? That wasn't the case at all.'

'Would it be like her to react like that? Most of the information we get about your mother is filtered through some other source. You were her daughter; I trust your judgement. What do you think? Her public persona is level-headed and calm. Whereas your dad is . . . slightly more temperamental, shall we say?'

Rosie laughed a little. 'Well Dad's a lot better now he's eased off the drink a bit. Him and Pip, back in the day? Oh my goodness, the trouble they gave my mum. And Ecco was another over-indulger. Rhea was a pill-popper. Mum was always the sensible one of the Sunflower Girls.'

'Your mum wasn't the kind of person who'd throw herself off a cliff because her daughter's thinking about researching her ancestry. Any mother of an adopted child knows that question will come one day. If it wasn't that, what was bothering her so much that she jumped?'

Rosie closed down, staring into the middle distance, looking at a memory that she was not willing to share.

Caplan smiled. 'In the pictures they took . . . on Saturday,' she hastily rephrased from her original thought *the day your mother died.*

'Was I Photoshopped out? Or was I two stone lighter? With nice hair and amazing skin. All done by somebody in an office in London. You should see the magic they work with Tron, no wonder he's not allowed out – somebody might see him. It's a shitload easier than real life.'

They both watched the old dog try to scratch itself, trying to get the hind leg to reach the back of his ear and finding that his old bones couldn't quite make it. Rosie called him over and kissed him on the top of his grey, hairy head, then started rubbing in behind the itchy ear, letting the dog lean his weight onto her.

'Rosie, what did you mean when you said you were responsible for the death of your mother?'

'Just that. I was worried that she had jumped, worried that I had upset her so much that she might have taken her own life. But I don't think that now. I see that in her mind, living a lie for twenty-three years is neither here nor there. We live lies every day of the week.'

Caplan sat down opposite her, moving a salt and pepper grinder out of the way as if they were chess pieces.

'Now mum has gone, who will protect Tron and Morrow? Cosmo and EB will be okay.'

'Protect them from whom?'

'From ourselves. It's a big wild world; fame only lasts until the next day. They build it up to tear it down. They'll rip you apart. You've tasted a bit of that. You're a has-been detective, sent up here because you messed up so badly in Glasgow. That picture of you all over the internet, leaving here yesterday, old and tired with *yer wee bun.*' Her faux-Scottish accent was mocking.

This was a new side of Rosie. Caplan said calmly. 'Well, fair enough, I am old and tired.'

Rosie looked her up and down. 'Yeah. I can see that.' Her voice softened, she turned her gaze to the dog. Caplan sensed a shift in her attitude, a player about to deal their best card. 'That's what mum was afraid of. Well, that's what she said. You see, I'm about to become very famous. The rest of them will not like that.'

'Go on,' encouraged Caplan.

Rosie pursed her lips slightly. 'We found out who my dad is. He's Angus McLeerie.'

Caplan felt her heart miss a beat. 'Angus McLeerie? The murderer?'

'He's not a murderer.'

Caplan looked out the patio doors onto the hedge that gave privacy from the hubbub in the bailey. 'Must be a different one, then. Because the only debate about Angus McLeerie is how many women has he actually murdered.'

Caplan walked across the bailey. The cross beams of the loggia had white flowers interwoven with the green, a leftover from the wedding. The heat was caught between the high walls but a hot draught was coming from somewhere, moving the stifling air around. Caplan made her way over to the small chapel which stood like a sanctuary in the shade, aware that many eyes could be watching from the tiny windows above her. She needed a cool space to think.

She slipped into the quiet of the chapel, the sun catching Jesus through the stained-glass window, and sat in a pew, grateful for the cold air and the darkness after the oppressive heat outside.

Angus McLeerie.

And Pomeroy had said nothing.

McLeerie was a name that would make somebody jump off a cliff.

He was involved in Koi's disappearance, her death – she was sure of that.

Who really had wanted to buy the castle? Who had wanted to pull back from public life? Who was the Fisherman?

Then in walked Angus McLeerie, and there was no way Pomeroy was going to miss the earning potential of a murderer in the family. The whole story of Rosie McQuarrie-Samphire panned out like a soap opera. Caplan messaged McPhee to get on to the Scottish Prison Service and find out McLeerie's status. McLeerie might be about to start on a release programme for all they knew. Where was he now? Where had he been on Saturday night? Outside the wall at Torsvaig, high on the cliff, waiting?

'You okay, ma'am?' asked her sergeant as he drove the 4 by 4 out through the gates, getting a wave from Perkins. Caplan wondered if they had been stepped up to a twelve-hour shift pattern to give twenty-four-hour coverage. Surely not.

'Why? Do I not look okay?'

'You look fine, ma'am.'

'Did you find a secret way out of the castle?'

'No. And I didn't get to speak to Tron or Morrow or Cosmo. But, well, the case has a new avenue to explore now.'

'Where are we going?'

'Twenty minutes down the road, to the stables. They're not far across the fields but it's a bit of a drive round.'

Story of my life thought Caplan, thinking fondly back to her days in Glasgow where the motorway cut through the city centre and was handy for a quick exit. 'Where Robyn works?'

'Yes, the proper girlfriend of the young man that DC Mackie is so fond of.'

'She's your cousin, you don't need to call her DC Mackie.'

'Second cousin. And I think it's good to interview this young lady while the . . .' Craigo paused, pursing his lips, trying to get as much disapproval into his tone as possible, 'other young lady's in the area.'

Caplan nodded. 'I see your thinking, DS Craigo.' She settled into the seat, clipped in her seatbelt. 'How was Samphire? Was his migraine genuine?'

'I'm not a doctor, ma'am. Could have been a hangover but he seems genuinely distraught. He has no memory of being in the dark passageway yesterday but says it's where he goes sometimes when he can't get peace. High up, it's drier, warmer, there's arrow slits that mean he sees nothing but the sea. He regularly goes up there.'

'And his dead wife?'

'Missing wife, ma'am. He can't believe she's gone. Said that she might have been a little odd, but she could be like that when Pip upset her, sometimes advising the kids to do things that Koi would rather they did not.'

'The photograph with EB and the sunflowers on her backside? I'd not have allowed that photo of Emma at sixteen.'

'He mentioned that photograph specifically.'

'That's what she'll always be known for.'

Craigo indicated and turned the vehicle towards the sea.

'If I said the name Angus McLeerie, what would you say?'

'It's thought he killed Daisy Evans at Limpetlaw Sands, years ago now, ma'am. He may have killed Sharon Baird but there's only mild circumstantial evidence on that. Then he got life for killing his wife.' Then he went quiet, his eyes on the road, but she knew he was wondering why she'd asked.

'If that comes up again act surprised, will you? I want to gauge who knows what. Is Robyn expecting us?'

'Oh yes, ma'am, we had a very pleasant chat on the phone. Basically, she's a groom at the stables but she looks after the bloodline of the Kinglass Clydesdales that are stabled there.'

'Like Charlie Campbell was?'

'Yes. Robyn was very upset about Mrs McQuarrie-Samphire, hoped she was at peace now. And an interesting thing about her character, ma'am: Koi was the lady who held Charlie while he was being euthanised. That takes a strong character, ma'am. She loved that horse.'

'My God. Losing the cat was bad enough,' muttered Caplan, letting the movement of the car rock her into silence. She heard her stomach rumble and wished she'd stayed for a cucumber sandwich.

Craigo turned a sharp left; Caplan found she was looking out to sea again, the woods having given way to fields. There were a few horses out enjoying the sun, swishing their tails to keep away insects. Some had fly nets on. Then they pulled into a yard, quiet on a Sunday afternoon.

Robyn was a chatty young lady, round faced with jet-black hair pulled into a messy ponytail. She waved at them and gestured that she'd be out in a couple of minutes, then disappeared into a shed that had the words 'Tack Room' above it.

Caplan had just got out of the car when Robyn re-emerged with a bottle of water. 'We'll be in the shade over here,' she shouted.

There was a grey mare tied onto a rail, enjoying the sun, her dappled coat twitching to dislodge the flies. Caplan gave her a wide berth and introduced herself to Robyn.

'I heard about Koi, bloody shame. Are you any closer to finding out what happened to her?'

'Following a few lines of inquiry,' Caplan assured her, regarding the young woman covered in dirt, and thinking about the partnership with the metrosexual, forensically clean Cosmo. Or was that an artifice as well?

'Yeah, she was a nice woman, genuine. No crap about her. I think Mo has taken it badly.'

'She calls Cosmo "Mo",' explained Craigo, in case Caplan wasn't following.

'Not spending my life calling him bloody Cosmo, am I? Has Shaz appeared yet? I heard a helicopter.'

'Yes, she has. Rosie was saying that they are both doing *Strictly*.'

'That'll be a laugh. I mean, Shaz'll be a good dancer and he'll be hopeless but he'll keep getting voted back on because the public want to see the battle between them. Mo has a lovely personality, has his dad's charm and naughtiness, his mum's charisma. The camera loves him, the audience will love him. Shaz looks like a painted doll beside him. I can see why the producers want both of them.'

'And with Koi passing? Surely Cosmo will—'

Robyn raised her hand to stop her. 'Pip'll say think of the audience figures, the column inches. Pip'll say he's advised Mo to pull out due to personal circumstances then the public will demand that they want him back. Then the money in the contract will be renegotiated because the viewer numbers will increase as they'll want to see the tears flow. Once Pip's been offered enough money, Mo will return and claim that he's doing it in his mother's memory. More tears and the judges will be too scared to mark him down. Little old ladies will take him to their hearts. That's his life mapped out between now and Christmas. I've heard it from Pip a hundred times.' She shrugged.

'Are you always this cynical?'

'That's not cynicism, that's reality – well, reality TV at least.'

'You knew Koi well?'

'Yeah. More than that, I think I saw her . . . the real her. I looked after Charlie for the last . . . oh, five or six years. He was at stables in Summerstown, near Tooting Bec. I met Mo there. I think Koi knew I could be relied on, you know, them being who they are. They operate an *omertà*, and that extends to me.' She laughed a little as she said it. 'But when they came up here, so did I. The family are a handful, but Mo's great, so's his mum.' Robyn stopped talking at that point. 'Obviously Charlie was old but Koi got a recip mare and a yearling for me to bring on, on loan, so I had a job. I guess they'll be going back now.'

'Recip mare?'

'Like surrogacy for horses,' explained Robyn.

'Back to Kinglass?' asked Craigo.

Robyn shrugged, 'Why would they pay for them to be kept here? The Kinglass stables are doing well, good for an endangered breed of horse. They're here to give the bloodline some space. Charlie Campbell was one. I asked them for the address of the other recip mares, as you sounded interested. There, you can photograph that.' She held out her phone.

There was a kissing of mobile phones and Craigo looked very pleased with himself.

Caplan was going to remind him that they weren't here for him to get new bloodstock for his farm when Robyn said, 'Well, I guess you're here to ask me where I was last night.'

'Of course,' said Caplan.

'I was in the house over there with the owners, Neil and Mary, and the kids. They went out and I was babysitting. Watched *The Curse of the Were-Rabbit* and put the kids to bed. I was texting Mo during the night. And there's cameras all over here so they'll have me doing final feeds and tuck-ins.'

'Were you invited to the party?'

'Oh God, no. And I wouldn't have gone. Well, maybe to play with Cawdor.'

'The dog, ma'am.'

'Do you want to see Tron? He's around somewhere, or he was. His bike's still here.' She whispered, 'They took the car off him.' She inclined her head towards the huge barn, 'I'll go and get him.'

Robyn disappeared into the darkness of the shed. They heard her shout for Tron, causing the grey mare to lift her head, ears pricked. When she reappeared, alone, she had a drawing pad under her arm. 'He's gone but he left this. Look how talented he is.' She showed them a pencil sketch of the tack room, finely detailed; the finished portion looked photographically accurate. 'Mo says that Tron goes places in Torsvaig where he's not supposed to go, exploring all the dark corners and dungeons.'

Caplan looked up, impressed by Tron's artistic ability. 'Has he ever mentioned finding another way out of the castle? A secret gate or something?'

Robyn shook her head. 'No. Nobody gives a shit where he is. And he has a drawing room up somewhere, near the top, I think. Good views judging from the drawings he does of it.'

'We found a room with a locked door in a dark corridor, which we thought was odd,' Caplan said.

'That'll be where Pomeroy stores his millions so the tax man doesn't find it. There's something in that place upsets Tron though. He'd rather be here with the horses, he trusts them.'

'Why?'

'Abuse? Fear? Does he think Pip and Gabe killed his mother, Rhea? Something Mo has always been puzzled about. I don't mean murdered, I mean like they didn't take measures to keep her safe. They are doing the same with Tron. He's not safe in that house. His mum was an addict. Mo says Tron drinks like a fish yet that bar sits there, unlocked most of the time. It drove Koi mad. As you've seen, Tron won't speak to you, he doesn't speak to strangers. He barely speaks to anybody. Mo says that since Saturday night, he's been drawing Koi. Don't say I said this, but Mo has always thought something, an incident, affected Tron. He was normal one day, then he was weird, saw something, heard something, witnessed something. It's one of the reasons Mo won't leave – he worries about him.'

'He's eighteen. He must have money, can he not just leave?'

'Oh, they're not allowed their own money, it all belongs to the company. And leaving didn't work out well for those that tried it, did it?'

Caplan looked at the young woman – so earthy and honest. But she'd been ready with her alibi, and Caplan was surprised how close the castle was to the stables, going over the fields. Thinking about Robyn keeping out of the public eye, and Rosie, desperate to get in it. She could see how the narrative with Pomeroy and Rosie might go. Angus McLeerie was big news, and Pomeroy wouldn't be able to keep his hands off it. Media traction he'd call it, beguiling Rosie with the promise of being centre stage. A book maybe. A Channel Four documentary. A young daughter keen to have a relationship with a man who could be a triple killer.

Then Tron, such a troubled youth. Had he been abused? He was definitely scared. They needed to speak to Cosmo and get some more information on the incident that had traumatised Tron so much. Was Koi the one who stood up for him? And the temptation of an unlocked bar? The piles of empty bottles up in his turret. How irresponsible was that for a youngster with addiction? The words 'not waving but drowning' came to mind.

What had he been thinking when he was on that cliff?

TWELVE

Leaving Craigo to park elsewhere, Caplan sat in her own car, window open, checking her messages before she entered Pilcottie station. There was a lot of activity.

Linden had phoned twice then sent a message with two attachments, plus links to a couple of articles. There was a picture of Caplan at Saturday's dinner party. The glass in her hand contained water but you couldn't tell.

The main picture was a famous one of Koi laughing, her chin cupped by her hand, smiling, her blue eyes crinkled with happiness. The contrast with a tired Caplan, drinking, looking as if she couldn't care less about the death of the last Sunflower Girl, was stark and cruel.

There was only one person who could have supplied them with that picture: the girlfriend of her son. Jade Browne.

After Linden had called, Spencer had phoned and he wanted his call returned immediately.

She put it to the back of her mind and placed her fingers on the handle of the door, then removed them as a car, a Mini, pulled in front of her. She could see two occupants, who were talking, quite animatedly. The woman in the passenger seat was DC Toni Mackie. Her driver had some kind of hood pulled up over his head, even though it was about twenty-five degrees.

Caplan watched, reading the body language and not finding it easy to interpret. Then Mackie got out, bending over to speak through the open door to keep the chat going. Then a man emerged; his height, broad shoulders and slim hips were not totally disguised by loose joggers and the lightweight sweatshirt, hood still up. He danced his way onto the pavement, making Mackie laugh. Halfway up the path, they turned to face each other. Mackie's face was serious, looking up into his. A quick nod, then she said something and got her phone out for a selfie. He leaned down and forward to give her a kiss on the cheek. Then he turned, walking towards the car, then stopped like he'd just remembered something. He put his hand in the pocket of his sweatshirt and pulled out a phone, handing it to Mackie.

She waited on the path until he drove away slowly, carefully indicating before he pulled out into the deserted street.

Mr Cosmo McQuarrie-Samphire.

The change in McPhee was remarkable. The case was doing good things for his mental health. He was even getting on with Wattie. His concentration and his application were getting back to the old McPhee.

Somebody, maybe Wattie, had brought in chips.

'Okay, children. We'll give Mackie here ten minutes to calm down and pull together the salient points of what I hope was an interview with Cosmo McQuarrie-Samphire.'

Mackie was staring into space, a huge smile on her face.

Wattie screwed up some paper and threw it at her, making her jump.

'Let's talk through these timelines. Who was or wasn't there. Just in case somebody did bump off their mum, stepmum, wife, cash cow . . .'

'Cash Koi more like,' muttered Wattie.

McPhee, perched on one of the wooden dining chairs, nibbled at a chip. 'I have information for the board.'

'Do tell?'

'Perkins thought Koi had no accent at all. Pickering said there was a hint of west coast Scotland. "Ironed out" was how he put it.' McPhee shrugged and stuck another chip in his mouth. 'Interesting.'

'Thank you, Callum.' Caplan took a breath and updated them on the results of the conversation with Robyn. 'So what do you have to tell us, DC Mackie?'

'Robyn called him, told him to get down here. We were talking about the situation with Tron?' Mackie shrugged. 'Maybe I was supposed to know what he was going on about but Tron really doesn't get on with Samphire or Pomeroy. There was an incident, but Cosmo doesn't know what it was. As to where he was when Koi died, his story is the same as everybody else's except he and EB downed a half bottle of Chivas Regal after they were told the news. Hence the hangover.' Mackie smiled. 'He took me out for a wee run in his car.'

'Youse were away a fair time if that's aw you got out of him,' said Wattie, folding his arms accusingly.

Mackie ignored him. 'He said that EB was wanting to take on projects outwith the Sunflower Company and that her man AZed really wanted to be taken under the Sunflower umbrella. EB and AZed together would sniff the money up their nose in a week. The only thing he said was, he thought his mum was unsettled, but didn't know what about. I suspect he thinks that she jumped.'

'Well, that's an interesting insight.' Caplan considered. 'So, he thinks that the main source of the Sunflower income, the face of the empire, went off the top of a cliff,' she said. 'The tracking of Tron's whereabouts is important, so Callum, can you keep a really tight spreadsheet on that?'

McPhee nodded. 'From my notes, Koi's "last seen" was at 23.34, a scream was heard at 23.52, probably her scream. Some of the locals say that the curve in the wall gives weird acoustics.'

'Mair like the sound's carried on the sea breeze, son,' said Wattie.

'Is it easy to tell where the noise would be coming from, does it bounce off those walls?'

'Ah've no fuckin' idea. Let's throw Mackie aff the cliff and find oot.'

Caplan ignored him.

'Samphire had been strolling around looking for her, walked past Pickering at 23.45 or thereabouts, up the castle steps, and Koi was dead at the bottom of the cliff. That's really all we know.'

'With all due respect, we don't really know any of that, do we?' asked Craigo, who had sneaked in the door after the other two with his silent creep.

'Don't we?' asked Caplan and Mackie together.

'Not from irrefutable evidence we don't. And we don't know whether she was alive after 23.34, but she's photographed on the rocks at 00.14.'

Mackie rolled her eyes at her distant cousin.

'Well.' Craigo did that slow blink of his. 'To be clear, we have a picture of her at the bottom of the cliff timed at exactly 00.14. And how easy is it to change the time stamp on a phone? And no pathologist has declared life extinct. Because there's no body. Yet.'

'So, are you saying that we stick to what we can prove?' asked Caplan wearily, knowing that Craigo was right, as usual.

McPhee looked at his notes. 'Okay, so seen at 23.34, not alive after that.'

'Not seen at all after 23.34.'

'So where is she, then?' asked Wattie. 'Ahm telling you, taken oot with the tide.'

They sat and looked at each other, nobody wanting to agree or disagree.

Caplan felt the mood of the room drop and was determined to jump-start it again. She clapped her hands, as if chivvying a group of toddlers to get out of the sandpit. 'Where are we on the placement of people? Tron was on the chapel roof at one point. But he's not when the video sweeps round when Koi leaves, as she's just hugged him. Pomeroy was – seemed – drunk all the way through, hardly capable of walking in a straight line. Samphire, in Craigo's opinion, is genuine in his grief, as was Cosmo. We also know exactly when Samphire went through the Welcome Gate.

'Tron is strange. EB was out of it; she collapsed on the table just before the time of interest. Rosie said that she, Rosie that is, went through to the kitchen. There's a situation with Rosie that I'll return to.'

'Did anybody see her?'

'Nope, and Morrow disappeared very early,' said Mackie. 'Cosmo is lovely. He's filming on the dance floor for all of the time we are interested in, and I know that because he took a selfie every so often and I've seen him dancing in that video many, many, many times. He saw his mum go off, and at that time Samphire was back on the video, dancing. What was the song again?'

'Grace Jones, "La Vie en rose",' muttered McPhee.

'That song, that version, goes on for about eight minutes,' said Caplan.

'The kids, well Cosmo and Rosie, had put together a playlist of the family's favourite songs. It went from the *Thunderbirds* theme to Taylor Swift. It's quite good, actually,' said McPhee.

'Utter shite,' pronounced Wattie loudly.

'Pomeroy's seen on video, drinking red wine and eating a leg of chicken. He's over at the buffet. Morrow is nowhere to be seen; EB is doing a weird dance before she collapses. Grace Jones is her hero, as you might have guessed.'

Caplan pulled the conversation back on track. 'Who else was there?'

'I checked, the chef they use for weddings was not on the premises at all, and nor were any other wedding staff.'

'What do we know about the guys on the Welcome Gate, Pickering and Perkins?'

'Background? Pickering's easy. Police records were on hand; he was solid, dependable, never a shining star but a good constable. He's sixty-five now, retired at fifty, joined the mountain rescue, hurt his knee, took up golf when his wife died of complications of diabetes. Then, fearing he was going to be stuck at home with the grandchildren, he took the job on security at Torsvaig, initially just for weddings, but more recently it was more hours and lots of them, especially in the last few months. And that was an interesting point.' McPhee sniffed. 'Perkins was not so easy, he was born in Taynuilt and joined the army from school, served in the Black Watch, was commended for bravery during Operation . . . – the other part of the text was redacted. He's fifty-one, has his army pension. He came home to look after his mother on the passing of his father. The armed services are not forthcoming with detail.'

Craigo made one of his snorting little noises. 'And the kids are home-schooled, ma'am. They don't get out unless it's an event. They have cars secured by the gates; they stay in suites of rooms. They fly off to go shopping and go on holidays, or to do filming, but I'm not sure how much real friendship they have.'

'Online maybe?' asked Mackie. 'I have Koi's phone to check too.'

'Good, but all their activity seems monitored. What twenty-year-old allows their social media to be monitored?'

'Right.' Caplan tried to sound businesslike; she wanted to put a hook in the water and see what she caught. 'So, the geography at . . . Torsvaig?'

'Limpetlaw's whit we call it,' said Wattie with a degree of defiance. 'Been Limpetlaw for a thousand years or more.'

Mackie rolled her eyes. 'Wouldn't want to get married at a castle called Limpetlaw.'

'Why? Is Cosmo asking?' asked Wattie.

Mackie ignored him.

'Wattie, do you think you could give us the background as succinctly as possible?'

There was a picture on the board of a beautiful sandy beach with a picnic area and with a map beside it, an area circled by red biro.

'Limpetlaw Sands?'

'Aye, that's the flat beach before the cliff where the castle is, it has lovely white sand,' said Wattie.

Caplan frowned, waiting.

'It was a nice beach. Trees and a picnic area and some big rocks, then the white sands, a long stretch of it at that point. Quite the little secret, but it was a popular place for locals. Well, it was back in the day, but then the body of a young woman was washed up on the beach, then years later two fishermen, same thing. The place got a bit of a reputation, campsite closed.'

'Was that recently? I mean, when was that?' asked Caplan. Her heart starting to jump.

'The two fishermen were what . . .? Four years ago. The boat, *The Girvan*, had sunk. Two were rescued, one was lost at sea and two were washed up on the beach, a day apart, I think, and about a week after the boat went down.'

'And the woman?' asked Caplan, carefully.

Mackie shrugged. 'Did she walk into the sea and drown herself? Get bashed on the rocks? That was about twenty, twenty-five years ago? Before my time, but you know the rumours run rife that her ghost still walks the beach at night.'

'Daisy Evans,' said Wattie.

'So, nothing directly related to the castle?'

'No, it's more related to the strong currents at high tide round here.'

Caplan blew out her cheeks and tapped her pen against the desktop. 'What else do we know about Daisy Evans? Anything?'

'Daisy Evans . . .?' Wattie screwed up his eyes a bit. 'She was shagging . . . who was it now? Angus McLeerie?'

'Really?' asked Mackie.

'So that was a known fact? In the village?' asked Caplan, her voice suddenly loud as everyone fell silent. 'Do the security guys know this? Pickering would, he was a cop at the time.'

'Hang on, hen,' Wattie said, raising a single finger as he pulled his phone out his pocket, selected a number from his contacts and pressed call. 'Just you watch the magic that is the WFP.' The phone was answered very quickly. 'Aye, it's me. A wee question for you. You were telling me about the Gabe bloke, about a conversation you had with him and then you spoke to me? . . . Aye,' Wattie nodded, encouragingly. 'One is one, but two is . . .' Wattie listened, his teeth nibbling at the skin of his thumbnail. Then he said, 'Ta, great, thanks,' and hung up.

Knowing the others were looking at him he kept his silence.

'So?'

'Last year Gabe Samphire asked Pickering if he'd ever come

across Angus McLeerie. That's McLeerie as in murdered his wife and got life up his arse? That McLeerie,' prompted Wattie to Caplan in case she wasn't getting it. 'The body washed up on Limpetlaw Sands? There wis another one on the golf course, Sharon something. Angus McLeerie was born in Oban. Cocaine habit, walloped his wife's head off a door frame. Fractured her skull. Carol her name was. Full life sentence. Daisy was 2001. Sharon was the year later.'

'So, Gabriel Samphire asked Pickering about McLeerie and then this happens to Koi.'

'What does that mean?' asked Mackie.

'Don't ask me, I'm fucking lost,' said Wattie. 'Angus McLeerie though. Shitey wee bastard.'

'Have either Perkins or Pickering ever mentioned the stalker, the Fisherman, to you? That might be something to ask more about. They have a non-disclosure clause in their contract. They have a sense of loyalty, but I'm not sure who to,' said Caplan.

'Is there something there to be investigated?' Mackie pondered.

'What's the point?' asked Wattie, or that's what Caplan thought he said but he had his mouth full of chips and pickled egg, so she wasn't sure. 'Daisy was pissed off and walked into the sea. The inquest could come up wi' nothing else but that. Now we have the Koi one, seen walking up the path alone, next thing she's on the rocks, nobody else there, so she fell, or she jumped. McLeerie's in the pokey, he got life for doing his wife. Nobody else involved with the Koi one. Case closed. Whit are youse lot doing here? Drinking ma tea? Eating ma Hobnobs?' He sucked some egg from between his teeth. 'Wasting taxpayers' money.'

'There's Hobnobs?' asked Mackie.

'It's not what we can prove, it's also what we can disprove,' said Caplan, looking at the board. 'If Koi is dead, and it's looking more likely that she is, there'll be a Fatal Accident Inquiry and we want all our ducks in a row. If we think it's suicide, then we have to show that we have explored every other avenue and present the evidence of the dead ends. If she's alive we need evidence of life.

'It's too early to look at lack of bank account activity. And don't speak to me about the amount of media coverage this is set to generate. And what does it mean if no body turns up? She'll join the ranks of Lord Lucan and Shergar, leading to endless, endless speculation.'

She took a deep breath. 'This goes no further than this room.

Rosie McQuarrie-Samphire is under the impression that McLeerie is her biological father. I don't believe that Angus McLeerie was Rosie's dad any more than I believe in the man on the moon. You do see the connections that Pomeroy will be very keen to exploit, don't you?'

Mackie muttered, 'Jesus.' Craigo was open mouthed, and McPhee looked very worried.

Wattie beamed. 'I'm starting to like you. Do you fancy a chip?'

Although it was a short detour on her route home, Caplan was driving out to look again at the geography of the castle and Limpetlaw Sands, now the tide was further out. This time she was intending to find where the caravan park used to be, the rocks that Daisy Evans had perished on. She needed to check for herself, and intended to walk through the wood to the sand, and then to have a look at the cliff from that angle, even if it meant scrabbling over the rocks to keep dry. She was fit; a little older than Koi, but not much. She wanted to know for herself that escape from the bottom of the cliff was not possible, if Koi was capable of movement after the fall. Spencer had one eye on social media and one eye on the reputation of Police Scotland. She, they, might be pushed to a higher threshold of evidence to prove what happened to Koi – that of the conspiracy theorists. Their policing was being controlled by social media.

She pulled the Duster into the lay-by. It was deathly quiet; the air was very still. This was the beach where Daisy Evans's body had been found washed up after either walking into the sea or having her head battered against the rocks by Angus McLeerie. As soon as that picture came into her mind, she thought of Koi's body, lying on the rocks, in the surf. She knew her brain liked connections and patterns, but this was just a bit too much of a coincidence – two women dead on the beach, within . . . what? A third of a mile. And Angus McLeerie being touted as the murderer of Daisy and the biological father of Rosie.

She turned the engine off and sat for a moment, looking at the map and thinking. Now it was even more important to get out and walk and be sensible about it. Before she did that, she called Mackie back at Pilcottie, informing her of her location and the time. As her constable repeated it back, she put the locator on her phone and made sure Mackie could see her, then said goodbye.

This was where the advert had been filmed. She could see the broken remnants of picnic tables and chairs in the long grass, an old bin hung from a wooden spike.

To the locals, this place had been the site of a small but popular caravan park, with the sandy beach a place of sunshine and fun, kids and holidays. This was still Limpetlaw Woods, the same woods where she had first met Morrow and Rosie, the woods that Samphire had run through to try to get to Koi via the beach. Caplan could remember how dark it had been underneath the dense canopy of summer leaves in the height of the day.

Caplan got out of the car, dropping her bag into the footwell and taking the collapsible baton from the glove compartment. She put on her sunglasses and checked the signal on her mobile again, just to be sure. To anybody watching she was walking through the woods that circled round the southwest part of the castle, maybe searching for any path to the beach that they didn't know about already. Which was exactly what she was doing.

She walked slowly, moving forward while listening for any noise coming from behind her. The trees got thicker, their trunks closer together. The ground underfoot was not that of a managed forest at this point, but she kept walking, not caring if she stood on fallen, diseased branches that cracked as she broke them. There was nobody around to hear.

The overgrowth became denser, jagging at her bare skin and pulling at her hair until she stumbled through onto a narrow border of harsh grass, then the white cushion of sand. The waves beyond were in gentle mode, merely tickling the beach. She did a hop, skip and jump over the softest of the sand, over the dried seaweed, disturbing the herring gulls and the sandpipers. As she looked out to sea, to her left was just beach, then a flat piece of land overgrown by bushes and small trees. Was that where the caravan park had been? Up to her right she could see the castle on the headland; it looked so close, she could almost reach up and pull it from the sky. The stark ruin of Mary's Tower pointed heavenwards. She wondered what stories it could tell. The round castle tower was just visible from here; she'd need to walk out towards the water's edge to see the rest of the castle, as any hopeful invader would have seen it. She could see the reason for the fortification now; this was the last point where the sea met the shore at ground level. Anything along from this involved climbing a cliff face, the tallest point being where Koi had fallen.

She took off her shoes and walked into the cold water, lifting her trouser legs up like a little kid. Turning to look inland, the castle wall was in full view. It looked impregnable. The rock outcrops, long jagged fingers, were just at the tideline at the moment. The tide was on its way in; it wouldn't be long before anybody in the cove would be cut off. She squinted, putting her hand up to protect her eyes from the sun, noting the viciousness of the barbed wire overhang of the Woodwall. There was no way anybody could gain access round that.

Years of volcanic activity, then erosion by sea water on soft rock had left this cove with its natural barrier against invasion. All mankind had done was to take advantage of it.

She enjoyed the view for a few moments. The gentle breeze was cooler here on the coast, but it was so quiet, so calm.

She was getting paranoid . . . this serenity felt eerie. Why did she feel that she was being watched again? A yacht out on the bay scudded past, its jib out catching the wind. Somebody up at the castle could be looking out. Morrow reading her book. Tron up on the ramparts, drawing. There could be any number of unseen eyes watching her from the woods behind. Her car bore witness to her presence.

She could sense Pomeroy's hands all over the McLeerie situation. Angus McLeerie was about to become Pomeroy's latest cash cow.

Did Pomeroy, with his perfect veneers and hand-made shoes, know how badly his dance with the devil could backfire?

She noticed a missed call from Sarah Linden, the ACC handling the media furore; Caplan often thanked God that Sarah was one of her oldest friends. She returned the call.

'How is the case, you little media sensation? They are asking why your rank is working a suicide? That's fooling nobody.' Linden sounded in a gossipy mood.

'That's how it seemed, to begin with, and there's nothing to say otherwise, but the family are a nightmare. Both a delight and a nightmare. Makes my lot seem quite normal.'

'Must be bad,' Linden retorted. 'Have you seen that Cosmo Samphire? He's a bit of all right. The hubby is okay except he can't keep it in his trousers. I met him at an awards ceremony for fuck knows what, he was defo on the Columbian marching powder.' Linden gave an unfortunate sniff of appreciation. 'He has a beautiful family though.'

'But not a happy one.'

'Who's happy these days?' asked Linden. 'Don't answer that, you with your wee house in the middle of Crunchy.'

'Cronchie, and it's miles away from the village.'

'So, Koi McQuarrie?' declared Linden, 'Jumped, pushed or fell? I have a bet on it.'

'No comment. ACC Linden?' asked Caplan.

'Okay Miss Whatever-rank-you-are-now-but-it's-less-than-mine Caplan. Anyway. That's not why I'm phoning you. You were on the system asking about McLeerie. I was a bit concerned about that, so concerned that I had a flag on it.'

'He came up in conversation. Would you know, off the top of your head, how long the lovely Angus McLeerie has still to serve? He was sent down on life licence in 2006?'

'Yeah, that's why I'm phoning. He's out, Chris, he has been for weeks.'

Shit. And shit again.

Caplan strode along to the rocks, the first or the last of the five fingers, depending where you were counting from. She reached the waterline and clambered onto the rocks, gaining a better view of the cliff from where Koi had fallen. Here she paused, listening to the seagulls; a few sandpipers bobbed across the wet sand.

Daisy Evans had been washed up at some point on this narrow beach.

Where was Koi?

That prescient sense of danger, a prickle on the back of her neck. She wasn't alone. Heart thumping, she pulled back into the shade of the rocks, watching as a man walked towards her.

He shouted hello and gave her a wave.

She looked up the beach, along the top of the distant cliff, the ruin of Mary's Tower rising like a finger, telling her to wait.

She let him get closer. A small man, pot belly, short arms and legs, thinning ginger hair scattered across his head, all furrowed in one direction with the removal of his hat, giving his scalp the appearance of a ploughed field after a poor harvest.

'DCI Caplan?' he asked. He sounded rather polite, his voice clear but lacking any authority. 'Christine, I need to talk to you.'

'Why are you following me?'

'I'm working.'

'Doing what?'

She didn't think this was McLeerie, but the photographs she'd seen of McLeerie were twenty years old or more. Like McLeerie, this guy was small. Caplan had already noted the frayed cuffs of his dark, striped shirt. His brown trekking boots had seen better days and his black jeans bagged from constant wear and looked like they hadn't fit him when new.

There was no prison pallor, but McLeerie had been released a while ago and the weather had been so sunny.

'Angus McLeerie?' she asked, standing her ground. He was unfit, old and suffering from the heat. A single push and he'd be on the ground.

'No, but I like your thinking. I followed you; I was up at the castle.' He took his mobile out of his pocket and showed her a website featuring his photograph. Andrew Knox, journalist.

Caplan handed back the phone and looked at her watch, then pulled out her own phone and read a message. 'Can I see your ID? Press card and driving licence, please, Mr Knox?'

'Andy.'

She held out her hand and he placed the two cards into it. After examining them closely, she returned them. 'So why were you following me?'

Knox pulled out a packet of Benson and Hedges and tapped one out, flicking it up to catch it in his lips. 'Do you mind if I have a seat on the rocks?'

'I prefer to walk.'

He squinted in the glare of the sun. 'You looking for where Koi fell?'

'Yes. Let's walk.'

She was much taller than him, longer legs. She chose a path on the hard sand, leaving Knox to either get wet or struggle on the soft sand.

'God, you're fit.'

'You shouldn't smoke. You wrote a piece about McLeerie and Evans?' She turned slightly to look at him. He was like somebody's bachelor uncle who had fallen on slightly hard times.

'That was ages ago, local stuff.'

'I think Pip Pomeroy referred to you as a tame journalist, the wordsmith for the great unwashed.' She looked at him, not warning him about the wave approaching the back of his legs. 'If you were so close to the family, then why were you outside the wall talking to the fans, rather than getting the inside track from the family themselves?'

He winced. 'He likes to think I'm tame.'

Caplan looked at his old shoes.

'I need the money.'

'Why are you following me?' She couldn't help the little surge of excitement that was coursing through her veins. He knew something.

'I'm a journalist and true crime writer. I was with a tabloid for twenty years then went freelance. I've written four books.'

'True crime and look where we are. Daisy Evans? McLeerie? Scrabbling around for an angle on Koi McQuarrie's death? What are you up to?' Caplan raised an eyebrow in what she hoped was a scathing manner. 'Working on a story about the Sunflower Girls?'

He thought before answering, hands in pockets, then started to walk on, looking up at the cliff. 'Not at first, no.'

'*The Sunflower Deaths*? That's a book I'd buy.'

'That's interesting.'

'So, what do you know about the residents at Torsvaig?'

'In a nutshell? Cosmo's normal, hence Robyn being so down to earth. EB's an addict, Morrow's anorexic, Tron's an alcoholic. Samphire misses his life in the danger zone and takes risks that he shouldn't. Pomeroy keeps juggling all the plates to squeeze every buck that he can. Rosie'll get more abuse by domesticity now Koi's gone. Then there's Angus McLeerie. Rosie and McLeerie? I think you and I are on the same page.'

'Looking at my picture in the newspaper today, I'm not so sure.'

'That was Carrie, Carrie Cowie-Browne. You know her daughter Jade. But I'm guessing you've worked that out.'

Caplan's heart skipped a beat; it was out her mouth before she could help herself. 'Pardon?'

'Another one of Pomeroy's soft journalists, but Pomeroy has a better nose for a story than I do and that's saying something. I've information that he'll spin if he gets wind of it, and that could be dangerous for . . . well, it could be dangerous.'

'For whom?' asked Caplan.

Knox bobbed his head about as if weighing something up then said, 'I thought there were two reasons why you'd pull in here. Either Koi or McLeerie. Or both. I'm checking a few facts.'

'We could check them for you,' offered Caplan.

'I'll pass, thanks. Let's go for more topical. Koi's death concerns me. I was keen to see what connections you've been making. Your team are good. I'm impressed. Can you answer one question?'

'I can. I doubt that I will.'

'Pearl Lilac Rose, Rosie to her friends – except she doesn't have any because Pomeroy makes sure of that. She's starved of life, that lassie. If she's been told Angus McLeerie's her dad, she won't let it go. McLeerie's writing his autobiography.'

'Nice to see our prison system working.'

'He's out.'

'Yes, I know.'

'He's represented for his book by Pip Pomeroy.'

'Is he representing your book as well? I'm presuming there's one coming. *Death on Limpetlaw Sands*.'

'I do some work for him, he's unaware of my bigger project. He's part of it. I think you have the measure of the man.' He sniffed. 'There's times I don't like the police.'

'There's times I don't like the media,' said Caplan.

Knox gave her a tired smile. 'Pomeroy's a slippery wee arsehole and McLeerie's a dangerous wee arsehole. You check on that backstory that you've been told, or try to, and I bet you won't get anywhere. Have a look at Daisy. And Carol. Then Sharon Baird. When you get nowhere, call me. I'm staying around. Here's my card. Spencer will have you on a tight lead. So, tread carefully. I can go where you can't.'

'Mr Knox, do you feel that McLeerie is involved in Koi's death in some way?'

'See how Daisy, Carol and Sharon got on? Tell me what you think. Do you use a murder wall these days? If so, his name should be on it. He started the drama that ends with Koi taking a long walk off a short cliff.' He sighed. 'He's poison. He might have just pushed Koi a wee bit too far – metaphorically, I mean.'

'Did you witness her taking a long walk off a short cliff, Mr Knox?'

'If I did, I'd be writing it up myself and selling the story for a hundred grand.' He licked his lips. 'But I'm telling you, there's a much bigger story here. The McQuarrie-Samphire empire is not *The Waltons*, it's a cult.'

They both stopped walking when they reached the far point of the rocks, seeing the imposing height, the darkness of the cliff face for the first time, the changes in colour of the high-tide mark. Caplan looked at that, then at the jagged rocks that bookended the tiny strip of sand they were standing on. Ten metres high, as sharp as the teeth of a chainsaw.

Nobody could have survived that.

THIRTEEN

Caplan heard her phone alert and decided to pull into the truck stop and have a cup of tea in the car. Parked in the shade of the trees with the windows open, watching the sparrows and chaffinches at the birdfeeders, she thought about Knox and what part he might be playing in this. He'd be up on the board as much as McLeerie. She opened her phone and, seeing the two missed calls and an email from Ryce, she pulled out her laptop and set the screen share up. The pathologist said she wanted to talk about the series of photographs from the scene of the incident. Series of photographs? Had Ryce gone back to Samphire and requested more? Surely Pomeroy wouldn't have let him do that. She had presumed that Ryce was going to say that the image was of no use; she worked with bodies. But something had piqued the pathologist's interest. Caplan was still struggling with the idea of Samphire having the presence of mind to take the photograph in the first place. His story of trying to get to her from the beach and needing a landmark made some kind of sense, yet he knew he couldn't do that with the tide in.

It sounded wrong, but folk were strange and twenty years in the police service had taught her that there was no point in predicting what anybody would do in any situation. A war correspondent had once mentioned casually how good it was to run towards an explosion, or an outbreak of gunfire; they were pre-programmed to get the story. Maybe Gabriel Samphire, a photographer, had simply taken a few images of the beautiful woman in front of him. It didn't matter that she was his wife or that she looked as if life was extinct; he simply did what he did.

Or had he known she had passed away, and he just wanted one more picture to mark the last time he saw her?

Or was he seeking proof? But of what?

Caplan's laptop beeped and she saw a request for her to let Ryce have access to her screen. Then her mobile rang. It was Ryce.

'How are you doing on this case that is not a case?'

'Do you have something for me? Please tell me you do, and I

can leave this for the Fiscal to wrap up – I'm too old to deal with Instagram LOL, YTA, FOMO and YOLO. It reminds me of how bad I was at Latin.'

'What's YTA?'

'You're the arsehole. That's what it means. I'm not saying that you're an arsehole.'

'ROFL.'

'Oh, I know that one, rolling on the floor laughing? And YOLO?'

'Tell me.'

'You only live once.'

Caplan could hear Ryce chuckling, the sound of her sipping something and the cup or glass being put down on the desktop. She saw the cursor move on her screen.

'I might have something for you.'

'How can you see anything in a photograph taken from that height on a darkish night?'

'Well DCI Caplan, ma'am,' Ryce's tone mocked her, 'I did think that myself. So I asked Russell, crime scene photographer – you know him?'

'I've a face in my head but I'm not sure.'

'Well, it's about the wonder of using a phone over a camera. I'd like to pretend that I knew this, but Russell explained it to me. A camera, like the one Gabriel Samphire would use, is like an instrument. It's a piece of equipment that does exactly what the musician tells it to do, or what the photographer tells it to do in this case. Whereas a phone camera is a bit more like AI, it sorts it out for itself. It's the technology inside the phone that senses the environment and adjusts accordingly. The phone camera automatically adjusts the picture to the best image it can give you. With a camera, it's the photographer who makes those choices depending on the effect he's looking for. The phone camera does the thinking itself. Russell said that photographers like Gabriel tend not to use their phone camera for their professional work because they're working in a studio with prescription lighting and a controlled environment. A landscape photographer might take a few initial shots with their phone, just to get the picture framed properly. But the big shots will always be with the camera. You don't want AI removing the mist, or tidying the halo round the moon, if that's the effect you're trying to capture. But these images are from an Apple iPhone 15 Pro Max, right?'

'No idea, I only use mine to take pictures of the cats.'

'Well, it's a top of the range phone camera. Can you see the pictures I've sent you?'

'I can. How did you get them?'

'I got Russell to ask Samphire to send them over. He responds well to flattery. And they are on the dark web, though he denies putting them there. Samphire, stressed and using his phone, took a series of images. We can be sure that these images are sequential. He's moving his hand around, bearing in mind he was standing close to the cliff edge, in an emotional state and probably slightly drunk. His missus had fallen straight down so she was on the rocks right at the foot of the cliff. She dropped like a stone, and that's not usual. She didn't take a run and jump at it, there's no forward trajectory. Do you want me to see if the tech guys can do a virtual reconstruction and see where the body would land?'

'Can they do that?'

'They have software for everything these days. I think it's worth doing.' Ryce took a deep breath. 'The images are not geographically sequenced, they're all over the place, but by placing them in chronological order you start to see something very interesting.'

'And what is that?'

'She blinks.'

'Blinks?'

'Yes, an opening and closing of her eyes.'

'So alive but dying?'

'I'm not sure.'

'And what would you need to be sure?'

'Have you a suicide note?'

'Nothing that we've found so far.'

'Or any sign of a struggle at the King's Reach?'

'We have no evidence of that and no evidence that anybody else was up there. Everybody is accounted for. There's no way up there without being seen by the security guys.'

There was silence at the end of the phone; in her mind she could hear the cogs turning in Ryce's head.

'Okay, off the record.' The main image on the screen retreated and was replaced by another. 'Look at her hands here, and here, and here.' The images flashed over and over. Ryce was manipulating the photographs so that the hands were enlarged.

'I'm not seeing anything.'

'She's holding on. Could be a reflex, but she's gripping the rock. Her fingers change position slightly.'

'Okay,' said Caplan slowly, just starting to see a glimmer of hope, followed by a sickening feeling of dread.

'And that's odd because if she fell backwards, you'd expect a degree of damage to the hands as they scrabble to grasp something. Rocky cliff in this case.'

'So, she was alive when she hit the bottom? There was a delay, you know, a delay because the air-sea rescue couldn't get there,' Caplan said. 'And, God forbid, if the conspiracy theorists got hold of this there'd be hell to pay.'

'I'd say the delay was the result of a well-considered decision given what they were told, but examining the micro-evidence if you like, then there are a few signs that all is not as it first appeared.'

'Would those signs enable you to state officially that she was still alive?'

'Absolutely not. It's an opinion and not one I'd stick my neck out for.'

Caplan sighed in frustration. 'Well, cheers for that.' She looked up at the sparrows dancing on the feeder, thinking of the shitshow from hell that Pickering had warned her about. She realised Ryce was still talking on the screen.

'Christine? There's something else. The bleeding on her face doesn't change when a wave goes over her. Her eyes close when a wave comes yet the blood marks stay the same. They should wash off.'

'What? What are you saying? It's fake?'

Ryce made an abracadabra gesture with her hands.

It was Caplan's turn to think. 'Okay, so she was a model; she'd done lots of videos and would have been on the receiving end of professional make-up? Yes? This happened after she was last seen in the castle, and she sure as hell didn't have blood on her face when she went out the gate.' She shook her head. 'No, there's no gap in her timeline to allow the application of all that. No matter how good or how fast she was at it.' In her mind's eye Caplan relived the footage, the scarf, the floaty dress. Koi had taken nothing up with her. 'Is it all exactly as it appears? She just fell to her death. Could the residual blood from those wounds be due to the simple fact that not enough waves had gone over her to wash her face clean?'

'Tell you what,' said Ryce. 'Bring her body in so I can put her on the slab and get a proper look.'

'I wish I could. Are you happy to put it on record that the injuries to her face are fake?'

It was Ryce's turn to think. She shook her head. 'I refer to my previous answer. It's an opinion. Bring me her body.'

Caplan's mind was racing. The fact that the incident had happened at the tallest point of the cliff, and at the point that was over the most dangerous of the rocks, at that time of tide, with the scarf flagging it up, so that the investigation team knew exactly where she'd fallen. Was that too obvious? Not only that, did it suggest Koi's intention all along was to make it very, very clear that she was dead? Did that mean she was alive?

The upper floor of Challie Cottage looked very welcoming in the fading sun; the lower floor looked exactly like the building site it was. Caplan parked the Duster beside the small green van and heard Aklen shout to her. He was round the side of the house, sitting in the swing chair, a sign that he was thinking.

'Do you want a seat?' asked her husband, patting the yellow cushion beside him.

'Do I need a seat?'

'Probably. I have news.' The grave look on his face gave a huge hint that it was not good. He took a deep breath and muttered three words. 'Jade is pregnant.'

'Pregnant?'

'Yes.'

'Shit.'

'Kenny intended telling us the evening before but didn't want to detract from Emma's news. It was unplanned but they are both delighted. Are you okay? You look a bit pale.'

Caplan let out a long slow breath. One of the kittens jumped onto her lap. 'Well, how is he feeling about it?'

'Like I say, he's delighted.'

'Are we delighted for him?'

'If that's what he wants.'

Caplan sank her head in her hands 'Do either of them have a job? Can they support the baby? Can they support each other? What am I saying? Jade was throwing back the wine on Saturday night.'

'She was. She was stressed. But if they're happy, then we need to leave them to get on with it.'

She smiled at her husband. 'I hope you're right. Bloody hell. Where are they going to live? He's in a flatshare above a café . . . Does she have her own place?'

'Still with Mummy, just the two of them. Kenny also asked if we could help out.'

'They don't have any money, then? Mum seems a successful journalist.'

'Well, he was asking about the caravan?'

'There's no way I'm putting a baby in that caravan. When's it due?'

Aklen shrugged. 'No idea.'

'Jesus, men!' She closed her eyes against the lowering sun.

'Then he asked what we were doing with the ground floor of the house.'

Caplan's eyes sprang open. 'You know what he's doing, don't you? He's giving us solutions that are impractical as well as useless. Why would a young woman with a baby move out to the wilds? And then I bet he came up with something we would find acceptable. Like we pay for a flat?'

'To be honest, he only wanted the deposit and three months' rent,' Aklen said, then added. 'For the West End – Jade wants a G12 postcode.'

'She can forget that. Do you know how much that'll be? That'll be the end of this renovation, that's what'll happen.'

'So, we leave the wee baby out on the streets?' said Aklen, mocking her. 'Our first grandchild.'

'No, we leave it until somebody makes a sensible suggestion. G12 postcode?' Caplan sighed, stroking the cat. 'You know how some women get pregnant deliberately just to catch the man?'

'I've heard of such a thing.'

'Well, it can't be that . . . because Kenny is absolutely bloody useless.'

Caplan couldn't sleep. It was too hot, and the gentle light seeping through the curtains made it difficult to sleep. And she was going to be a grandmother. She climbed out of bed and sneaked into the kitchen, getting her laptop out, then her phone, and sent a message to Lizzie and Sarah, her old friends, asking if they were online. It was a quarter to midnight, but crisis talks were needed.

Sarah Linden responded immediately. 'Is somebody dead? Apart from the skinny Sunflower Girl. I know about her.' She sounded as if she'd had a few glasses of Chardonnay.

'No, quite the opposite. FaceTime in five minutes?'

Caplan got a bottle of water from the fridge.

'Quite the opposite to being dead?' typed Linden. 'Skinny Sunflower Girl is still alive?'

'No, well . . . no.'

'Somebody's pregnant?' asked Lizzie Fergusson, her happy face appearing on screen.

'Yes.'

'Aklen is pregnant?' Linden's face was suddenly there, in a box, but with her features filtered through the glass of white wine that stood between her and the camera on the laptop.

'You are intoxicated, Sarah.'

'Yes, I am. But my daughter isn't up the duff,' she replied with the singsong cadence of the very drunk. Linden was sitting at the island in her kitchen, a glass in her hand as usual, and the bottle beside her was almost full, so it probably wasn't her first of the evening.

'You don't have a daughter and it's not Emma, it's Kenny.'

'Kenny's pregnant?' asked Linden, sounding genuinely confused.

'Sarah, be quiet,' said Fergusson. 'His girlfriend is pregnant? The nice girlfriend?'

'No, he ditched the nice one and took up with this one.' Caplan took a sip of water. 'And I don't like her. Not one bit.'

'Well, you can't say anything, Chris. It's his choice, you have to be supportive and let them get on with it.'

'I think most of our support will be of a financial nature. I just feel that I'm due a little breathing space to get the house done. And I feel bad for thinking that.'

'Then don't give them money, Chris. They need to stand on their own two feet. Do you want her arrested?' asked Linden.

'Sarah, you really are very drunk.' Fergusson, tired after a day of being a single parent and working a full-time job, tended to get annoyed at Sarah's overindulgence.

'Ha, ma kid didn't get some wee lassie knocked up.'

'You don't have any kids, Sarah,' said Fergusson. 'Chris? He's your son, you have no option but to support him. What's her support network like?'

'Chris? They can live on the ground floor of your building site, or Aklen can make them a teeny, tiny house for their teeny, tiny baby,' butted in Linden, swaying slightly.

Fergusson and Caplan looked at each other, then Caplan said, 'I think she just has her mum. Don't know if her dad's on the scene. Mum's Carrie Cowie-Browne.'

'Testicles for earrings time,' sang Linden.

'How far along is she?'

'This is Aklen we're talking about, he got no information.'

'Useless twat of a man.' Sarah Linden raised a glass to the screen. 'He may be useless, but he's good-looking. I'd fancy him if he wasn't yours.'

'I'll remember to pass that on,' answered Caplan wryly, knowing Aklen was scared stiff of ACC Linden.

'You know, Chris – Granny – there's nothing you can do until they come to you. If they want to do it themselves, let them. Even if they make a mess of it. They aren't kids any more.'

'True. I just always thought it would be a girl I liked. Jade hates the police. She's already posted some stuff online about my career, something less than glowing, and it got picked up by somebody and it's now "out there".'

'Yeah, Sarah, get her arrested.' Fergusson raised her cup and pulled up the collar of her PJs. 'What was it this time?'

'Oh, just that I need supervision and that I'm not up to the job. But I will never be able to talk freely in my house if she's there. I don't want to spend my life like that.'

'Ah, that solves a mystery – I was wondering where this vendetta was coming from. So, it's from inside the henhouse.'

'The good news is that I think we might have a seam of info re Torsvaig. I was talking to a journalist called Andrew Knox.'

'Oh him! He did that book about miscarriages of justice. What the fuck was he talking to you for? The only sniff of corruption near you was you losing that evidence on the Brindley case.'

'Knox and I were discussing the current case. The Brindley thing was years ago.'

'Christine, it's in the media this morning, i.e. today, so it is a thing.'

'Bloody hell, I gave a bag of evidence to a young cop who lost it. It had no evidential value . . . and—'

'You were such a superstar before that, now I'm ashamed to know you . . .'

Fergusson broke in, 'Look, I need to go, I hear the patter of not so tiny feet – I've woken up one of the kids.'

Her screen went black.

Sarah Linden held her glass close to her screen, suddenly appearing very sober. 'You see, I've noticed that before. You defend yourself and she pisses off.'

'Your imagination.'

'Fucking hope so, because if you lost evidence that had something to do with Brindley and our very good friend Liz? Me? I'd look the other way, but Andrew Knox is a journalist, and he will not.'

Caplan stared at her.

'Oh, no denial, then?' She held her glass high. 'For those that are about to die, I salute you.'

'Oh, fuck off.'

FOURTEEN

Monday mornings were never good but breakfast that Monday was particularly awful. The heatwave was continuing without a let-up. People were sleeping with windows open. Crimes of housebreaking were rocketing as were hospital admissions for heatstroke. Three children had died on the west coast over the weekend in accidents involving inflatables and water.

The gentle breeze from the Sound that usually cooled the coast at Challie Cottage was imperceptible. The bright glare off the water, even first thing in the morning, indicated that this day was going to be another scorcher.

The Caplans had slept with the windows closed, due to the lack of midge nets. When they had gone to bed the night before, Aklen had seemed okay. He was cheered by the news, welcoming a new baby into the family. It was left to Caplan to worry about her son, about the money, about the future, so everything in the Caplan marriage was where it always had been: Aklen the optimist and Chris looking at the practical implications. And Lizzie was right, of course they would support the young couple in any way they could. They were family.

Aklen had spent the night tossing and turning. He got up looking pale and tired, then nibbled at a slice of toast before giving up; the same scenario that had played out in the Caplan household for the six or seven years when depression had robbed Aklen of every bit of energy he had. And then it had started to eat into Caplan's.

Jade and Kenny might have gone but they should have realised that it was too much for Kenny's dad. Kenny should have seen the risk of the mental strain they were putting on Aklen. The burst of socialisation, the news of the engagement, the news of the baby; then, because Caplan had been working late, he had driven Kenny and Jade into Oban station, something he had not done for many years. He was still shaking from his nightmare after he had woken up. He looked deathly pale, and had that hard look of strain around his eyes, a tightness in his mouth. He had picked at his toast, looking at his medication as she handed it over as if she was trying to poison him.

Right before her eyes, she could see him retreating into that dark place at the bottom of his soul.

He trundled off back to their makeshift bedroom.

Caplan went out to the balcony, breathing in the fresh air, and looked out onto the beautiful morning. The sea was crystal blue, the sky as clear as far as the horizon between the islands. She texted Mackie and said that she'd be in later, maybe in an hour.

How much communication was there between Pomeroy and Jade, via Carrie Cowie-Browne? Jade and Kenny had met by pure coincidence in the bar where he worked. But journalists were opportunists. No wonder Pomeroy knew all about her. Kenny was a chatterbox. Oh yes, Caplan felt Pomeroy's hands all over what had been leaked to the press.

But if he thought that would derail her, and the investigation, he was wrong.

Linden called. 'Hi Granny Caplan.'

'What do you want, ACC Linden?'

'Have you seen it, this morning?'

'Oh shit. What now?'

'It's hysterical.'

'No, it's not.'

'It is. Well, apart from another picture of you knocking back a clear liquid? It says that you were responsible for DS David Harris getting shot a few years ago. His wife Marie seems to have a lot to say. It's all on record, from Harris himself, that he acted without your permission or consent.' There was a pause as Linden took a breath. 'Look, everybody here loves you. Don't worry, nobody gives a fuck. The more interesting thing is – who the hell put these two ideas together? Because that person has some questions to answer.'

'Am I not supposed to be the paranoid one?'

'Using publicity and unsavoury half-truths to derail a police investigation? Let me think who I can talk to, because I can get your budget increased with this. Somebody is trying to undermine the efficiency of DCI Christine Caplan in particular, and Police Scotland in general. The only person allowed to do that is me. Don't worry, I'll take care of it. If anybody asks you just agree with what I've said, i.e., the response to that picture of you holding a drink is: yes, this is DCI Caplan enjoying Scotland's national drink, our fabulous tap water!'

'Oh, right.'

'If somebody asks you if you drink water, just say yes. Okay?'

Caplan could only manage a weak thanks as she hung up, not wanting to imagine what havoc Linden could wreak if she was annoyed. She hadn't thought of Happy Harris for ages. Out of the corner of her eye, she saw the fridge door opening. Aklen was getting a drink. She watched him stand for a moment, as if deciding what to do next. Then he turned and shuffled over to join her on the balcony. His crumpled T-shirt matched his crumpled face.

Aklen squeezed her shoulder, sitting beside her. 'Jade took that picture, you know.'

'Oh, I know.'

'Want me to have a word?'

'What good will that do? I'd hope Kenny can see the damage that this might cause. I really want to have it out with Jade myself, but I think that would be seen as intimidation.'

'He might need it spelled out for him, his head's all over the place at the moment.'

'You're right. You go back to bed. You were entertaining other people most of yesterday, you've been peopled out, you need to rest.'

'Peopled? How long since we used that word?' Out on the balcony seat, Aklen looked over her shoulder to see her phone screen. 'And what are we saying to Jade and Kenny about the baby? He will call me and ask what you said.'

'He can call me himself,' retorted Caplan.

'He's too scared, he thinks you won't approve. And after this,' he tapped the phone, 'he'll really be too scared.' Aklen sat down. '*Do* you approve?'

'More disappointed. I wanted a daughter-in-law who'd get on with Emma and me, but I doubt that's happening. I wish it had been somebody else. There'll be a future of perennial disapproval by both parties. Or Kenny being led . . . well, away from us.'

'It could be much worse.'

'There you go, Mr Glass Half-full.'

'And while we were arguing about the glass being empty or full, a realist crept in and drank the contents.'

'Hang on, Toni's calling.'

'I thought her mum had just passed away?'

'Yes,' Caplan smiled at him. 'But she wants to be at work, and unfortunately this case is about a deceased mum. It's very close to home. And, being Toni, she's enjoying the eye-candy up at Torsvaig. She'll say something inappropriate at some point and get us into trouble.' Pressing to accept the call, Caplan glanced at the time. 'She's either in early or she has been there all night.'

'I came in early, ma'am.'

Caplan winced; Mackie must have heard the tail end of the comment.

'We were just talking about you, whether you should be at work at all.'

'Oh, don't you bother yer skinny wee arse, ma'am.' She added, 'It's fine. Have you seen your picture in the paper? I've my good dress on today in case they want to photograph me. Instead of you, I mean.'

'Well, that's an idea. Nothing to do with the fact that Cosmo might pop in.'

'Oh, I wish! Was that photograph taken at your cottage, ma'am? You're wearing the same clothes that you had on at the castle that night.'

Caplan didn't know what to say.

'If you've got an issue with anybody, you let me know. I'll sort it.'

DC Toni Mackie, like Craigo, was not as daft as she looked.

'Thank you, Toni.' Caplan pulled a face at Aklen, knowing he had overheard. Mackie could be scary when she wanted to be.

'And my third cousin three times removed has been on the phone.' She mimicked him. '"I don't know what to do about it."'

'Craigo doesn't need to do anything about it.' Caplan quickly moved on. 'I'm just about to leave, see you at Pilcottie station in what? Half an hour?'

There was a snort at the end of the phone. 'From Challie Cottage it's more like three-quarters. It's a bad road during daylight hours when you'll meet traffic coming the other way.'

Mackie had a point. 'Okay, so while you're waiting, imagine yourself as a supermodel, one of the most photographed women in the world. Why would you move up here, to the land of midges and single-track roads? What was she running away from? Or what was she running to?'

'Well, ma'am, she didn't get very far running away from her family, did she? She brought the rest of the manky wee buggers with her.'

'But Cosmo, he's family?'

'Oh aye. But while he's family, he's not a manky wee bugger, is he? Nope. He's a sexy mother fu—'

Caplan ended the call.

On the drive into Pilcottie, Caplan checked with the Coastguard and the search co-ordinator. There was no sign of Koi's body. She had been wearing white, and the visibility on the water was excellent. The co-ordinator explained how good the computer programs were at predicting the behaviour of a body in local tidal waters. The implication was clear; they should have found the body by now, if it was there to find.

By eight-thirty Caplan had arrived at the station, and was retrieving her paperwork from her rucksack, finding a single A4 sheet of paper with 'Granny' scribbled on it, and a smiley face sketched by Aklen's brown-ink fountain pen. She suppressed a smile and put it back, before eagle-eyed Mackie spotted what had been written and drew the wrong conclusion. Mackie finished sticking a photograph of Andrew Knox on the wall, then sat down on the broken end of the sofa and almost disappeared. Caplan decided that the rickety dining chair on the opposite side of the table was a safer option.

'Who's that, ma'am? Do we have a suspect?' McPhee studied the photograph carefully.

'Ah know him!' Wattie sniffed. 'Who is he?'

'Before that, ma'am, can I have a go?' asked Mackie. 'Please?'

'Yes, but keep it short.'

'I went round the net. These conspiracy sites are really something else. All about Koi McQuarrie and what happened to her,' Mackie exclaimed, waiting for a response from her audience.

'Yes, that's what we are supposed to be finding out,' Caplan reminded her drily.

'So, I've been crawling everywhere over social media and I'm going through what the conspiracy nuts are saying. It's fabulous. Number one theory . . .' Mackie did a drum roll on her thighs. 'She was abducted by aliens.'

Caplan sighed, then glared at Craigo when he wrote it down in his notebook.

'Number two, eaten by a shark.'

'But she fell first. Yes, that's an "ended up in the water" one and then eaten by a shark, which is why we can't find the body. Sorry, ma'am, that's still a jumped or pushed situation,' argued Craigo.

'Number three, this one has a whole website to itself. She crawled into a cave, waited until it all calmed down, then climbed out of the cave and ran away. You know there was a time gap when Samphire made his way back down to the Welcome Gate, when she was alone? Well, he took the pic, she climbed off the rock into the cave. She did pole dancing, ma'am – they have a pole in the room that she and EB use as a gym. She might have had a bad knee, but she had really strong arms.'

'Okay, so where is the cave?' Caplan looked nonplussed, 'Have we missed something?'

'No, ma'am, it's four miles further up the coast.'

'Too far to swim, so why are they mentioning it now?'

'It's a popular theory in Australia – they think Scotland is very small. The next theory is that she was airlifted out by helicopter.'

'The helicopter was there weeks before, that's somebody getting their dates a little mixed up.'

'Taken by the Lord.'

'Well, you never know . . .' said McPhee in grave reverence.

'Next,' Mackie said, 'she throws a mannequin on the rocks, then runs away with the gamekeeper.'

'I think Ryce and Spyck would have noticed if the photograph was of a mannequin.'

'She had a stunt double, threw them off the cliff then ran away with the gamekeeper.'

'I'm not sure they have a gamekeeper, ma'am,' pointed out Craigo. 'They have no game.'

'Is that the best comment you can make on that theory?' Caplan asked her sergeant.

'Is there any sense in any of these?' said McPhee. 'I don't see a lookalike agreeing to be thrown off a cliff. But if she were to run off with somebody else, who would it be? She doesn't *know* anybody else.'

'She doesn't indeed.' Caplan thought about the phone call last night with Sarah and Liz; those social networks that made life bearable. 'Okay, do you think she had any pals, anybody that wouldn't treat her like the supermodel she was? Koi was discovered and became famous, there was no time in between. She doesn't seem to have known anybody before that, anybody who knew her for herself. So, who was there now? Anybody? Anything on her phone?'

Mackie shook her head. 'It's used to track her fitness and to phone or text other people in the castle. She calls Robyn. She's Koi No-mates.'

'What does she do if she wants a haircut?'

'She texts Pomeroy and he arranges it. A car. Security. All that.'

'No other activity? No friend?' asked Caplan.

'No,' Mackie sighed with an air of disappointment.

'But if she wanted, needed a friend outside the circle. Who would that be?'

'Somebody online?'

Caplan shook her head, 'There are no devices that either Pomeroy or Samphire don't have access to. Everything up there is interconnected.'

'Somebody she must have met?'

'But who? She didn't go anywhere that they didn't take her. She never drove, she was always driven. Nothing happened to her that Pomeroy or Samphire didn't know about, she was a celebrity 24/7. I doubt she'd any control over her money.'

Craigo sighed. 'I was just thinking about the lady, ma'am. She was in isolation in many ways. In company, but on her own. I'm thinking about the way Agatha Christie disappeared for a few days. Have you thought of that?'

'I can see your thinking,' said Caplan.

Craigo tilted his head, looking at the photographs on the wall. 'I was thinking how much we have dug into the lady's life and how little there is.'

'Apart from the family, the designer clothes, the gorgeous food, the houses and the travel all over the world. The luxury lifestyle. You mean apart from all that, she doesn't have very much?' asked McPhee.

'We've been talking about finding somebody who knew the lady from outside that circle. We can't find anybody. And we're having trouble tracing her actual family. Pomeroy's lawyers just aren't having any of it.'

'From the life they live, I can see why. There's an artifice of perfection with Gabriel and the children. The last thing Koi wants is reality to come along and slap her in the face. That could halt the gravy train,' said Caplan. 'Surely if there was a sibling, a relative, they would have come forward. As nobody has, maybe there are no relatives. Many people would be happy to walk into a new life where nobody knew their name.'

'Yes, ma'am, I'm sure that's true, but it also leaves you very vulnerable.'

Mackie agreed. 'It's a weird mixture of being popular and isolated. I mean, AZed and Shazamtina have now arrived to support EB and Cosmo. AZed is EB's boyfriend and a complete arse. He has silver tattoos on his face, wings round his eyes. He's a poet and street artist.'

Caplan saw Craigo frowning. 'And?'

'Just interesting that Cosmo's girlfriend was flown up by helicopter while AZed was left to travel by train.'

Caplan's eyes narrowed. 'And?' she repeated.

'He's up to his eyes in debt. EB makes a fortune doing her content and her influencing. The real revenue comes from the advertising it carries. The sex tape scandal generated profile and that generated income. AZed thought that Koi withdrawing from public life, i.e., leaving the kids to do their own thing, was madness. The older generation earn, and control, the big money.'

'Scared the gravy train might be at the last stop?' murmured Caplan. 'Maybe Koi coming north was her trying to step back from her fame. But having met Pomeroy, I think that as soon as that affected the balance sheet, he'd get her right back out there.'

'Instead, they have AZed wanting his clothing brand, and his knitted wellies, to come under the Sunflower umbrella, but they refused. Obviously.'

'Who refused?'

Mackie shrugged. 'Just the company. Don't see Koi and the brand going for that.'

Caplan was quiet for a moment, listening to the silence. 'What's the feeling of the rest of the family?'

'I think they just ignore what Koi wants and carry on as usual. She was in that final photograph,' said Mackie.

'What about the locals, what's their take on it all?'

'Positive. A wedding venue instead of noisy hen nights and corporate shite they had before, plus they allow the helicopter parking space—'

'Helipad . . .'

'. . . to be used by the rescue services. Then there's this kind of thing from MisChief666,' Mackie said, pressing play on her phone.

Today on the Living Their Life *podcast we are looking at the eternal bridesmaid, the daughter of two of the most beautiful people on God's earth and why, sometimes, they are impossible shoes to fill.*

This podcast tells a story of a girl called Rosie. Miss Rosie McQuarrie-Samphire is worse than the bridesmaid who was never the bride; she's the fat employee. Probably on minimum wage.

Her job is to stand to one side and watch as the glamorous bride emerges through the doors of her own home – a 1,000-year-old castle. The bride is beautiful in a fifty-grand dress – who wouldn't be! Each seed pearl has been sewn onto the raw silk by hand.

Any of the wedding party who notice Rosie are nice to her, because it's always good manners to be nice to the 'staff'.

I wonder how much Rosie watches the world around her. Does she look through the arrow slits, spying on the bride and groom as they walk into the ornamental gardens for photographs? Does Rosie watch the happy families? Does she see their disregard for smudged lipstick and nobody caring if the photographer catches their good side or not?

It's all a castle in the air for her.

I suspect she sits up on the ramparts, preferring to listen to the happy chatter drifting up to her from below, because then she can imagine that they are small and fat and ugly like her.

If they come into view again, does Rosie torture herself watching them – the beautiful, happy people, thin and lovely. Maybe she could do with taking a leaf out her sister's book and eat nothing for a few days.

Rosie wants a bride to ask her to be in the picture with them, the way they do with her famous mother, Koi McQuarrie.

They never do. They never will.

Pearl Lilac Rose McQuarrie-Samphire is never the bride, never the bridesmaid, she's the hired help. She'll grow into a bitter—

A podgy finger slammed onto the pause button. 'That's fucking horrible. Who wrote that shite?' Wattie was furious.

'It's important,' said Mackie, getting to her feet, defensive.

McPhee shook his head. 'That's really nasty, ma'am.'

'It is,' Caplan agreed. 'The nastiest thing about it is that it's been written by somebody who knows their way around the castle and knows what's going on in there. It's one of them.' She looked along the pictures on the wall, but they remained silent. 'Anyway, we've two new faces on our board. Andrew Knox and Angus McLeerie, similar age, similar build as young men, but pertinent to this case in very different ways. Callum? Wattie? Grab a coffee while you can. And one for Craigo,' said Caplan, and explained to them who Andy Knox was, and why he had been hanging around so much.

McPhee said that he'd read one of Knox's books about miscarriages of justice, *Tipping the Scales*, and thought it was quite good. Wattie said that he might try to read one. Mackie said there was no point as it had no pictures.

Caplan looked around the room. 'Sorry, who did I give McLeerie to?'

'Me, ma'am,' said McPhee. 'Well, it's one of those cases. The teams who investigated the deaths of Daisy and Sharon knew exactly who had done it. He confessed to Carol's. But they got nowhere near the threshold required for a successful prosecution for Daisy or Sharon. Of course, Daisy preceded McLeerie being convicted of killing his wife and they reviewed Daisy's case at that point but it was still no-go.'

'What is he like?'

'There's a psych report in the file. I didn't have the time to go through it all, but the summary is quite enlightening. He was just a nervous wee guy who couldn't take pressure, who was being bullied at work. His mum was old and depended on him. He used to relax by having a quiet drink in the pub, then someone gave him some cocaine and that was the start of it. With regard to Daisy's death, the owner of the campsite . . .'

'Ann McIlroy.'

'. . . saw him go down to the caravan. She was sure he was still there when Daisy came back, and then Daisy's body was on the beach. The time spent in the water removed all forensic evidence from her. There's evidence McLeerie was in the caravan, but he admitted that he often was. He had visited her on that night but she wasn't in, so he went home. He was supposed to run her to the train station, but he was early. No provable alibi.'

'And the other one? If he didn't kill Sharon Baird, then he must be the unluckiest man alive.'

'Well, they were both attending the same rehab support group. He has said that he hoped the death of Daisy was the jolt he needed to give up the cocaine, but losing his friend was a hard blow. The support group was important to him. Four of them walked home together every fortnight. Two of them dropped off at various places en route, leaving McLeerie and Sharon to walk across the golf course; he always walked her back to her front door as he lived another ten minutes' walk further on. But on that night, she was found dead at the side of the fairway, her head battered in with a heavy branch. All forensics relating to him could have been explained by their physical proximity.'

'That's quite interesting too. Three women: one battered her head against the wall, one battered her head against the rocks and one with her head battered by a branch. Nothing premeditated, nothing brought to the scene, all possible with the flash of anger that McLeerie is reputed to possess.'

'Where is he now, Angus McLeerie? McPhee?'

'I'm still waiting on word back, ma'am. I've had to go through his welfare officer, who referred me here, there and everywhere, but basically the Detective Super is not keen unless we have substantive evidence. I was thinking if you spoke to Linden or Spencer himself, that might get things moving.'

'Who is his welfare officer?' asked Caplan.

McPhee checked his notes. 'A Colin Reese?'

Caplan nodded. 'Colin's an okay bloke – if he could help, he would. But it does mean McLeerie's in Glasgow. They're keeping him away from his previous area of operation.' She closed her eyes and sighed. 'The fact he could have been visiting Torsvaig on Saturday night is not substantive evidence. We've no evidence of that at all. I can hear the media screaming harassment.' Caplan mused, 'Do we think McLeerie could be the Fisherman?'

'Doesn't quite fit the psychology, does it?' said McPhee.

'Aye it fuckin' does. He controls women with violence when they are there in front o' him. If they arenae, he sends them a letter.' Wattie tapped his forehead. 'He gets inside their heid.'

'Is that Freud? Gets inside their heid?' mocked McPhee.

Before Wattie could bite back, Caplan asked Craigo if he'd anything to add. 'Preferably physical rather than psychological.'

'Not on the Fisherman, ma'am no, but on Tron.' He held in his hand three pieces of A4 paper that had been printed off elsewhere and had been folded up and put in someone's pocket, probably Craigo's judging by the dirt on the crease lines.

'Is this relevant?'

He shuffled it a little, 'It looks like it could be, ma'am. It's quite interesting. It's about the young lad, Triton. Seemingly when he was young . . .'

'He's eighteen, how young are we talking?'

'Younger than he is now.'

Caplan wondered why she bothered.

'He was wanting to learn to drive and had been driving around on some private land. Then he decided to take Pomeroy's car, a Porsche Boxster, out for a joyride, and it was after midnight and for some reason he decided to go through a housing estate and crashed into a fence killing the dog that was in the front garden at the time, and knocking over the old lady who was accompanying the dog on a before-bed walk.'

'Sad for the dog. but better that than the other way round.'

'Better that it hadn't happened at all.'

'Yes of course,' said Caplan. 'Why is none of this on record?'

'We're looking into that. It's disappeared. I suppose money talks, or something, but there were no criminal charges made. The family, the Sunflower Linen Company, made a huge donation to the dog and cat home, then paid for the old lady to have her broken wrist fixed in a private hospital and then threw in a set of new teeth just for goodwill.'

'Can this family pay their way out of anything?'

'Technically he was insured to drive the vehicle because he works for the company, on paper at least, and the vehicle is a company car, and the lawyer took a long time to go through that and point it out in the very small print. And the lawyer was very expensive. And the owner of the vehicle isn't going to complain seeing as the culprit is the son of his business partner or whatever.'

'What a load of pish,' exclaimed Wattie, 'fuckin' back handers going on there. Old boys, Masons and all that.'

'For once, I find myself agreeing with PC WFP,' said Caplan.

'Since then, I think the young chap's mental health has been deteriorating. And a mental health diagnosis is . . .' he searched for the right word, 'a good way of deflecting attention.'

Caplan looked at the date on Craigo's paperwork. 'His behaviour is all put down to him losing his mother and that it was sad all round, but did something happen just before the incident with the Porsche? That sounds like teenage rebellion, the one thing that the others are not allowed. Well, not that we know about.

'We'll keep digging until I'm 100 per cent convinced that something criminal did not happen to that woman, but if something criminal did and Tron was involved? He's just as isolated as Koi was, in many ways.

'And maybe much more vulnerable.'

FIFTEEN

Craigo and Caplan drove to the castle, parking down at the car park, having been told by Spencer not to attempt to drive up to the Welcome Gate the way the family did, the way Wattie did. Pomeroy had complained.

It was Perkins on duty. Caplan could see the signs of his being military rather than a cop in a past life – something about his accent, his bearing, the wariness in his eyes. Like most security men, he wore black. Today it was a black T-shirt, trousers with side pockets and a radio clipped to a utility belt, sunglasses on top of his head.

He welcomed them with a smile, asking if they had any news, which Caplan took to mean had the body been found yet. She explained that the search was ongoing. They were there to see Morrow and Tron. He gave them a curt nod and wished them luck.

Caplan let Craigo chat to him, finding out he was also a gardener, a groundsman, odd-job man. There was a connection here. Craigo saying something about getting to school by snowplough when he was a lad. Perkins saying that he had sometimes gone to school by rowing boat. Caplan thought of her mother's 3 Series BMW waiting outside the school gates, the warmth and smell of the interior as she climbed in with her schoolfriend who went to ballet class with her, as the rain ran in sheets down the windscreen. Then Craigo began to gently probe Perkins as to why he was helping out on security, what kind of security was needed. Caplan stood back and pretended to look busy with her phone.

'I was in the forces for years, then came back to look after my mum when my dad died.'

'I'm sorry. Was that recent?'

'Couple of years. Lack of public transport is the problem with these places. My mum doesn't drive. Makes it very difficult.'

'And before that?'

'Black Watch, Fort George.'

Nothing further was said, no more information forthcoming.

'Did you like Koi?' asked Craigo, catching Perkins off guard.

He didn't answer, just looked away, his eyes narrowing on something that he didn't like. His fair hair was going grey, making him older than he looked, but it was still a face with a degree of character. 'Sure, I liked her, she was . . . grounded. But I don't think anybody got to know her. Seen them a bit in my time, damaged women. Oh, she could turn on the smile but there were times I thought, well, just that it wasn't all easy for her. So yeah, you want Morrow. I'll track her down, the castle is too big a place to go wandering around looking for people.' He glanced at his watch, made a quick call, listened, then said. 'She's outside on the north rampart. Go up the steps on the wall there and keep going, turn left at the top. There's a wooden walkway with steps, just go up there. You'll find her, just out of the sun. Make sure she knows you're coming. Don't give her a fright.'

Morrow McQuarrie-Samphire was sitting tucked under a wall, out of the glare of the midday sun. Sitting on a cushion, her book, *The Children of Men*, close to her face as if she was short-sighted. A large, floppy blue hat hid her features, but not the skeletal thinness of her legs.

'Hello, Morrow.'

'What do you want?'

'Just to have a chat. We didn't get a chance to catch up yesterday. Morrow is rather a beautiful name. Do you know why they called you that?'

'Because they liked calling their kids wanky names. It rhymes with sorrow, so that's good.'

'It's part of tomorrow, so that's good as well.'

'Have you found Mum?'

'Not yet.'

Morrow's slender hand reached up and pulled the hat from her head. 'My mother was one of the most beautiful women in the world. Full stop.'

Caplan searched for a reason behind the non sequitur but couldn't find it. 'And with that goes privilege and responsibilities – her words carried weight.'

'That's shite. She never said anything, never actually spoke out loud. It's against the rules. We don't say anything unless Pip tells us to.' She smiled. 'But you know that.'

Caplan leaned against the wall, her hands feeling the rough stone and the heat held within. She turned her face up to the sun, eyes closed, then turned back to Morrow, folded up now against the bottom of the wall, withdrawing into the shade. Caplan waited until her eyes adjusted.

'I thought that everybody is kind to the beautiful. It's one of those unwritten laws of nature. Maybe everybody thinks that you will be kind because you're pretty.'

'That's what my mother had – her face was lovely, and she was lovely. She wasn't haughty and fucking nuts like Ecco, or intense and crying all over the place like Rhea. She was just her, and if you've never met her, you can never understand that.'

'I'd like to have met her. Nobody that I've spoken to has a bad word to say about her.'

'And they won't because she was nice. She was Mum.' A slightly odd look came over Morrow's face as if she was thinking about getting angry but was too tired. 'She never spoke back, she never stood up for herself, you know. We don't eat – we are given our food, but we don't eat it; beautiful people don't eat you see. We just exist. We went somewhere, no idea where it was. A hot island, somewhere sandy, and we were in a huge hotel, the restaurants were amazing. There was everything you could want, but we ate nothing, because we have to stay beautiful, because guess what? Nobody would be interested in Mum as a human being unless she looked like *that*, if she didn't look like *that*, she failed to exist. It was horrible.

'When we get old, we may as well just die. On that photo shoot Pip drove us away from the hotel, and only two miles from all this luxury there were kids living in huts and starving. All our food was photographed, then flung out.'

Caplan had heard this argument before, many a time, from Kenny. 'Well, there will always be kids starving, you not eating will not put food in their bellies.'

'No, but it makes me feel better about the situation.' She stretched her skeletal arms, moving into the warmth of the sun. She withdrew them as if she'd been stung.

'Maybe you should eat and get strong, then really do something about it. You have fame, you have a weapon you could use to benefit those who are vulnerable – should you choose to.'

'Pip wouldn't allow it. And it doesn't work. They only ever wanted my mother. And I don't have what it takes. Look at Cosmo and EB. They have it, the thing. The thing that Gabe and Mum have, Tron and I don't have it, so we're diagnosed with something, so we don't have to try. That excuses us from doing a load of shit. And then there's Rosie who is stuck, stuck in the middle like a fat pig. They call her that in the media, you know, the fat pig.'

Caplan said, 'Yes, I had noticed the fat pig bit, but stuck?'

'Your constable – she's fat, ugly and she smells but you know, I look at her and envy her and despise her at the same time. She can eat, and she laughs.'

Caplan remained tight-lipped; this was a teenager with very little experience of real life and too much experience of an unreal life.

'If you want stuck, you should speak to Tron, but I bet Pip doesn't let you. Because Tron knows stuff, he's weird. He knows about Rosie. Pip won't let you speak to Dad either, so don't wait around drinking tea with Rosie. She's stuck here and is stuck being Rosie. She's so fucking miserable, and she doesn't even know it.'

'Does Rosie have any friends?'

'Nope.'

'Did your Mum have any friends, anybody come to see her?'

'Nope. Everybody who wanted to see her wanted to make money from her.'

'And what about you, Morrow? Have you got a close friend?'

'Nope! I'm going to disappear without Mum to hang on to, I think I'll just fade away.' It was said matter-of-factly, a little wistfully, but far too dramatically.

'What do you think happened to your mum?' asked Caplan, straight out, without warning the subject first.

'I think she left me behind. I wasn't enough to keep her here. Here, on the earth. She's gone now. And she was the one who did the good stuff, the charity stuff, the Children in Need, Comic Relief. The Kids' Hospice – she did a lot of work for that. Gabe and Pip went along with it but now Mum's gone, it'll never happen again. None of it will.'

'Well, you could walk in your mum's footsteps.'

The eyes, deep in shadow, turned on Caplan. 'Nobody will ever walk in my mum's footsteps.' The hat was placed back on the head, the book was picked up.

Caplan knew she was being dismissed, said goodbye and walked away. By the time she got to the top of the steps, Morrow had put the book down; her chin resting on her knees, deep in the shadows, she was still hiding from the sun, from life, from herself.

* * *

Caplan jumped as a figure stepped out of the darkness. 'Jesus, Craigo, I didn't see you.'

'Didn't want to interrupt, ma'am.'

They walked along the rampart until they stood in the bright sunlight, looking down at the grass of the King's Reach. Then they followed the length of the Woodwall which ran across to the cliff edge where bundles of razor wire had been thrown many years ago. The trees were crammed together, growing over the top of the wall on the other side. Below they could hear the gentle lapping of waves. The beach, far along to their left, was a golden ribbon lying in the sun. It looked like the border between two worlds.

If a ghost was going to walk it would walk here, Caplan thought. If it was Lady Mary's ghost, this would be the view she would come to see, looking out for her husband to come back to her rather than losing him to the waves forever.

She looked up and around, considering. 'The drone footage would have picked up anything going on in the woods. Wouldn't it?'

'Well, the trees are in full leaf so the drone wouldn't see the ground, and nobody can get over the wall from here anyway. Can they?' Craigo looked puzzled as he asked the question.

'And the IT guys have examined the files from the drone and seen nothing, have they? Koi was wearing that white dress, it would be easily seen.' She looked at the height and the breadth of the ancient stone wall; it looked as impenetrable now as it would have eight hundred years ago. 'All it is, is a wall. It seems such a simple idea, just put stones on top of stones. Yet it's still a true defence.'

'Just ask any Mexican, ma'am.'

'Someone mentioned that Tron likes to be high up. To be high up you do need to climb.'

Craigo waggled his pencil, conducting an invisible orchestra and harmonising his thoughts. 'There was also mention of him being in two places at one time – outside and inside the castle wall – which is exactly the circumstances required to have committed this crime.'

'He could have sneaked past the security, found a way to escape being caught on camera. It might be nothing more than that,' said Caplan.

'Do you believe that?' asked Craigo.

'Sherlock Holmes once said that there's nothing more deceptive than obvious fact. The fact is that Tron was up on the King's Reach. The fact we can't get him there doesn't alter the fact that he was.

If he sneaked out the gate, the security camera would get him. If he managed that, and walked up the King's Reach, somebody would have spotted him. Ghost sightings are more frequent. Something vague about a woman in white . . .

'Or a young man, longish hair, dressed in the Sunflower white linen? Have we viewed all that security tape? Have they given us it all?'

'I'll check, ma'am.'

'Please ask Pickering, don't ask Pomeroy,' said Caplan, turning full circle, thinking about that Gerry Rafferty song, rewriting the lyrics in her head: stones to the right of me, woods to the left. Koi would indeed have been stuck in the middle.

Craigo coughed in polite interruption. 'I think we should be a little more careful with our terminology, ma'am. Inside and outside the castle. Especially when talking about the path.'

'Yes, but the path belongs to the castle, doesn't it? It's on their land.'

'It belongs to the castle but it's not part of the castle, not at all. And the public have right of access.' He looked down again at the tall grey stone wall that dropped below them. 'And if we were standing down there, back in the day, we'd be getting all kinds of implements thrown at us, shots fired, rocks hurled, hot oil poured on us, the odd arrow coming this way. It's the very definition of being outside the walls.'

'And your point is?' asked Caplan, closing her eyes, dizzy from looking down too much.

'Well, people keep pointing out that there's no way in from here.'

'There's not, you have to go all the way down the path and through the big gate, the Welcome Gate, and then up to the Castle Gate to get into the bailey before you are in the castle itself. It's a long way. It takes twenty minutes.'

'So how did Tron get past us without us seeing? He was in the castle, and now he's over there, on the clifftop.'

They looked at the slight, hunched figure sitting on the edge.

'I wish he wouldn't sit there. Did Perkins let him through?'

'They let him through on his bike.'

'But that was to visit Robyn – he's allowed to go to the stables. Robyn phones when he gets there, phones when he leaves.'

'That's understandable. But how did he get up there? Are we the only ones who see the importance of it?'

'Well, imagine your best soldiers are trapped up on the King's Reach, I'd imagine you'd want some way of bringing them in, without the enemy knowing what that was.'

'And that is?' asked Caplan, imaging the loyal soldiers cornered here, a choice to fight or go over the cliff. She saw Craigo scribbling in his notebook. 'What are you doing?'

'Making a note to find out, ma'am.'

'Okay. Let's ask Tron if he knows. We'll retrace Koi's footsteps and prove that nobody coming down can get past us going up.'

It took them thirty minutes to walk, strolling because of the heat. Mostly in silence except for Craigo pointing out some interesting moss formations on the wall.

On arrival at the King's Reach, Caplan looked along the top of the cliff; Tron was nowhere to be seen. A frisson of panic went through her, but a quick check over the cliff proved he hadn't come to the same fate as Koi. Taking a few breaths to calm herself, she looked round the base of the Woodwall and then the castle wall.

'He's not here, is he, ma'am?' said Craigo, scratching his head. 'So where did he go?'

'Where indeed?'

Caplan had just walked into the Great Hall when she heard a voice say, 'Hey, I was looking for you.'

Even in leggings and a thin jumper, EB caught the eye. She was sitting on a stool near the bar, and while still very beautiful, she seemed a little jumpy. There was, Caplan thought, just a touch of redness round her nostrils.

As if reading her mind, EB sniffed and looked away,

'I gave you my number,' said Caplan.

EB shrugged and lost whatever little train of thought she had.

'Did Koi give you anything, a present, recently?'

'Well, was it a present if it was already mine?'

Caplan asked, 'Already yours?'

'Stuff my mum had. She gave me that back. Was mine anyway.'

'What are your memories of her?'

'I was less than a year old when she fell. I've heard many stories. I've heard she was wild.' Her fingers came up to form quote marks, waggling a cigarette in the air, raining ash on the flagstones: '"A party girl who got out of her skull." She was so loaded with coke her heart arrested and she . . . well, for a long time, I believed that.'

'And now?'

A slow, thoughtful draw on the cigarette. 'I do wonder, I really wonder. Was she wanting out? She had a baby. She had me and she wanted me.' EB looked over her shoulder, through the open door, but dropped her voice even further. 'So that arsehole Samphire's my dad but there was another guy my mum really liked, or so Koi and Rhea told me. DeVries?' EB smiled like she was seeing Caplan for the first time. 'Do you know where he is?'

'My colleague's tracking him down. What do you think happened?'

'I think she'd taken a line, went out onto the roof garden of the flat to join the party. There was dancing. She fell. Or her heart stopped. She fell. Mum, Rhea and now Koi. And I'll be next if I'm not careful.' Her face creased up and Caplan thought she was going to cry for a moment. 'Do you think Ted DeVries will remember me?'

'Of course he will,' lied Caplan.

'I'd like to speak to him, to somebody who knew my mum, really knew her. Knew her real name. We all get a new name. Imagine being called Mary. Looking like a goddess and stuck with Mary. You can see why we get a better name. My name's not EB.'

'Ebony Blanc?'

'My name is Elizabeth. Elizabeth Bria Middlemass, not EB McQuarrie-Samphire. That was Pomeroy's idea. They never adopted me.'

'Elizabeth? That suits you, it's regal.'

'What's your name?'

'Christine.'

'That what your mum called you?'

'Yes, mostly.'

'Koi was—'

Then Cosmo bounced in, a breathless ball of energy, a more nervous energy than before, Caplan thought, and he smiled.

Caplan looked around, wondering if there was a camera somewhere and Cosmo had been summoned to stop her talking to EB.

He said hello to them with that easy grace and then offered the information that Tron was supposed to be resting in his bed, as much as anybody could keep Tron anywhere. Doctor's orders. 'He's just visited,' Cosmo whispered with his sexy smile.

'Has he?'

'Yes, he's just left. I'm afraid you've missed him.'

'Dr Rowe?'

'Indeed, I can only give you his name and his number. You'll need to ask Pip for more than that.' He gave a little laugh, a slightly nervous laugh.

'Name and number only,' snorted EB, then looked at Caplan. '"Mary, Jesus and the wee donkey." He said that in a TV show.' She punched her half-brother gently on the arm. The arm then slid away through the archway at the far end of the bar, into the darkness of the castle.

'Of course,' Caplan said softly. On her way out into the brilliant sunshine, she stopped beside Cosmo, looked him straight in the face. Then, outside in the patchwork of sunshine on the courtyard, she looked back into the handsome features. 'Thank you for talking to DC Mackie. And I want to reassure you that I will find out what happened to your mother.'

'I'm sorry if we appear less than helpful. It's a lot to cope with.' A flood of genuine contrition flowed over his face; maybe he was even holding back a tear. He said quietly, 'EB tends to cope with these situations . . .' He searched for a word.

'Chemically?'

'She was bad before the revenge tape, she trusted the guy. She's much worse now. There's no way Pip will allow you access to the family's medical records. He's like that.'

'And you – how are you?'

'Like somebody who has lost his mother. Has a slightly useless father and people depending on him.'

'Of course, family comes first. But all I seem to hear is how it will affect the business, how it will change things. Is that fair?'

'Things were changing anyway; Mum was getting older and getting tired of it. That's . . .' he stuttered slightly, 'why she did what she did. I'm sure of that.'

'Cosmo?' The voice was female and unpleasantly squeaky, coming from somewhere above them, in the hall, at the top of the stairs. For the second time, Caplan was subjected to the sight of a beautiful woman with endless legs, this time dressed in shorts and a bra top, making her way down the central stairway, a strappy shoe reaching slowly for the next step, then a pause, then reach and repeat. She was not the natural beauty of the McQuarrie-Samphire DNA; this was colour and artifice. Caplan looked at Cosmo, who appeared to be captivated by the scene, then he turned to look at her and gave her the tiniest of eyerolls.

'That's my onscreen girlfriend,' he whispered conspiratorially. Then he winked. 'I was taught never to lie to the police.'

She held his gaze, then spoke very quietly. 'Does Pomeroy know you spoke to us?'

The smallest shake of the head, a look in his eyes. Pleading? *Say nothing*.

'Cosmo? Honey?' The slow progress of the blonde down the stairs halted.

'I better leave you to it.' She nodded to the figure on the stairs. 'What about Rosie? Downstairs? I'm a bit worried about her. The adoption thing?' Caplan let the question lie.

Cosmo switched his smile back on. 'There's always been a family joke that Mum wanted a baby, but Dad wanted to keep her working, so he went out and bought her a baby to keep her quiet. Rosie might have just realised that Dad didn't want her at all.' He nodded, more to assure himself than anybody else.

'Dahling?' More soft footfall on the carpet.

'Be with you in a mo,' Cosmo shouted over his shoulder, then said quietly to Caplan. 'Mum wasn't allowed to turn down work, but when I came along, I was worth it, commercially.' He paused. 'By then the Sunflower Linen Company had a good campaign behind them, a maternity clothes range and babywear. It sold well. With Rosie, I think the issue might be more where there's a father, there must be a mother. Pip might not have thought that through.'

'And who is that?'

'We have no idea. I assume Pip knows. Well, I really need to go and amuse my celebrity girlfriend. Excuse me.'

Caplan walked out to the bailey, approaching the patio doors at the rear of the hedge. With her fingers on the handle, she looked through the windowpane to see McPhee making Rosie a cup of tea. He was just about to sit down at the table, opposite Rosie but facing Caplan. It was obvious that Rosie was crying, and that McPhee was giving her tea and sympathy. She saw him put his hand out across the table. If he was holding out a tissue, that was allowed. If he was reaching for her hand, then maybe that was not so good. She took a step back from the patio doors, thinking that she might have to stop him from coming up to the castle. Mackie wasn't the only one who needed protecting from themselves.

SIXTEEN

Caplan called Pomeroy to ask him to arrange a meeting with Tron, saying it was important. The call went to voicemail.

Koi. Every time she thought she had a clear picture of her, something happened that put her just out of focus, just out of reach.

She kept making the mistake of thinking of Koi as a normal woman in her early forties, but she couldn't be. The Svengali would have started his work on her, Rhea and Ecco twenty years earlier. Their pasts obliterated, given a new name, they were chosen to fit – the blonde, the redhead, the person of colour.

Did anybody know them before that?

And had EB just told her that Koi's first name was Mary? That wasn't enough to go on, but it was a start. She knew there was a day when a tall young blonde walked through an airport, and maybe that was the last time that somebody called Mary was heard of.

It was easy to forget how young the Sunflower Girls were when they were first discovered, how naive and innocent. How could they have known what would become of them at the hands of two older men who knew the business inside out, on the lookout for a new project to exploit. They had no idea that it would end so tragically for them. Caplan was ruminating on the end result, when Rhea and Ecco realised they had had enough, when they wanted to walk away and have their own lives.

They had died.

Her phone pinged. She looked at it, thinking it might be Ryce, but it was a cyber specialist from Glasgow. They had traced the device that had released the series of images of Koi's body to the dark web. She said thank you, then called Craigo to tell him to bring the named party down to Pilcottie.

Pip Pomeroy looked faintly ridiculous sitting on the small black plastic chair at Pilcottie police station with his white hair sticking to his skull with sweat. The white flannel trousers and yellow Hawaiian shirt identified him as exactly what he was: a fish out of water. Caplan had thought the change of venue would unsettle him, and away from the comfortable red leather of his captain's chair, his red wine cellar and the polished rosewood of his office desk, his discomfort was obvious. Despite Mackie's best efforts to clean the place up, it was all Pomeroy could do not to pull his ironed white handkerchief from his breast pocket to avoid touching anything with his podgy pink fingers.

Caplan looked calm and unruffled despite the heat. Unlike the man sitting opposite her, her hair was still immaculate, every strand in its place.

'Why am I here?' he asked, jerking his head a little, indicating the office/interview room/kitchen/dining room at the unmanned police station.

'Because the station at Oban is surrounded by reporters and rubberneckers trying to get a look at Cosmo or EB. It's a celebrity thing, seemingly,' said Caplan, deliberately misunderstanding. 'Can you turn all of your mobile phones off for the moment?'

'They've snapped me being driven out by the police. You know what they'll be saying.'

'I know the feeling, Mr Pomeroy.' She put her own picture, taken outside the walls of Torsvaig, in front of him.

He looked at it. 'Good picture. Good lighting. I thought they might have gone down the Cruella de Vil route with your looks, but no, that's good. But back to my question, why am I here? And I don't mean here at Pilcottie, I mean here rather than my home?'

'Your home? Your home at the castle? The castle owned by the Sunflower Linen Company? I knew exactly what you meant, Mr Pomeroy, I was being obtuse to prove a point.'

'And that point is?' Pomeroy pulled the handkerchief from the pocket, refolding it to pat his forehead, trying to mop up the rivulets of sweat running over his pink skin.

'I want to speak to Tron.'

'You can, when he's better or sober. The doctor was out today to see him. He's in his bed. Dr Rowe will send a letter to whoever needs one. Leave him alone until he's better.'

'He was back out, on top of the cliff. I could argue that he's vulnerable and you're not looking after him too well. If he's on a clifftop on meds.' Caplan shook her head. 'I'll get on to Spencer, clear the path for an interview.'

'I've been on to his boss, and you won't get an interview.'

Caplan gave him a smile that could chill the blood. 'I'm sure you know why I am up here,' she whispered. 'I don't always obey the rules. Why did you post the pictures of Koi's dead body on the dark web? You knew it would get picked up. Was that part of keeping her relevant? Keeping her profitable?'

'What's the dark web got to do with it?'

'Can you answer the question? I'm a member of the police service and we tend to keep things on a need-to-know basis. Mr Samphire, in good faith, gave one picture to the CSI. The rest in the series? Well, they went to the entire world. Surely that was beyond human decency?'

'She was dead. DCI Caplan, is it? I'm used to dealing with more senior officers. Like Adam Spencer's boss.'

'Yes, so am I.'

Pomeroy licked his lips, thinking. 'Okay, I'll level with you.'

'Please do.'

'I agree with you. She was dead. It was horrible. But that picture was going to go out anyway. I wanted to wait. I wanted to take the tack that you are taking and once it was out, we could react with moral outrage, and get column inches and sympathy that way. But Gabe?' He shook his head. 'He didn't want that picture bouncing up in a week, a month. Who would know when or where? Gabe wanted it out to get it over with. So, I got the series out on the dark web, to a site called Dead Famous. Ninety seconds later it was round the planet. Can you believe that?'

'Yes.'

'Ironically, it's now reported that they are the official police photographs.'

'Of a body we didn't find. That's impressive.' Caplan scowled at the lack of logic. 'But why the Dead Famous site? Why, full stop?'

Pomeroy sighed. 'Because people are fascinated by fame, beauty and death.'

'Why did Mr Samphire make that decision when he was drunk?'

'This was before he was that drunk. He wanted to fix on the idea that she was dead. When her body was washed off the rocks, we guessed there wasn't going to be a pronouncement of life extinct that we could release as a statement. So, what do we do to prevent endless, and I mean endless, pages and pages in the newspapers speculating about where she was, and saying that she wasn't dead?'

'You couldn't have known her body was going to be that difficult to find. You could have waited.'

'Gabe wasn't for waiting. He saw her. She was dead. Imagine how Morrow was going to feel waking up every day and hearing conspiracy theorists talking about her mother being alive? Where there's a gap, ignorant, mindless people fill in the blanks with their tedious little theories. Gabe wanted to close the door on that sort of speculation.'

'Like that she was abducted by aliens.'

'Like she was an alien all along?' He gave a wry smile. 'You think I'm a monster.'

'I do.'

'I work in PR. Once the horse called Rumour has bolted there is no getting it back. Denial fuels flames. The best policy is damage limitation. God knows, the family make mistakes.'

'They do, but rather than manage their mistakes, you create them. You engineer untruths to put out there, and the only reason I can think of is so you can respond. Respond to something that was never an accusation in the first place? I'm confused by that.'

Pomeroy patted his face a little more but nodded in agreement, happy to go along with a statement that was perfectly accurate.

'I'm seeing a young man distraught at losing his mum being publicly comforted by somebody, yet he's engaged to somebody else. At the stables . . . She describes . . .' Caplan considered for a moment, 'something akin to a code of silence.'

'Robyn's a good kid, we like her. She's allowed to stay part of the brand. She plays by the rules.'

'Plays by the rules?'

'Yeah, it's a bit like being in the royal family. She knows what side her bread is buttered on. Koi McQuarrie, the Sunflower Linen Company, are a brand. It's a business. You need to keep that in mind. Shazamtina is a successful model. Cosmo is a model who'll be a successful actor. He's had a few bit parts in . . . what was it now? . . . a London-based crime drama where a pathologist does all the investigating, and the cop from the Met drives a brand-new BMW wearing designer gear. Can't recall what it was called.'

'You're not narrowing it down,' Caplan smiled.

'Cosmo'll get more decent parts; he has some very expensive suits.' Pomeroy was proud of his nestlings and was very keen to protect their earning potential. 'We'll do something about Robyn presently. But for the moment he remains romantically attached to Shazamtina publicly. He's a celebrity, a real celebrity, not one famous for doing nothing. He's his mother's son, no need to tell you about nepo babies. But he has the look, the style and the personality. Like his mum, he has the ability to come across as a very genuine human being.'

'Come across as?'

'We're all complex personalities, DCI Caplan. Gabe and I are extroverts. Koi and Cosmo can turn it on when they need to, then they tire and revert to their natural state which is going out with the dogs or sitting in front of the fire with a good book. He's so professional, he's hiding how devastated he is over the death of his mother, but I know him and I know he needs to be kept busy. We're doing a high-value shoot with him and Shazamtina, scattering flowers on the beach where Koi died, dressed in Sunflower Linen, posed against the sea, the blue of the sky, white clothes on the sand.'

Caplan took a short breath. 'There's commercial value in the death of his mother? Are you serious?'

'Entirely. Hot topic. Everything has a price. For the moment Shazamtina will support him, and we'll deny that she's cancelled a huge contract to come to Torsvaig and comfort him. Then their careers will inevitably pull them apart, then they'll be on, then off again, then they'll get engaged. There might be a baby, we haven't decided yet. Then they'll split up, but they'll remain good friends. In a few years' time, he'll be settled down with Robyn. There's a woman who could win the Grand National without a horse. The demographic of his fans will be a little older, youngsters at the age of settling down. He'll stay relevant. Cosmo is really happy with Robyn at the stables. Don't forget, I've lived with that boy for every minute of his life. He's genuinely like a son to me, and the Sunflower Linen Company is still a family business.'

'Would the fictitious baby not be a problem after nine, ten months?'

'Babies can be totally fictitious. All the sorrow of a miscarriage. We can play that in many ways, just as long as we stay empathetic. This is all mapped out, it'll get picked up by the glossies.'

'Is nothing genuine?'

'I've always found real life rather boring.'

'I wish mine was,' said Caplan, leaning forward, her voice quiet and calm.

'I bet you do,' Pomeroy said, deadly serious.

'You let it be known that Triton, Tron, has a problem. Social media picks up on the drug and alcohol shame of the eighteen-year-old and the virtue-signalling hatred starts. Then you issue a statement: "Oh yes now is the time to face up to the issues he has and get him the help he so desperately needs." There's media mileage in him getting treatment for a mental health issue that he's had for years. Probably since the death of Rhea Doonican, who was his mother, remember. Rhea, not Koi.'

Pomeroy put his palms up in submission. 'With Tron we had to predict something that was going to happen, his mental health was deteriorating. Instead of speculation, which would have been cruel and unpleasant, we managed to get a story out there that appeared to come from a source of law and order. There was an incident with a knife.'

'Was there?'

'Of course not, we just made it up, told old-what's-his-name and word got out. Tron's . . . complicated, he's not dangerous.'

'When you say "old-what's-his-name", do you mean Wattie?'

Pomeroy nodded.

Caplan wondered if this was Pomeroy laying the groundwork for a defence. Tron might have made it outside the bailey, outside the castle grounds when Koi had gone over the cliff. Koi being the woman who had stepped into the role of his mother.

'What was Koi's real name?'

Pomeroy folded his arms across his chest. 'I can tell you it wasn't Mary. Do you want her passport? Her birth certificate?' And there was that viper smile. 'Take them and see where it gets you.' He spoke slowly, as if talking to a child. 'Money can buy anything. But you wouldn't know that.'

'And it's not strictly true. We're tracking her down. Where is EB in all this?'

'As in exploited or exploiter? Believe me, she could teach me how to play the game,' snickered Pomeroy. 'She needs no help from us. Until she goes too far. One arrest with a little recreational cocaine was enough for us to make a statement that she needs help. We spun it that she was trying to cope with the death of her mother. In reality, I doubt whether EB has ever looked back on her mother's life with any depth of emotion. EB's very like Ecco. It's all about the here and now, no impulse control at all. EB will not go gently into old age.'

Caplan remembered the way EB had slunk down the stairs, placing her arm round Cosmo's neck, a lovely and loving gesture to a man she had known as a brother, and shuddered. Was there a wee kid in EB, still hurting? No, Caplan thought, Pomeroy was wrong about EB. She may appear to be tough, living for the moment, but she had grown up the hard way, without her mother.

'It's my job to protect those who live behind the walls at Torsvaig. I'll do that in any way I see fit.'

'Funnily enough, that's my job as well.' Caplan leaned forward. 'What happens when they step out of line, Mr Pomeroy?'

'They don't.'

Their eyes met.

'And that, DCI Caplan, is the first time I've seen you speechless.'

Returning to the back room of Pilcottie police station, grateful for two minutes' peace and quiet, Caplan was eating an egg mayonnaise sandwich at her desk and thinking about Pomeroy. Whatever he said to the contrary, if he hadn't wanted that picture out there it wouldn't have been released.

Koi had been taken by the waves. It would have been so much easier if there had been a body as proof of death, and all the legal issues, like the release of insurance money and the triggering of the will, would go away instead of waiting for seven years, or pushing through court with a 'no proof of life' ruling.

Unless the insurers accepted that photograph as confirmation of death.

It was proof, but proof of what?

If Caplan spent a huge budget proving Koi could have escaped somehow and then her body was pulled up by a fishing boat, the whole police service would look stupid. Equally, an experienced pathologist had queries.

There was a middle ground of course. A body in water, not being returned by the tide, maybe due to a change of weather, or the body gets hit by a boat and chopped by a propeller.

Caplan knew how easily that could happen.

Or did Koi get herself off the rocks and out of the cove in a way she could not fathom? And more than that, she had appeared to be dead, and that had been planned. But the only evidence for that were the photographs, and how did she know Samphire would take them? Caplan argued with herself that the question was moot. Her job was to find Koi alive, and then she could ask her.

Her inbox pinged and there was the picture of Koi on the rocks again. This time it had been scribbled over by Dr Leonora Spyck, Ryce's colleague.

Caplan video-called her. Spyck was having a cup of tea and eating two ginger nuts at once in front of a very messy desk.

'This is an interesting one this, isn't it?' mused Spyck.

'I'd prefer less interesting and more clear-cut.'

'Look at that picture.'

'I've looked at it many times. I'm not sure what it shows. Blood on her head from lacerations in the skin? There's a twist of her knee. She had a bad knee, you know.'

'She had very good muscle tone in her arms though. A swimmer?'

'I think so, and also did some pole dancing to keep fit.'

'You know, some crime scenes are very difficult to interpret.'

'But it is a crime scene?' Caplan wanted confirmation.

'The reason for my call is because we might have solved the mystery of the blood that doesn't wash off.'

'Okay,' said Caplan carefully.

'I was thinking some type of make-up used in films where people get bitten by a shark but when the body pops up, it still has blood on it, that kind of thing. I've asked around in here, and they said to look at the brand name FXHorror. They do special-effects make-up, a waterproof spray-on blood that's applied through a template.'

'I'm lost.'

'Okay. Scene one, day one. You hit . . . Spencer on the forehead with a hammer. That lesion is modelled from a template with holes in it. It's placed on the face and the synthetic wound is sprayed on. Then another template is put over that, black dried blood sprayed on top and so on. It appears to be one small, multilayered lesion; the pigments dry within seconds. Then the next layer goes on top. That way, the replication of the precise bloodied wounds, day after day, is very easy, and much quicker than hand-painting. I'm wondering if that's what Koi did.'

Caplan was quiet. 'Tins of fake spray blood and templates? She had nothing on her when she left the party. But she didn't need it when she left the party, did she? She needed it at the top of the cliff. So, where is it?'

'That's your department. But why not look through their social media? I bet somewhere they'll have some sexy Halloween posts. If they did it, they'll have filmed it.'

'Leonora? Was this photo staged, yes or no?'

'Not sure. Look at it this way: time is passing. If she survived, where is she? If she died, where's the body?'

'A wave must have knocked her off her rocky ridge. She was light, the tide is powerful. It makes sense.'

'Good timing, you must admit though,' said Spyck, 'to jump in at the precise time of very high tide, on the correct night. Maybe she knew that and was just making sure she died. If she'd walked along the clifftop for what, another two minutes, she would have landed in water and sand. Though maybe that's not what she wanted. Maybe she wanted to be sure. Remind me, the fall was from how high?'

'Ten metres or so. About thirty feet?'

'That's survivable if the landing is soft, but McQuarrie's wasn't. It's not the height of the fall but the landing that would be fatal. If she'd landed on the rocks there'd be punctured internal organs, fractured pelvis, fractured ribs, fractured vertebrae. In the photo she's lying as if there's nothing wrong with her. I mean the position of her limbs suggests somebody who's just fallen asleep on a jagged crop of rocks. It looks awkward but not fatal. Even in death she's beautiful, even alluring.' Spyck looked back at the image on the screen, tilting her head. 'You remember when she snogged the wee guy from *Coronation Street* for Cash for Kids?'

'No,' said Caplan sharply.

'It was so funny; she was rather sweet.'

'So I keep hearing.'

'Before we saw the blood, what was your theory?'

'The more I hear about her life, the more I think she might have jumped. If she did, I wouldn't blame her.'

Spyck looked up at Caplan, her eyes wide in genuine surprise.

'I can't explain . . . it's more like a feeling.'

'Feelings are valid, Christine.'

'I can't tick a box in my report about my feelings, can I? I'm thinking about Rhea Doonican and how she lost her life. And before that, how Ecco Middlemass lost hers. Koi seems to have had it all, including the children of her two best friends, and yet has lost her life.'

'Closer than sisters?' quoted Spyck.

'That's been said about the Sunflower Girls before.'

'What can I say, I was a fan.'

'See, you know the story, the PR line. On the surface, Koi had everything and yet actually, she had nothing. She was an icon of natural beauty and clean living, but she was empty. That was the first word that came to mind. The woman was taken and used by Samphire and Pomeroy to be Koi the corporate identity. Somewhere in there I think she might have lost herself.

'There are no issues with the timeline, with the dress, with the shoes, when she was seen. And with Samphire being at the top of the cliff and the time stamp on the image. If I found a way I could get her on and off the rocks safely, what would you say?'

Spyck sat back again, looking at the ceiling, popping a couple of Maltesers into her mouth. 'We know she left the gathering and went up the cliff herself, but . . . she's famous for being a mother. You're a mother. Why would a mum walk away from her kids like that?'

'You haven't met her kids. Your kids are a lovely age, they're not yet capable of destroying your life, your carpets and your bank balance, but give them time.'

'At the moment they are only destroying my sleep.' Spyck slammed her hands on the top of her desk. 'Oh, I heard about the engagement. This Allanach bloke, does he not own most of the west coast? And he's very handsome, in a posh-boy kind of way. Christine, your daughter is made for life. Even if it doesn't work out, she could divorce him and take him for the odd island or two.'

'He doesn't swear. He wears sandals. He doesn't go on holiday. He's weird and lovely at the same time.'

'Does he make Emma happy?'

'Yes. She's not the ambitious young lady I thought she was.'

Spyck asked, 'Did you grow up to be what your mother thought you should be?'

'You know damn well that my mother died thinking that Darcey Bussell stole my career.'

'My mother wanted me to be a doctor.'

'You are a doctor.'

'Not a proper one, with live patients. Now she thinks that I should give up work because of the wee ones.' Spyck took a deep breath. 'But Koi loved her kids, she loved the kids of her friends, she took them on when they died, that's a commitment to live for.'

Caplan smiled. 'Did she take on that commitment? Or was she

landed with it? All those children are a challenge. They're still in her house. She can't get away from them – it's not as if they are going to university and leaving. Imagine that.'

Spyck thought of having her three children at home until their twenties and groaned slightly.

Caplan sensed her change in mood. 'Samphire and Pomeroy engineer situations, and Koi was the one that had to deal with it all. She smiles in front of the media. I just thought that maybe she had managed to get away.'

'Maybe she did exactly that.

They looked at the picture: a broken doll lying on the rocks, the sea of white foam swirling around her.

'Even in death, she's stunning. You know, Chris, it's the blood that says to me it's fake. But maybe what she was trying to fake went badly wrong. Die young, stay pretty,' said Spyck.

'That's been said before.'

'Let's go with "I did it my way". Maybe her death was the one thing in her life she had control of.'

'We've evidence, anecdotal evidence that she was saying goodbye. Giving away her jewellery and mementos to special people, saying goodbye to the dogs. It looked to me like she was cleaning her life with a view to bowing out, on her terms. By jumping off that cliff, at that point, she made 100 per cent sure that it'd appear that she would not survive. Her life was a runaway train, maybe she wanted to stop it.'

'She could get off the train without stopping it, she could get away from her life without ending it, Chris.' Then Spyck added, 'Millions of folk think Elvis did exactly that. Look at Koi's DNA, the blue eyes and the chiselled cheek bones. What was her real name? I presume she wasn't born Koi McQuarrie.'

'We're still working on that. She could be Mary, but she's not Mary McQuarrie. And we've checked all female McQuarries in that age group in Scotland, in case Koi was a nickname, but nothing.'

'Koi a nickname? So, what? Born in the water feature department of a garden centre? A pet shop?'

'No, it's legally her name now but the family are saying nothing more. It's futile, as we will get there eventually, but that's where we are at the moment. It's an elimination game.'

'Why won't they tell you?'

'Because to them control is everything – well, it is to Pomeroy. He spins everything to make money. Samphire's a puppet who dances to Pomeroy's tune; that double act has been going on so long neither of them notices it.'

'Try Marie rather than Mary. Put it out on the wire, see what comes back. She would've been born . . . 1985? Five years either side of that? Within a fifty-mile radius of . . . yes, I see your problem. But somebody'll remember her or wonder what became of that tall, lanky lassie. Then there's Gabriel Samphire.' Spyck rolled the words around her mouth, tasting them on her lips. 'As if that can be his real name. I'd love it if he was actually christened Barry Boyle.'

'Who the hell is Barry Boyle?'

'A young man we pulled out a ditch earlier today – I'm draining his brains into a bowl.'

Caplan stopped chewing her egg mayo. 'Nice.'

Before Caplan got in her car, she got a text message from Aklen saying that he was turning his phone off and having a lie down. Emma had visited and she knew the situation. When Caplan got home an hour later, she let herself into the house quietly and fed the cats, though she had a sneaking suspicion they had already been fed and were lying to her. She made herself a cup of tea and sat out on the balcony, then quickly retreated from the midges. Up at the castle Caplan had seen three or four midge eaters, but she could bet they had a lot more of them to cater for summer weddings where the dancing in the bailey went on into the night.

She sat down on the new sofa they had upstairs, in the room that would be the dining room but for now was storage for boxes, the sofa and Aklen's big desk chair.

There was a pile of A4 paper, a packet of ten pads. Aklen had cut it open and taken the top one from the packet. Caplan slipped her hand into the plastic sleeve and slid out the one underneath. She lifted the top sheet, revealing a pristine leaf of white paper. Then she leaned over to a small pot and lifted a ballpoint pen.

She lay down on the sofa.

She wrote the name Samphire on the page, thinking about the family, where they were now, what they had been through. She clicked on the next podcast.

Today on the Living Their Life *podcast we are still looking at the famous, or should that be infamous, family who now reside in the castle on the cliff.*

It can't be easy being the children of two of the most beautiful people on God's earth. Who would want that pressure in their lives? And how are they coping now that they have left the bright lights of London behind and are living in a tenth-century castle with walls eight feet thick and four towers to protect them. Not to mention the ghost . . . oops, did I mention the ghost? Well, I'm too far away to be haunted by her, she walks the headland, romantically named the King's Reach, as she calls out for her husband who was lost at sea.

My question is, what else haunts the family? The relationships that we know about are bad enough. What else is hidden behind those walls?

I'm taking a look at the McQuarrie-Samphire family in detail, hopefully just a quick peek behind the façade as well as the castle gates because dear listeners, I can assure you that all is not well on the castle on the hill. The reasons they left London are . . . well, exactly as you would expect with a supermodel who has attracted all kinds of male attention over the years.

But what kind of attention has her running for the hills? Literally, in this case. Let's say that the tax man was happy. She's more scared of the kind of attention that warrants a couple of specialist security agents to stand at what's basically their front door. Who wants that for a life?

Not me.
Maybe not them.
From MisChief666 causing Mischief 24/7.
Laters

Then she looked at the Amazon reviews of Andrew Knox's books, which were full of praise. The books about Madeleine Smith, Oscar Slater and Peter Manuel had been thoroughly researched and had sold well. *Tipping the Scales*, the book about miscarriages of justice, had been sparked by the notorious Oscar Slater case. She stared at the picture of Knox, sitting on a log pile in wellington boots and Guernsey jumper. He was prematurely grey. He had his arm round a bright-eyed Border collie. She googled him, finding a rather good article and interview that traced his career along the typical trajectory of success, drink problem, divorce from all three wives, money issues and years trying to claw it back. She was still thinking about that when she noticed the drawing Aklen had been working on lying on the desk. Reaching over, she lifted it up and studied it, always impressed by the accuracy and detail of architectural plans. It was another layout of a tiny house. This one had a toilet with a shower that was less than a square metre. Then she looked at the bed, tucked high under the roof, and the tiny ladders, mere slats in the wall, that allowed access.

Tiny ladders.

She opened up the photographs Craigo had taken of Tron's pictures and was still looking at them, deep in thought, when Aklen came through with a chilled bottle of Oxford Landing Sauvignon Blanc. Things must be bad if Aklen thought that she needed that.

SEVENTEEN

When Caplan walked into the station at Pilcottie on Tuesday morning, two things in the news had already caught her eye. One was the hot weather update, with older people and those with certain medical conditions being warned to stay indoors. The other was her own picture, which was out there on social media, but this one was accompanied by another of her son, Kenny, looking worse for wear. It was an old picture of him, one from his wild days in Glasgow before he had chucked university, but in it he could have been anything from late teens to late twenties.

'Good picture of you this morning, ma'am. Nice top,' said Craigo.

'Thank you,' Caplan said, looking round, sensing her team didn't know what to say.

'Is he a wee arsehole then, yer boy?' asked Wattie, emerging from the hall, having come from the toilet, still doing his zip up.

'Och, if Wattie wasnae a cop he'd be in the pokey,' said Mackie, nodding at her boss to pledge her loyalty.

'Okay, let's not get bogged down by distractions. What are we doing today? Security footage? Drone footage? Any information about the state of Koi's knee? The state of her mind? McLeerie's whereabouts? Knox's activities? Come on, what do we have?'

Mackie was in first. 'Right, well, I've been speaking to Louise Kendall, the wedding planner. She was useful for background info but there was no sense of her being a confidante to Koi. She said that none of them have friends, said they don't get the concept. She and the chef seem to be the only two people that were inside the castle with any regularity, a few visits to cover the eight weddings they have hosted so far. All the other staff were called in by the catering company. Neither of them told me anything that we didn't know or suspect. I've located the last bride, we have a Zoom call with her in . . .' she looked at her watch, 'ten minutes.'

Caplan remained quiet. She felt guilty about not sharing with her team, but it was unofficial. The supporting evidence would come to light if Ryce's hypothesis was correct. And Ryce had said that she wasn't so sure that she would go on record. Caplan had to respect that.

'Have there been any sightings of the body?' asked McPhee.

'None, and that troubles me,' said Caplan.

'Well, I've tracked down Ted DeVries, Ecco's old boyfriend,' McPhee offered. 'He's a sound engineer now.'

Caplan watched her young constable closely, hoping he was going to say something that might offer EB some comfort. Or something Caplan could trade to get the young woman's trust.

'He wasn't easy to find online, I caught up with him at seven this morning. He's been offered a fair amount of dosh from the tabloids over the years for the story of his life with the Sunflower Girls. In an article published the week Ecco passed away, he said that the only way out of the Sunflower Girls was to die.'

'To die?' repeated Caplan.

'Jesus Christ,' muttered Mackie.

'He says he wasn't allowed into the inner sanctum. He says DeVries and Ecco were broken up by Pomeroy. He says Pomeroy is a bastard. Samphire is a bastard. And that Samphire is the father of the children. All of them except Rosie,' said McPhee. 'She's his daughter legally, but not biologically. EB and Tron are both Samphire's DNA. But legally only Cosmo, Rosie and Morrow would inherit. Not so sure about EB and Tron if Pip leaves everything to Samphire. Rhea's and Ecco's money has been swallowed up.'

'All the money might be channelled to Koi's three children?'

'Yes, it appears so.'

'DeVries was saying that he's tried to get in touch with EB over the years – you know, to pass on a few memories of Ecco. She refuses to have anything to do with him.'

'Does she?' Caplan said doubtfully. 'I wonder who told him that? Is he a good guy?'

'Who knows anything for sure?'

'Did he split with Ecco because she got pregnant with Gabe?'

'Yes.'

'Did she try to leave the Sunflower Girls, so Gabe seduces her, and ties her to the family forever?'

Caplan sat quietly for a moment, thinking over a theory that she didn't want to voice just yet. Ecco dead. Rhea dead. Had Koi been scared of something or somebody and planned her escape? If so, did she manage to do it? Did she have help? Caplan realised that she couldn't get a grip on the woman at all because she didn't know her; that face, that body, the good works, the smile, the beautiful, helpful nature – all that was available to the public. But she knew nothing about the books she read, the TV she watched. How bright was she? How gullible? Somebody in all this had a heart of solid stone. Was it her?

Caplan pondered what Koi McQuarrie would have done if Cosmo had got a girl pregnant and the girl didn't want to join the family. How far would she go to protect the brand? How far would Pomeroy go to safeguard the clan? She realised she had nearly quoted Knox and said the word 'cult'.

'Back to basics. How do we get access to Tron? To repeat, we need to find out for ourselves how he gets in and out. What's the smallest a rope ladder can be to get up a wall that height? It's not rocket science. Come on, guys. Craigo, you've been looking at Tron's drawings of the castle?'

'I'll reconcile them once I get a layout of the castle from a reliable source.'

'And how are you doing with that?'

'Getting nowhere.'

'I could ask Rosie to get a meeting with Tron – with an appropriate adult present and all that, ma'am,' said McPhee. Craigo and Wattie caught each other's eye. Something was going on.

'I have a rare clip of Koi talking, unguarded, off the cuff. Not an easy thing to find,' said McPhee. 'I'll get it on the laptop after the Zoom call. And we're expecting more security footage any minute.'

'It'd be good to hear her. We need to get a grasp on who she was. She exists as a media statement or somebody behind a castle wall. Nowhere else. What's this note stuck here?'

'You're meeting Daisy Evans's sisters tomorrow. Did you not see that yesterday?' asked Mackie.

'No,' snapped Caplan, suspecting it had not been there. 'Anything else? To get us moving?'

Mackie jumped. 'We've got our call with the last bride; she might give us a different perspective.'

'Who? Unterweger?'

'No, the last normal bride, not last celebrity bride. McPhee, give us a hand setting this up, will you. This is the bride, Betty Wilson. This was the wedding before the big wedding, on the first to the second of June.'

The screen lit up to reveal a woman in her late forties or early fifties, her pleasant face plump, with large blue eyes. She smiled with nervous humour.

'God, it's awful, isn't it? Koi, well, she saved our wedding. She was so nice, so full of life, you know?' She paused a little. 'It's my only wedding day; I wanted to have what I had always dreamed of. A Highland wedding. It was going to be a small affair, with relatives coming over from Canada.' She coughed. 'And at Torsvaig we could all be together, for three days, and we had the run of the place, except for the upper floor where the family live.'

'Did you expect to meet the family on that first day?' asked Mackie.

'Not at all. I wasn't sure they were there until we got the phone call that my hairdresser and make-up artist were stuck in traffic behind an accident on the lochside. I was going to be in my wedding photographs with bad make-up and frizzy hair. I was a basket case; Mum was knocking back the gin, Dad didn't understand what was going on. My dress was brilliant white, and the make-up girl had advised warm tones on my skin to stop me looking like the bride of Frankenstein. I was ready for calling off the wedding, then Mum talked to Louise to see if we could get married and have the meal, then come back and do the photographs with Mr Samphire on a different day.' She paused dramatically. 'There was a quiet knock at the door. I really snapped *"Yes?"* Who else is going to come in here and give me bad news? Koi McQuarrie came in. I nearly died. I was so stunned by . . . well, she was here. She was so pretty, beautiful clear skin and the brightest of blue eyes. She was so nice . . . I knew who she was, not a make-up artist or a hair stylist, but she's been at hundreds of photo shoots, right? And she starts talking – she was so calm, had me sitting at the mirror with me explaining how the hair was supposed to go, how the flowers were to be, how my make-up was supposed to be done. And Rosie, her daughter, came in with straighteners. They styled my hair, put the flowers in, then did the make-up. I had a wee glass of champagne to calm me down. I looked so good, couldn't believe it!' Betty laughed.

'Was Koi good at doing make-up?' asked Caplan.

'Oh yes, and she was funny. I was saying about my dress and my skin tone. Rosie said that they had done a TikTok video dressed up as the Addams Family, and that she enjoyed doing that kind of thing.' Betty laughed. 'She asked if Morticia was the look I was going for. I nearly said yes for the hell of it.

'Plus, we had paid a lot of money to get Mr Samphire to do the photographs.' She held out a small picture, held it up to the screen. 'There you go, I carry that around with me. It's beautiful, isn't it?' Mackie stepped up to the screen to get a closer look. 'When Mr Samphire appeared, he was definitely in charge, in a good way.

'But yes, Koi calmed me right down, saying there was nothing that couldn't be fixed. She sent Rosie off to get my mum a coffee and a sandwich to absorb the gin. She did my mum's make-up and then at the photographs at the end she came up and stood in with me and Colin, my new husband. He couldn't believe it, arm in arm with Koi McQuarrie. Here she was in my wedding picture!' She held up a framed photograph this time. Bride, groom and one of the most beautiful women in the world.

Caplan noted that Rosie, once again, had not been invited to appear in the picture.

'She was very down to earth . . . very nice. It's very sad she's gone. Do you know what happened to her?'

'We're still investigating. Did you meet any of the other family members?'

'No, I only spoke to Rosie, to Koi, to Mr Samphire, when we were talking about the photographs, the lights, the set-up. He was making sure we got the shots we wanted.'

'Accent?' asked Caplan.

'He was Londonish. She was softly spoken, Scottish. I thought she said she was from round that way. Or did I imagine that?'

Mackie had been typing furiously on her keyboard, then turned her laptop round to show Caplan that she'd found the TikTok video.

'Can we just back up a bit? Did you say that Rosie did the make-up for the Addams Family?' asked Caplan, causing the others to look at her.

Betty Wilson nodded. 'Yes, why?'

'It might be pertinent to the case, that's all. Thank you for your time. You've been very helpful,' said Caplan, leaving McPhee to do the final sign-off.

'You narrowed your eyes earlier, when we were talking about Koi dying.' Craigo turned in his seat. 'What do you know that we don't? What is it about the make-up, exactly?'

Caplan cursed herself. 'Okay, so this is information not to be shared or recorded. It's only a tenuous theory, and I was hoping the team would find evidence to back it up. That picture might be posed.' She pointed at the photo from Samphire's phone, pinned to the wall above a picture of Koi's face. She explained about the eyes, the blood, the distance of the body from the base of the cliff. 'But it doesn't make sense. Koi's still at the bottom of a cliff as if she had fallen just before he got there.'

'Maybe Tron scared her?'

'That would explain the scream.'

Craigo bit the corner of his mouth, then gave his slow blink. 'What are you saying now, ma'am? That she's still alive?'

'Until we find a body, we have to consider that a possibility. If some special make-up has been used – a long shot, I know – it could explain why the blood didn't wash off. If Rosie is the one who is skilled at using this stuff, I presume it's hers and in her possession. Would Rosie even notice if it had been used? She's not been out of the castle for God knows how long. Koi could have flung it to the waves.' Caplan shook her head, 'I can't imagine being cooped up with my family behind those walls and never getting a chance to go out.'

'Maybe that's why Koi did what she did, ma'am. Why she ended her life.' Craigo looked at her and smiled. 'Or do you think it was an illusion?'

'Fair and dandy, but no fucking use if yer still deid at the bottom o' a cliff.' Wattie said. 'And yer McPhee lad there looks like he gets on good wi the wee lassie Rosie. Least she's no' a psycho bitch like his last one.'

'Yes, she seems nice. I think she'd join me in Greggs for a caramel fudge doughnut,' said Mackie.

'And no just the wan, fae the look of the two of ye.'

'I wonder what kind of life she has,' asked Mackie. 'Callum, what were you saying about her not being allowed friends?'

McPhee looked up. 'Oh, it was just that she'd met a group of girls at a fashion show. She thought they were friends, until Pomeroy told her that they were using her to get into the family, to get her money, to get them access to the best clubs and onto the best invite lists. He banned her from seeing them. I wasn't sure if that was Rosie being naive or Pomeroy being protective or controlling. But Rosie was quite upset.'

'I'm just putting it out there, but how upset would you be finding out that you were adopted and that your "mother" had been lying to you for your entire life? And Koi might not have been thrown from the clifftop – it could have been a push, a loss of footing, and down she went.'

'And then the family cover it up.'

There was silence in the room. Caplan studied Mackie for a moment, then said what she was probably thinking. 'Rosie doesn't strike me as being that devious. I think if that had happened then she would have come running down that path screaming. Tron though, he's a different matter. The family have closed ranks for him before.

'I want to know what make-up was used and if Rosie still has it in her possession or if some of it has disappeared.' She saw the look on McPhee's face. 'Why don't you go, Callum? Ask her where she keeps it, follow her and call me when you find it.'

'Why?' asked McPhee. 'Why me?'

'Because if she's in possession of the make-up and templates, then Koi knew about them. Koi could have taken them and used them to falsify those facial injuries and . . . I don't know what then. And don't tell me she had no time to do it, I'm aware of that. But one step at a time, eh?'

'Here we are, ma'am. How good is that?' said Mackie.

The screen was dark, then the familiar finger snaps of the Addams Family theme tune popped out of the speakers, a spotlight picking up each hand. Then there was EB as Morticia, slinking around in the skin-tight black dress.

'Oh, look,' Mackie squealed in delight, as Cosmo appeared as Uncle Fester, and then Koi as Lurch, almost unrecognisable. EB was playing it seductive and straight. Koi and Cosmo could hardly stop laughing as they did the Addams Family dance.

Caplan leaned forward and pressed pause, pointing to Cosmo's face, and tapped on the screen. 'That's a white skull cap, anaemic-looking foundation and black teeth, but those eyes, the bits round there . . . that's sprayed on, I think. The same technique that Koi might have used to create the illusion of injury.' She pointed at the image of the supermodel at the bottom of the cliff. 'If Koi did that, she's bloody good.'

'Hence why I'm asking Rosie if she has that kind of thing in her possession?' smiled McPhee.

'Without distressing her,' emphasised Caplan. 'Don't make it obvious what we're thinking.'

'Aye, use yer chuffin' charm fur once,' said Wattie, but McPhee was already heading for the door.

'Can we watch it again, ma'am?' asked Mackie, zooming in on Cosmo.

'No. Do you have the audio clip that Callum found?' Caplan said, as the door closed behind McPhee's hasty exit.

'What's wi' him and the Rosie lassie?' asked Wattie.

'Nothing,' said Mackie and Caplan in unison.

'This is McPhee's audio clip about Koi's accent. Morrow mentioned it to the boss, and a friend of McPhee's mother put him onto it.' Mackie had her finger over the start button of a sound clip on the laptop. 'These are some kids at primary school talking to Koi. An *EastEnders* actress on tour was supposed to appear and do a Q and A, but she called off at the last minute,' Mackie explained to the blank faces of her colleagues. The soundtrack rolled, halfway through the question: '. . . is tall and skinny, what would you have been?'

As quick as a flash Koi's answer came back: 'Poor.' There was laughter, the audience sounding in awe of their superstar visitor. 'To be serious, I'd probably work with animals. Maybe a vet nurse – I'm not bright enough to be a vet.' More laughter. An older voice asked her if she had animals at home. 'We had a dog, and an old horse who lived in fine style. That was all we could have in central London, but now I'm home, we have a couple of dogs and maybe we'll get some more horses.'

'And who would you like to be?' asked a voice that sounded very young indeed.

'Who do you want to be?' Koi asked back, a little unnerved by the innocence of the question, maybe because she herself was a construct.

'Elsa from *Frozen*!' the young voice said.

'Do you? I think that'd be a fun person to be. But me? Well, I think I'd be Rapunzel with long, long hair and my prince would climb up the Rapunzel steps, and . . . do the dishes! Who here helps with the dishes at home?'

'Now I'm home?' repeated Caplan, pausing the recording.

'And that's a Scottish accent – it's had the rough edges taken off but it's defo from up here,' Mackie said.

'More east coast though?'

Mackie shook her head. 'Play it again. Just listen to that – she's local. She sounds like that posh woman who works in Greggs. It's the roll of the r. I'm good with accents, ma'am, she's from up the coast from here.'

'And what the hell are Rapunzel steps?'

Craigo was busy. 'Googling ma'am, I'm googling.' He was quiet for a moment. 'Okay, ma'am, it's any way of getting up and down a wall, a covert ladder, but you can only see them if you know where to look. *L'escalier de l'amour* to give them their proper name. The French use them for climbing into their lady's window. It's very interesting, ma'am, just a series of hand holds, side pulls they're called, perfectly positioned for the reach of an average man or woman. Once your hands have found one, it's easy to move onto the next step. The weight is supported through the feet, but the stability is through the hands . . . you see, it's very easy and so . . .' he looked around.

'And?' asked Caplan,

'Then I was thinking about the Queen Mother. Was it the Queen Mother? Somebody royal had a castle with a monkey in it.'

'Craigo, what are you getting at, exactly?'

'There was that case in Glasgow, the house with the extra floor where the kidnapped wee boy lived for years.'

'Johnny Clearwater? If there's a way out, there's a way in. I see what you mean. Do you think Torsvaig has Rapunzel steps?'

'It's a castle, ma'am. It'll have a labyrinth of passageways and dungeons, and things that nobody knows about. Except Tron.' Craigo leaned forward, waving his pencil in the air as he spoke. 'Do you know what might be going on here?'

Wattie swore and asked the Lord to give him patience.

'That Koi made it back into the castle after climbing the cliff?' asked Caplan.

'With her bad knee? Either in bare feet or heels?' Mackie was incredulous.

'Maybe she exaggerated how bad her knee was. She was dancing at the party, and she left the castle without a limp. But it's a long way up to the King's Reach, and where the hell was she intending to go?'

'Was there another man in her life?' Craigo looked thoughtful.

'Nobody we can find. And how would she manage any liaison?'

'So where else could she be? She's being looked after by somebody after a bad fall? Who?' asked Caplan.

'You mean she survived the fall, and somebody got her back up into the castle without anybody seeing, like Rapunzel in reverse maybe?' said Mackie.

'I would like to know how long she has been pole dancing. If we doubt her sore knee, maybe she could run and walk perfectly well. If we doubt the sore knee, was she a strong enough swimmer to beat the currents and get beyond the rocks before the drone was up?' said Craig.

'Who was chasing the GP's notes? Who was doing that for me?'

'Nothing re GP. He quoted patient confidentiality but added he never saw her. Pomeroy said there was a referral to a knee specialist in London where she had an MRI scan, looking for a tear in the medial meniscus. The results were inconclusive. She got that injury when she tripped on her dress – it had been raining on the flagstones, she took a right tumble. He was happy to offer that information.'

'I was thinking more about upper-body strength and hand grips on a pole. Could she have put a rope down, got to the bottom and then climbed back up it? That's the only thing I can think of. Climbing ropes nowadays are incredibly strong and very thin, easy to transport. But the overall question is why. Why would she do that . . . why would she do that to her family?' asked Caplan.

'And what would she tie the rope onto?' said Craigo.

'I think if I had that family, I might be doing all kinds of things to protect my mental health. Did she have another agenda?' Caplan pressed the palms of her hands into her eyes. 'I think we're being manipulated by the family for the sake of the media. Everything is a game to them. I think Agatha Christie's disappearance was a genuine psychotic episode, but this does have some echoes of that.'

'I think you mean, ma'am, that this could have a totally different interpretation if we consider that Ecco Middlemass and Rhea Doonican are both dead, with the Sunflower Company receiving all their funds. If Koi dies, all her funds go to the Sunflower Company. That means to Samphire and Pomeroy.'

'Pomeroy's killing the goose that lays the golden egg.'

'Or does everything that she's done become more valuable because she's dead?'

'Or believed to be dead,' muttered Craigo.

'Thae pictures oh her at the bottom? She's deid! Ah know yer pal has the university and all that, but I know a deid lassie when I see one.' Wattie sat back, arms folded over his pot belly. 'Aw that stuff on her face is neither here nor there. The lassie is deid! She didnae get oot that water, thae currents'll skin you on thae rocks.'

'She's a lot cleverer than you are though,' said Mackie.

'Where did she go? And could she make it up that cliff? And down the cliff before she went up?' Craigo gave his slow blink again, then looked at Caplan. 'I'm just saying, ma'am, that it's a pity we don't know a fit, thin lady of Koi's age who could see if it was possible to get up and down the cliff, before we think about getting her into the castle. And do it all in the time Koi had to do it.'

'Aye, Ah'd like to see that, DCI Caplan, ma'am,' said Wattie. Everything about his look and his tone of voice was a challenge.

'I beg your pardon, DS Craigo?'

'You wouldn't need to wear the frock, ma'am.'

'Oh naw, ye need the frock for realism,' argued Wattie.

Caplan glared at him for some time, and continued to do so as she spoke to Craigo. 'I've no head for heights. I'd fall to my death and you lot would have to work for a change.'

'I see what you're saying, ma'am, but it would remove one big doubt in everybody's mind, one question they'd have at the inquest.'

Wattie shook his head and blew out his cheeks. 'You'd need some level of protection and expertise. Ah can get the lads at the climbing club to climb it wi you, they do the mountain rescue. They'd pick you up if you fell off.'

'I'm not doing that.' She looked at the three pairs of eyes staring at her and realised that she probably was.

'I'll get that organised for tomorrow morning.' Wattie could not contain his glee.

Joe Perkins was leaning on the main gate of Torsvaig Castle, his arms folded, chewing a piece of grass in the corner of his mouth, a man relaxing in the sun. As Caplan and Craigo approached, he lifted his sunglasses to rest them on the top of his head and placed his hand on the lever of the gate, but he didn't open it for them.

'I've been told not to let you in. I've been told to stay out here.'

'And we've had a phone call from a member of our team that he's being obstructed in his duties, so . . .' Caplan said. She was guessing that Perkins would be on the side of law and order.

'That would be Callum, then.' Perkins lowered his voice. 'Pomeroy's just mad that you took him down to Pilcottie and that

Wattie's gloating about it. Mr Pomeroy likes the comfort of his own office. Maybe if you flashed your warrant card at me and insisted, I might have to let you in. I'm not ex-job like Pickering, I don't really know what rights you have.'

There was an urgency about the way he opened the gates that make Caplan and Craigo exchange a quizzical glance. As they neared the bailey, they heard Pomeroy's voice raised in anger.

They could smell burning.

Caplan pointed. She'd be quicker going through the castle, so sent Craigo round the outside of the Great Hall. She was panicking that something had happened to McPhee. She had sent him up here on his own, his mind confused with his trauma and his thoughts about 'poor Rosie', and all Caplan could think of was a young woman pleased to have a serial killer for a father and the mocking way she had said, *yer wee bun*. Rosie, like the rest of them, was a product of her environment and her upbringing.

She burst into the bailey, seeing McPhee at the patio doors, his mobile phone in his hand. Pomeroy was standing at the firepit, ripping up Tron's drawings and throwing them into the flames, one by one, while ranting abuse at the boy. Caplan caught 'fucking stupid', 'fucking useless' and then 'no wonder nobody wants you', then 'useless' and 'turd', then 'even your own mother'.

That was enough. 'Stop this right now.' Caplan walked over, warrant card held out, trying to keep her anger in check. She stood in front of Pomeroy, looking round, assessing the scene. Taking in the tableau, she saw Rosie, watching with her arms folded, a smug smile on her face. Rosie stared back at her defiantly. Turning around, stepping out of the way of the smoke spirals, Caplan's eyes passed over her young constable, his face immobile but his hand, holding the phone, moved ever so slightly.

Then she saw Tron, tears rolling down his face as he stared at his drawings burning in the flames.

Pomeroy had his hands on his hips, sweating profusely and breathing hard, trying to let the fury within him calm.

'This stops now,' Caplan said very quietly. 'Tron? Do you want us to take you away from here? I can get Callum McPhee to take you anywhere you want to go.'

The pasty face looked up, a small shake of the head. Then he darted off, past the constable and through the patio doors, no doubt to hide in some dark corner of the castle.

Craigo ran into the bailey and stopped abruptly. Caplan looked from him to Pomeroy, then to Rosie. Nobody spoke. The drawings crackled and curled in the fire as they burned. Then she saw McPhee lift his phone to film the reality of the perfect family.

'We'll return to this later.' She stepped up to Pomeroy, their faces inches apart. 'Just so you know, we've filmed that, all of it. Threatening language, verbally abusing a vulnerable young man. I guess the shares in the Sunflower Linen Company might plummet in value if that footage finds its way onto social media.'

Pomeroy didn't apologise. The stand-off lasted a long moment, then he turned and walked away. Rosie watched him go, then she, totally ignoring Caplan and McPhee, went up the two steps and into the shadows behind the patio doors.

Caplan thought about following them, trying to track down Tron in his sanctuary in the castle, but if he didn't want to be found he knew best how to stay hidden.

Instead she looked at the fire. The drawing of Koi in her chair with her dog and her book was curling and blackening, slowly succumbing to the flames.

'Let's go back to Pilcottie. Craigo, can you write this up? I think McPhee should go home, as will I. I think I want to speak to my family to get some sense of normality.'

EIGHTEEN

The three guys from the climbing club had been at the King's Reach since six-thirty a.m. and were sipping tea from a flask. Joe Perkins, the security man, was with them, helping them navigate the cliff edge, pointing down, to the left and to the right. Around them, to Caplan's untrained eye, was enough rope to hang a herd of elephants. The crew looked young, relaxed, tanned, as if they never got stressed about anything. While Caplan was impressed by the amount of equipment they had, she wasn't that pleased to see that Spencer had signed off on this operation.

During her sleepless night, many things had been running round her head: about the emotional abuse of Tron, the destruction of Koi – as that was how it had seemed to her. And about that final hug she had given the troubled youngster before she came up to the King's Reach. If Koi could do this climb, then she could too. If that woman, who appeared to have everything, had to force herself to do this to get away from that life, then so could she.

And Aklen had thought it would be a great story to tell the grandchildren.

Gary and Donnie, who ran the Hard Rock Climbing School, were the experts. Gary reckoned they could get down the cliff within a few minutes. It was the getting up again that would be hard. 'Would she not be better using a prusik knot?' he asked.

'I doubt Koi would know what a prusik knot was if she tripped over it. What we are testing is if it's possible with only a knotted rope,' said Perkins, looking a little concerned. 'Do the family know you are doing this?' he asked Caplan quietly.

'We are outside the castle wall, and if they're interested, they can ask us,' said Caplan, 'though to be honest it's pretty obvious that we are re-enacting something, that's all they need to know for now.'

They secured Caplan with a harness and gave her two pairs of very good gloves. They gave her a single rope knotted at various intervals.

'We've found nothing to tie it onto, so we've put a TR, a top rope, in. There are five anchors for the two of you, so if one falls you're okay. Keep the rhythm, just get a rhythm in your head and go with that,' Perkins said, plonking a hard hat on her and strapping it tightly under her chin. It was heavy.

'Joe has shown us where he thinks she fell, so we've our ropes beside you. We'll be abseiling down, then coming back up the ropes, so we'll be right there.'

'And Gary here is controlling your rope,' said Donnie reassuringly, then added, 'If you fall, it's likely you'll swing away. He'll let you dangle for a bit, then let us know if you want brought up, but you should be able to get back on the rope.'

'This is where she went down,' said Gary. 'The headland juts out, so you have a negative space. The rope will swing under the cliff when you get to that point, just keep going.' Perkins smiled at her. 'You'll be fine. Starting is the worst bit. You've faced worse,' he said, with a wry smile, and she wondered what he knew about the incident at the firepit. Then he added, quietly, 'I saw Tron on the top of the chapel late yesterday. He seemed quiet. Calm.'

Caplan nodded. The boy had been on her mind.

'Being splatted over the rocks will be the worst bit,' said a voice, cackling. Toni Mackie had turned up to witness her discomfort.

'No rocks here,' said Gary, 'only smooth sand, but still, try not to hit it at high speed.'

She backed up to the top of the cliff then felt the weight of her body descending into fresh air as she tried to feel for the first knot. Mentally she couldn't do it. No matter how much her brain told her about the safety harness, and that she was in the hands of experts, her fear was too much.

'Gary? Just give her a bit of slack.'

They decreased the tension on the safety rope so she wasn't fighting against it as she leaned over to find the first knot, gripping it hard. She realised the benefits of the thin gloves as she slithered her legs over the top, thinking, again, how desperate Koi must have been to do this.

She dangled for a moment, not able to catch the rope with her feet.

Then, without looking down, she jammed it against the rock face, and managed to bring her feet together, the knot in between. She was amazed at the weight it took off her arms. Slowly she felt down for the next knot and gripped it, the words 'as if her life depended on it', coming into her mind, and down she went, the rope slipping through the instep of her boots.

It was quiet, strangely so, and immediately dark when she swung into the shadow of the overhang. She was aware of the two guys beside her, but didn't want their help, instruction or interference. She was concentrating on her descent, hand over hand. Undo feet, let feet come together and slip hand over hand, feet come together and slip. It was easy to get into the rhythm. She dared not look down, but knew the cliff face she was now looking at, given its appearance, was low enough to be covered by water at high tide, so she was already nearing the bottom.

Then her heel hit solid but yielding ground.

She was standing on terra firma.

'Great,' said Gary. 'All you have to do now is climb back up again.'

Caplan smiled, genuinely proud of herself. She looked up at the blue of the sky and the overhang of the rock face above her, thinking that the noise in her ear was the breeze echoing around the water and the cliff.

She tried the reverse process and got about four feet from the ground when the burning pain in her arms would let her go no further. She dangled there, helpless and spinning in the air. She saw Gary's feet come into view beside her, then his hand indicating that she was to go back down.

Then she saw the drone, filming every move.

She thanked Gary very much for the offer to pull her up, and explained that she'd like to keep her feet on terra firma.

Gary gave her a wink and said, 'You're braver than I thought. I had money on you refusing at the last moment.'

'See you at the top,' said Caplan, deciding to jog along the firm sand. The sea breeze tempered the early morning heat a little and for the first time in the investigation she could appreciate the beauty of the place. She could see why Tron liked to sit up high and just gaze on nature's beauty. Something people had done for millennia, she guessed, although this generation with their nose stuck in their phone screen, maybe not so much.

She had a good look at where Koi had landed, the rocks now grey, the drying wrack already attracting flies. Maybe she'd see something different without Knox wittering on. But the landscape unsurprisingly stayed the same. There was no wee hidey hole, to use one of Emma's favourite words. No gap in the rock face, no recess in the cliff wall where Koi could have crawled and waited, away from the battering waves while they searched frantically for her thirty feet above. Her arms were aching and tired, but she'd managed the climb down relatively easily. And she was reasonably confident that if she'd been used to climbing, she could have made it back up again. If Caplan had six months' notice that her life would depend on a climb like that, and like Koi, had access to a small gym, she'd make sure she was strong enough to do it. Like Caplan, Koi was slim; there wasn't that much weight to lift.

As she went through the woods she mulled over the beautiful seclusion of the place and how irritated she would be when it was invaded by a wedding party. Caplan had felt annoyed at her own family interrupting their little haven just outside Cronchie. The red Hilux was waiting for her in the car park. She jogged over and jumped in. Craigo just nodded, strangely silent, as if he hadn't quite approved of what had gone on.

'Well, that was an experience,' she said, 'but not one I'd like to repeat.'

Craigo put the Hilux in reverse and glanced in the rear-view mirror. 'But what did it prove exactly?'

Caplan felt like pointing out that it had been his idea but instead she said, 'That Koi knew weeks, months, ahead that she was going to do it; she wasn't a climber, but she turned herself into one.'

Caplan and Craigo found the two sisters sitting at the back of the café in the pedestrianised part of Oban town centre. Each sister was cradling a cup of tea – a pot for two sat on the red table cover in front of them. One sister was old before her years. Her blouse was buttoned up to her neck, grey hair curled perm tight, and she had a light rain jacket on the table beside her despite the current heatwave. The other was dressed too young in a pair of yellow dungarees and an LGBT T-shirt. Her pleats of brown hair were streaked with bright-red highlights. Despite that, anybody could tell they were sisters: they had the same brown eyes, the same steady stare that evidenced a defiant character. Caplan said hello, asking if they wanted anything else; her sergeant was getting a bacon roll anyway.

They both relaxed. It couldn't be an easy thing, to be reminded of the death of a much loved, much younger sister.

'Thank you for getting in touch.' Caplan moved the cutlery that was directly in front of her to the side. She had prepared this speech. 'I'm DCI Caplan and I'm investigating a death at the cliffs just along from Limpetlaw Sands. I believe you felt you had some information for us?'

'I'm Heather.' A hand with a single wedding band, a small stone in the engagement ring, flew to her chest, 'I'm not sure we're doing the right thing.' She then added dismissively, 'This is Ivy, she thinks you need to know.'

Caplan nodded and said nothing, letting the story unfold, mostly from Ivy's sympathetic point of view. Ivy had been closer to her young sister and had helped her through her troubled times. Heather, who was a teenager by the time Daisy came along, was more of the mind that Daisy might have been better standing on her own two feet, and if the rest of the family hadn't constantly indulged her, she might have been a bit more responsible. Ivy was more indulgent of her little sister's rather chaotic lifestyle as she moved from rental accommodation to rental accommodation, a series of badly paid jobs, mostly bar work, which were beneath her capability, and a chain of men who lived off her. One of those men had introduced her to cocaine, and to feed the habit she had started dealing. She tended to move in with a new boyfriend after dating for only a couple of months, then would reappear a few weeks later, begging for the use of a spare room from whichever sister was geographically closer. All the time, promising she'd never do it again.

'That's why she was staying in the caravan. Angus McLeerie had found out where she lived so we moved her into a site. We thought he wouldn't find her there, in winter.'

'Out of season and very cheap,' said Heather. 'Ann, the owner of the site, was away for September to December, just back a week when Daisy's body was found. Ann even gave her a few pounds for cleaning the vans ready for the new season. And we told her, until we were blue in the face, that she wasn't to tell any of her men friends where she was. And she does!' Heather threw her hands up in disgust.

'She started to invite McLeerie back,' explained Ivy. 'To be fair, we thought that he was different, he had a steady job.'

'He was a junkie,' snapped Heather.

'He had a steady job, he looked after her. For a year, we never heard a cheep from her apart from happy phone calls, you know? We thought this guy was okay.'

Heather snorted. 'It was always okay until next time.'

'She thought Andy was different. On that night he followed her to the caravan. We think she tried to get away from him, along the beach. He must have battered her head against the rocks and then left her for the tide.'

'Andy?' asked Caplan.

'Yes Andy,' said Ivy. 'Why?'

'But that's why we got in touch. He killed her on the Five Sisters at Limpetlaw. And now you have another woman, dead on the beach in the same place.'

'The fatal accident report said that she sustained injuries from repeated impact on the rocks,' said Caplan and took a long sip of her tea, letting that statement settle.

'We didn't say he was daft,' muttered Heather.

Ivy shook her head. 'But that is where the model was found, the Sunflower Girl? You see what we are getting at here? And now he's out after killing his wife.'

'How do you know he's out?'

'Because he was standing at the bottom of my allotment on Thursday. I'm sure it was him. Twenty years older, a bit tubby. He doesn't scare me. Never did.'

'Was it just the name Limpetlaw or do you know of any connection between McLeerie and Koi McQuarrie? McLeerie and the Sunflower Girls?' asked Caplan.

'Just the place. The journalist, Andrew Knox, phoned and said you might want to know.'

Caplan nodded, her mind dwelling on a fantasy of flinging Knox off a cliff.

Ivy explained, 'McLeerie was physically abusing Daisy, she never said but we knew it was him. I'd put money into her bank account so she could travel to Liverpool where I lived at the time. She was getting a train on the twenty-third, but she never made it. We think that she'd gone out to get her laundry. Ann, the owner . . .'

'Ann McIlroy . . .'

'Well, they'd had a chat earlier that evening. Daisy wanted late-night access to the laundry because she was leaving soon.'

'Wanted to use the tumble dryer, last minute as usual,' Heather tutted. 'She didn't want to stay with me in case she put my family in danger too.'

'You didn't ask her,' Ivy nodded, 'and Liverpool was that bit further away. She thought she'd be safer there. She nearly made it. Twelve hours later and he'd never have found her.'

A silence fell upon the table as they shuffled along to let Craigo in with his tray, a tea, a coffee and two bacon rolls.

'I didn't ask for one,' said Caplan.

'I didn't get you one – they're both for me, ma'am,' Craigo said, smiling at his companions.

Ivy placed an envelope on the table, pushing it towards Caplan with a fingertip. Caplan picked it up and took out three pictures of a pretty, dark-haired girl with huge brown eyes.

'She's a very pretty young lady,' remarked Craigo between bites, covering Caplan being rendered speechless at seeing a picture of Rosie McQuarrie-Samphire in another incarnation.

'She was, unfortunately,' said Heather, wincing slightly as Craigo bit into his roll, a slice of bacon escaping from the corner of his mouth. 'She deserved better.'

'They always do. I'm sorry, I'll let you know what happens,' reassured Caplan. 'I'll look at it again. I promise.'

'Can you . . . well . . . we think that Daisy might have had a baby,' said Ivy.

Heather butted in. 'We've wasted enough of your time.' She nudged Ivy.

Ivy remained sitting. 'She was away for eight or nine months. They said at the post-mortem that she'd had a baby. And we knew nothing about it. Ann McIlroy was away for the last few months of Daisy's stay in the caravan. Can you tell us if that's true? And what happened to the baby? It's been over twenty years.' She wiped a tear away. 'It'd be nice to know what became of him or her.'

Heather rammed her chair back from the table and went to pay.

Ivy mouthed the word 'Please,' and made a praying gesture with her hands as she left.

Caplan picked up her mobile and stabbed out Knox's number. 'Mr Knox, DCI Christine Caplan here. I'm not, under any circumstances, doing any investigation into any connection between the deaths of Daisy Evans, Sharon Baird or Carol McLeerie. Thank you.' She punched the 'end call' button with her forefinger, wishing she had a handset to slam down.

'Angus McLeerie worked for the bank, very helpful on the mortgage help line. Daisy was a minor drug dealer, she was always trouble, had a history of—'

'Don't blame the women, Craigo.'

'I'm not, ma'am. I'm wondering why such a mild-mannered bank clerk would kill—'

'Three times? Rage, Craigo. Just rage.'

'He was only charged with one. Not Daisy. He either walked her down to the shore and battered her head against the rocks, or she walked into the sea and sustained similar injuries. The pathologist could not determine what the power behind the impact to her skull was. Power of the sea or power of the human hand.'

'And then Carol McLeerie – he killed her.'

'And admitted it, immediately. Phoned the cops himself after calling an ambulance.'

'And Sharon Baird? She gets dragged across a golf course and murdered.'

'He was never charged with that. Now he's out. And writing a book. He applied for parole. Somebody gave him a roof over his head.'

'I should get on to Spencer, as McPhee said.'

'Maybe Knox does know something that we need to know, but humble pie never tastes good, does it? You need some reason to reopen the investigation.' Craigo began tapping on the middle of the three photographs, where Daisy was as old as she ever got to be. 'It's obvious, ma'am. We have a Heather, an Ivy, a Daisy, and now we have a Pearl Lilac Rose.' Craigo narrowed his eyes, peering at the counter with the cakes. 'Interesting.'

'During the year when they didn't see her, and she was only in touch by phone? I don't think I'd go home and explain to Heather that I was pregnant. I'll speak to Ryce. Bring your roll with you if you want. And Craigo?'

'Yes, ma'am?'

'Do you have any cousins called Angus?'

'Yes, two. Both men, ma'am.'

'Does Angus ever get shortened to Andy?'

'No. That's my cousin Andrew.'

'That's one of the more normal things about your family. I wonder why they shortened Angus to Andy.'

'Unless there was an Andy and an Angus?'

Back at Pilcottie, Caplan got Mackie to phone Cosmo and ensure that all was quiet at Torsvaig. Then she sent a text to both Ryce and Spyck, asking for some information. It was Spyck who called back after a short delay.

'You know, DCI Caplan, normally when an SIO gets in touch and asks for historical PM reports, something in my heart dies,' said Spyck, munching away at something, making Caplan wish that she had eaten a bacon roll at Oban. 'The answer is yes. Daisy Evans had given birth to a female child, less than a year before her death.' Spyck shoved a Malteser in her mouth and washed it down with Irn-Bru. 'Is that what you expected?'

'Yes.'

'Oh. I like to surprise people. But this time you are obviously on trend. That information has been requested twice this week.'

'Who by?'

'Both Detective Super Spencer and Cold Case in Glasgow.'

NINETEEN

DCI Caplan was watching the clock, waiting for a Zoom call that Detective Superintendent Spencer had arranged, and he was late. As she sipped her tea, watching the panel on her screen, waiting for a familiar face to appear, she listened to another podcast on her phone, with its familiar phrases and nasty nuances.

Today on the Living Their Life *podcast we are once more looking at the famous, or should I say infamous, family who now reside at Torsvaig Castle.*

Where does it all end? With the first scandal? With the first wrinkle? Burn-out? Or do they fade away?

It looks like the McQuarrie-Samphire business model might be sinking. Well, sinking is the wrong word, it's more contracting. Following the money, as I have been doing, it would seem that the riches are making their way along the web, back to the spider.

And there is a lot of money. There's the Sunflower Linen Company – the home of the tediously boring Little White Dress. There are the images of those three women, now dead, but those pictures never stopped earning. Look at the estates of Marilyn Monroe, of James Dean.

And the children, of very mixed motherhood but single fatherhood. They were all signed up at a young age to the company and that company still owns them. Don't argue legal documents signed by their parent or guardian, or conflict of interest. This is family.

This is The Family.

But it's not a family tree, this is a family circle and it's the money that goes round and round and Philip Pomeroy takes a cut whenever it passes Go.

And his lover.

But you've figured that out by now, haven't you?

Of course you have – they are the last ones standing.

From MisChief666 causing Mischief 24/7.

Laters.

Caplan saw the screen change on her monitor and Detective

Superintendent Spencer's face appeared on the Zoom call. He was sitting at his desk, the Police Scotland logo behind him. His office was tastefully designed in frosted glass and beech wood. Through the clearer glass of his office wall, Caplan could see a roomful of officers, typing away, ears to their phones, having meetings in corners, chatting over the water cooler. Doing the sort of thing, living the sort of life that she used to.

Her eyes drifted over the room at Pilcottie, to the laptop, the wallpaper and the pictures of Cosmo Samphire above the picture of EB's butt cheeks.

'You seem to be making quite a stir up there.'

Caplan took a mouthful of tea. 'My working theory is that Koi McQuarrie got down the cliff, then posed at the bottom for that photograph. Ryce and Spyck both think that the blood was make-up. Difficult to prove, but it certainly didn't behave the way recent bleeding behaves after a few waves of seawater have washed over it. And . . .' She paused.

'And?'

'Ryce and the tech forensic guys have software to reconstruct the fall, calculating weight and wind and updraught. Each time the simulation has the body much further out. Every time. They could not replicate where Koi landed.'

Spencer didn't respond at first. 'Food for thought.'

'And, sir, I really need to know about Angus McLeerie. He leaves a trail of dead women behind him, and he could be Rosie McQuarrie-Samphire's father.'

'Ahh, now that is overstepping your remit and—'

Caplan interrupted. 'I think you and I both know that's not true, sir. Was that said in a budgeting meeting? I'm fed up saying that we need to investigate to find the evidence and yet—'

'You need the evidence to get the funding. You are working on the Koi McQuarrie case, nothing else.'

'So why are you and a Cold Case team already reinvestigating Daisy Evans?' Caplan stared at him. Through the internet and from a distance of a hundred miles, it worked.

'Arrange an interview with McLeerie. Prepare well and don't waste it. Make sure he has advice and representation. If you find evidence that warrants a further investigation, then it joins the long queue at Cold Case.'

'Could it make its way to the front of that queue?'

'It could.'

'Thank you, sir.'

'Before you go, I've had a very short conversation with the Samphire family lawyer, and they want to be left alone to mourn. You are annoying them. The lawyer told me that Mr Pomeroy caught you snooping without a search warrant.'

'Pursuing inquiries, sir. And we were invited.'

'No more without a lawyer present.'

'The lawyer will be acting on the advice of Pomeroy, i.e., the one person who is exerting harmful control on vulnerable members of the family. My argument is that we ignore that legal advice and gain access by the consent of another family member.'

'Jesus.'

'My team will back me up on that. If we're invited in by a family member then we're clear. In fact, I'll send you something sir. Just to show you who we're dealing with. And also, the family, the company, do not own any of the land outside the castle wall so they cannot dictate what we can and cannot do.'

She reached for the phone and a minute later Spencer was watching the tortured face of Tron as his artwork burned.

'You've made your case.' Spencer put his hands up in surrender. 'Any connection between McLeerie and the other Sunflower Girls?'

'No. Just that Daisy Evans might be the birth mother of Rosie McQuarrie-Samphire. So the only connection leads to Koi.'

'Might be?'

'I refer to our previous conversation. No definite proof, but there's the name, the timing. I trust Pomeroy as much as I trust my cat with a field mouse. All he needs is social media to believe that McLeerie is Rosie's dad. And he'll do that by denying it.' She took a deep breath and tried to sound nonchalant. 'I've requested the notes on the forensics at the caravan. It was reported by an eyewitness that there was somebody in there.' She didn't let Spencer reply. 'And, what about Andrew Knox? If Pomeroy wants to make the news, he literally makes up the news. Why does he need a journalist in his back pocket? Especially one so local. The family are more Aspen than Appin. Why was he so keen on Rhea's death being thought of as an accidental overdose? Good PR, but was it suicide? Overdose? Ecco Middlemass fell from a height, heart stopped by a high level of circulating cocaine.'

'Can you connect those two incidents?'

'The main players were present. The money all moves in the same way.'

Spencer nodded his head a little. 'Do you think that somebody murdered Rhea and Ecco? And if so, who? Who is the brains, the ego, behind it all: Koi, Gabriel or Pomeroy?'

'You've seen the video, what do you think?'

'Don't spoil my illusions, Caplan. Koi was a beautiful strong woman who did the correct moral thing – the way she took Tron and EB on board, that was a lifelong commitment.'

'Maybe she was or maybe the kids were foisted on her for Pomeroy to . . . exploit, really.'

'But she still has them with her. Would you do that? And Rosie's now going to be touted as the daughter of the serial killer? I'm not convinced.'

'I think Larkin got it wrong; I don't think your parents fuck you up – pardon my French – it's the kids that fuck up the parents. And that's what you have to look at.' Caplan continued, 'It's interesting that they called the company, I mean the company they bought was called the Sunflower Linen Company. It remains that way, so it's not intrinsically bound to them. It's not the Koi Company, or the Rhea Doonican Foundation. Pomeroy masterminds it all. They were like the three musketeers, all for one and one for all.'

'So, no matter who dies, the money goes in the main pot?'

'Exactly,' Caplan said. 'I've read what I can about the deaths. I just think the cases bear similarities. I'm getting the sugar-coated version from the Koi fan club up here, but there's a background of recreational drugs. I'm seeing mental illness, an eating disorder right in my face, everything seems to be controlled in an attempt to make life perfect. That kind of pressure makes folk buckle.'

'Do you think Koi buckled and tried to escape?'

'I find myself hoping that she did. I'm hoping she placed herself at the bottom of the cliff for that photograph. What happened then? I'm not sure. But if she's been watching Pomeroy for the last twenty years, she's had a masterclass in getting the media to believe what is not true.'

Spencer put his head back and looked at the ceiling for a long while. 'I'll trust your investigative team and look forward to reading the report. What about Ecco Middlemass?'

'I think she had the toughest life before they met up. Addiction's never easy, and it's expensive, it makes people unpredictable. I think all three of them were vulnerable when they became the Sunflower Girls. With Ecco and Rhea that vulnerability might be addiction. But I think Koi came from the back end of nowhere and was naive maybe.'

'Okay, DCI Caplan, go forward as you see fit. I'll back you if Pomeroy kicks off.'

'Just tell him you've seen that clip of film. He really won't want that going viral.'

Caplan sipped a cup of tea and eased out the crick in her neck. She was reviewing Cosmo's tape of the party, taking it slowly and trying to see something, anything, that they had missed before. Caplan had been at it for over half an hour and was going cross-eyed. It was a young person's job, that obsession with watching people, being interested in every move and every gesture. Watching Koi was easy. An elegant woman in a long white dress, her blond hair twirled round the top of her head, enough of it teased down over her ears to frame her beautiful face. How was life when you were that good-looking – was it a blessing or a curse? It must have made some things easier, and others almost impossible. Samphire, the man she had married twice, the man who had fathered her friend's child. The man who had been with their manager for years before he met Koi. Had she been another career move for him? For them?

Caplan knew her life was in a bit of disorder at the moment, but she couldn't imagine Aklen fathering a child with another woman, and her staying friends with that woman. How could that not have an impact on a friendship? Yet Ecco Middlemass and Koi seemed as close as they ever had been, for the very short time Ecco was alive after EB was born. Caplan repeated that phrase to herself; the *very* short time Ecco was alive.

Was that significant?

She watched Koi, now dancing near the firepit. Tina Charles, 'I Love to Love'. The Greek goddess was spinning around – elegant, beautiful, yet somehow very human, very approachable.

She drew the eye. The music stopped and Koi shimmied out of shot, then returned with something in her hand, some treats for the dogs from the buffet. Then she bent over and gave the old dog a big hug. The video moved off closer to the firepit where Pomeroy was sitting holding a very large glass of red wine, apparently telling Rosie, standing with her back to the firepit, a long story. Swinging back, Koi was still with the dogs. It struck Caplan that Koi was taking a long time to say goodbye to Cawdor and Thane.

Then there was that hug between Koi and Tron. She'd never seen him respond in this way to another human being yet here he was, like a scared wee boy cuddling his mum, which might be exactly what he was. Mackie was right, he was holding on to Koi as if his life depended on it.

Then somebody shouted 'Mum!' Cosmo started dancing to 'Sweet Caroline', the chorus of do do do's floated all over the party. The view of the firepit flames was interrupted by arms and hands waving in the air, the singing more enthusiastic than it was tuneful.

The person filming was distracted by something. Koi was now visible only at the edge of the screen, then she disappeared completely only to float back in when they panned back to the dance floor under the stars.

By this point EB was lying across the table. Koi's phone was already there.

Koi's height, her grace and her natural beauty made her mesmerising to watch. Then Gabriel Samphire appeared, dressed as he was when Caplan had first seen him. They spun around, laughing, Samphire making a mockery of himself with his dad-dancing. Then something changed. Caplan leaned forward. Was she imagining this? It could have been a word out of context, God knows it happened enough in her own family. It had happened that night when Emma had announced her engagement.

They left the dance floor, walking towards the chairs at the side, holding on to each other. The video moved away, leaving them outside the image. She turned the sound down, looking over Rosie's shoulder, watching the two main stars, Mum and Dad.

They embraced in a long warm hug, a few whispers exchanged. Gabriel grabbed the upper arm of his wife. They both stepped away from each other, then he made another grab for her, but she slipped away from him, walking away, then there was the long arm hold. He was watching her leave, she refused to turn round and look, then she was gone from view. Then he smiled, a slow, wide, knowing smile. Caplan peered at the screen, as if by looking at him she could see what he was seeing. But she knew that look, she knew that expression.

That was a man saying goodbye.

He knew.

He had known all along.

'La Vie en rose'.

She paused the video, freezing him once more, then letting him move away. She was about to lean down to pick her handbag up from the floor when she saw Samphire flick his wrist and look at his watch. More than a quick check of the time, more like a check of timing.

She replayed it. Again.

And again . . .

'You can get a sense of how fit they would be – you know, the soldiers marching up the hill.' Craigo parked the Hilux outside the gate, a grin on his face as he looked at the castle. 'How strong they must have been to carry a sword, a targe . . .'

'Tuberculosis, syphilis . . .' added Caplan quietly, getting out of the vehicle and starting to walk. 'We are going to follow in Koi's footsteps, while it's quiet.'

'Looking for what, ma'am?' asked Craigo, jogging a little to catch up with her.

'Anything that has been missed. Koi said goodbye to Samphire and came up here. He followed her up and took the photograph. He expected her to be alive, posing. Now we re-examine the scene with that in mind so we need to . . . Oh, look.' She glanced over.

'The castle gates are open and unmanned, ma'am.'

'So I see.'

'Shall we . . .?'

'Let's go in on the way down, eh?'

If anything, the breeze blowing over the King's Reach was hotter than before, the walls of the castle, the object of Caplan's study, looked more impenetrable in the golden afternoon sun.

'I can't see anything. If I go close to look . . . well, more closely, I don't see enough of the wall to see a pattern and my neck hurts. If I walk too far back, I'll be off the cliff. I don't know what I'm looking for.'

'Can we ask Tron? Surely after the display of familial devotion over the fire, he'd—'

'I've been thinking that we should get him out of there. Koi was his anchor and he's struggling with her loss. That's what I don't understand, why she'd leave him and Morrow.' She took a deep breath, thinking it through. 'Unless, as I said, she felt she was the problem.'

Craigo was bending over and peering at the grass. Caplan sighed and turned to look out to sea. It looked very calm. Even with the breeze, this high up on the cliff the air was stifling. There would be a downpour of rain soon. And the earth would be glad of it. There had been hosepipe bans in the south for over a month now and the ban was moving northwards. Yet standing here, and looking between the islands, there was water and more water, a continuous body of it swirling around the islands, pushing for the line of least resistance to the shore.

Caplan turned back to Craigo, who was now peering over the edge of the cliff, as if he was going to dive down head first. Then occasionally he turned around and looked over his shoulder to let his eyes settle into the distance.

'You okay?' she shouted. 'Not thinking of jumping, are you?'

'Oh yes. And no.' Then he had his head down again, now peering at the grass.

She took another deep breath of sea air, enjoying the sun on her face and the quiet moment, wondering why life couldn't be filled with moments like this.

For a thousand years the rocks, the cliff and the castle wall had repelled invaders. How did Koi get up the wall? If she climbed up the cliff, there was nowhere for her to go; she couldn't get back down the Queen's Rise without being seen. But these walls were impregnable. The castle had been lost in marriage, lost in inheritance and lost in a game of cards, but it had never been lost in battle.

'Are you seeing anything? I'm thinking of calling it a day here and preparing the interview with McLeerie.' She looked around her, feeling again that she was being watched by unseen eyes up on the wall of the castle.

'Ma'am?' Craigo called. 'Seriously, ma'am, you need to see this.' He was bent over slightly, pointing at something in the ground. 'This is what we were looking for.'

'What is it?' asked Caplan, looking at a bundle of rope and plastic strips lying in a shallow hole where a sod of earth had been. Then she made sense of it. It was a tightly coiled rope ladder, stuck tight under the sod, hard against the rocks at the base of the castle wall.

Caplan looked at it and said, 'Really?'

Craigo said, 'It was that metal stanchion that gave it away. Where there's an anchor, there's something to anchor.'

'She *did* get back up? Bloody hell.' Caplan crouched down beside the nest of coiled rope, once red, now a faded salmon pink. 'Did they not see this yesterday? Did they not dig a hole because they had no anchor?'

'They were searching over where she was lying, ma'am, not over here. And while I'd like to agree with you, ma'am, I need to point out that this rope hasn't been disturbed for many years. But this . . .' he pointed, 'is the excuse we need to search the castle, and to talk to Mr Samphire again.'

'That's a substantive piece of evidence. Don't touch it – we need to get CSI to photograph it *in situ*. Can you video yourself with the ladder in frame, time-stamp it? Samphire can have his lawyer present if he wants, he can have the Pope there for all I care. We'll threaten Pomeroy with a search warrant, and see how that makes him feel. Because Koi is somewhere.'

'You think in there rather than out at sea there?' he tipped his head to the horizon.

'Dressed in white, miles from anywhere, with her face all over social media, the internet chattering about her. And all the conspiracy theories. So, she got up that cliff face with Samphire's help? Then somehow up that wall? There's a lot we don't know. Maybe there's a very good reason why they are no longer talking to us – maybe it's because not all of them are good liars.'

'Good time to find out, ma'am, the gates are still open. No security around.'

'After yesterday, we'd be negligent in our duty if we didn't check that all was well.'

As soon as they walked into the deserted bailey, the hairs on the back of Caplan's neck started to prickle. 'Where is everyone? Perkins? Pickering?' She looked around her, nothing. Deathly quiet. Everything still, frozen in the sun.

She glanced over at Craigo, making a tacit agreement to go in through the castle doors that lay slightly open, then they waited for their eyes to adjust to the relative darkness. The older dog was at the bottom of the stairs, tail wagging slowly. It turned its head, regarded them, dismissed them as unimportant then refocused on the stairs.

'Ma'am?' Craigo nodded at an empty space in the wall of armour. Four axes; the fifth – the bottom one – was missing.

'Christ. Keep together, eh?' She pulled out her warrant card. No protection from the blade of an axe but it was all she had. Pausing on the step, she pointed in the direction of Pomeroy's study.

Craigo nodded; he could hear it too. Voices slightly raised, in panic but not in anger. Sobbing, then a burst of hysterical crying. Then she heard Pickering's voice, taking charge, commanding. They followed the noises to the study and found the door broken down, the axe lying on the floor in a pile of jagged fragments of wood.

Caplan and Craigo stood at the doorway to what looked like a bloodbath. Pomeroy was staring out of the window, Samphire was slumped over a settee. EB and AZed were cuddling each other, weeping loudly. Then Caplan's brain registered the overwhelming smell of red wine. Koi's picture had been torn down, the cellar door was open. Perkins stood at the far sofa, leaning over Tron, two fingers on the boy's neck, monitoring his pulse. Tron was unconscious, in the recovery position with frothy liquid dripping from his mouth and nose. The room was awash with red wine, the Sunflower Girls in the flowery meadow were now spattered in light purple, as if caught in a shower of purple rain. The floor was covered in smashed bottles, puddles of precious Penfolds soaking into the Persian rug.

Cosmo bumped into them as he rushed into the room, unfolding a tinfoil blanket before his hand flew to his mouth, holding in a scream.

Perkins looked up, held out his arm to take it.

'Have you called it in?' asked Caplan. 'Cosmo, go down with Craigo,' she said, remembering the difficulty she had finding the castle on that first night. 'Get the Hilux on the road at the corner, so the ambulance driver doesn't overshoot.'

'ETA less than ten minutes now.' Pickering didn't say, *I hope that's quick enough*. He didn't need to.

'Where are you, DCI Caplan?' Spencer was on the phone.

'At the Lorn. Tron Doonican's seriously ill. He was rushed through A & E. I can't tell you the mess this family are. Thank God Perkins has a cool head, but some of the family followed us, phones out, recording their weeping and posting it. Samphire has disappeared. Rosie's in hysterics. I think Morrow, AZed and Shazamtina are still at Torsvaig. Pomeroy is at hospital admin to see what they can do about keeping away the crowds of concerned fans and well-wishers now that Joe Public have been alerted to the situation, by him.'

'Pardon?'

'Sir, you have no idea. I'm going to stay here a while then I'm going to find Samphire. After that, I'm talking to McLeerie and Knox.'

'A respected journalist and a convicted murderer? I've already warned you about overstepping your boundaries.' Spencer's voice had lost the weighty admonishment of before.

'I'm talking to Knox because, although he is a true crime journalist, he was interested in Daisy Evans before her death hit the papers. Look, I need to go and speak to the medical team. I do not trust this family.'

'You have an evil mind, Caplan.'

'I just recognise exploitation when I see it. Bye.' She ended the call.

The hospital had cleared all the family out of the treatment room. Triton Doonican was, at first glance, the odd one out of the family, pasty faced with a pale imitation of his mother Rhea's famous brilliant green eyes; his hair was a washed-out strawberry blond rather than her deep auburn. The sprinkle of freckles across his nose and cheeks gave him a boyish charm. Caplan thought that he looked very young under the hypothermia blanket, and the nasal tubes that were aiding his oxygen uptake.

She heard a commotion outside the door; a doctor came in and introduced himself. 'I guess this young man was rebelling about something.'

'It might have been sparked by Mr Pomeroy's setting fire to his art. So he, in turn, smashed all the bottles in Mr Pomeroy's wine cellar.' Caplan looked at the small, slim figure on the bed. 'He had a lot to rebel against. Feel free to get hospital security to remove them.' She indicated the family on the other side of the door.

'I believe it's in hand. Too much disruption.'

'How is he?'

'Well, he's suffering from acute alcohol poisoning. He's been fitting. We're a bit concerned about aspiration of vomit. We'll keep him stable then move him to QE2 in Glasgow. His blood oxygen was very low, and we can't seem to get that stable. He has numerous cuts from the glass, especially to his hands and feet. Whoever put that blanket on him knew what he was doing.'

'Mountain rescue-trained.'

'We see too many youngsters misusing alcohol these days, though never with red wine. Usually it's Glen's vodka or Buckfast.'

'That wine cost over a hundred pounds a bottle.' Caplan asked to be kept up to date with any changes and handed over her card, suggesting that no member of the family should visit the boy unless the visit was supervised. The doctor gave her a quizzical look but didn't disagree. 'Cosmo is the sensible one, if you need somebody.'

She sat at the bedside as the doctor left, thinking about the psychological abuse Tron had suffered. Cooped up in this castle, before that in a rambling house in Chiswick.

He had no siblings, no friends, no school pals, no football team . . . The more Caplan thought about it, the more irresponsible she thought these parents, these people were. But it was Pomeroy Tron seemed to be targeting with the Porsche, the trashing of the wine cellar.

Koi and Gabriel? He seemed to have nothing against them. She remembered the hug he'd given Koi. The detailed drawings he'd done of her.

She left a note by his bedside saying they had pictures of most of his art that could be printed out. It wasn't the same, but it might give him some comfort. Caplan stood at the door, listening to a calm, polite voice telling the family that they'd be moved to the nearby hotel for privacy at this time. While Caplan waited for the arguing to be over, she texted Craigo to ask where he was.

'I'm watching Mr Samphire, ma'am. He's sitting round here in the car park. If you want a word with him, now's a good time.'

Her phone flashed. One unread message from Sarah Linden and an email with some documentation attached. She downloaded it and read the letterhead. It was a children's home outside Oban, about a girl called Mary McDonagh. She had left their care, aged sixteen, and had never contacted them again, had never been in trouble and had never sought any help from social services to aid independent living.

And nobody had come looking for her.

Caplan looked at the date and the attached grainy photocopy of a picture of a stick-thin girl with eyes too big for her head and short fair hair. Had she then bought a cheap flight to London?

She felt she knew exactly what had happened to Mary. If Samphire had shown her how to reinvent herself once, she could have done it again.

The corridor outside was suddenly quiet. She opened the

message from Sarah, a screenshot of a social media post of a tearful EB next to Tron's masked face, looking close to death. The caption read: 'Pray for my brother.' It already had over ten thousand likes.

Gabriel Samphire was out in the hospital car park under the watchful eye of DS Craigo, who was sitting in the Hilux, window down, arm hanging out, tapping out some rhythm on the door.

Caplan walked up to Samphire and leaned back against the fence, her eyes on Craigo. 'It's the scariest thing in the world to see your child like that. Helpless, utterly helpless. My son once took a drug that he shouldn't have. He thought he could fly. He climbed up onto a monument in the park and threw himself off the top.'

Samphire turned to look at her, shock on his face.

'It wasn't very high, he wasn't very badly hurt, but it was terrifying. And all the terrible possibilities run through your mind.' Caplan blinked slowly. 'You do everything you can to protect them but, in that moment, when I was needed, I wasn't there. And like you, Mr Samphire, I was partially responsible for my son being in that situation in the first place.'

'How so?'

'My job. We are not so different. On that film, Koi hugs Tron so tightly.' That made Samphire close his eyes; he didn't want that memory. 'Koi was the one he related to. Certainly not Pomeroy, and maybe not you. Is there a reason for that?'

Samphire looked away.

Caplan resisted the temptation to call him a coward. 'Do you know what happened to Koi? Because that young man up there is suffering. Not knowing is a terrible burden. He's the one sitting out on the clifftop, as if he's waiting for your wife to return. Is she going to return? Or is a better question, did she ever leave?'

'Tron doesn't need to know.'

'Not know what, Mr Samphire? Because anything must be better than what he's going through now.'

There was no response, just a narrowing of the eyes as a noisy motorbike came into the car park.

Samphire's phone pinged. It was Pomeroy, telling him to get to the hotel so they could issue a statement.

Caplan waited until he made the decision not to answer it, and they stood for a moment, in the hot sun and the gentle breeze.

Then Caplan showed him the photograph of the rope ladder on her phone, in its bed of earth, still rolled up.

Samphire looked at it as if he needed some time to make sense of it. 'That's been there for years. My wife was dead on the rocks.' He started to cry, his hand covering his eyes. 'It wasn't supposed to happen. It wasn't.'

He sniffed loudly, backhanding the tears from his eyes then slowly placing his hand in his trouser pocket and pulling out a single key, attached by a fine chain to his belt loop. He unclipped it and dropped it delicately into Caplan's palm, then closed her fingers around it. 'That will unlock the door on the musicians' gallery. I think you'll find out all you want to know in there. Well, maybe not, but it'll explain a few things.'

His phone pinged again. 'Pip wants me over at the hotel.'

'Either that or sit outside your son's room. Tron will want you there when he wakes up.'

Samphire looked doubtful. 'You think?'

'I know.' She patted him on the shoulder. She could feel every bone. 'Do we have your permission to enter the castle, do what we need to do?'

'You do. How was your son after the fall?' Samphire turned round to look directly at her.

'Broken. Scared. But there was a face he knew when he woke up. Me or his dad,' Caplan lied. In reality Aklen had been unable to cope and had taken to his bed. When Emma had been in a coma, Sarah and Liz had helped her keep her vigil waiting for the swelling in Emma's brain to go down. Emma's slight limp was a constant reminder. 'There will always be a feeling that, as a parent, you could have done better.'

Samphire took a deep breath, looked at the hospital then back at Caplan. 'You know where Morrow likes to sit?'

'Yes.'

'Same location but in the West Tower. That was where Koi was trying to get to. You have my permission to kick the door in.'

TWENTY

Caplan and Craigo made their way up the staircase and onto the musicians' gallery, leaving Wattie at the gate with Pickering. From there Craigo went through the velvet curtain, to the modern door they had found, the locked door.

The key on the chain opened it very easily, suggesting frequent use.

'Well, look what we have here,' said Caplan as the door swung open, sticking slightly on the thick, plush carpet inside.

The room was dominated by a huge double bed, covered with eight pillows, a bedside table on either side. A desk, a mirror, one big brown aged leather wing-backed armchair, with *Words of Wisdom and Warmth: 31 Speeches* by Ruth Bader Ginsburg upside down on the arm, placed there as though the reader had been disturbed.

She looked out of the window. They were in an older part of the castle. The view was right out over the sea and the islands beyond. This was a window to sit and stare out of, a window of contemplation.

Yet it looked like a hotel room that was occupied by a short-stay guest. Not enough clothes storage. Nothing lying around.

She stood at the far side of the bed, Craigo at the other.

'Two glasses, ma'am. Who sleeps here?'

'I'd have thought that was obvious.' She smelled the pillow; two people had laid their heads here. She could smell two scents, the type of people who put on scent before they went to bed. Bending over, she looked along the surface of the fabric of the pillowcase; there were two grey hairs, six or seven inches long. And another, much longer, darker.

'Mr Samphire, I'd guess,' said Craigo.

'And Mr Pomeroy.'

'At the same time?'

'Of course.'

'Oh.'

Caplan stood in that room for a long time, the chess pieces in her head moving around the board, then she lifted her phone and took a few photographs of the room, then a few more in the narrow bathroom, an en suite that had been built within the original footprint of the room.

'It's the scent, isn't it? That's what Gabriel Samphire wears. Clive Christian?' She read the bottle sitting on the narrow over-sink shelf.

'I don't know him, ma'am.'

'No, on our salary I wouldn't expect you to.'

They were moving slowly down an old corridor that stank of sea water and dead fish. It was bitterly cold despite the heat of the day.

They had taken a few wrong turns before they came across a warm passageway, with light coming in from a faraway window, a refurbished stairway going down from the landing they stood on.

There was a doorless recess to the right, nothing more than a big storage area with photographic equipment placed carefully against the wall and spreading into two corners. There were many camera stands, light screens, old computer carcasses; some long and heavy-looking metal struts, black and dusty, that looked like old lighting rigs. There were two surfboards and a row of pegs on the wall from which hung miscellaneous old coats.

It took Craigo and Wattie about five minutes to lift the items from the wall, checking for signs of recent work before they found a door.

'We have permission to open it – you are allowed to batter the door down. That's the only reason we brought you, Wattie.'

Wattie immediately pointed to something that looked like a folded stand for an old video camera. 'I could ram it with that?'

Craigo looked around the room, rummaging through things, lifting toolboxes and metal cases full of God knows what. 'Or we could use these.' He held up a small wallet full of screwdrivers and set about unscrewing the lock from the door.

It came out easily, and the first thing that struck Caplan on entering the room was the smell. Fresh and light. She felt the thickness of the carpet, soft and deep underfoot. It was new and a very rich green. She gestured to Craigo and Wattie to hold back for a moment. They all smelled fresh paint; the long hallway was lined with natural stone, cold to the touch on one side, and modern plasterboard on the other. The floor was uneven, and creaked as Caplan stepped forward, ducking her head to avoid bumping it on the ceiling. Her mind wandered to how this might sound at night, the ghost walking above, creaking the floorboards, maybe even gentle voices sounding across the air. No wonder Morrow was half scared to death. She went down two steps and pushed open a small internal door with no lock, no handle. Through the door the green carpet continued up two steps to a raised platform where a double bed sat, duvet smooth as a millpond, six pillows beautifully arranged at one end. It had a touch of Koi about it. The bed sat on a raised platform, a small ottoman separating it from the small living area where there was a folded futon and a television. She could see a microwave and an air fryer in the adjoining room. Towards the outer side of the building was a door leading to a small toilet.

Caplan walked up to the deep-set window, pulled back the light-green curtains with their blackout lining. This was the only window in the room; it looked out to sea. A fluffy cushion rested on the ledge, and outside, about three feet down, was a stone balcony, part of the old ramparts, a mirror image of one that she had seen near Morrow's apartment.

It would be easy to open the window and sit on the ledge with your legs dangling outside. It would be a direct climb up from the King's Reach, if it was climbable.

She heard Craigo whisper, asking if she was okay. She answered that she was, but he wasn't to come in yet. She didn't want to disrupt the air of privacy. This was where Koi had come to escape.

She opened the window, wondering how much of this was visible from the King's Reach. She would still be hidden if she climbed out and sat on the wicker chair tucked in the corner of the rampart. Using the rampart like a balcony, somebody could sit here all day, watching the sky, watching the sun. The view was over the sea and to the islands. She could hear the waves beating against the cliffs, but she couldn't see the strip of grass above them; she'd need to climb through and look directly down for that.

Was this place a sanctuary for Koi and Gabriel? The weight of public interest in them was intense. As a couple they must have needed somewhere to go that was away from the business and the rest of the family.

But were they a couple? Or was that Pomeroy and Samphire?

She closed the window again, pulling the old iron handle down to lock it into a new aluminium catch.

In the kitchen was a tiny fridge. The cutlery was four of everything – a cheap set bought somewhere local, not like the stuff they used in the wedding venue.

There was nothing in the fridge except bottles of water, nothing in the cupboard but tins of consommé. She went to the bed and found the drawers underneath, half full of clothes, all women's, all size ten; the leggings were 'long', big jumpers, casual trousers, Ugg boots. No anoraks, no jackets, no men's clothes.

Samphire knew about this place. Yet there was no sign of him being here, or being wanted here.

Did Koi want to be away from him? Did the girls know about this? Did Cosmo?

Or was Pomeroy in the know?

For the first time in her career, Caplan didn't really know who the right person to talk to was, so she talked to herself.

'God, faking your death then disappearing shows some kind of desperation. She didn't want to be here for another single moment, so she ran. Yes, she ran but where to? Why is her real identity a secret? And why didn't she make it back here?' She called over her shoulder. 'Craigo, can you come in here? Get somebody to photograph all this, the contents of the cupboards, the books, the photographs and any luggage that's here.' As Craigo walked slowly round the room, Caplan thought how small it was. Aklen was researching how one person doesn't need a lot of space to live in – the travelling people in caravans, those that yearned to live in a tiny house. Aklen had been watching a programme the other night about a climber who hated hotels so lived in a truck for eight years. Alan Bennett's neighbour had lived in a van, and here was a snippet of paradise, a little nest high up in the castle.

Her eyes swept along the books on the bookshelf, most of them having the appearance of well-read favourites. John Stonehouse's life story popped out at her, then her eye swept sideways through the crime fiction to *Out of My Depth* by Anne Darwin, wife of John Darwin, who had faked his own death.

How many more books had she read on this topic?

She saw Thomas Paine's *Rights of Man*, *The Gulag Archipelago* volume one, beside another Solzhenitsyn book, plus the whole collection of P.D. James, including *The Children of Men*.

Caplan looked at them, realising how much she may have underestimated the woman she had been trying to understand.

But had their plan gone badly wrong?

Or had she changed her mind?

Had fate intervened and she had simply slipped onto the rocks?

She needed to talk to Leonora Spyck again. If a pathologist couldn't tell the dead from the living, then there was no hope for any of them.

Gabriel Samphire looked very uneasy sitting in the interview room of Cronchie police station behind a black-topped table with a single glass of water in front of him. Tron had not regained consciousness and the transfer to Glasgow was scheduled for that night. There was an air of resignation about Samphire, a sense that whatever ordeal had been stressing him so much was almost over. The decision had been made to bring him down here, away from his environment and, more importantly, away from Pomeroy, who had appeared at Pilcottie shouting the odds. Wattie had given as good as he got.

Caplan was sure that Pomeroy's next move would be to get hold of the best legal defence he could find in Edinburgh or Glasgow. She had explained to Samphire that they were interviewing him as a witness who had, they believed, been holding on to information that should have been divulged in the interests of the investigation.

Expecting a solicitor to be on the phone at any moment, Caplan didn't mess about. She placed the file on top of the table and said, 'Did you really think you would get away with that?'

'I'm not sure what it is I was supposed to be getting away with.'

'Okay. Let's start with the room at the top of the West Tower.'

When Samphire spoke, it was very slowly and deliberately; not quite rehearsed, but it felt as if the speech had been on his mind, as if he knew that this day was coming. 'Koi was very stressed, she was worried about the kids, about money, about the Fisherman. I also think she just wanted to disappear. Rosie had mentioned the Agatha Christie thing a few times – you know, when she went off to that hotel in Harrogate.'

'Yes, the similarities have been mentioned.'

'Koi had read about that and thought how wonderful that must be. Being somewhere where nobody knows her, where she could be on her own. But it was never going to happen. So, rightly or wrongly, we decided to fake her death.' He nodded when he finished that sentence. 'There, I've said it, I know how bloody awful it sounds and how bad it must seem, but that was all that was behind it, a fresh start.'

Caplan sighed. 'I'm presuming the rope ladder was used to get her down and up the cliff? But how was she going to get up the castle wall and back to her wee room?' She tapped the table for his attention. 'Where are they? The Rapunzel steps?'

'I don't know. She never told me.' Samphire gave her a wry smile. 'There's some folklore about them being a secret passed from woman to woman. Years ago, I did a photojournalism feature on free climbers in the Highlands, in Canada, in North America. I know a few things about handholds and I've looked everywhere round the castle for those steps. They're not there. I've seen them in castles in France, a set of steps consisting of nothing but a series of stones sitting proud.' He closed his eyes, his hands lifting from the table, as he recalled his search. 'But no matter how much I looked, I couldn't see them at Torsvaig. Did Koi ever show me? No. She kept that secret to herself.'

Caplan leaned over the desk towards Samphire, 'And you have never kept a secret from her? I presume she knew about you and Mr Pomeroy? I find it hard to believe she didn't. Why the secrecy?'

'It didn't suit our profile.'

She folded her arms, 'Oh, of course. Please continue.'

Samphire shook his head. 'Once over the wall, she'd go down into the flat in the West Tower. Then we were going away together. She and I, not Pip. She was very definite on that.' He was fighting back tears now.

Caplan pushed the glass of water across the table towards him.

'We had the money, we were going to live a different life somewhere where nobody knew us and . . . But that didn't happen. She fell. So don't ask me any more, I've told you what was planned. But instead, she fell. She was dead at the bottom of the cliff, what else can I say? My wife is gone.'

'The photographs on your phone?'

'Part of the plan. That was our proof.' Samphire palmed away a tear. 'When I got to the top of the cliff, she wasn't there. I saw her lying at the bottom, as planned. I took the photograph, but even then, I knew. I just knew something terrible had happened, the way she was lying, in that position. I thought she would be at the bottom of the cliff in the shallower water, and then she'd climb on the rocks and pose and then I would photograph her. But she looked dead. Then I saw the ladder wasn't there. She'd fallen before she got it out.'

Caplan gave him a moment then asked, 'What was to happen, then, if it had gone to plan?'

'I was supposed to go down the walk, hold back Pickering and Perkins, so they wouldn't rush to the top of the cliff and catch her climbing up the rope ladder or rolling it up and putting it away. They've both worked for mountain rescue. We didn't want them to try to climb down to offer assistance.'

'And you definitely didn't see the ladder?'

'I looked around. Nothing. No ladder. No Koi. Just grass and fresh air. I could hear the music from the party. I knew they would have heard the scream. Then I looked over the edge. I thought her knee had let her down, then I remembered her knee wasn't as bad as she was making out. She just wanted it to be thought that she couldn't climb, when she could.'

'What kind of person does that to their children?'

Samphire gave a bitter little laugh. 'The kind of person who loves their children. DCI Caplan, we created a monster. The brand, the Sunflower brand, was a toxic weed that was strangling her, and the kids. If she was gone, the monster would die and she thought the kids would be free to live their own lives.'

Caplan, thinking about the distress of Morrow and Tron, considered the point. 'But do you really think that one of the most famous faces in the world could disappear and we would sit back and pay no attention at all?'

'If she ate normally for a month, she'd look very different. I'd be able to visit her any time I wanted. There are plenty of noises in this castle – we wouldn't need to keep quiet, nobody would know we were here. We'd thought it all through. In three months, she'd leave and go somewhere else. I was to follow her. Leave all this behind and live our lives.'

'I'm not sure I believe that. It might have been her idea, but I can see you going along with that plan then pushing her off the cliff. Then you'd have a properly dead wife and you'd be able to claim the insurance.'

'Her scream was long before I got there. And she cancelled her insurance.'

'You two could have agreed when the scream was to be beforehand. She could have still been at the top when you got there. You could have thrown her off. I've seen the footage of you when she leaves the party – you check your watch carefully.'

'I didn't kill her.' He sulked. 'I don't think that's very fair.'

'Well, I don't think throwing your wife off a cliff is very fair either.'

'You're wrong, believe me, you're wrong. I know what was supposed to happen. I'm just not sure what did.'

'Who is the Fisherman?' asked Caplan, her voice light. 'I know, but I'd like to hear it from you.'

'Pip. It was a ploy to keep Koi around, to show that she needed the protection of the family. I told her it was Pip and that there was no real danger. She was furious. She felt Pip was pressuring her – he was writing the scripts for the MisChief podcast.'

'Written by Pip, yet he comes very close to accusing you, and incriminating himself as being involved in the deaths of Rhea and Ecco.'

'Yes, all for publicity. People will always wonder how they died, why they died. Why the beautiful die young. They just love a conspiracy theory.'

'So Pip's attracting media attention to the family, while Koi's trying to safeguard their privacy?'

'He was safeguarding our income, the storyline kept us relevant. Pip was trying to keep Koi safe, keep her with us where we could protect her. But all she dreamed of was getting away.'

'And you and Pomeroy? Long-term?'

Samphire nodded. 'From way before Koi. He was getting fed up with her. She was fed up with the pretence. It was a three-person marriage. Then Tron caught us, Pip and I, once, together. It was only much later that he realised what he had seen. I don't think he has coped well with that.'

'If at all. Here's another idea, Mr Samphire. Do you think that Mr Pomeroy found out what you and Koi were planning, attempting to get away? Considering what happened to the other two Sunflower Girls when they tried to leave.'

Samphire closed his eyes.

Caplan kept her voice low and engaging. 'If you have any doubt, any suspicion at all that he was in some way responsible for their deaths, then now is the time to speak. He is the master of PR, but nothing will save him if we and the Met put our heads together and re-examine the files on the deaths of Rhea, Tron's mother, and Ecco, EB's mother. Two women you were intimately acquainted with. I think the kids deserve better than your silence – your kids, Mr Samphire.'

He opened his eyes and looked her straight in the face. 'No. They were very damaged women. Pip helped them, protected them from their demons, if you like. When they left, he just couldn't do that any more. I tried, I really tried to bring them back, but no. Ecco's addictions got worse. Rhea was just depressed and . . . empty, really. I was there the night she died. If only I had stayed . . .'

Gabriel Samphire put his head in his hands and sobbed.

On the board was a photograph of the rope ladder tightly coiled up in its hole in the ground, and then another image with it covered by the mound of earth and grass. They would never have seen that, on the night in the semi-darkness. Samphire was keeping to his story. Koi was supposed to use it to get down and up the cliff, then roll it up, climb the Rapunzel steps and hide in her room. It wasn't a feat for the faint hearted, but Koi had been training her upper-body strength. She had been prepared. She could have climbed it easily. But that was not what happened.

The rope ladder was never uncoiled.

Koi was at the bottom of the cliff.

Caplan jumped when Craigo asked. 'You think she knew he was gay, bisexual?'

'Oh, she knew. The couple that have been together the longest are Pomeroy and Samphire. Koi got fed up, broke up with Samphire. Pomeroy was there first.'

'It's all about image. And there's a twenty-year age difference. Gay, and a twenty-year age difference? There'd be a lot of stigma around that,' said Craigo.

'Pinky and Perky have a degree of empathy, for the kids at least.'

'Just might be difficult for them, being an ex-cop and ex-services. They are seeing the kids and Koi struggling and they are helpless to put it right.'

'Do we think there's anything in Morrow's statement?' asked Craigo. 'She said that she sees a ghost floating around on the wall of the battlements. Do you think there's something in that?'

'I would, if Koi had ever made it up to that room, but I don't believe that she did. I'd love to think she was alive and well, reading her books and taking a walk along the battlements at night like Lady Mary. And nobody's going to believe Morrow, are they? Which was maybe the point, come to think of it.'

Caplan looked at the empty page in front of her. And wrote down 'Koi'. Getting away from a life of fame, getting away from children that were becoming what? More famous? More independent? More of a burden?

The kids, all of them, appeared to love Koi. Especially Tron, who was the obvious one to resent the woman who had replaced his mother.

Yet Koi had said goodbye. She had fully intended to leave them all behind. She had been drawing her old life to a close.

Nobody had expected her to die.

Her report to the Fiscal was short and factual. In the absence of evidence to the contrary, the death would be considered accidental. Caplan hoped that Koi cancelling her huge life insurance policy before she disappeared was one final defiant gesture to her husband.

They had thought it through so well, then she had accidently fallen and the whole thing had turned into a real-life nightmare.

'What are you doing? You've been very quiet. I thought it was all over.' Aklen was sketching on his pad; Caplan was trying not to let the scratching of the graphite on the paper get to her.

'It's a file called "Caravan Evidence".'

'I suppose that's easier to search than an entire castle.'

'I'm scrolling through the evidence of a caravan that may or may not be involved in a crime.' She picked up her glass of wine. 'And that crime was a murder.'

'Are you looking for more work? Do you not have enough?'

'Why would you dye your hair?'

'Why?' Aklen stopped drawing, regarding her for a moment. 'Some guys do it to look younger. Maybe to attract women, not to look too old in an unforgiving job market. Don't see the point myself.'

She returned to her scrolling, Aklen to designing the under-bed wardrobe for a Toaty House. Looking at the list of forensic samples taken from the caravan, and the accompanying documentation of how they had been processed, it was obvious that the investigation team had given a lot of credence to the evidence of Ann McIlroy, the owner of the caravan site. A dark, deserted location at night on the twenty-second of December. She had stated that McLeerie had been there in the caravan. She had seen him leaning against the kitchen unit, waiting for Daisy to come back. If she had known what his intentions were, she would have called the police, but she had no idea. Nobody did.

Caplan ran her finger down the screen, looking at the list, pausing now and then. It showed McLeerie had definitely been in the caravan, but he'd never denied that Daisy was a friend and a supplier of his cocaine. McLeerie claimed Daisy had a few customers in the caravan site in the summer months. He himself just needed something to help him with the stress of his job.

That was a relationship that was bound to end badly.

And there were Border collie hairs in the caravan.

She read that again. And thought of the land around the caravan site – no sheep there.

Did Ann McIlroy have a pet dog? Did Daisy?

She read on. The answer to that question was no. And neither did McLeerie.

'Aklen, I need to make a few confidential phone calls.'

Today on the Living Their Life *podcast we continue to look at the famous, or should that be infamous, family who now reside at Torsvaig Castle or Stalag Torsvaig as it's known outside the walls.*

Koi Castle, Limpetlaw, Torsvaig, call it what you will. A prison is still a prison, no matter how neat the grass is. Adored round the world, but how much do they, the McQuarrie-Samphire family really desire anonymity? Maybe they thought they would get that in their quiet little village where a stolen sheep makes the headlines in the local newspaper.

Desiring anonymity is one thing but putting yourself all over the front of the papers, appearing on TV shows and in soft-porn photographs is not a usual route to a quiet life.

How much do they envy the freedom of the yachts that sail by, into the unknown?

Koi we know is a tragic figure, and that's how we shall always remember her. Ecco was never going to enjoy a long life, dead after partying with Koi, Pomeroy, Rhea and Samphire. And Rhea? Was there more to that story than meets the eye? Rhea, who was dead after spending the evening with Samphire? Koi was invited but didn't go, clever girl. Pomeroy was Samphire's excuse for leaving. Rhea passed away soon after he'd left. By her own hand or by someone else's. And then Koi, dead after partying with Pomeroy and Samphire?

It's like the Agatha Christie book And Then There Were None.

As for their endless search for anonymity, I'm not sure that being dead is the best way to do it.

It doesn't allow a lot of feedback.

From MisChief666 causing Mischief 24/7

Laters.

TWENTY-ONE

DCI Caplan felt her deductions about McLeerie were reasonable. She'd read the documentation Central Records had collated for her. Caplan already knew much of it. McLeerie had killed his wife in a drug-induced rage and had gone to jail on life licence, but from reports in the media, he'd become a new man. He had evolved into a pleasant human being.

He had apologised for his actions to the family of his wife. He had studied Buddhism. He wanted to speak to those who would listen about the evil of drugs.

She could remember the pictures of Carol at the time. She had looked very young, but strong. As McLeerie was a skinny wee bugger, the drug rage must have been immense.

Caplan was in an unfamiliar toilet at another station. They had borrowed an interview room, and she had not been told where in advance; a driver brought her and Mackie. Now she was smoothing down her hair, checking her make-up, running through her questions in her mind. McLeerie had agreed to the meeting, but he wanted a venue away from Oban. He had refused the offer of counsel but had requested the presence of his criminal justice social worker, the man that Caplan knew from Glasgow, Colin Reese. He was good at his job, reasonable and fair, but would be no walkover.

Caplan wanted justice for Daisy, twenty-two years old when some monster had dragged her into the waves and banged her head against the rocks. There just wasn't enough evidence to convict. And Caplan wasn't sure they had the right monster.

'You nervous, ma'am?' asked Mackie.

'A little.'

'You scared of him?'

'Oh no, I'm not scared of him. He's not worth it, you wait and see. He'll be a little grey man. And that's all.'

'He could be a triple murderer, and that's the victims we know about.'

Caplan turned around, seeing in the mirror that Mackie's hands were shaking. 'You okay?'

'Feel a bit rusty, ma'am. Been a while since we did this . . .'

'Just don't lose your temper and hit somebody.'

They shared a smile and walked down the unfamiliar corridor, following a uniform called Bob who had been detailed to look after them.

'Interview room four – it's one of the family rooms, as requested,' the uniform said, 'They are already in there. I've put some water on the table. Plastic cups, I'm afraid.'

Caplan said thank you, took a deep breath and opened the door.

McLeerie was even less of a presence than Caplan had expected – older, smaller, thinner – but there was a brightness about him. No bravado. No fear. He was . . . interested in what she had to say.

Reese nodded at Caplan, introductions were made. McLeerie shook hands, a warm handshake; he gave a brief nod, a glimmer of a smile.

'Mr McLeerie has written a statement for you,' Reese started.

'So not amenable to interview, then?' said Caplan, placing her pen down very deliberately and precisely on the desk in front of her.

'He'll answer any questions you want to ask after I've read his statement.'

'Is he going to tell us if he killed Daisy Evans?' asked Caplan.

Reese smiled. 'I think he might have that covered.' He cleared his throat. 'I was in a business relationship with Daisy Evans for over two years at the time of her death. She was my dealer; she supplied my cocaine. I had an expensive habit at the time. She was a troubled young woman, but good fun. We never had a romantic relationship. We were friends. I had a girlfriend at the time. Not to say that we didn't hook up once or twice when we were both blind drunk. Then Daisy got pregnant with her man and was too scared to tell her family. To be honest, I think she was scared to tell him as well.'

'Does he have a name?'

'Not that I knew. You lot went through all this at the time—'

Caplan put her hands up and halted his speech. She slowly picked up her pen and wrote something down. 'Continue.'

The two men looked at each other. Mackie sighed in irritation.

McLeerie shook his head, asked for his statement back and folded it up.

'Okay, so I didn't have anything to do with the death of Daisy Evans, nothing at all. I had nothing to do with the death of Sharon Baird.'

'You did know them both.'

'I knew them through my addiction. Daisy as a supplier and Sharon as part of a group I attended to help me get off the cocaine. It was an NHS group, there were about twenty people there, give or take. I told the police that at the time.' He looked away, pursing his lips. 'I did kill Carol, my wife, in 2005. I put my hands up to that. I phoned 999 as soon as I heard her skull crack off the wood. Every time I close my eyes, I can hear that noise. I've never, ever denied what I did, the state I was in then. I was out of control, my life was shit and I had all sorts of issues with . . . well, trusting life really. As would you if you had lost two people that you knew, and all kinds of folk came out the woodwork and said you were places when you weren't, and that you were sleeping with people when, in reality, all you did was share a cup of tea on a Wednesday night with fifteen other people.'

'Why did you kill your wife?'

'A perfect storm of work, anger, frustration. I was under a lot of pressure, bullied at work, passed over for promotion. We needed money, my mother was ill. I wasn't sleeping, I was throwing up. It was a perfect storm. I was suicidal, but I lashed out at her and killed her. It was over something really daft.'

'She burned your toast, and you smashed her head against the door frame.'

'Yes, I know. But I was lashing out against everything, and she happened to be there. My life was awful. I'm sorry, I did love Carol. And I never laid a hand on Daisy or on Sharon. I think if I had admitted I played a part in their deaths, I would have been out long before now. But I didn't because it's not true.'

'It is unfortunate though, the way the other two deaths followed in your wake.'

'I felt like somebody was taking bits of my life.'

'Why were you talking to Rosie McQuarrie-Samphire?'

McLeerie gave a little laugh of disbelief. 'Aye, right.'

Then he realised Caplan was serious.

'Now, you wait a minute. I had nothing to do with the death of Koi McQuarrie.'

For a moment, Caplan got a glimpse of the handsome young man he had been.

'I've never spoken to any of the McQuarrie-Samphires.'

'Have you ever spoken to Philip Pomeroy?'

'I don't think so, who is he?'

'Are you writing a book, Mr McLeerie?'

He looked sideways to his lawyer, who gave a nod.

'I have to write a diary for my counsellor. I do it every day, but that's all.'

'No intention to publish it?'

'Oh God, no, nobody reads it but me. It's my homework.'

Caplan nodded. 'To backtrack, was anybody giving Daisy hassle?'

'Of course, she was a dealer. And she'd had the baby, and no, I wasn't the father. I don't know who was. He might have been married, but she was wary of him. She had asked me to run her to the train station, she was going down south to visit her sister, I think.'

'You were in the caravan on the twenty-second?'

'No, I wasn't. Not that day. I'd been there in the past, many times. But when I got there that night, she wasn't in. She was late for everything, was Daisy. I didn't hang around.'

'Did you have a key?'

'No, she was a friend. 'Course I didn't have a key.'

'The woman who runs the caravan site says you waited for Daisy.'

'I came back again the next morning, to take her to the station. Again, she wasn't there, and when the police knocked on my door, I knew why. And that woman said I smoked, which I don't. I never have.'

'Okay. One minute she's going to stay with her sister but the next minute she's walking by herself, across the campsite, through the woods, across the dunes, onto the beach and then walking into the sea where she fell over and was battered to death by the waves? No alcohol in her bloodstream, nothing to impair her judgement.'

'It wasn't me. There was somebody else there. Somebody who smoked.'

'And that person also killed Sharon Baird?'

'I don't know but I know it wasn't me.'

'Why would someone do that? You must be the unluckiest man in the world, having somebody kill people you know.'

'Not as unlucky as Carol, Sharon or Daisy.'

'That's a good line.' Caplan nodded approvingly. 'Do you like dogs?'

'Not really. I'm a bit wary of them.'

Caplan sat back, folded her arms and stared at him.

He stared right back.

'We have your DNA in the system. Would you give us another sample? I'd like to do just one comparison test, then it will be destroyed. You have my word on that.'

'Why?' asked Reese.

'Paternity.'

For the second time in twenty-four hours, they were sitting opposite a suspect.

Andrew Knox was being helpful, still sniffing after his story. Before he said anything he'd slipped a photograph across the table towards Caplan. It was a print of her, in a black tutu, the one taken in the dark studio with the single light. The session that had made her feet bleed.

If he thought it would unnerve her, he was wrong. She ignored it and slid McPhee's copy of his book towards him.

'Have you always smoked the same cigarettes Mr Knox? My husband gradually weaned himself off, then he gave up and started drinking.'

'I'm down to about ten a day – can't afford it any more,' said Knox.

'What do you know about the hate mail and the Fisherman?' asked Caplan.

'That's something I'd like to keep to myself, if you don't mind.'

'This could be part of a murder investigation, so we don't allow people to withhold information that could be relevant to an investigation.'

'Well, I've been studying this family for a couple of years now.'

'So you're an investigative journalist, but if you have information that is pertinent to the inquiry then it is your duty to hand it over.'

He sat back, thrust his legs forward and started twiddling his thumbs. It was incongruous when his round, cheery face broke into a smile and he nodded as if confirming that Caplan was quite correct, but still his lips remained tight.

'Are you stalking the McQuarrie family?'

'No!'

'Did Rosie tell you who they suspect her father is?'

'Yes, she did. So, it's obvious who's stalking them. Maybe ask the security about why they were actually employed?'

'I feel it was a bit of an own goal by Pomeroy to decide on the story that Angus McLeerie was Rosie's father.'

'Do you have any idea where McLeerie is?'

'I know exactly where he is.'

Knox tilted his head slightly, regarding her as if she was an interesting but unidentified specimen. 'Rosie might like to know.'

'Yes, she might.' Caplan sat back. 'I think she's travelling to Glasgow. Because of Tron. Now he's a real victim of social media, PR people, ex-journalists et cetera. Like MisChief, the podcaster. I know who Mischief is. I know the smell of misogyny. Pomeroy, Samphire, Cosmo? They get off quite lightly, but Rosie, Koi, Morrow and EB? Remind me, how did it go? The bit about Samphire and Pomeroy. She turned to Mackie who started to read aloud.

'This is The Family.

But it's not a family tree, this is a family circle and it's the money that goes round and round and Philip Pomeroy takes a cut whenever it passes Go.

And his lover.

But you've figured that out by now, haven't you?

Of course, you have – they are the last ones standing.'

'Tron heard it, and he put two and two together. The boy is not blind, I imagine hearing those words suddenly shed a different light on something he saw, maybe when he was too young to see it.'

Knox gave a little shrug. 'I'm not responsible for their behaviour.'

'You're not responsible for the podcast either, but you write up what Pomeroy tells you to, then your eloquent words are read by an actress.'

'What can I say? It pays.'

He was two years older than McLeerie, similar build; the difference was this man's arrogance, and the other man's fear. Caplan knew which one she'd prefer to be stuck in a lift with.

'I was looking to fill the gap in our investigation. Looking for the one who helps spread the celebrity gossip to the lower echelons of the media. You know, not a good journalist, one who's a bit past it. One who doesn't like women. How many times have you been married, Mr Knox?'

'Twice.'

'Three times, actually, divorced each time.'

'And each time I get poorer.'

'I know – I've seen the state of your shoes, I can guess the state of your bank account. You're on the market to be bought.'

'You're good.'

Caplan shook her head. 'My sergeant is good. There were dog hairs on the seat of the caravan that Daisy was in.'

'And?'

'Border collie hairs.'

'I don't have a dog.'

'But you did then, a Border collie. She's in the photo on the back of your book.' She turned the book over and showed him his own photograph. 'My sergeant has a farm. He's always talking about bloodlines and collies, especially working collies. Your dog was from show stock rather than working stock, wasn't it?'

'It was over twenty years ago.'

'Wife number one. It was her dog. She took her in the divorce, and she'd bred that dog herself. She still has them – different fathers, but the mum is always the best female pup from the litter. The current thirteen-year-old is the grandmother of the two-year-old you had when you were married. The DNA rules are the same, human or canine. We can get that tested. We can place you in the caravan.'

Knox laughed. 'The caravan was cleaned regularly. It was a rental van; anybody could have been in there.'

'No. Ann was a friend of the family, remember. It was her business. She gave her friend's sister the use of a new caravan in exchange for deep-cleaning the rentals between September and December. At the end of December, she was going south. You know she had a baby in the previous August, a wee girl.'

'Yes, it's McLeerie's.'

'Maybe. Maybe not.'

Then Knox was quiet. 'She said it was McLeerie's.'

'Maybe she was too scared to tell the real dad about the kid, maybe she wasn't sure how he'd take it. Maybe he was married. Maybe she was scared he'd get violent. Why do you dye your hair, Mr Knox?'

'I prefer it.'

'Really? Well, I think you killed Daisy. I think you were at the same addiction meeting as Sharon and McLeerie. And for the record, if I put a picture of you in front of Daisy's sister, would they identify you as Andrew Knox? Or do they think that this face,' she circled the tip of her pen at him, 'belongs to Angus McLeerie, after all those years in jail? You have similar age and build, except you have the belly, not him. He's stick-thin; Daisy's sister called the man she saw at the end of her allotment 'tubby'. If I got Rosie to listen to your voice, she'd say you were McLeerie too. Interesting, eh? DC Mackie?'

'Yes, ma'am?'

'Can you arrest Mr Knox, read him his rights?'

'What charge, ma'am?' asked Mackie, cheerily.

'Oh, let's start with the murder of Daisy Evans. Then the Fiscal can add Sharon Baird when they're ready. Okay?'

'Good to go, ma'am.'

'Indeed we are. Thank you, Mr Knox, we'll meet again. You'll be the one in the dock. I'll be the one who put you there.'

McPhee walked in and slumped into the vacant seat.

'This is very big, ma'am.'

'You never know how big until you start digging,' said Caplan. 'I'm thinking, poor Koi, she's gone and who can blame her. Samphire hates talking without Pomeroy telling him what to say. He thinks McLeerie is Rosie's dad because he thinks Rosie has been talking to McLeerie. They privately adopted Rosie as a very young baby. Her mother handed her over, not naming who her dad was. This was in September 2001. They took wee Rosie back to London. Her mother was called 'something flowery'. Prompted, he said Daisy. When they came to Torsvaig, it clicked that the girl who died was Rosie's mum.

'One of them is Rosie's dad. But I think Knox killed Daisy and got that close to framing somebody else. He started the rumours that McLeerie and Evans were a couple. It wasn't true. We need to reopen Sharon's case. Knox must have thought all his Christmases had come at once when McLeerie killed Carol. He could lump Sharon and Daisy in there as well.

'If McLeerie had died in prison, Knox would have got a good book out of it. He probably still will. The fly in the ointment is the DNA would prove paternity, except nobody had Knox's DNA sample, so no match. He had to be clever about it. Once we get the DNA then place Knox in the same self-help group as McLeerie and Baird, then the case is as complete as it can get. They were moving through the addiction support services in this health board at the same time. They would have come across each other. Knox is sulking in a cell and Baird's not here to comment.'

'Do you think he'll get convicted?'

'Yes.'
'What will you do then?'
'Have a day off probably. Or a glass of white wine. Or both.'

'Any chance of getting any more evidence? Something we can use in court?' Harry at the Fiscal's office had left a voicemail message for her. 'You have a lot of holes in the narrative here.'

'It's that kind of case and it's an interim report,' muttered Caplan, swiping her phone off before turning to Craigo. 'If Koi reappears, alive or dead, then we will know. We don't have the budget for much else. The Fiscal is still not accepting the evidence we have detailed in the report. He wants to know why the software always places the body further away from the cliff than Koi was. He wants more. He's happy to sit in his office and tell us that any inquiry is also going to want more. We have to prove that Koi died at the bottom of the cliff. Or prove that she did not.'

'But there's no body.'

'Yip. And they want us to prove that Koi could not have got up that cliff. Or prove that she did. They don't want to come out and look, so we're Torsvaig-bound one last time.' She rubbed her eyes.

'They're pissed off that they're under pressure to open the Daisy Evans and Sharon Baird cases again.'

'Well, they should have investigated it thoroughly the first time around. Anyway, the clifftop at Torsvaig. One good look around when the place is quiet and we aren't disturbed by anybody.'

Craigo took a deep breath. 'Are you sure she's dead?'

'We explored the possibility that it was planned, and we've proved that. But it went wrong, and she died. Sad though it is, the last Sunflower Girl is no more.'

Craigo looked confused. 'But there's no body.' He repeated.

'I'm aware of that, DS Craigo. That is the Fiscal's point, but I can't just produce a body on a whim, can I?'

'It's out on the tide, ma'am.'

Caplan sighed.

'Well, you explain that to the Fiscal.'

If Koi and Samphire thought they could fool them all, could Koi have fooled Samphire?

Caplan hoped to God that she had.

But there was no other ladder. The castle was well fortified: one way in and one way out, as far as they knew. Anybody carrying a rope ladder down the cliff path would have been seen.

Otherwise, it would still be *in situ*.

And the Rapunzel steps. Was that part of her fiction?

Caplan looked at Koi's face on the board, maybe seeing something, an intelligence she had missed before. *What did you do?*

Caplan looked back at her laptop screen, trying to find something of evidential value to support one theory or the other. They came here from London. Did they expect Pomeroy to follow the way he had? Or, to be more correct, did Koi expect him to follow? Maybe that was the last straw. Keeping all of them together – whose idea was that? Pomeroy had said this was their home, this was where they pulled up the drawbridge and kept the outside world exactly there – outside.

But it kept them inside.

In London there could be anonymity amid the masses. But not here.

Maybe Koi wanted a home but here they were running a business again. Everybody was a commodity. Again, Koi was at the centre of the very thing she had tried to escape from. Somebody was stalking her, threatening her life, threatening her family. When she closed the door, Pomeroy opened it. Samphire and Pomeroy. Caplan wrote down both names and tapped her pen across them, thinking of the room that Samphire and Pomeroy shared. So, what was Koi, what was her role in that relationship?

She had never got off the rocks. Yet it was Ryce, the pathologist, who had first mooted the idea that she wasn't dead. So why were they now so readily accepting that she had perished on those rocks?

Round and round the theories went.

The finding of the rope ladder that had never been used, and the room at the top of the turret that had remained unoccupied.

And if Koi could outfox her husband, her family? Could she outfox them all?

Slowly her pencil wrote down all the suspects, then added a few more names of anybody even loosely connected to the family. She drew lines and circles, rubbed them out and started again. Then her pencil stopped at one name.

Something she had not thought of before.

God, she was tired, but she knew. She hoped that her hunch was right, and in some ways, she hoped that she was wrong. Rosie did the domestic work. The company brought in staff for the weddings; Pomeroy didn't let the family come into close contact with anybody else in case they started thinking for themselves. Missing from her list was a gardener. Who was it who cut the lawn in stripes with such precision? Almost military precision?

TWENTY-TWO

Caplan was sitting in the car at Torsvaig. She'd be glad to see the back of it, and the entire family. She'd heard that Tron wasn't doing well, and she bore some of the guilt for his condition. She could have intervened, but she hadn't.

Still having a few minutes to wait for the others, she picked up her phone and felt physically sick when she read the online article. She now knew why famous people never googled themselves. The words 'hatchet job' came to mind. The journalist didn't quite call Caplan corrupt, but the implications were there. Failed dancer, lost evidence, embarrassment to the force, fellow officers killed on duty because of decisions she had made, exiled to the Highlands. None of it was untrue, but that didn't make it accurate.

And she knew who had written it before she looked. Carrie Cowie-Browne. That woman had the ability to destroy Caplan's career if her readers believed her; and with the current lack of confidence in the police, they probably would.

Out on the ramparts for the last time, she enjoyed listening to the wind and the sound of the waves rolling and crashing below. The sky appeared a little darker; it was a little colder. Was that real or was that just the way she was feeling, the tiredness creeping into her bones, the sense of sadness and futility she often felt at the end of a case? Or the sickness she felt after reading the article.

Maybe the world was just a little duller without Koi McQuarrie in it.

Maybe she'd put that in her report for the Fiscal. She didn't blame him for not quite understanding the difficulties of the case. These were not normal people.

She pondered how Koi had migrated from the successful model in her London town house to being at the bottom of a cliff, all because she wanted to get away.

Her first attempt had been foiled when Pomeroy moved with them. He had reinvented her stalker, pushing Koi further in her desire, her desperation, for anonymity.

Koi had then turned to her husband, and they hatched the plan of the fake death and the hideout in the small flat in the castle. That smacked of his romanticism rather than her common sense. Then Samphire told Pomeroy.

Not even Koi could think that it would end in a lovely new life once the coast was clear. Even in another version, with an Agatha Christie twist, the one where she re-emerges, Pip would book her into a clinic for treatment for an emotional psychotic trauma and there would be lots of material there for glossy magazines, a book, maybe even a film of her life.

And she'd be trapped again.

Pomeroy was both her saviour and her tormentor.

The only way to be free was to free herself.

Caplan turned to McPhee who was looking down at the King's Reach, following the line of his gaze. She wasn't surprised to see Rosie sitting on top of the cliff, her bare feet over the edge, leaning back so she was looking up at the sun.

'What do you think will happen to her, out of her castle, away from the sand and the sea? There could be a great new adventure for her.'

'She needs to escape, Callum.'

Rosie pulled her knees up, shifting her weight back from the edge, keeping an eye on the horizon. Was she thinking what tomorrow would bring?

The two police officers walked along the ramparts, 'What do you think did happen, ma'am? With Koi?' asked McPhee.

'She got as far as putting the blood on.'

'Then she fell?'

'What did Samphire say? *Where is she?* To me, that grief was genuine. Yes, Koi's dead,' she sighed. 'But then again, nothing about these people is genuine, absolutely nothing. Everything's an act.'

'If the Fiscal decrees that they want further evidence and start going through Pomeroy's papers, that's what they will find,' said McPhee.

'What?'

'Absolutely nothing.'

They stood for a moment, watching two herring gulls perform acrobatics mid-air. Caplan's eyes scanned the horizon.

'Do you think Pomeroy killed Ecco and Rhea?' McPhee asked, staring at the constant motion of the waves.

'Not so much killed. More like he didn't stop it. Well, he didn't stop Ecco. I'm not sure with Rhea. Did he give Samphire something to drop into that wine and then called him to get him out the situation? Who knows? Both women had started to free themselves from the Sunflowers. It proved fatal.'

'Poor Tron. It's carnage, isn't it?'

They both turned at the sound of huffing and puffing behind them. Craigo wiped the sweat from his forehead. 'So, I have spent some more time on the King's Reach and found something of interest.'

'Have you? Another ladder?' Caplan knew he wouldn't say until she asked.

'A single groove at the cliff edge, ma'am, right on the edge where it's crumbling. It's recent and deep. Just like the ones you left. I have a theory. I was here very early this morning.'

'Good for you. Does your theory depend on secret steps found on the walls of French châteaus?'

'Yes.'

Caplan and McPhee exchanged a glance and an eyeroll.

'It was what Perkins said about a prusik rope, or a friction hitch.'

'It's a climbing thing with a single rope,' explained Caplan to a confused McPhee, thinking back to that morning when Joe Perkins was being very helpful, showing Gary where they thought Koi had fallen. Why had it not struck her at the time, the art of misdirection?

'And easy to tie, ma'am.' Craigo stood between them, bright as a button. 'I know how she did it, ma'am. The friction hitch and the steps. We know about the plan to hide up in the room. What if she wants Samphire to think that his plan has been in play for as long as possible? She needs to go up to the King's Reach, put on the fake blood, then get down the rock face.'

'And how did she do that?'

'Single rope, just like you did.'

'And where is it?'

Craigo shrugged. 'I presume she took it to her new home. It could have been up here, waiting in a bag with the make-up. I've found a single groove in the earth at the edge of the cliff about twenty feet to the right of where the grooves were made by you and Gary. Just a single rope. Not dangling where Samphire expected to see the ladder, but much further along. After he takes the picture, confused and concerned, she climbs back up.'

Craigo looked at her.

Her face was expressionless.

'The scarf was there as another misdirection for us to look in the wrong place. Samphire can't quite make sense of it. He wants to go back up to the secret room to see if she's there, but he couldn't do that with the timing they had planned. If he didn't raise the alarm immediately, it would look suspicious, as everybody had heard the scream. They wanted the place to be swarming with police to back up their story.

'She climbs back up her own single rope which was hanging down at the far end of the cove, hidden by the way the high cliff projects.'

'And she did that with her bad knee?' asked McPhee, scathingly.

'There's no evidence that she has a bad knee. One story is she hurt it pole dancing, the other is she hurt it when she tripped over her frock on the path, ma'am. It's all misdirection. This was very planned, very clever.'

Caplan stayed quiet, then said, 'Go on.'

'She climbs up, pulls the rope up and—'

McPhee jumped in. 'Then what? She goes where? She can't go anywhere. There's water, a cliff and a wall. She can't go back down the path as anybody could be on their way up to help search for her.'

'She went over the wall.' Craigo blinked.

'She couldn't get up the castle wall. She's not Spiderman,' said Caplan slowly.

'Wrong wall.'

'Pardon?'

'The Woodwall, ma'am. She couldn't go round it with all those coils of barbed wire round the end of the Woodwall on the promontory of the cliff, so she had to go over it.'

'And how did she do that, get over the wall and through the dense woods?'

Again, Craigo looked at him, then turned to Caplan and smiled.

'The Rapunzel steps? Don't tell me you've found them on that wall?' she asked.

'It's a more recent construction. Well, two hundred years more recent, but the idea is the same. For brave warriors trapped on the King's Reach? They went over there and hid in the woods, not up here. And the thing about the Rapunzel steps is that they are laid out in reverse.'

'Oh God,' muttered Caplan.

'Seriously. They are easily seen from above. Not so easy from the ground up. These walls were built by master stonemasons for the protection of the lairds of the land. They can be built either way round, angled up or down. It's very clever, ma'am.'

'But the steps are to get soldiers back into the castle, are they not?'

'Why? Tired and injured soldiers would get over the Woodwall to escape through the cover of the wood, much easier than climb away up there.'

Caplan refused to be persuaded. 'As Callum said, it's a dense wood, it's not been thinned for hundreds of years. She wouldn't get through that.'

'So we were told, ma'am. The plans have been a long time in the making. It's not unheard of to make a path through woods. And the one thing we forgot about Koi was Charlie Campbell. She was a good rider. Do you know how far a small pony can go in thirty minutes, even winding its way through thick trees? I think if you looked at the roads going into Limpetlaw Forest Park from the far side, miles away, on the night in question, there'd have been a horsebox or something, for the last leg of her journey and—'

Caplan sighed. 'But this is conjecture. Can we prove this, with evidence, beyond reasonable doubt?'

'No, ma'am, you see the—'

They all turned at the shriek that pierced the air.

'What the hell was that?'

'It was out there,' said McPhee.

Down on the King's Reach, Rosie was on her feet, screeching for help.

Looking down, they saw the two dogs around her. Thane jumping up, sensing the excitement. Cawdor was closer to the edge of the cliff, looking out to sea, his pricked ears focused on something.

'Shit,' said McPhee.

Caplan was trying to see what she was screaming at and shouted down to her.

They didn't catch the answer as the young woman's face turned up to them, her words lost on the sea breeze, but her distress was obvious. Her pointing towards the sea grew more panicked.

Craigo took off towards the steps down to the bailey.

McPhee climbed up on the ramparts, looking for a way to get down the castle wall. 'No, Callum, don't, you can't climb down there, you just can't, so don't even try.' She got her phone out. 'I'll call Perkins and Pickering. They're closer. You'll fall and break your neck.'

While calling she leaned forward, looking down the side of the wall to see if Rosie was on her own or if there was somebody there that they could get a rope to. Then she saw it. Leaning low against the top of the wall and looking down, she saw a stone that was slightly proud of its neighbour. Then she looked along from that and, just below, was another, then another, then another – a sloping tiny stairway. There was a sequence, all the way to the top, all the way to the bottom.

'Callum!' she shouted, pointing. 'This way.' She ran along the top, calculating where the first stone might be. The uppermost stone was worn a little smooth compared to those on either side, hundreds of years of a palm resting there to heft the body over.

McPhee looked down, colour draining from his face.

'Once you start going down, just feel for the next grab hold. About a foot between each stop there's a handhold, that's what guides you. The small steps take your weight. If you don't want—'

She was too late though. McPhee was climbing over the wall, sitting astride it then dropping one leg over until he felt the stone that sat proud of the others with his foot. Caplan closed her eyes as McPhee's head dropped slowly behind the wall, thinking what on earth she was going to tell his parents if he came to more grief.

Cautiously, she peeped over, seeing his fingers hooked into a stone, then letting go in a controlled manner. For every step down, he had to go two steps across, but he was making good progress, moving with confidence and ease on his descent.

Then Caplan saw the reason for Rosie's distress. Out on the bay somebody was swimming out to sea, a slim figure making her way slowly through the waves. On her way to nowhere. And the tide, again, was high. Even as Caplan watched, she saw the swimmer tire. They stopped swimming, then the slow arm cycle started again, the elbows barely breaking the surface.

Caplan got back on the phone, dropping her rucksack where she stood while trying to reach Perkins. Or Samphire. Or Wattie.

It was the best she could do for now.

Then she ran, clattering her way down the wooden steps, then the stone steps, through the bailey and running at full speed down through the castle doors, to the Castle Gate and onwards to the Welcome Gate, pulled open far enough to let a person through, no more. She slowed slightly, paying attention to the pounding in her head and the burning in her lungs before she started on the climb to the King's Reach.

Then round onto the path and she started jogging, keeping her breathing regular and deep, her mind floating back to her dancing days, that feeling of fatigue in her legs.

Two strides then a step up, two strides then a step up . . . on and on, her thighs began to burn, but she was nearly there. She was at the viewpoint; the whole cove lay in front of her. McPhee had made it down the castle wall and was now making his way down the cliff on the old rope ladder. As Caplan watched he jumped the last few feet, pulled his shirt off and started clambering over the rocks, trying to reach the water without getting himself thrown back onto them by the next wave. He disappeared under the water, then his head popped up. A flick of his head to get the water out his eyes, then he was swimming after the distant figure, a strong breaststroke, slow but beating the power of the current.

TWENTY-THREE

It had been a week.
Just seven days.
With all that had happened in those seven days, the one constant was the strength of the sun in the sky. A week ago today she had crossed this street on her way into the laundrette, before her daughter got engaged, before she knew she was going to be a grandmother.

Before Morrow McQuarrie-Samphire had tried to end it all, and was now safe in an NHS hospital psychiatric unit, her fractured psyche starting to heal. She had refused Pomeroy's offer of a private London clinic.

Before McPhee had been admitted to Lorn and Islands hospital with saltwater aspiration. There was talk of him getting a commendation for bravery.

Seven days after Koi McQuarrie 'died' there was an alert out for her to all police forces in the UK, all ports and airports.

The official and final statement was given by Sarah Linden at a press conference. Caplan's team had watched it at the station in Cronchie. Media Liaison had crafted a speech stating that Koi McQuarrie remained a missing person. No foul play was suspected. The McQuarrie-Samphire family wished to thank Police Scotland and all Koi's friends and fans for their support over the last few very difficult days. And then came the clincher. 'With a special thanks for the courageous and tireless efforts of the men and women of air-sea rescue.'

Public opinion was that she had perished in the waves.

'She your pal, ma'am?' asked Mackie.

'I went through college with her, yes,'

'So, wit diz all that mean, then? Like Lord Lucan, wur still lookin',' said Wattie, who was promptly reminded that he should get back to Pilcottie.

The team had said their goodbyes and gone their separate ways, sad at the lack of conclusion in the death of the Sunflower Girl but content that the deaths of Daisy and Sharon were being reinvestigated.

It had come to light that Pomeroy and Knox went way back, before he knew Samphire. Pomeroy had wanted a patsy in the media; when he met the war photographer Samphire, Knox was dumped.

As she closed the boot of the Duster, Caplan wondered if there could be more to be gained in pursuing Pomeroy for the deaths of Rhea and Ecco. Definitely not – she'd been told that officially now – but still, it was a puzzle her mind liked to play with. She stepped out of a shadow and into the sun. The breeze now had some force behind it, blowing in from the sea, carrying salt in the air, refreshing but not yet with the chilling bite that would come the minute a cloud went over the sun. But at the moment the sky was cloudless.

This end of the street was devoid of traffic. Outside the hotel two waitresses were standing by the front door, vaping. She noticed a couple of tables in the bay window of the dining room – one empty, the other occupied.

She had to look twice to confirm who she thought she had seen. It looked like Mackie in her blue summer frock fanning herself with a hat, with a man sitting opposite her. His hair was combed to the side, flattened down, wearing a shirt that showed the geometric crease marks of having just come out the packet.

So that was what Wattie from Pilcottie was doing in Cronchie.

Caplan was smiling to herself as she glanced at her phone. It was a text from Aklen. She wasn't expecting him to text, so she opened it immediately. It was short and sweet.

Can you come home?

What had happened? Who was in hospital? Her brain raced around, catastrophising as it usually did, reliving the time when she'd got the call that Kenny had been hit by a car. Was history repeating itself? Had the recent exposure on social media brought something awful to her door?

'Shit.' Was this something to do with Jade?

She phoned. Aklen answered immediately.

'Hi Chris, can you pop home?'

'Pop home? What's happened?'

'Just come home, can you? Nobody's hurt, everybody's okay but you're needed back here.'

'Give me a hint, Aklen, you're scaring me.'

'Kids.'

'Is Emma okay?'

'Everybody's okay.'

The scariest thing about it was Aklen's steady tone of voice. She'd be more comforted if her husband was panicking.

The house was empty; she walked around, then looked out at the caravan. Why would they be in there? She walked through the garden, going wide, approaching the caravan on the diagonal, then the door opened and Aklen was gesturing to her that she should come in.

Kenny was sitting on the settee but leaning back, his head against the wall and his eyes fixed on the ceiling. He looked exhausted.

Exhausted and defeated.

'What is it?' she asked, Aklen slipping his arm round her waist, preparing her for bad news.

'It's Jade,' Aklen said.

'Is she okay? Is the baby okay?'

Aklen looked away. Kenny remained staring at the ceiling, then Aklen looked pointedly at his wife and then at his son, his face a mixture of empathy and confusion. He shrugged and said, 'Best if I leave you two to it.'

He left, closing the caravan door behind him. It took a while for him to walk out of Caplan's line of sight from the side door to the window at the front of the caravan. He had gone outside to take a moment to steady his nerve.

The only noise she could hear was the yowling of Pavlova out in the drive.

'So, what's happened?' Caplan sat down opposite her son. He looked pale. Dark eyed, both upset yet furious, the tight line of his lips said that he was restraining himself so that he didn't punch something. 'Jade?'

He nodded, biting his lip as he did so, a small bubble of blood appearing as his snaggle tooth pierced the skin. 'She's terminated the pregnancy.'

Then he burst into tears.

The next day, they slept in. Kenny had stayed the night, and they had sat up into the small hours of the morning, talking the subject round and round, but the fact that they could not ignore was that the act had taken place. There was nothing that Kenny could do about it other than learn to accept it. On more than one occasion, Caplan met her husband's eyes, both of them thinking that in other circumstances, if Jade had felt comfortable speaking to them, the words abortion or termination would not be crossing their lips.

In the end they had made Kenny a mug of hot chocolate, the way he had liked it when he was a kid, and Caplan had sat on the bed with him until he had gone to sleep.

The next morning was sunny – a new day, a new start. She had missed ten calls on her mobile phone. Plus six messages, all to do with work.

'Something's up. I hope it's not about McPhee,' she said to her husband. 'Can you make sure that the door is closed, in case it has to do with Kenny and . . . her?'

Sarah Linden had called three times, Spencer twice. She called Linden back first.

'Chris?'

'Yes, you called?'

'Have you seen the online news feed today?'

'No, I'm just out of my bed.'

'Okay. Do you have a patrol car at the front of the house?' She could hear the fear in Linden's voice.

'Should I have?' She opened the patio doors out to the balcony and then stepped out into the fresh air. The end of the drive was devoid of vehicles, but then a flash of red caught her eye. There was a familiar red Hilux parked by the rocks on the road past their cottage. On the other side, tucked into the bushes, was a Land Rover. 'What's going on, Sarah?'

'Nothing much, but somebody has done a further hatchet job on you in the paper, this Carrie Cowie . . .'

'. . . Browne?' added Caplan.

'Oh, well, it's all here and it's personal: your terrible marriage, Kenny's drugs, Emma bagging a millionaire, your dealings with organised crime. McPhee fighting for his life . . . again—'

'My what?'

'Oh, don't worry, it's all above board and it's nothing the service doesn't know about. There's a photograph of you enjoying yourself climbing some mountain when you should have been investigating the death of a national treasure.'

'What?'

'Yes, I know what you were doing, but the world is thinking differently. You need to get out of there. If I can work out where you live from the way it's written, then God knows who else can.'

'I can't just—'

'Yes, you can. I'm flying out to Cape Town tomorrow, come and stay here.'

'I've cats to feed.'

'Can they not look after themselves? I thought cats were the epitome of independence, can they not use a tin-opener?'

'Kenny's here,' Caplan explained. 'That journalist is his ex-girlfriend's mother.'

'Of course.' Linden's voice had that hard edge to it that made Caplan shudder.

'And Pomeroy mentioned her – she was one of their tame journalists. Bastard.'

'Pack your stuff. Get here before two p.m. Bring Kenny. I've a cleaner, a wine fridge and a jacuzzi bath. And a seventy-five-inch TV. He'll have a ball. And security. Caplan, I've security. It'll keep the press away until they find somebody else to victimise. You've put a lot of bad guys away, Christine, let's just let this pass.'

Caplan swore profusely.

'Oh, and that picture of you dressed in a black tutu is all over the internet. Very fetching. You were quite the thing back in the day.'

Caplan came out of the shower, her long black hair hanging loose across her shoulders, her thin cotton pyjamas open at the neck because of the heat of the night. Aklen was lying on top of the bed in a T-shirt and shorts. It was too hot.

'If we were home, we'd be getting eaten by midges.'

She flopped onto Sarah's bed, got up, threw five bolster cushions onto the floor and lay back down again.

'Of course, it's just too bloody hot to think. God . . .' Aklen paused, stretched, then yawned. 'So, what do you think of our son, then? Do you think we brought him up to be too idealistic?'

Caplan snuggled up beside him. He automatically dropped his hand to hold hers. 'What do you think?'

'I asked you first.'

'I wonder if she *was* pregnant.'

'You're so cynical.'

'Pomeroy said during an interview that there "might be a baby, we haven't decided yet". A fictional child to provoke a reaction.

And you know what DC Mackie is like, she has her ear to the ground with any celebrity stuff. She says that Jade's mum, Carrie Cowie-Browne, is not so much a feminist as a misandrist. Her boyfriend left her the minute she was pregnant with Jade. She's had a tough life as a single mother. Makes me wonder if Jade was testing Kenny. Or forcing him away. Surely if she felt anything for him at all she would have spoken to him. But he didn't walk away from his responsibility. Maybe she didn't want to speak to him because lying to somebody consistently is difficult.'

'Do you really think she's capable of that?'

'I have a much lower opinion of people than you do, Aklen. It's the way she was drinking at the party. Pregnant women just don't do that. I could be wrong, it's just a feeling.'

'Bloody hell.'

'She made whatever decision she made for whatever reasons. Kenny is the one who has to live with it.'

'Still, it's rather impressive, the way he's dealt with the pregnancy, and the fallout.'

'I doubt that he has dealt with it – it's a lot to process. But one day I will look her in the eye, and I will ask her. I'll know if she's lying.'

'You see, she was right about the police oppressing the masses,' said Aklen.

They lay in silence, feeling the warmth of the night air drift in through the window, waiting for a sleep that evaded them because of the heat that crept through the dark outside, the unusual noises of the hot city night. 'If it's true and she was pregnant, then I confess that I'm surprised how hard this hit me. At the back of my mind, when I look round the table at Mags and Emma's anniversary, I'll know that there's one missing. When Kenny gets married, when he has kids, I'll know there's one missing. I'm sure he will too.'

'Do you think he'll be okay?'

'Time will tell. I hope he doesn't drift back to his old habits.'

'Time will tell.'

'We need to get blackout curtains at the cottage.'

'I rather like watching the sunset from up there, it's lovely.'

More silence.

'I'm rather proud of our son.'

'So am I.'

'We brought up a rather principled young man. He would have stood by Jade no matter what. But she didn't give him the chance.'
'We did indeed.'
'He gets it from his mother.'

EPILOGUE

Aklen and Mags's small design company, Toaty Houses, got an unexpected publicity boost because of the disappearance of Koi McQuarrie. Aklen found his role as husband of the celebrity detective hard to take.

Caplan took the view that there was always a silver lining.

To the outside world, the investigation had been a failure. The disappearance of the last Sunflower Girl would remain an enigma, a welcome feast for the conspiracy theorists. Pip Pomeroy was already in talks with a production company about a documentary with Knox now in the role of the killer father. The song 'He's Got the Ohhh' by Three to Please was back at the top of the charts and introduced a whole generation to the Sunflower Girls. Sales of the Little White Dress rocketed, the classic was reborn.

As for the case, the media began to concentrate on the missing body. Why were rescue services not on the scene sooner? Ask the woman whose son had been airlifted off the side of the mountain with a fractured skull and a swelling brain, ask the crew of the yacht towed into port after a broken mast and engine failure.

EB and AZed were preparing to get married at Torsvaig. Then fell out. Then got back together. Caplan could smell Pomeroy's hands all over that one. There was a rumour that Ted DeVries had taken EB out for a coffee, but it might only have been a rumour. Rosie had moved out of the castle; her father was probably about to start a long sentence. Torsvaig was hired out to a film company as a location for a time-travel Scottish fantasy.

Knox was facing one murder charge and another one was building nicely.

Morrow and Tron were still under the care of the NHS and hidden from public view. Cosmo was everywhere, mooted as the next big thing in Hollywood, as the new team coach for the national football squad, the new First Minister of Scotland if he wasn't careful. Strangely, he was the one who kept in touch with Caplan, keeping her updated on his siblings.

Caplan relaxed by going out for the day, looking for out-of-the-way places that might be suitable for a Toaty House. Aklen knew there was an ulterior motive and that some of these locations had horses: Clydesdale horses. Clydesdale horses of the Kinglass bloodline.

On another hot day, near the end of July, they set off again with Caplan driving. Aklen had the passenger window open, his elbow on the ledge, enjoying the drive and not thinking about the renovation of Challie Cottage that was falling further and further behind.

This property was smaller than the others. This was no riding stable or farm, just a smallholding on the lochside, with a blue rowing boat nestled into the short wooden jetty. They had parked the car and walked a single path to a small bay with an old cottage painted brilliant white, pastel blue round the doors and the two windows at the front. An older lady, in her sixties or seventies, came out of the front door, a basket of wet washing resting on her hip bone, and walked slowly towards the neatly mowed lawn where the rotary drier waited.

Caplan leaned forward, telling Aklen to wait, before retreating into the shade of some trees. She watched as another taller figure with long grey hair, wearing a baggy top, old jeans and crocs, walked to the short jetty that ran out over the loch, then sat down. She took off her crocs and let her feet slip into the water, and put her glasses on.

Caplan could see she had a cup of something in her hand. She dipped a biscuit in it and took a bite, then she gave her dog a pat and took out a book, opened it up. The mug was placed down beside her, and she began to read.

Caplan pulled out her phone and took a picture. Then, shielding the screen from the sun she spread her fingers, enlarging the features of the person she was looking at.

It was a scene of contentment.

In all the twists and turns, the lies she had been told, Caplan had been right. Her first instinct was to go down to the jetty and confront the tall grey-haired woman who was dressed as if she was spending the day tending to the vegetable garden.

The figure on the jetty was rubbing the collie's tummy.

She and Aklen walked back to the Duster, Caplan thinking of returning with a lot of questions.

Before Koi McQuarrie had died that day, she had fallen from the top of the cliff and suffered life-ending injuries on the rocks, and then her body had been carried out to sea, never to be found.

And after? The woman on the jetty had been born: grey-haired, heavier, happy to live a quiet life with a dog and a good book, with two Clydesdale fillies to look after until they matured, working to keep the bloodline of Charlie Campbell alive.

A man, tall with fair hair and broad shoulders, walking with the air of one who had served king and country, emerged from the shadows, taking the washing basket from the woman old enough to be his mother, and carried it across the garden for her. Caplan allowed herself to smile; she had wondered who cut the grass up at Torsvaig.

Aklen walked towards the car. Caplan took a final look at the sea, at the mist that was now shrouding the horizon.